I0734986

VIGILANTE JUSTICE

A GRIEVING FATHER'S REVENGE
CREATES A SERIAL KILLER

MARK MILLS

Copyright ©2020, Mark Mills

ALL RIGHTS RESERVED.

No part of this publication may be reproduced, stored in a retrieval system, or transmitted in any form or by any means—electronic, mechanical, photo-copy, recording, or any other—except for brief quotation in reviews, without the prior permission of the author or publisher.

ISBN: 978-1-948638-63-0

Published by

Fideli Publishing, Inc.
119 W. Morgan St.
Martinsville, IN 46151
www.FideliPublishing.com

Dedicated to my wonderful son, José.
You are a strong beacon of light and I love you very much.

CHAPTER 1

Six o'clock. Quitting time almost put Dan in a good mood as he glanced past the clock to the reporters typing their stories and talking on the phone outside his cubicle. It was gray and it was drab and it was full of smoke from the cigarette he had just sneaked in his no smoking office. "Almost quittin' time for the hack," he muttered to himself as he absent-mindedly switched on his desk fan to clear the air. *Hack* was the name he had been sarcastically calling himself since the day he started working for an online newspaper in Washington, D. C. After getting out of the Army, he started graduate school, majoring in history and Middle-Eastern Studies. At the same time, he started working for the paper, covering Washington, D. C. news and writing stories about the wars in Iraq and Afghanistan. Dreamily, he leaned back to let the cigarette do its nerve-soothing work. But it was not to be, as the telephone's musical ring split the haze like a scalpel, breaking the nicotine spell.

"Forester," he answered dryly, fully expecting another routine call from a wearisome source with a boring story to tell. But it was anything but that.

* * *

1280 miles away in Omaha, Nebraska, no one at KNOC-TV knew yet who Dan Forester was. It was a hectic day, even for the newsroom. Reporters ran to and from the producer's desk with scripts. Tape editors raced videotapes to the control room and in the midst of it all, the assignment editor barked out orders to the field crews through his two-way radio as the police scanner crackled out its garbled chatter. Everyone rushed around hurriedly as though theirs was the biggest story of the day. Everyone, that is, except News Director Bob Manson and Senior Reporter Susan

Jensen. They had learned long ago that getting all hyped up over a story wasted valuable energy. They chose to take a more serene approach ... even to big news.

"Reporters are hooked on the adrenaline-rush," Susan liked to say, "They like the frenzied pace and a lot of 'em act this way even with more routine, humdrum stories. Urgency makes them feel important, even when their story is of absolutely no importance. After all, if you're in a big hurry what you're doing must be important ... right?" But that wasn't the case on this day in this newsroom.

* * *

"Dan ... Cole never came home from school and I'm going out of my mind! I called all his friends and the last they saw of him, he was walking home!" Jan spit the words out all in one breath. It was her voice alright, as Dan subconsciously visualized her worried-but-beautiful, slightly freckled face framed by flaming red hair. But so terrifying were her words that, to him, the last few sounded like they were being spoken through a megaphone from the other end of a tunnel. He had a sickening feeling that this would be a tunnel of no return.

* * *

After five years of doing stories about the search for a missing Omaha boy named Jeremy Fenner, the big day had finally arrived. His remains had been found and KNOC-TV Reporter Susan Jensen was on it like a pit bull. The child had been kidnapped, mutilated and murdered. Authorities suspected a pedophile. Every TV newscast in the state was leading with the story and the Omaha stations were devoting most of their early newscasts to it. But because of Susan's efforts, KNOC was better prepared than the competition.

Susan had followed the Jeremy Fenner story the closest. Every step of the way she produced stories and special series reports on missing children. Twenty-eight years old, pretty and shapely, she looked like a cross between a beauty queen and a college professor. Her smooth, golden hair ended in soft curls that bounced around a ravishing-yet knowing face with penetrating eyes that seemed to look right through you. This was a beautiful and intelligent woman whose love was her job. Fenner and the missing children issue had become a cause for her and she had spent years researching it. She had also grown close to Jeremy's parents. Some of her colleagues thought too close.

* * *

Normally it was just a good-looking, well-built man with jet-black hair and a fiery-yet-icy stare inside Dan Forester's office window. But at this moment the glass housed a tight-skinned mask of horror as every muscle in his body went instantly taut and a blaring alarm shot off in his head; a silent but deafening siren that only he could hear. He felt panicked and paralyzed and it was several seconds before he could speak. "Are you sure he didn't go home with one of his friends?" he finally managed to ask his wife.

"Yes, I called them all ... and besides, you know he wouldn't do that without calling me," came Jan's inevitable answer.

Dan suddenly went hollow as if the breath was being sucked out of him by a high-powered vacuum. It was his worst nightmare. As a soldier, he had seen too many children permanently damaged by war and as a reporter, he saw too much child abuse.

A familiar odor then slowly began creeping into his nostrils. A subtle, metallic scent that he hadn't smelled in a long time. It was frightening, yet he couldn't quite place it. "Could he have stayed late at school for something?" he asked apprehensively, wanting to explore every hopeful possibility.

"That's the first thing I thought, but ... but I called the school and ... he didn't," she stammered.

What's that smell? It was foreign, yet familiar and he was afraid of the answer.

* * *

Like many people Ross Huggins wanted better cards than life had dealt him. His was a little-known job with the FBI doing background research on all kinds of strange and mysterious subjects. Most of the bureau's employees were involved in some type of research at one time or another, but Ross was given the really off beat stuff to look into. It could be interesting work, but he often wished he was out on the front lines of investigation instead of buried in the bowels of the Bureau's dark, dank, vomit-green research basement in Quantico, Virginia. He longed to get away from his cave, as he called it, and get into the real world of FBI fieldwork. Three times he had requested a transfer to a field investigation unit, but had been told each time he was too valuable where he was. This is irony, he thought. He figured if he wasn't so good at his job he would be investigating instead of back-grounding. But he had the patience of a fisherman and day after day he did his job in an office strewn with books and papers alongside the most advanced computer hardware and software available. He did it extremely well, waiting for the break that someday would make him a field investigator.

Unfortunately for him, he looked much more like a research librarian than he did an FBI field agent. At a slight 5" 8' with a crew-cut and glasses he didn't exactly cut an imposing figure. But the key to Ross was his eyes. They were calm, yet intense. Most people who knew him would have been surprised to learn that along with an IQ of 148, Ross had a black belt in karate and knew how to use his deadly skills. His job wasn't glamorous and he often got bored stiff. But things were about to change as his boss Don Westerhoff walked into his office.

* * *

It hit Dan like a hard slap right to the jaw as he heard his wife whimper on the other end of the phone. The odor in his nostrils was fear itself and he hadn't smelled it since just before his last fierce, death-ridden firefight in Iraq. His buddies had thought him crazy when he told them he had actually smelled fear. "More of Forester's cosmic crap," one of them snarled, referring to his natural tendency toward existential philosophy, which often seemed out of place in the harsh, cruel reality of war. Dan was probably the only deep-thinker in his company and most certainly the only one who often put his deep feelings into words, both in conversation and in the journal he kept. But he was also the first one to charge an enemy position or go after a sniper. He had always been contradictory, combining firebrand behavior with well-read, intellectual awareness. But at the time he knew what he had smelled. It was so vile that he had lain awake nights saturating his cot with sweat and worrying that at any moment the fetid sewer of horrors, as he called it, would wind its sickening way back into his nostrils and take its unsweet time to leave.

Even now, as he gazed dumbly at his busy co-workers through his office window, he felt the sweat again. His shirt stuck to him like wet paste and the telephone receiver slid on his ear.

"Are you sure he's not over at Bill's?" he asked hoping Cole may have gone to the neighbor's house.

"No, I checked."

"Think hard a minute Jan," Dan pushed, "Is there anything you might've missed?"

"No! You're not listening ... I already told you ... there's nowhere else he could be," Jan sputtered between choked sobs.

Scenes of horribly dismembered children in Iraq tumbled over each other in his head, battling for his attention. He had thought Iraq was as hideous as life could get, but he was wrong. Reporting the news in Washington, D.C. had shown him more inhuman, brutal treatment of children than he had ever imagined possible. Now it could be his son and that terrified him.

* * *

"I've got a weird one for ya' this time," Don Westerhoff said as he absent-mindedly looked around FBI Researcher Ross Huggins' messy office.

"What now?" Ross whirled around quickly.

"They want you to do a profile study on pedophiles."

"But we already have one," he told Don.

"Yeah, I know, but you know the boys upstairs. They've decided the old study is outdated. They've ordered a new one starting from scratch. You'll have to profile it all, from the pedophile's childhood to the cause of his death and everything in-between."

"Man, Don, this one's gonna' take some time."

"Well, if you've got the time we've got the queer," joked Westerhof, mocking an old TV beer commercial, as he walked toward the door hesitating just long enough to see if he would get a laugh out of Ross. He didn't.

CHAPTER 2

"Call 911. Tell 'em Cole is missing. Say a neighbor told you he saw a man grab him and shove him into his car," Dan blurted out all in one breath. The institutional gray office walls closed in on him like a man-size vise as the sickening fear-smell once again filled his nostrils.

"But ... why lie about the man?" Jan asked innocently.

"Because if you don't, the cops will think Cole stopped on the way home to play, or just ran away and they'll drag their feet." He knew police procedure and he struggled to breathe, trying to override his confused whirlpool of emotions and get himself under control.

"But I don't want to lie."

"I know baby, but if you don't it could hurt Cole."

"There's gotta' be another way."

"I'm all ears," Dan said softly, trying to couch his rising anger, "You tell me what it is." Ire boiled up inside of him as it did when someone else couldn't see what was so obvious to him. He loved his wife and tried hard to keep from losing his temper with her as he had done too many times before.

Jan often accused Dan of always thinking he was right and much of the time he did. Because of his keen, perception, he often was, or at least he believed he was, and he had little patience with anyone who didn't see things his way. Jan sometimes accused him of having an incredible amount of unwarranted self-esteem.

"Oh, I don't know..." Jan murmured, searching.

"Well, I do!" he said firmly, "Just make the call and we can argue about it later!" The familiarity of his sudden anger helped him catch and then dominate the horror that welled up inside him. It also helped to dilute slightly the repulsive fear odor that had steadily grown stronger.

"But," Jan said.

"Every time you say *but* you could be putting another nail in Cole's coffin," he blurted, regretting it even as the words came out of his mouth. As a policeman he'd picked up the habit of being direct and graphic, and he knew he'd just made his wife more anxious.

"Oh, Danny!" Jan shrieked.

"Just make the call," he snapped, the guilt about upsetting her leaving as quickly as it had come, "I'm coming right home. I'll be there in half-an-hour." He slammed the receiver down with a clang that reverberated around the closet he called an office.

After several months he had stamped nothing of his personal touch on the cubicle. There were no pictures on the walls, no cute little sayings pinned up anywhere. It was as if he didn't plan to be there very long. He ran one hand through his thick, coal-black hair, which he wore longer than most insurance men, while with the other he grabbed his black leather jacket and headed for the door. Even under the sudden suffocating pressure that gripped him, he sensed the contrast between the cold, colorless office and the warm, soft crackle of his leather coat as he put it on.

* * *

Douglas Glassman was a good husband to his wife Sandra and a good father to his two daughters Kate and Kelly. Wearing glasses and sporting a few too many pounds, the only thing striking about his looks was how utterly plain they were.

With brown hair, brown eyes and no distinguishing features he was the type of person that no one really noticed. The type that blended in with the background wherever he was. He had sold insurance for the same company for the last 20 years. He belonged to the Chamber of Commerce and to the Elks Club in Fort Wayne, Indiana. He coached little league baseball and soccer, even though he had no sons or daughters on the teams. Everyone who knew Doug Glassman considered him to be a model citizen, and he was, except for one dirty little secret.

* * *

Why can't she ever just do what I ask instead of arguing? Dan mindlessly asked himself as he sailed down the gray hallway on his way to the parking lot. It was a question he had asked himself before, but it seemed especially critical now, when every second might count. He was painfully aware of the child sex abuse cases, which had ended badly because authorities had moved too slowly. But with a tornado of emotions whirling around in his head he was already regretting his impatience with his wife. And on top of it all was Jan's maddening tendency to question anything and everything he did, no matter how small or trivial ... or crucial it was.

Dan believed that in times of crisis any decision, even a bad one, was better than wasting time dwelling on the predicament and discussing which action to take. His was the attitude of the combat soldier. It worked well in Iraq where he served as a special-forces marksman and demolitions expert. Later it was what made him a good investigative reporter. But it also caused problems he wasn't aware of, since he often leaped into action where a more thoughtful approach was needed. It was his instinct to instantly prioritize the problems and then quickly solve them one at a time, in their order of importance, using different tactics for each. Unfortunately, in doing this he tended to look at each tactic individually instead of together as a whole, which meant he often overlooked the probable overall consequences of his actions. It was this instinct for instantaneous reaction that had served him well in the deserts of Iraq and on Washington's tough streets, though not always so well in everyday life. Dan's feeling was that sometimes overreaction is the best reaction. But whatever it was, right now he felt like his brain was on fire as he slammed the car door shut.

* * *

Douglas Glassman first noticed he was different at age 12 when his younger brother, Jason, had a friend stay overnight. He accidentally saw the boy in his underwear and became aroused. That was the beginning of an emotional roller coaster he was forced to ride. Much of the time he struggled to rid himself of his desire for young boys, yearnings of which he was deeply ashamed. On an emotional level he was literally sickened by the idea, but intellectually he knew he was a pedophile. He had, however, managed to mostly repress his pedophilia over the years. Consequently, at the age of 40 Doug had spent a lot of time indulging in self-hatred as well as exercising self-control. He was getting psychological therapy for the former, which was helping him with the latter.

"The weird thing is that I honestly do love kids," he told his therapist, Dr. Christine Johnson in their first session. "Oh, I don't mean in a sexual way…I mean in a love way. I love being with them, helping them and teaching them. Sometimes I think I just carry this love too far and it gets mixed up with sex."

"Well, that's improbable because you are only interested in sex with the boys, and not the girls. If your theory about extended love for children was correct, it would follow that you would desire sex with girls also," came the doctor's reply.

"Yeah ... I guess that makes sense. Maybe I'm just grasping at straws."

"That's often how we get answers Doug, so please don't stop grasping. In fact, both of us will do quite a lot of grasping to get to the root of your problem. You must understand that it took forty years to reach this point and we won't figure out how you got here in just one day."

The fact was that Doug really did love kids. Besides coaching the little league teams he was a big brother to several under-privileged children and helped out in the anti-drug program at his daughters' elementary school. He loved children and genuinely cared about their welfare, but his deep, dark secret was that he craved little boys and that was something that at times nearly drove him over the edge. He was so disgusted with himself that at age 23 he had thought seriously about suicide.

Then he met Sandy who, without knowing his problem, gave him reason to believe that he might be able to bury it. It had stayed buried for years, through marriage to Sandy and the birth of their two daughters. Then, however, Doug's natural love of kids piloted him toward little league coaching and other children-related activities and his long suppressed, inner monster began to surface.

* * *

After 11 years of marriage Jan Forester was well aware of Dan's *jump-start* character, as she called it, and it was a big reason she questioned many of his decisions. But she often did it in unimportant situations where one decision was as good as another, and sometimes just to irritate him. It always worked and their relationship was tumultuous. But as Jan once told a friend, "The highs are higher than the lows are low." As turbulent as their marriage often was, they were very much in love.

When Dan cruised through the newspaper office area, more than one head would turn as the office secretaries were keenly aware of his rugged countenance. His face looked like it had been carved out of solid granite with chiseled, stony features that screamed *man*, and his deep, steely eyes looked as if they could burn two holes right through you. His lean body was muscular except for the incongruous, but slight beer belly, evidence of his fondness for beer and whisky and he looked like he would be more at home in a saddle than at a desk.

"He isn't exactly handsome," several women had agreed over after-work drinks one evening while they rated the men in their office, "But he sure is sexy." He was unanimously voted the man they would most like to sleep with. Whatever he had, Dan wasn't aware of it, and that probably made him even more attractive.

* * *

After looking all over KNOC-TV for Bob Manson, Susan decided he must be in the general manager's office. She didn't like going up there because News Director Manson and General Manager George Abbott argued too much. But she had to talk to him about the Jeremy Fenner story so she headed upstairs. Thinking about the sad scene of the dead boy's remains, she was about to knock when she heard loud voices coming out of the office. Deciding to take advantage of the secretary's absence she stood in the outer office and took in every word of the heated discussion. She also wanted to make sure that in their heated argument Bob didn't tell George about a major plan they had hatched.

"News you can use. That's what people want Bob," Abbott said in his used car salesman voice, "Stories on things like health and finance. You tell 'em how to be healthier and richer and they'll watch." George Abbott was a short, balding, roly-poly man. He had the look of someone whose life had been too easy.

Bob Manson was tall and lean with a mop of unkempt salt-and-pepper hair going in all directions. He looked like he had smoked too many cigarettes and drunk too many beers in his life and the massive quantities of coffee he consumed daily just added to his face's pallor.

"You just made a better argument for the blood-sucking consultants than they could ever make for themselves. Come on George, you're a smart guy…can't you see these guys for what they are?"

"Oh, I guess I'm just stupid Bob, but I suppose you're gonna' tell me."

"Yeah, I am. You pay 'em fifty thousand bucks a year to tell you what they've found to work in other TV markets and you automatically think the same things will work in this market. I think deep down inside, you know they're wrong, but you've paid 'em so much money you can't justify not taking their advice. Well, I'll say it again, what works in New York or L. A. is not gonna' work in Omaha."

"And I'll say it again Bob! People are people and viewers are viewers wherever you are."

"Not so. I tell ya' … this state is better educated than most. Nebraskans want good, solid, hard news. They don't want the flash and trash New York and Miami shit where if it bleeds it leads or L. A. gossip, where the big story is Liz's 29th marriage. You forget that Nebraska students always have some of the highest basic skills test scores in the country." Bob chose not to mention the rumor that some teachers teach the contents of the test beforehand, which was the subject of a Susan Jensen investigative report that would soon air on KNOC news.

"And you forget that the ratings dropped in the last book."

"One lousy point or two, depending on which book you look at … and you know the figures are only accurate within three points. So, whatever they are, they could be wrong by three points one way or the other and I'm sure that's the case here. This has happened so many times before I can't even believe you care."

"Well, Bob, all I can say is ... I hope you're right because you seem to be the lone voice. The rest of the industry is going with shorter and lighter stories with a little glitz and drama while you insist on the same old tired city and county news. You even bore the crap out of the audience with statehouse news. We've all got to change! These are different times. I just hope you're not letting your stubbornness cause you to be left behind."

Listening outside the door Susan thought, *George you've been reading too many TV trades again.*

"Thanks so much for your concern George," Bob shot back, "But that is really the point isn't it? I'm the one who's been in the news business for 20 years, not you, and certainly not the consultants who're getting rich off your lack of confidence in me." Bob thought about the fact that most general managers like George had worked their way up to the position as TV advertising salesmen, and the fact that you can't make a salesman into a newsman.

"Well, maybe you're too close to it Bob. Maybe you need an outside opinion from someone who doesn't have a news background ... someone who is more like the typical viewer."

"Someone like ... let's see ... like maybe you George?"

"Yes ... like me."

"Yeah, and maybe I need an acid enema too. Boy, I'll tell ya,' if you would've given me that $50,000 instead of squandering it on consultants, I'd have produced special series reports that would knock your socks off. Oh, and your ratings would be a lot higher than they are now. But you've got the purse strings. By the way, you're going to get just the kind of news you're looking for tonight. Sex, death, blood, tears ... the whole thing. They found Jeremy Fenner's body ... or what's left of it. So, tune in and watch. Your tired old, heavy-handed newscast is going to get you the highest ratings of the year tonight. Gotta' go, bye." Bob loved making a dramatic exit and taking one last shot at George on his way out the door. But this time, as he left he walked right into Susan and knew instantly that she had heard every word of their discussion.

"We've got a problem with the live van and Leon says he can't fix it," she said matter-of-factly. There was no need for embarrassed courtesies between them. They both knew she was an eavesdropper. What good reporter wasn't?

"Can't or won't?" Bob asked pulling a pack of cigarettes out of his pocket and offering Susan one. "I'll take care of it ... I'll be damned if I'm gonna' let that pissant screw with this newscast." George Abbott wasn't the only pain in Bob's neck. The news and engineering departments were often at odds too. Bob liked to say that there are men and women, and then there are engineers.

Mainly, however, he knew this newscast with its many angles on the Jeremy Fenner story stood a good chance of winning all the major news awards that year. Almost as if he had sensed what was coming, two weeks earlier he and Susan had supervised the production of six background stories relating to the missing boy. Three concerned Fenner himself and the search efforts made to find him and three concerned missing children in general. When KNOC-TV News hit the air that night it would have most of its newscast already in the can while its competitors would have to scramble helter-skelter to put together a news show. Bob and Susan both liked winning awards, but Susan had another special reason for wanting this newscast to be the best it could be.

CHAPTER 3

Leaving work early was not unusual for Dan, but recklessly gunning his midnight-black '89 Mustang out of the parking lot and roaring down the street was. He loved the car he had bought shortly before he went into the Army and had taken painstaking care of it. He had even stored it in an air-conditioned garage in his hometown while he was in the service. The car represented a simpler, more innocent time; a time growing up in Baltimore, Maryland where life was uncomplicated. Things were more black-and-white then without so many gray areas. He had grown up tough, attending inner city schools and he remembered much of his youth as a continuous battle between right and wrong, good and evil, strong and weak. Iraq blurred all those lines and shaded Dan's sight with permanently gray-colored glasses.

"Please God, say Cole just stopped to play and lost track of time, not that he was grabbed by some pervert son-of-a-bitch," he desperately mumbled to himself as he raced down the pot-holed street, completely unaware of the irony of using curse words in a prayer. Then, as he ran his second red light, not an unusual habit for any Washingtonian, he offered the inevitable deal, "God, if you make Cole O.K. I'll really start living a good Christian life." Dan still hadn't learned that God doesn't make deals.

As he careened down New Hampshire Avenue the dreaded fear-smell returned. Call it warring soldiers' collective anxiety sweating out of their pores and vaporizing into a stench that only other soldiers can smell. Call it an unexplained, clairvoyant vision manifesting itself in a doomed scent. But whatever you called it, Dan knew it, and he knew it to be the incense of fear.

Like the putrid odor of burning flesh, the smell of fear is hard to shake. No one knew just how hard better than Dan as he had smelled so many burning bodies blown up in IED explosions in Iraq. It simply wouldn't go away. With every ounce of his strength he forced himself to live with fear and eventually to actually relish it. As one entry in his journal read, "I've finally made fear my friend and as long as we're friends I see everything with a new, crystal sharp clarity and I feel I can do anything." He had hoped, though, that after coming home from Iraq he would never have to smell the terrifying odor again ... and he hadn't ... until now.

* * *

"Have a nice chat with Abbott?" Susan Jensen baited her News Director, Bob Manson as they walked back to the KNOC-TV newsroom.

"You oughta' know ... you heard every word of it."

"Yup ... same old crap from the same old fart."

"Yeah, and I'm sick to death of it."

"I don't blame you."

Susan had served in the Peace Corps in Ecuador after college, then settled down to concentrate on her career goal in journalism: to become a network correspondent. But just as she began making good contacts, the network news industry began scaling down. Her aspirations dimmed. Now she worked, half-satisfied, for Bob Manson, her news director and mentor. She felt he had forgotten more about news than she would ever learn. The only thing that made her job bearable was that Bob gave her more freedom than most reporters enjoy.

Some considered him a dinosaur in the present form-over-substance trend in TV news and he often felt like he was fighting a losing battle over cosmetics-versus-content. The winners, it sometimes seemed, were the George Abbots and the blow-dried, good-looking anchors who could read, but who often didn't really understand what they were reading. The appearance of a newscast had taken priority over its content and TV consultants were doing a booming business telling their client stations how their news shows should look. Bob Manson, however, still believed in just plain hard, investigative news with few frills and didn't like a lot of anchor personality interjected into his news shows. Some called him old-fashioned and he did look somewhat like a character from an old comic strip. With sharp features hardened and softened by the pressure of years of serious journalism, Bob looked road-weary but wise. His skin had the pallor of a chain smoker, which he was, and he had a curmudgeonly look that seemed to be a perfect fit for his personality. A wiry man of six feet, his black and gray hair often fell in uncombed clumps over his strong and sometimes fiery eyes. The fire was still there whenever it was needed. The coals had just cooled over the years.

Manson had had his fill of station-hired consultants who told him on a regular basis to change his hard news philosophy. "It may be good, solid news Bob," more than one had told him, "and it may be the most solid news show on TV. But what's the difference how great it is if no one's watching?" Consultant after consultant finally convinced Bob's bosses that if they didn't change to a more glitzy, soft and light newscast with more entertainment value their ratings would end up in the toilet. So far that hadn't happened, but the ratings had slipped a couple of points recently and some of KNOC's higher-ups were sure the final flush would happen any day. Bob was tired of battling the Abbott types and Susan shared his frustration. But unlike Bob, Susan felt she may be on the verge of a major career change and it all revolved around Jeremy Fenner and children like him.

* * *

At their modest, colonial, white-with-blue trim Wheaton, Maryland home Jan Forester was just getting off the phone with the Montgomery County Police Department. She nearly panicked when the voice at the other end asked her for the name and telephone number of the neighbor who had seen Cole being abducted. But wisely she said she didn't know the person's name and asked that they please look for her son now and ask questions later.

It worked. The authorities put out an all-points alert for Cole and sent two squad cars and a canine unit. As Jan hung up the receiver she half-expected to see her heart bulge out through her skimpy, yellow halter-top with each booming throb. It roared in her ears like a resounding bass drum in a 4th of July parade. She briefly wondered how nervous she had sounded on the phone. Then, she realized her nervousness might have made the lie about not knowing the neighbor sound more convincing. She sobered when she thought that if Dan wanted the lying call to be made so bad he should have made it himself and she should have told him to make it. "As usual," she said out loud, "I think of these things about a half-hour too late." And with all of this racing through her mind, she threw her softly flowing, scarlet hair back into a ponytail and headed out the door to retrace Cole's eight-block walk to school. Not once did it occur to her that the story about the neighbor sounded more plausible coming from her. Dan was right again and subconsciously it made her mad.

Her legs felt like boat anchors as she trudged up the sidewalk glancing in all directions. She knew Cole wouldn't stop to play and besides, he was a loner and didn't have anyone to play with. Anyway, she thought, after all the lectures and warnings about how important coming right home is, that's not what happened. She felt like she was sinking into the sidewalk with each step. It was like running in a slow-motion dream, her energy being devoured by terror bubbling up inside of her and by the ever-hungry concrete beneath her feet. Then, the guilt started creeping in as she began facing up to a possible reason for Cole's disappearance.

* * *

As FBI Researcher Ross Huggins sat at one of the office computers his fingers typed away but his mind wandered. His slight-but-slick good looks complimented his nice guy disposition. Blonde hair and a mustache accentuated an oddly boyish face. He was one of those rare, genuinely nice people who actually had compassion for those around him. His kids loved him and his wife, Sara, knew what a wonderful husband she had. He had a good job that paid enough so that she didn't have to work if she didn't want to, and he was basically the all-American family man. Several of the FBI field agents that knew him called him Mr. Clean and sometimes joked that Ross was the nice guy he was because he had never had to go undercover, as they had, and mix with society's lower elements. This characterization galled him to no end since undercover work was exactly what he wanted so desperately. He was bored with his job, but good at it, and it was no accident that his bosses had chosen him to do the pedophile study. He didn't know it but he had become somewhat of a legend in the research department for his analytical talents. He had a knack for finding what others would consider insignificant bits of information and turning them into major pieces of an investigative puzzle.

* * *

Block 1

Backtracking Cole's route, guilt seemed to grow stronger with each step as Jan thought about how they fell into an unfortunate category when it came to school bus transportation. They lived close enough to their son's school that he wasn't eligible to ride the school bus, but far enough away to question the safety of walking. Neither of them liked the idea of Cole walking, but Dan worked early hours at the newspaper and Jan's hours as a nurse at nearby St. Christopher's Hospital were usually early and always unpredictable. Driving Cole to school was out. In another time and another town there would probably have been a number of neighbors to pitch in and help ... but not here.

Block 2

Jan reflected that she had been the most vocal in her opposition to Cole walking. She had suggested he take a taxicab to and from school each day. Dan had logically argued that they couldn't afford it and that taxis in the area just weren't reliable.

Block 3 and no Cole.

"Oh God, how I wish I had stuck to my guns and not let Dan win that one!" she cried out-loud in her horror, as her heavy feet seemed to sink further into the concrete. "We should have gone with the taxi or come up with some other idea ... but no ... as always it was easier to go along with Dan than to fight. Now my weakness may have killed my son."

Block 4

She thought about how at first, they had filed a special request with the school district to make an exception. The answer had been a simple no.

Block 5

They appealed the first decision and got a second no. They talked about filing another appeal, but by then the school year was close at hand and it didn't seem it would do any good. "Why didn't we get an attorney and push it the whole way?" she asked herself out loud in the way many parents often ask themselves why they didn't fight the system harder for their children's welfare. The sidewalk now felt like quicksand, swallowing her legs like an insatiable, hungry beast.

* * *

The case of the execution style murders of a large number of Asians on the West Coast was a good example of FBI Researcher Ross Huggins' intuitive and investigative talent. From San Diego to Seattle, Asians kept turning up dead with no clues other than a strange, undecipherable design of a circle inside of a triangle branded into the palms of their right hands. It was Ross' dogged research that identified the design as an ancient symbol last known to be used by a Japanese clan of smugglers in the early 1900's. The Shangsitsu Clan ruthlessly killed anyone who got in the way of its enterprises and its victims always turned up with the circle and star brand. The purpose was apparently to show others who might be thinking about defying the clan what would happen to them if they did.

The clan had gone out of existence around 1916 and no one had heard of them since ... until now. With Ross's information FBI investigators traced the symbol to a modern-day group of very well-organized heroin smugglers operating out of Japan, Hong Kong and the West Coast of the United States. Their aim was to take over the heroin trade in the western

U. S. and they didn't mind killing all their Asian competitors to get the job done.

The FBI received personal accolades from the President of the United States when, after a long investigation, it arrested 52 members of the drug syndicate and charged several of them with the Asian murders. Ross Huggins' name was never mentioned, but he didn't mind. He knew that his branch of the bureau was one that could never receive a lot of attention. He often thought the American people would be quite surprised to learn of some of the taxpayer-funded research he and his department did.

* * *

Block 6

Several months of Cole walking to school went by without incident and the longer it continued the more used to it Dan and Jan got, and the more they forgot about the possible danger. It seems to be human nature to assume that when things are going well they will continue to go well, as if potential hazards initially acknowledged somehow magically disappear. But the danger hadn't disappeared and it was now hitting the Foresters square in the face like a wrecking ball through a Japanese paper wall.

Block 7

Jan was so distraught and filled with anxiety that she heaved her lead-weighted legs up out of the pavement and ploddingly ran the next block to the schoolyard.

Block 8

The last block. No Cole, but a flood of desperate sorrow drowning her heart and her legs disappearing into a swirling pool of guilt.

After talking to the school secretary, who confirmed that Cole had been in school that day, but that she had not seen him leave, Jan searched every inch of the school yard. She then walked what seemed like the longest eight blocks of her life back to her home asking everyone she saw on the street if they had seen him. No one had. In the back of her mind this confirmed what she had suspected after living in the Washington area for several years. In big cities, as a defense mechanism, people tend to subconsciously tune out many of the things going on around them. She knew because she had done it herself.

* * *

There was the study, Ross Huggins reflected, on how many grams of street cocaine it takes to kill the typical intravenous drug user. Another was done to find out how much money the average mafia hit man spends on clothes annually. A third was Ross' all-time favorite; research to ascertain how many married Capitol

Hill politicians were having extramarital affairs. All these he put down in his who cares category. But as the father of two, how could he not care about child molesters? At least, he thought, as his fingers moved nimbly over the keys, this study was something he could get his teeth into. Just as the thought entered his mind a strange feeling came over him that it would turn out to be much more than that.

CHAPTER 4

"Are you Jan Forester?" Police Detective Jack Adams pulled his squad car up beside Jan just as she reached her house, simultaneously rolling down his window. Jack was a solidly built man with prematurely graying hair, bushy eyebrows and a large, puffy nose that looked like it had been inside more than one glass of liquor. At the same time, however, he carried the air of a very professional and competent law enforcer. But above all he was a man and he instantly noticed Jan's ravishing, but pure and innocent good looks.

"Yes," she nearly screamed. She whirled around with tears streaming down a pretty face suddenly filled with a hope that replaced a little of her numb, heavy feeling. Please God, she begged silently, say they found him!

"I know this is difficult, but could you go inside and bring us a recent picture of your son and a piece of clothing he has recently worn that hasn't been washed?"

"O. K.," was all Jan said as the numbness returned. She walked up the sidewalk past the azalea bushes Cole had helped her plant, absent-mindedly brushing a low-hanging cherry blossom branch out of her way. Just before opening her front door she noticed another squad car and a police station wagon that said Canine Unit pull up behind Adams' car. A minute later with Cole's picture in one hand and one of his shirts in the other she was greeted by Officer Adams and two other policemen standing in her front yard, one holding a leash connected to a big bloodhound.

* * *

"Why do you think you have a sexual attraction to young boys, Doug?" Dr. Johnson asked Douglas Glassman during their third therapy session.

He thought about that one. "I was hoping you'd tell me," was his honest response.

"Perhaps I'll be able to ... in time. But we have a lot of exploring to do before we can answer that one." Dr. Johnson believed that finding the root of a psychological problem was essential to resolving it. She also believed that a pedophile could be rehabilitated through psychoanalysis.

"My problem is that I have this urge to have sex with boys, but I hate myself for it. I think men having sex with kids is sick and totally repulsive. But still ... I sometimes have the desire. I just want to get rid of it."

"Doug, just knowing it's wrong is a good step toward recovery. I've had several patients with the same desires as yours who don't see anything wrong with it at all. I think their cases were more difficult to deal with than yours will be."

With those words a light bulb suddenly went on in Doug's head. He didn't fully comprehend it, but a message was trying to work its way through in the form of a nagging question he had kept buried for many years.

* * *

"Mrs. Forester please give the shirt to Officer Anderson ... he'll let the dog smell it and then they'll go around the area and try to pick up your son's scent." Jan did as Officer Jack Adams asked. "And, if you would, please give the picture to my partner, Officer Simms, and he'll start driving around looking for Cole." Again, Jan robotically did what she was asked. The officer took the photo with a thank you and left.

"Now, we've got to do one more thing," Adams said as he walked back to his car and reached inside, pulling out a laptop, "If you would find another recent picture of Cole I'll scan it and email it back to the station. They'll distribute it to units in the out-lying areas so we can get everyone looking for him." Jan instantly went into the house to retrieve another picture. Five minutes later, Cole's picture was printed out at police headquarters. "Now," said Adams with practiced, yet sincere empathy, "Let's get all the information so we can find your son."

* * *

In spite of the resurfaced question in Doug Glassman's mind, the fact that Dr. Christine Johnson had dealt with pedophile patients before gave him confidence in her abilities and gave him hope.

"I know it's going to take a while to psychoanalyze this, but, what I really need is something that can push these perverted thoughts about children out of my mind when I get them," he told her.

"I know and I have three meditation techniques I'll show you. If you work hard, one should help." Dr. Johnson then showed Douglas three separate techniques, all based on the transcendental meditation method of relaxing your mind, but each with its own unique approach. "The key here is to work hard at these techniques and you'll undoubtedly find the one that's best for you. But you must also do physical exercise ... jogging, bicycling or whatever ... until you're too exhausted to think about these cravings. I recommend regular exercise anyway, because the old adage healthy body, healthy mind is more true than most people realize."

"Anything to get rid of these desires."

"Doug, for us to make progress in your therapy I may have to ask you some hard questions and it's important that you be honest with me. O.K.?"

"O. K."

"The first tough question I have to ask is, have you ever acted out your desires?"

Doug nervously looked around the room. He fidgeted in his chair and his face turned beet-red.

"It's important that you be honest with me Doug," she said soothingly.

"No ... I haven't. It's too sick."

Now the voice in Doug's head was back pestering his subconscious with the nagging question.

* * *

Tires squealed around the corner outside of the Forester home as Dan wheeled his Mustang to a stop right behind Officer Jack Adams' squad car. As Jan looked out the window the sun's reflection off of the car's over-waxed, shiny chrome bumper seemed to blind her. She reflected subconsciously that when your mind is racing ... everyday things can take on a new intensity.

"Must be your husband," Adams said with a sympathetic half-grin. At that moment he took full and detailed account of how uncommonly attractive Jan was, with crimson hair cascading over svelte shoulders and full red lips that didn't need lipstick. A hint of freckles accentuated her tear-stained face with its natural glow and sharp features. Her saucy figure showed some heavy workouts at the health club. *Enough horny stuff*, Adams thought guiltily as he snapped back to reality, this woman's in pain and I've got to help her, not fantasize about her. Having two children of his own he felt for Jan.

Sitting at the Foresters' kitchen table, Adams asked Jan to explain the events of the last two hours several times. Looking around he noticed how the bright and cheery kitchen decor contrasted with the dark and solemn mood in the room. He correctly figured that the blue and white wallpaper with multi-colored birds flying in all directions was Jan's and not Dan's work. Dan, meanwhile, sat with his 6' 1" frame rigidly planted in a solid oak kitchen chair which he had never found very comfortable and found even less so now, as he uncharacteristically drummed his fingers on the table.

"Let's go over it again," he heard Officer Adams say for the third time. He was getting frustrated, but his personal fear combined with his professional experience made him sense the urgency beneath the tedious routine. Beads of sweat formed on his brow and the acrid reek of fear, which had somewhat abated, crept slowly and horribly back into his being. It rose up inside of him again like volcanic lava boiling up through the earth's crust trying to find a way out so it can blast through to throw pain, death and destruction everywhere. In the back of his mind the only comparable feeling he could find was the horror and carnage of Iraq, for which nothing in nineteen years of life could have prepared him. But this was worse than Iraq because there he was only afraid of dying; now he was more afraid of living ... without his son.

Finally, Dan couldn't take it anymore as the dreadful fear worked its way through his self-control. He stood up and said softly, but firmly to Officer Adams, "I appreciate your need to know the facts." His volcanic voice slowly began to rise. "But wouldn't it be better if you were combing the neighborhood right now look-ing for Cole," it reached a pinnacle of loud, intense frustration, "Instead of sitting here making us repeat everything a hundred times!" It erupted in an explosive cre-scendo spewing rage all over the room's gaily pictured walls, drowning the colorful birds in a gushing sea of angry despair, and startling Jan and Officer Adams. But Jack didn't miss a beat.

"First of all Mr. Forester," he said calmly, "I have a son of my own. I know what you must be going through. Secondly, a police dog is combing the area trying to pick up your son's scent and my partner is searching this neighborhood right now while another squad car is looking in the surrounding area. And thirdly, please trust me when I tell you that having dealt with this type of case many times in the past, this is the best course of action. The reason I'm having you repeat the story so many times is that you may remember something important the third or fourth time around that you forgot the first few times."

As much as he hated to admit it, Dan knew from his own crime-reporting experience that Adams was right, but he found it hard to look at this case with professional detachment. What if that were my kid were the words that kept racing through his mind because those were the exact words he had said to himself every time he worked on a missing child story. Now it was his kid and he had a feeling his worst nightmare was just beginning. Jack Adams felt compassion for both Dan and Jan, but he felt something else too.

* * *

Doug Glassman left his afternoon therapy session with Dr. Johnson with an anxious spring in his step and headed straight for his blind box at the post office. It was there. Chicken Little, the child pornography magazine he had been expecting and he was excited. He sat in his car and poured over the pictures and stories of men having sex with boys and boys having sex with each other. One picture of three men and a boy having sex so excited him that he reached for his genitals when he suddenly remembered he had baseball practice in 15 minutes. Hesitating only for a moment he tucked the magazine under the seat and drove away with his groin throbbing and the long-buried question finally emerging from his subconscious. It was a voice screaming with full force and he could almost hear it asking the long-buried question, *Is there really anything wrong with it*? His parents didn't know. His wife and children didn't know and the people in his business and social circles didn't know. The only person who knew Doug Glassman was a pedophile was his psychologist. Well, there was someone else.

* * *

In missing child cases like the Forester case many law enforcement officers often suspect the parents first. But with this one, thought Officer Jack Adams, there is more to it than that. Every time he asked Jan about the neighbor who saw Cole being dragged into a car she hesitated, looked down and said she was so upset that she hadn't asked the neighbor's name so she didn't really know who he was. Even more suspiciously, she didn't seem too interested in finding out who he was. It just didn't make sense that she wouldn't do everything she could to find the only witness to her son's disappearance. Besides, if the neighbor knew Cole, then Jan should know him too. Adams took a chance.

"There really is no neighbor is there, Mrs. Forester?"

Up until then Jan had maintained a white-knuckled grip on the edge of the oak kitchen table. When Adams asked the question her hands quickly slid off the table leaving two large pools of sweat. The color drained from her face as if all life had gone out of her body leaving her limp as a wet rag, while at the same time she felt like a gigantic burden was lifted from her mind. "No ... there is no neighbor," she said choking back the tears, "Dan told me to tell you that so you wouldn't drag your feet getting here." Time stood still. Yet, a strange sense of relief settled over her because, above all else, Jan prized honesty.

"Jan!" barked her husband who shot her a look as sharp as a knife. Unlike Jan, Dan knew that cops often suspect the missing child's parents of foul play and this certainly wouldn't help matters. The next 15 seconds seemed like 15 years to them.

The tension in the room was thick enough to cut with a dull blade as the three of them sat frozen, brought together by horror.

* * *

Doug Glassman had lied to the good doctor. There was someone else who knew about his problem. It was the young boy he had sexually molested, Bobby Segal, the 7-year-old first baseman on his little league baseball team. Doug thought about Bobby as he left Dr. Johnson's office and drove down the street. Bobby's parents were in the middle of a very messy divorce when he first joined Doug's team and Doug could tell he was having a tough time dealing with it. So, one day after baseball practice Doug sat Bobby down and they talked things out. After that, these after-practice discussions became a regular, innocent event with Doug often giving Bobby a ride home. Bobby's mother was happy that her son and his coach had become good friends because the only other man in his life, his father, had moved out of the house.

Then, one day Bobby was more upset than usual and after practice he told Doug through tear-stained eyes that his father was moving to California and he was afraid he would never see him again. Doug's heart genuinely went out to his young first baseman as he instinctively put his arms around him to comfort him. How could any father leave this little guy? he asked himself. He only wished he had a son like Bobby.

But then, without intending it to, his affection for the boy took a more physical form. As he held the whimpering lad in his arms all the years of repressed desire suddenly welled up inside him and exploded into one great, uncontrollable eruption of love and lust. It seemed to Doug like it was natural and right. Yet, he knew somewhere in the dark recesses of his being that it wasn't. Although he tried to stop himself Doug found himself succumbing to his instincts. Suddenly he was fondling Bobby's genitals outside of his clothing, and a thoroughly confused Bobby did nothing to stop him. Doug then took Bobby by the hand to his car and performed oral sex on him in the front seat while masturbating himself. Afterward, filled with remorse, shame and guilt Doug explained to Bobby that he had done what he did to make him feel better and that he shouldn't tell anyone what had happened because they wouldn't understand. He also promised him that it would never happen again. A baffled Bobby agreed, still not entirely sure just what had happened.

Now, as Doug turned into the park the thoughts of his experience with Bobby had a contradictory effect on him. The sex had him aroused, but the weight of what he had actually done to the boy made him physically ill. He finally had to stop the car, hang his head out the window and retch. "I am a monster," he choked, "I love him and I violated him. I don't deserve to live!" He pulled into the parking lot next to the baseball diamond and wept for Bobby. But Bobby wasn't the only one.

* * *

Police Officer Jack Adams knew that duty required him to include the Foresters' lie in his report. *But duty to who*, he thought. His duty, he felt, was more to these parents than to his superiors and their bureaucracy. Looking at the Foresters' faces, something told him that the only thing they were guilty of was loving their kid. Besides, he knew that if the lie was included in his report, police investigators would look more for the parents' culpability than they would for Cole.

"Dan was right," came Adams' decision, "We'll just leave out the neighbor."

"Thanks officer," was all Dan could feebly say as he nearly collapsed with relief. He had taken a gamble and won, something which Jan missed entirely as she struggled to hold onto her self-control.

Adams went on, "The big question is are either of you involved in anything someone would have a reason to kidnap Cole for?"

"No," was the combined answer.

"No child custody dispute from another marriage or relationship?"

"No."

"Do you have money kidnappers might want to extort from you?"

"All we have is $50,000 in an IRA account that I inherited from my father. Other than that, we barely have any money in the bank," was Dan's answer as he glanced at Jack and thought he recognized a look of understanding of the poverty cops and journalists often have in common.

"Do either of you buy or take drugs?" Adams asked thinking drug dealers could be involved.

This time the answer was a combined and firm "No." Both of them loathed anything to do with illegal drugs.

"Have you noticed any adult who has recently taken a special interest in Cole?" Adams went on.

After giving it some thought the answer was again "No."

"Are you aware of any problems Cole has been having at school lately?"

"No," Jan answered, "Cole has always gotten along well at school and the teachers and kids like him."

After a few more questions Officer Adams shut his notebook and looking up at the two tortured faces said, "Now for the tedious part. My partner and I are going to talk to each and every person who lives between here and the school and in a six-block radius to see if anyone saw anything. While we do that you two should make a list of anyone who even remotely knows Cole and call them. Make a list of questions to ask and ask each of them the whole list. The first question, of course, should be do they have any idea where he might be? The second question should be did they see him at school today? Did they see him leave school today and did they notice anything different or strange about him? The third question should be does he take drugs and if so who does he get them from and where can that person be found?"

"But Cole doesn't take drugs," Jan blurted as she looked up from the note pad on which she was writing Adams' instructions.

"I know, I know, but you would be surprised at how many times I've heard that and it turned out to be wrong. Besides, we've got to cover all the bases," was Adams' reply.

A reluctant "O.K." was all Jan could muster as she continued taking notes.

"Then, ask if they have seen Cole with any adult, probably a man, recently, at school or out of school. Ask if they know of any problems of any kind Cole was having. And finally, ask if anyone has heard Cole ever, and I mean ever, talk about running away from home and, if so, what destination he might have mentioned. Add to those specific questions any of your own that you can think of dealing with Cole's life. Think of specific problems that he may be dealing with and ask if any of these people have ever heard him talk about them. Finally, sit down and think about the last few months and try to remember if Cole ever mentioned anything to you about any adult male, something that you may not have thought too much about at the time, but that you may be suspicious of now. If you come up with anyone call the police dispatcher and have him patch you through to my car radio. I'll tell him you may call. I know this is painful, but often times it is a man that somehow gets involved in a young boy's life."

Up to this point Jan hadn't seen this as a possibility and hearing Adams say it just intensified her terror and produced sick, twisted scenes in her mind. Dan, on the other hand, had seen this possibility right away and the idea that his absence might have driven Cole to any kind of relationship with a man was eating away at him.

"There will be another officer here within the hour to hook tape recording equipment up to your phone just in case this is a ransom kidnapping," said Officer Adams not really believing it was. "The calls to people who know Cole are very important, so write down the answers and I'll pick them up later. Above all, hold your faith that we will find Cole." He gave each of them a sympathetic look and walked out the door into the crisp night air with a heavy heart leaving them alone with their excruciating pain.

CHAPTER 5

"I can't just sit here," Dan told Jan anxiously, "You make the calls and I'll go out looking for him." His nerves were as taut as a tightrope and he knew he had to get out of the house and do something. "Besides, you know more of Cole's friends than I do," he rationalized as he got up and reached for his jacket.

"But what if the kidnappers call?" came Jan's desperate response. Dan already knew the answer to that question. There were no kidnappers and there would be no call.

"If the kidnappers call just do whatever the cop with the recording equipment tells you," he said mechanically as Jan followed him to the door. "Just agree to whatever they ask. I'll be home later and we can go over it then. We really have no choice but to agree to whatever they say." He hugged Jan with the little consolation he had left, which wasn't much since he was rapidly using up whatever he had on himself, and gave her a tragic kiss on the forehead. "I'll be back, hopefully with good news," was all he could say as he closed the screen door behind him. He reflected, as he left, that he really did love Jan. In fact, she was the only woman, and there had been plenty, that he had ever loved. But he knew somewhere deep inside himself that this whole thing was going to be bigger than both of them or any love they felt for each other. All he could see as he pulled away was his wife's tortured, anguished face at the window, a sight that would haunt him for years to come. Fighting her way through the tears Jan began numbly making the list of calls. She heard Dan's car burn rubber down the street and wondered where he was hurrying.

* * *

The cigarette tasted stale in Lieutenant Derek Lindsay's mouth. But after his all-nighter it was the only thing standing between him and sleep, which wouldn't have been a good idea as he sat in on the morning briefing in precinct 11 of the New York City Police Department. A sandy blonde with deep blue, baggy eyes and a sagging husky physique, he looked like life had beaten him up one too many times as he slouched in his chair, eyelids half-mast. He appeared older than his 45 years and when someone inevitably commented on his seasoned look he would often say, "It's not the age it's the mileage," and he'd been all over the road.

"I hope we're not keeping you up back there, Lindsay," quipped Officer Luis Seldano, an old friend who reveled in razzing him about his rough and tumble lifestyle.

"Well, you are," Lindsay predictably responded, "But go ahead anyway."

This was a typical morning briefing, at least when Derek was in attendance. He made this one only because he had stayed up all night drinking and playing stud poker with some rather nefarious characters. He figured if he went home before going to the police station he might fall asleep and miss work completely.

Derek Lindsay was one of the NYPD's best detectives. He had broken a lot of big cases and put some heavy hitters in the crime world behind bars. But his success had had a price. At age 40 he had an estranged wife and a 15-year-old son, Gary, who didn't really want him around much. Dealing with criminals and deviants all day, continuously witnessing his fellow man's inhumanity, and frequently being frustrated by a justice system that often seemed to favor the criminal over the victim had left Derek an angry man. Too much of that anger had come home with him until his marriage couldn't take it anymore.

* * *

Dan Forester had no idea where he was going. As always, he just wanted to do something, anything to actively pursue the situation, even if it meant driving blindly down the street. He knew that even though he desperately wanted to stay and comfort Jan, if he had stayed in the house he would have short-circuited like an over-loaded fuse box. So, he drove around the area looking everywhere, searching for any sign of the only thing that had ever given his life any purpose and meaning. The tears were now uncontrollably streaming down his face for the first time in many years.

Sitting at a stop light several hours later Dan was lost in despondence as car horns blared behind him. The clamorous din slowly filtered into his consciousness, intruded upon his reverie, and woke him up to where he was and what he was doing.

Looking first behind him and then ahead, he noticed an old family sedan driving by. It was painted fire engine-red with black and blue racing stripes. *What a joke*, his wandering mind mused as he subconsciously thought about how stupid it is to try to make a big, clumsy car look like a sports car. No matter what you do, it's still a big clumsy car. He unconsciously pushed the gas pedal and cruised through the intersection, looking at his watch as the high-pitched chorus of horns faded into the backdrop of his rear-view mirror.

He had always hated wearing a watch and had tried several times to go without it. To him it was a collar of slavery strangling his wrist, enslaving him to a schedule and choking any spontaneity out of him. He had always wanted time to be fluid and flow with no sense of urgency or rush and when he went without his watch he felt freer. The only problem was that during these watch-less times he was usually late for appointments, so he always put it back on. He told Jan once that a watch was like one-half of a set of handcuffs holding him prisoner. He said he felt trapped by time and his watch was the jailer. After a few more scotches he told her that his life could never be carefree and untroubled as long as he was chained to a timetable by a wrist watch like a dog tied to its tether. "Welcome to the real world," she had said, "and stop mixing your metaphors." Nevertheless, he didn't want his life to be dictated by a timepiece, but it was.

Now, as he looked down at his jailer he realized he had been driving aimlessly for three-and-a-half hours. It was time to pack it in, and feeling his world crashing down around him, Dan pulled back in front of his house late in the evening with nothing but a near-empty gas tank to show for his efforts. He wanted to go into the house to see Cole sitting there and find out it had all been a big mistake. But he knew that wasn't going to happen and the fear of what he would find inside kept him frozen to the car seat, paralyzed with dread.

Finally, he found the courage to pry himself out of the car. As he walked up the sidewalk to his house he looked up beyond the cherry blossom tree in the front yard and noticed the overhead black clouds pregnant with rain. They looked as if they were sagging downward from the weight of the water they contained.

They looked like he felt. But there was something else about the clouds that Dan couldn't quite put his finger on. It almost looked like an obscure face in the clouds. Then, suddenly a shudder shot through him with incredible force. He didn't know what it was but he knew it was bad. It was all he could do to open the door and walk in the house.

Jan's telephone calls had turned up no useful information. No one had noticed anything out of the ordinary about Cole, and she now sat stiffly waiting with a policeman and his tape recorder. She shot Dan a hopeful glance but seeing no encouragement she went back to staring at the telephone. It was as if she expected to see the spark of a call from Cole or his kidnappers come flashing through the wall and trailing up along the cord to explode into a hopeful ring in the phone itself. Just then the telephone rang.

* * *

"I love you and will always love you," Detective Derek Lindsay remembered his ex-wife Julie saying. But then she also said, "What I don't love is what your job turns you into." It was an old story about a cop who had to be street tough and mean just to survive on his job, but then was expected to turn back into a sensitive, loving husband and father when he got home. Like so many police officers, Derek had a hard time keeping his two worlds separate, though he tried desperately.

But in the three years since his divorce Derek had finally figured out that he was a cop and nothing could change that. Now he slumped in his chair half-asleep and half-listening to Officer Seldano run down the day's activities. "One more thing," said Seldano, "We've got a report of a child-stealing ring operating out of Manhattan. We've got no details other than that homeless kids are being kidnapped and sold to rich foreigners. We don't know who or where and we don't even know if it's true. But shake your snitches down for any information you can get."

Derek raised an eyelid and suddenly came out of his fog. One of his best informants was connected to the kiddie sex trade and while he hated dealing with him, he sometimes provided a wealth of good information. "Gotta' check with Sammy," he thought as he half-staggered out of the briefing room.

CHAPTER 6

The tape recorder was rolling and the police were listening as Jan picked up the telephone receiver. But on the other end of the line was one of her nursing colleagues asking if she could work a shift for her. The dreaded, but hoped for call never came and after one week the police investigators disconnected the recording equipment and told Dan and Jan they would continue working on the case. What they didn't tell them was that they were suspects in their son's disappearance, although Officer Jack Adams didn't share the suspicion.

The hours turned into dark days and the days into even darker weeks. Jan spent the first ten days after Cole's disappearance hanging onto desperate hope. When it became apparent that unrealistic hope was all she had, she broke down in a fit of anguish that lasted for weeks. She did nothing but cry and in the rare moments when she wasn't crying she just stared straight ahead and would not talk. Her only baby was gone and there didn't seem to be much reason to go on.

Dan went numb. He felt empty and hollow inside and only felt any emotion in his frequent nightmares. Some nights he dreamed that Cole was trying to tell him something, but he couldn't quite make out what. One night he thought he heard him say, "Don't do it daddy. Wait for the prophecy."

He dreamed that he asked, "Don't do what?" and "What prophecy?" But Cole didn't answer and only shook his head as he disappeared into the haze of his cloudy unconsciousness. In the morning, Dan figured it was just another dream. He tried to fill the void with his own private investigation into his son's disappearance and got a one-month leave of absence from his job to do it.

* * *

"C'mon Sean ... throat the bagel and let's hit it," Derek Lindsay yelled at his partner, Sean Casey who was nursing a serious hangover.

"Where's the riot?" Sean asked.

"Gotta' go see Sam the Man."

"O. K. I'm coming," Sean sputtered as he wolfed down the last crusty chunk.

Once in the car Derek told Sean what Seldano had said about a possible pedophile ring. "If there's anyone who would know about a child stealing ring it's Sam."

"Yeah," said Sean pensively. The subject of children reminded him of his own disintegrating domestic situation. His wife was divorcing him and he was about to lose his son John. "Ya' know ... life sucks."

Derek instantly knew what his partner and friend was thinking about. "Ya' think?" was all he said.

"It's not like I was a bad husband or father. I was always there as much as I could be and I've been a pretty good father to Johnny."

"I guess pretty good isn't enough these days. We're supposed to be super dads or somthin'."

"Ya' mean like the dads on TV?"

"Something like that."

"Yea, but I never even pulled half the crap on Joanne that you pulled on Julie."

That one hurt because Derek knew he hadn't been the ideal husband and father and that's what had led to his own divorce. The last shoe had dropped three years earlier when he and Sean busted a drug house in Brooklyn. They found a trashed-out row house with feces on the floor and several bags of heroin and crack in the closet. They also found two gaunt little girls whose prostitute mother had been pimping them out for drug money. That night Derek tried to drown the sickening sight in a pool of whisky at the corner bar. The only problem was that he forgot his son Gary's birthday party, which he was supposed to come home to right after work. When he dragged in late and drunk Julie laid it out that it was over. The next day he moved out.

"I know I was a prick to forget Gary's birthday," Derek said as they waited in a sweaty traffic jam, "But for crying out loud there were some extenuating circumstances and she didn't even want to hear about 'em."

"I know. After a while Joanne didn't really want to hear it anymore either. They can't really understand it unless they go through it themselves," said Sean thinking about his own impending divorce, "In fact, no one can. But then, no one else is stupid enough to risk their lives and be exposed to all this scum for a lousy fifty-grand a year."

"Yeah, but don't forget the overtime!"

"Yeah ... right."

* * *

Jan cried herself into an almost comatose state. She cried until there were no tears left and then she just sat and stared numbly out of the window. It went on for weeks with her parents and everyone that knew her worried that she might kill herself. Numb himself, Dan tried to help but couldn't. The best he could do was to urge her to get psychiatric help and arrange her appointment. Dan's self-help, meanwhile, came more and more in a bottle.

"I really see no reason for living," Jan told her therapist, Dr. Joan Simmons, in their first session. "My only child is gone. He could be dead. And even if he's alive, he's probably been through so much hell, he'll never be the same again."

"Even when things seem hopeless," Dr. Simmons had matter-of-factly told her, "You can't give up on Cole." After several sessions Dr. Simmons realized that if Jan lost hope, no matter how irrational that hope might be, she could easily slip into a deep, suicidal depression. So, she held out hope and put off worrying about what to do when hope ran out until the time when it actually did.

"There are two kinds of psychoanalysts," Dr. Simmons told her in their second meeting, "Those who believe the best road to mental recovery is to explore all of the underlying causes of the patient's problem and address them one-by-one ... and then there are those who speculate on the various roots of the sickness, but concentrate on treatment or cure more than on cause. I fall into the second category."

"Recognizing the possible underlying causes of your depression is fine," she went on, "But first of all, we pretty much already know what they are. Secondly, if this state-of-mind continues and graduates into chronic, long-term depression we might track down many subconscious causes. But it could take years getting the right one, and by then we may do you further damage by concentrating more on the roots of the problem than on its solution."

Dr. Simmons immediately put Jan on an anti-depressant but warned her that it might make her nervous at first and could take six to eight weeks to really kick in. She also warned her of the possible side effects, one of which was a decreased sex drive.

* * *

Derek Lindsay and his partner Sean Casey drove on in stony silence.
"Why do we do it?" Sean broke the solemn mood.
"Like you said, stupidity."

"Well, I'd like to say it's duty or protecting the public, but we both know that's a load of shit. None of us really wants to admit it, but I think we crave the action."

"Oh, I don't know if I crave it all that much."

"Sure, you do. Somewhere deep inside you need it and love it. Other guys lost that craving when they realized just how vulnerable they really are. But us ... like you said ... we're stupid. We never lost it and we've had it so long we got sort of addicted to it 'til there's no other way."

"You always get on this shit when you're hung over. You're like trying to convince yourself you shouldn't be a cop anymore."

"O.K. O.K., but tell me the truth ... do you ever think about your civic duty and the good you're doing as a cop anymore?"

After a long pause the simple answer was, "Not really."

"I rest my case. But I do wonder sometimes why we keep putting ourselves through shit like that bust. How can a mother starve her two kids and then sell them out to child molesters?"

"I can name that tune with one word ... drugs."

"Yeah. Yeah. They're so addicting and all that crap. I think if a woman abuses her kids like that, it's just in her and she'd do it to get money for anything."

"That one really got to you didn't it?"

"Yeah ... and I know it got to you."

It hit too close to home and Derek shrugged it off. "But you've seen shit like that before and even worse. Why that one?"

"I don't know. I guess with my family life shot to hell I'm thinking more about parenthood these days ... know what I mean?"

"Yeah, I do," Derek said as they turned off onto a side street. They came to a stop and parked behind a bar where Sam sometimes hung out. But Sam was about to give them a lot more than they bargained for.

⚔ ⚔ ⚔

Three months of therapy and it was not going well. Dr. Simmons saw Jan sinking deeper and deeper into the pit of despair and knew she had to do something. Up to now the anti-depressants and the therapy had helped her keep her hopes up that Cole might be found. But now hope had run out.

"I just can't do it anymore," she said in one session.

"Do what?" the doctor asked.

"Live."

Dr. Simmons had learned over the months that Jan did not say things like this lightly and she instantly realized that if she didn't give Jan a reason to live she was going to have a dead patient and friend on her hands. *But what*? Then it hit her. Jan needed a purpose.

* * *

Omaha's star reporter Susan Jensen stared numbly at her computer screen. Because she had covered the Jeremy Fenner story so closely and because she had actually become friends with the Fenners, she felt the discovery of Jeremy's body was a real milestone in her life as well as in theirs. It was a sad climax to an even sadder situation in which the boy's parents went through five tortuous years of not knowing their son's fate and imagining only the worst. Susan followed the case every step of the way. She felt the Fenners' pain and became deeply involved in the story, something her professional ethics had never let her do before. She grew close to Jeremy's parents and passionate about abused children.

Perhaps her own childhood had made her relate strongly to the issue.

* * *

It was Dr. Simmons who made Jan see that she was not doing her son or herself any good by wallowing in self-pity and grief. So, even though she knew it was unrealistic, she suggested to Jan that she begin an organized effort to find her son. Something, anything to give her hope and occupy her mind.

"Oh ... I don't think I could do anything like that," was Jan's initial reaction. But Dr. Simmons pressed on and after a few sessions convinced her that it might save her life and that she might even find Cole.

Jan took her suggestion and started the Find Cole Forester Foundation, turning her home into a clearinghouse for clues to her son's fate. She had a special telephone line installed and put the phone number on posters with Cole's picture on them which were distributed all over Washington, Maryland, and Virginia. A family friend helped her build a Web site dedicated to Cole and she had the picture and number put on milk cartons, semi-trailer trucks, bill boards and anything else that would be seen by people all over the country. And she paid for it with Find Cole Forester Foundation money that she raised on the Internet and from the increasing number of speeches she was asked to give on the subject of missing children.

There was no doubt that Jan desperately wanted to find Cole. What most people didn't realize was that one of her principle reasons for doing all this was to stay sane. Subconsciously, she knew now that if she sat and thought she might well sink into a suicidal depression. To anyone seeing and hearing her on the telephone and giving speeches she seemed fine. But in reality, she felt numb. The depression and the anti-depressant had left her a walking zombie going through the motions, afraid to stop lest she feel the pain that lurked just beneath the surface. Work, thankfully, kept her mind occupied.

Dan was also numb, but for a different reason. Having seen all this effort come to nothing in numerous cases while on the crime beat, he had now given up hope of ever finding Cole alive. Like the police, he had come up dry. Often during his investigation, he had the eerie feeling that someone was trying to tell him something, but he didn't know who or what. He wasn't having as many nightmares as before, but he still sometimes dreamed that Cole was trying to tell him something. One night it sounded like he said, "It's God's providence, not yours," whatever that meant, but he marked it all up to stress. There was simply nothing left to do and he knew it.

So, he went back to work, but now he spent his days sipping whisky out of a hidden bottle at his desk, nearly always inebriated, but somehow still able to do his job. In earlier days Dan had learned well how to be intoxicated without showing it. When he returned from Iraq he went to the University of Virginia and there he learned how to handle his alcohol. At U. V. heavy drinking without drunken behavior was a sport. If you acted drunk you were weak, but if you were drunk as a skunk and able to carry on a complicated, philosophical discussion you were admired. Even with that talent, however, it wasn't long before everyone at the newspaper knew what was going on. Most simply felt sorry for him and said nothing.

* * *

Susan Jensen's own childhood undoubtedly made her more sensitive to child sex abuse than most. She had gone to live with her father in Tampa Bay, Florida after her parents were divorced and her mother remarried. But her younger sister, Jenna, had stayed behind with their mother and stepfather. Sitting at her computer terminal trying to write a story about Jeremy Fenner, Susan reflected back on the night when Jenna was visiting her and her father in Tampa. "Do you and daddy ever lay in bed naked?" Susan still shuddered in horror at her sister's question.

"No! Of course not! Why would you ask such a thing?" she reacted, hoping she wouldn't hear what she suspected was coming.

"Oh, I just wondered," said Jenna.

* * *

Sitting in her favorite chair and gazing listlessly out of the living room picture window, Jan reflected on how ironic it was that in her home the weak had come out strong and the strong weak. She was channeling her grief into work, while Dan was channeling his into self-pity. But she thought to herself, she did not have the same psychological baggage her husband had. She had grown up in a small town in Illinois where life was much simpler than it was for Dan in his Baltimore neighborhood. While Jan was learning simple lessons like "you work, you eat," Dan was learning the more complex lessons of survival as a white boy in a school that was predominantly black.

As she watched a whirlwind of leaves and dust swirl by the window she drifted back to her childhood days in Illinois. It was a blue-collar town where everyone worked hard to scratch out a living. Her father was the president of his labor union when he was offered a lobbyist job at its Washington, D. C. office. He packed up the family and they moved to Laurel, Maryland. At 20 years of age, had just completed two years of nursing school while living at home and decided to go with her family to Washington. She felt she could go further in nursing with a four-year degree and decided to finish it at the University of Maryland in College Park.

* * *

Susan Jensen was still reflecting on her sister's experience when she remembered that later that evening, upset by Jenna's question, she had told their father. Immediately suspicious, he went to his younger daughter. "Honey, it's O.K., tell me ... do you lay in bed naked with anyone?"

There was a long silence. "You can tell me, baby. I won't be mad or disappointed or anything like that," he said hugging her tenderly. "If anyone has told you your mother or I would be upset with you they're wrong. Now, honey, have you ever lain naked with anyone and has anyone touched parts of your body?"

Then it came, first just a drop and then, as the dam of secrecy broke, a torrential flood of the anguish Jenna had felt for three years, experiencing something she somehow knew was completely wrong, but which her stepfather had told her was very right.

"He said it was what all fathers and daughters did, but that I still shouldn't tell anyone or mommy and daddy would hate me and give me away. He said it was just something all fathers and step-fathers did with their daughters, but that they couldn't tell anyone." Now the tears, which had started as a trickle, turned into a raging river overflowing the banks of Jenna's shame. She shook uncontrollably with the sudden knowledge of something she had suspected: that she had been defiled and debased in the worst way.

* * *

Back in Wheaton, Jan continued her daydreams. Her mind now drifted back to when she met Dan. Her political science instructor had invited him and several other Iraq war veterans to talk to the class about the war from a first-hand perspective. Dan wouldn't normally have agreed to talk about it and he hated any veteran who blamed the war for his problems. He was stoic and believed he was in control of his feelings, not some troubling mental imagery. But at the time he was reluctantly seeing a therapist to try and work through some of the anger and lingering PTSD problems she believed were related to his combat experience. It was the therapist who suggested it as a way of getting some of his feelings out and Dan agreed to it begrudgingly.

"You never knew if each mile of patrol would be your last," Jan remembered Dan saying to the class. "Bombs going off everywhere and shooters you never saw killing everyone around you. You never knew who was friend or foe. That was Iraq."

What he didn't tell Jan's class was that the worst part of it all was risking his life for his country and then coming back to a nation that thought he was just another crazy vet who could go ballistic at any moment. And besides, what he really felt young people should know is how much folly the war was ... how it was all about the oil and nothing else. "It wasn't an honorable war," he would say.

"Hell, it wasn't even a real war ... war was never declared ... it was simply to protect American oil companies' interests."

He also didn't mention the fact that, like many veterans, he had problems for which many people blamed the war. From the day he returned to the United States after eighteen months in country he had felt lost, like his life and all life had no meaning. When he got back he felt like an animal out of its natural habitat. He had gotten so used to living on the edge in a constant struggle for survival that life in the states seemed overly-sedate and frivolous.

He also went through periods of intense rage. He was mad at someone or something, but he didn't know who or what. He sometimes suspected that he was subconsciously enraged by how the war had affected his life, but this object of his fury was so intangible it gave him nothing to focus his anger on and that enraged him even more. He was also angry at himself that something as petty as a daily life and death struggle might have had such a profound effect on him. He had seen and done things in Iraq that would haunt him for years to come. It was a war like no other war before it and it had left its mark on many men like Dan, leaving them to flounder between periods of empty depression and raging anger.

When he had first arrived in Bagdad he felt he could handle anything that was thrown at him. *After all,* he thought as his troop plane touched down at the Kuwait Airport, *I just finished four years in another kind of war zone.* Dodsen High School in inner-city Baltimore. At Dodsen about half of the students carried weapons of some sort and often needed them. It was at Dodsen that Dan learned how to fight for practically everything he got. But it was after he landed on that Kuwait runway that he learned what a tea party high school had been compared to the horrors he experienced in the 130-degree madness of Iraq.

Jan remembered how she was struck hard by Dan's rugged good looks and felt his pain as he talked to the students about his wartime experiences. It was almost as if his war for survival resembled the no-bloodshed war her father had fought to survive. In each case she wasn't sure who won or lost. After class she nervously went up to him and asked him some more questions.

* * *

The day after her sister's revelations Susan Jensen's father reported it to police and charges were filed against her stepfather who denied everything. In the trial that followed Jenna had to testify against him. His attorney tried to depict her as a little girl with a very big imagination. In the end the jury found him guilty, but his sentence was little more than a slap on the wrist: two years in a minimum-security prison and then 5 years of probation and psychiatric treatment. Jenna's father sued for custody and won. The two sisters were back together again living in Tampa. Neither they nor their father could ever forgive their mother for not knowing about the abuse. They had rarely communicated since the trial ended.

Susan knew how hard life had been for her little sister since then. She often woke up screaming from nightmares. When she turned fifteen she began a life of promiscuity searching for the sexual approval she had gotten from her stepfather. She drank and took drugs and was in trouble with the police until finally at age 21 a routine blood test showed that Jenna was HIV positive.

Whether it was from a dirty needle or one of the many men and boys she had slept with would never be determined. Susan had no doubt about who was to blame. Had it not been for her stepfather, Jenna could have had a successful, fulfilling life like her own. Instead she was doomed to a life of constant medication and fear, all because of a sexual pervert whom society seemed to tolerate. As for Susan, the thought of sex made her shudder as she had the night of Jenna's revelation. More than one of her boy friends had accused her of being frigid. She often went through the motions without enjoyment because she thought she should. She felt a personal attachment to sexually abused and missing children and produced excellent reports on the subject; reports that won national awards. In fact, with News Director Bob Manson's support she had spent the last year putting together a one-hour documentary on missing children using the Fenner case as a central focus. The plan was to air it if and when Jeremy was found.

"Now's the time," Susan said out loud as she came out of her reverie and she was talking about more than the documentary.

* * *

Staring at nothing out of the window, Jan thought back to Dan's speech to her class and how he had waited outside of the building and acted as if it was an accident that they ran into each other. It almost made her smile. They both knew instantly that there was an intense chemistry between them. He asked her out on a date and the rest could have made the Guinness Book of Sexual Records, if there was such a thing. Dan called it lust at first sight and, in fact, they literally could not keep their hands off of each other. Jan held out for a month, but after that their love and lust for each other exploded into a passionate frenzy.

Jan shared a College Park apartment with two other nursing students who both worked the night shift at a nearby hospital so she and Dan spent most nights in her bed, where they got very little sleep. The downstairs neighbors would often pound on the ceiling because of the hammering of Jan's bed on the floor above them. But then, Jan reflected apathetically, they didn't really need the bed. The bathtub, sink, kitchen counter, dishwasher, stove, balcony and every piece of furniture in the apartment had served as a lovemaking setting. Even when Dan came to pick her up for an actual date, as soon as she kissed him at the door it was like throwing gasoline on a smoldering fire and they usually ended up in a pulsating, erotic human sculpture of arms, legs and other body parts gyrating all over the living room.

Their sexual encounters were intense and acrobatic, and Dan often joked that they were ruining his health. They seldom made it to the intended movie or restaurant. They were hopelessly in love and the sex was beyond belief. This was the first real sexual relationship Jan had ever had. Losing her virginity shortly after her eighteenth birthday, she had slept with three other former boyfriends and enjoyed the carnal relations with each immensely. In fact, two of them broke up with Jan because they felt they couldn't keep up with her sexual appetite. But it wasn't until she met Dan that she discovered real passion.

Dan, on the other hand, had had sex with dozens of women, some short-term girlfriends, some one-night stands, and a lot of prostitutes while in the service, several of whom caused him to visit the infirmary more than once. Never, however, had he experienced sensual pleasure like he did with Jan and so, he confided to his police partner one day, "I think this is the real thing."

Their marriage pushed Dan's monster of meaninglessness into the cluttered back room of his mind giving him an unaccustomed happiness, but only temporarily. Jan now reminisced that once the novelty of their blissful union wore off, the dark, depressing feeling returned to its home just beneath the surface of Dan's consciousness, now and then rearing its ugly head. This went on until their son was born. When Cole came along, Jan pondered, Dan seemed to snap out of his doldrums. She guessed that finally he had something that gave his life meaning. But the sudden intrusion of her son into her drifting memories was too much for her so she forced herself to get up and turn on the television ... anything to get her mind off Cole.

CHAPTER 7

Not too far away, at FBI Headquarters in Quantico, Ross Huggins was doing a little pondering of his own on life and the surprises it often holds when his musings were interrupted.

"There he goes again tilting at windmills." The sudden intrusion of his friend, Roy Bellizi, as he walked into the office both annoyed and pleased him. "Who're ya' gunning down this time?"

"No one you son-of-a-bitch. I'm typing out a study outline."

"Don't give me that. I can tell you were somewhere else."

"Well, any place would be better than this rat hole," Ross motioned around his drab surroundings, "O. K. So I want to be a field agent. Is that so terrible?"

"Another wannabe. What ... we don't have enough of 'em already?"

"I'm just sick of all this. I want some action." As corny as that sounded, Ross felt he could be honest with Roy.

"Well, buddy ... it's not all it's cracked up to be. At least you don't have to get down in the dirt and become part of the degenerate crowd." Ross braced himself for the speech he knew was coming. "I'm telling ya', you don't realize what a nasty effect deep cover can have on you," Roy said staring off into space. He was a big, dark-haired, good-looking Italian who had once gone undercover for three years as a lieutenant in an organized crime family in New York City. His work netted the Bureau 30 arrests and convictions of some of the family's top leaders and he was looked upon by other agents as a genuine hero. He had never really talked to anyone about his three years in the mob, but he felt unusually candid today and what he had to say didn't sound all that heroic. "To be convincing I had to actually become a criminal. For three years I had to think and act like a mobster. Believe me, it leaves its mark on you. I also got personally close to several people who were very fine folks, except for the fact that they were murderers, pimps, and pushers ... and then I had to betray them."

"Yeah, but look what you accomplished. You're the envy of every agent in the bureau. You almost single-handedly broke up one of the biggest crime families in the country. And now you're back to your normal life with that accomplishment under your belt. That has got to feel good," said Ross admiringly and with more than a little envy.

"Oh, don't get me wrong ... it does. But I'm not sure the price I had to pay was worth it. I had to see things that no one should ever have to see. I had to do things that no one should ever have to do. Hell, I was in Iraq and Afghanistan and it was nothing compared to some of the vicious shit I saw during those three years."

"That's just my point, Roy, by doing what you did you helped put those bastards away and spared a lot of people the misery of becoming their future victims."

"I know, but I can't help but think that for everyone I put in jail there are three more just waiting in the wings to do the same shit to those future victims, so did I really save anyone?"

"Yes, you did."

"Well, besides, all you see is the adventure, the excitement of going under cover. What you don't see is the pain that comes with having to become the part you're playing. And believe me, you do have to become that part and not just play the person or they'll find you out fast. But it destroys your whole personality, the person you have been up to that point in your life, and it really screws up your sense of identity. Man, for six months after my deep cover I didn't really know who the hell I was. I didn't let on that I was having problems, not even to you, but I was. And to make it worse, I still have problems reconciling myself to the fact that not only did I stand by and let really bad shit be done to innocent people, I did some of that shit. Believe me buddy, it plays tricks with your head that you don't need."

"I can understand what you're saying," came Ross' standard reply, "but I just know I'm going to have to find it out for myself some day or I'm never going to be satisfied."

"Well, if you ever do go under cover, let's hope it's in something like a nice old fashion drug syndicate or a car theft ring and not something like child pornography. Remember Joe Carnahan."

* * *

"How was your day?" Jan asked as Dan came through the door at his usual late hour after having spent the evening drinking at his reporter's bar.

"How's any hack's day?" was the standard reply as he headed toward his nightly, mind-numbing ritual of television and whisky.

Knowing that it was futile Jan tried anyway. "Honey, how about not drinking tonight and we just talk?"

Dan looked at her, both respecting and hating her for her strength, but at the same time loving her as much as ever as his soul mate and the only thing left to remind him of his son.

"Sorry ... you cope your way and I'll cope mine." There was no belligerence or anger in his voice, just sad resignation as he walked into the den, ice cubes clinking in his whisky glass. Now it was just him and the mind-numbing TV until he passed out in the easy chair.

* * *

Ross Huggins and fellow FBI Agent Roy Bellizi looked at each other and then glanced away as the name Joe Carnahan sent shivers down both their spines. Their friend Joe had spent two years in deep cover with an organization that made child pornography movies and sold them all over the world. After busting the pornographers and their entire distribution network, Joe had testified that in addition to the movie-making most of the people involved in the operation had, themselves, routinely had sex with the children involved, mostly little girls. No one had proof, but from the change that came over Joe during those two years, many at the bureau suspected that he had committed some of the kiddie sex himself. Maybe it was to maintain his cover, maybe it was to test his own moral boundaries, or maybe he liked it. Whatever it was, Joe walked from his last deposition into the courthouse bathroom and shot himself to death. "He just couldn't live with what he'd seen or done," was all Roy could say.

"Yeah, if and when I ever do get an undercover assignment I hope it has nothing to do with kiddie sex. Now, adult pornography I wouldn't mind," Ross chuckled, trying to lighten the heavy, somber mood. Roy laughed too because they both knew he was probably the most faithful husband in America. He would undoubtedly win the contest for the least likely to commit adultery no matter what the situation.

In spite of Roy's admonitions Ross knew that it was his destiny to work under cover. He had known he wanted to do this kind of work since the age of twelve when he devoured hundreds of detective novels. As a child, of course, he just saw the adventure of being an under-cover agent or a spy and none of the harsh realities of such a life. But even as an adult, after looking at it in a more realistic light, he still desperately wanted to do it. For now, he bid Roy good-bye and settled back into his pedophile study outline. He knew that to conduct an accurate study he had to be objective and detached and make no moral judgements about child molesters. But dedicated father as he was, his first thought was that it would be nice if he could find something that would help catch them.

* * *

Cole wasn't the only casualty in the Forester household. His parents' marriage slowly disintegrated as intimacy between them disappeared along with their son. Depressed as he was, Dan had not lost his sex drive, which had always been considerable. Jan, on the other hand, now had none.

"I just can't," she whispered to him shortly after they went to bed and he reached a hand over to fondle her breasts. She hadn't had any sex drive since Cole's disappearance, but still Dan found it hard to accept this from his formerly ultra-enthusiastic bed partner. He continued hopefully, waiting for her nipple to stiffen between his thumb and forefinger.

"No, No, No," was all he got in response.

"What's the matter?" he asked ingenuously.

Jan was astounded by his stupidity. She pulled away. Dan, as usual, went to sleep angry and proceeded to dream dreams he would never remember. Some mornings he did feel something significant had happened in his sleep but he didn't know what. It was almost as if someone was trying to tell him something important but he couldn't quite make out the message or the messenger.

* * *

After FBI Agent Roy Bellizi left, Ross Huggins sat at his desk trying to keep his mind on the pedophile study outline. But his thoughts began to wonder again and he started thinking about his original job application to the Central Intelligence Agency. He figured his Master's Degree in Criminology with a heavy emphasis on statistical analysis gave him a good chance. But when he received the form rejection letter mentioning recent budget cuts and a full department, scrawled across the bottom was a note saying, "Try the F.B.I." So, he went to the Bureau and his degree and genius-level I.Q. landed him a research job with a promise that he would be considered later for a field position. Now, even after Roy's warnings and Joe's suicide, it was still the only job he wanted. If the truth be known Ross was very simply bored with a capitol B. Oh, he loved his family but at the age of 30 he was beginning to ask himself if this was really all there is.

As he sat staring at his busy computer screen his thoughts now meandered back to the days of his youth. His high school years in a little town near Medford, Oregon called Holliwell were spent as a minor juvenile delinquent, always pushing the boundaries of the law, but never quite crossing them far enough to get caught. Numerous school counselors had asked him, "Why do you cause so much trouble?" And the honest answer was always, "Because I get bored and it livens things up." School was too easy and his peers were too witless to keep him interested, so he pulled pranks to keep things cooking.

There was the time, for instance, when he caught 20 bats and turned them loose inside the school building. Or the time he replaced the mirror in the girls' locker room with a two-way mirror. The boys' locker room was on the other side of the wall and got pretty crowded during girl's Physical Education classes. And then, there was the motorcycle gang called The Mighty that came to town.

* * *

"I can't believe he doesn't understand," Jan told Dr. Simmons the day after rebuffing one of Dan's nightly sexual advances. Sitting in the doctor's tastefully decorated office with fine art on the walls and expensive furniture on the floor, Jan's feelings now poured out as easily as the tea they both drank every session. "Besides, I know how broken up he is over Cole ... how can he have any sex drive?"

"My dear, it is a sad fact that men too often think with their genitals. It has been my experience that, in general, men are just better able than women to separate their mental state from their sexual appetite. And, sometimes I think they might have the right idea," said Dr. Simmons as she put down her second cup of chamomile. "But you can't get by your DNA," the doctor went on, "We are the ones with the cycles and we do feel amorous when we're ovulating ... we just don't when we're not. Men don't have cycles."

"Well, in a way, he actually has a point. Before Cole ... uh ... disappeared, I ... I had a very intense sex drive. Actually ... I often initiated it." "On the average, how many times a month did you and Dan have sex?" Dr. Simmons asked casually, picking up her pen.

"Oh, three or four times ... a week."

"Wow!" Dr. Simmons erupted, dropping her notebook and not hiding her sudden interest. "Well, that certainly puts you over the once-a-week average for most couples. I guess the sex was obviously good?"

"No, good isn't the word I would use. Great is more like it. It's kind of hard to believe now, but after all these years of marriage we still had every kind of sex imaginable and for two hours at a time. We would often spend an hour or more just in foreplay." Somehow Jan and Dan's sexual chemistry had survived the years.

* * *

Ah yes ... The Mighty, Ross Huggins reminisced. They pushed the town folk around and scared the local police who just tried to avoid them. The only one unafraid was Ross.

One night while most of the gang was in the local tavern and their Harley Davidsons lined the parking lot in the center of town he filled a high-pressure weed sprayer with gasoline. He hand-pumped the five-gallon reservoir-tank for maximum pressure and crept close to the motorcycles, unseen. From several locations, hidden from view by the large evergreen bushes surrounding the parking lot, he sprayed a thin, silent stream of gasoline on as many of the bikes as he could reach. He left trails of gas on the pavement between Harleys. He then skulked out of the bushes just long enough to remove the gas cap of the nearest cycle and hang a gasoline-soaked rag out of it. Silently stealing back to the other side of the bushes he calmly and deliberately lit another gas-soaked rag hanging out of a pop bottle half-filled with gasoline and tossed it onto the parking lot. As he ran away into the night he heard the crash of the bottle breaking on the concrete and then the whoosh of the burning gas followed by the inevitable explosion as the first gas tank ignited.

Hearing the noise, the gang came flooding out of the bar. Seeing the ball of fire rising from their bikes they knew instantly what had happened. By that time, however, they were powerless to do anything but stand there and watch their beloved choppers explode up into the air one-by-one in flames. It sounded like popcorn amplified by a factor of 1000. As the fire spread, the air was thick with acrid smoke. The town's volunteer firemen were called out, but, when they saw what was burning and that there really wasn't any danger to any nearby buildings, they moved quite a bit slower than usual. In fact, by the time they sprayed the first stream of water the once menacing-looking motorcycles were just charred hulks of metal. The now not-so-mighty salvaged what they could, which wasn't much, and just disappeared. Ross commented later that "they apparently were nothing without their motorcycles, which were the obvious phallic extensions of the manhood they lacked." He was never one to brag, so no one ever knew that he had been the arsonist. That was the way he liked it in high school. But then, there was college.

* * *

"Boy, do I have some women patients who would envy you!" Dr. Simmons was still trying to collect herself after Jan's sexual revelations.

"He used to say there were two kinds of women who give oral sex," Jan went on, "The kind that do it because they know the man likes it and the kind that do it because they like it, and when you find one like that, you marry her. I do and he did."

"Anything kinky?" the doctor asked with a little more than professional curiosity, taking the teacup from her lips and leaving a speck of saliva at the corner of her mouth.

"Well, I guess that depends on how you define kinky. I sometimes wore a garter belt and stockings with no panties on under my skirt and in the evening, while Cole was watching TV, Dan would come up behind me in the kitchen or some other room, bend me over and do it to me right there. Of course, that was just a tease for what was to come later. Sometimes, after Cole went to bed we would go out in the front yard and make love, but I had to stifle my screams because I tend to get vocal. We often used a vibrator and believe it or not we had anal sex at least once a week. Is that kinky enough?"

"Ohhhh!" Dr. Simmons blurted out as her hand involuntarily twitched, spilling tea on her five-hundred-dollar, feminine-but-business-like suit. "Kinky enough for me to think about leaving my husband to get that kind of sex," she replied, quickly covering her excitement with the weak joke. "Did you always achieve orgasm?"

"Only three or four times ... every time we did it, except for the quickies in the kitchen." Now even Jan was getting a little titillated.

"My gosh!" Dr. Simmons could no longer hide her astonishment or her envy and she gulped her nearly full cup of tea in an effort to calm her growing excitement, "why do you think the sex was so good?" she asked as she strove to contain herself once again.

"I don't know. Dan is a lot of things. He's stubborn and opinionated ... but he is really ... really a man. Ya' know what I mean? He's a strong man and I don't care how liberated a woman is, I think, sexually, that's what most of us want."

"Many women do ... or think they do. It's probably evolutionary going back to the ancient animal kingdom when females would choose the strongest male mates who they thought would produce the strongest offspring."

* * *

In college Ross Huggins had been equally daring, but more sophisticated. He once hacked into the university's computer system and programmed it to send memos to all departments canceling classes on a Friday that he wanted to take his girlfriend to the beach. For two years he operated his own illegal, low power FM radio station broadcasting a mix of rock and classical orchestra music along with the latest gossip about the school's teachers. He punctuated each segment with farts and belches and his own stream-of-consciousness philosophies. Whatever sounded good to him at the time, in whatever state of mind he was in, he broadcast.

But the best stunt of all was probably when he landed a rented Cessna in the parking lot of a downtown shopping mall at 2:00 o'clock in the morning so he could urinate on the sidewalk. He took off just as two police cars arrived with lights flashing and sirens blaring; too late to get the plane's I.D. number. Those were the fun days, Ross thought as he drifted out of his reminiscence and got back to work. He wished he could re-live some of that excitement. Little did he know he was about to do just that.

CHAPTER 8

"I want to follow up on our last conversation," Dr. Simmons told Jan in their next session.

"Yeah, you just wanna' hear more about the great sex," Jan said almost playfully. She and the doctor had gotten to be fairly good friends over the months of therapy.

"You bet I do," Dr. Simmons said with a laugh, "but if I'm going to earn my money we better get to the things behind the great sex. You said last time that you think it's a man's strength that attracts women."

"Yeah … it is for me, but it's contradictory."

"How?"

"Well, it seems like at the same time I'm wanting Dan to be strong I resent him for his strength because it makes me feel weak. So, when he's strong I strike back and needle him to make myself feel strong again. At least I used to … now I don't do much of anything."

"How did you do that?"

"Well, he's always complaining that I have something to say about everything he does, whether I know anything about it or not … and actually he's right. I think I come by that trait kind of naturally since my mother was the same way. But I also think, subconsciously I do it just to get even with him for making me feel weak or to show him that I'm not subordinate to him … that I know as much as he does about everything. That's probably been the root of most of our arguments. Sick huh?"

"No, just human. You've just described what's probably the number one cause of the battle of the sexes these days. It's tough for present day women because we're supposedly equal to men, but the world still expects us to be feminine, sweet and sexy ... still the weaker sex, if you will. It's a constant inner battle between the two people you're supposed to be, but you always end up the loser because you're really only fighting yourself. Is it any wonder that more women than men suffer from depression? After all, men haven't had their identity ripped out from under them."

"Then ... I can blame Dan?"

"No, I'm afraid not. You can partially blame the way of the world, but not Dan."

"O. K. That all sounds good ... but what's it got to do with why I don't want to have sex?"

"Well, there could be a number of psychological reasons. It could be that subconsciously you relate the act of sexual intercourse with the birth of Cole whose disappearance is causing you all the pain. Your mind then automatically lumps these two distinctly different elements together and you connect pain with sex. Or it could be guilt. Subconsciously you may feel that it is wrong to enjoy yourself and feel good in any way while your son is missing and might be in pain. It could just simply be your depression. As you well know, depression drains you of your energy and your interest in many things and sex could just be one of them. It could be the anti-depressant. Or it could be his booze breath. A drunk isn't that titillating, is he?"

* * *

Back in Omaha the KNOC-TV station management was delighted with the newscast the day little Jeremy Fenner's body was discovered. More surprisingly, they were thrilled with the following night's documentary. A few salesmen grumbled about the lost revenue incurred by pre-empting network programming. But the two nights' ratings were the highest for the year. Once again News Director Bob Manson's keen news sense had won him the right to continue doing the news as he saw fit.

But station management didn't know that he had helped his star reporter, Susan Jensen use her reports and the documentary to apply for a $500,000 grant from the Children's Protection Society to produce a series of 1-hour documentaries about child sex abuse. The goal was to air them first on public TV and later on network television. If she got the grant Susan planned to take a leave of absence from KNOC to produce the documentaries. Bob had promised her he would give her any help he could. She had done nationwide research on the issue of sexually abused children and kept track of all the reports of missing children across the country. The latest case she had come across was a missing young boy in Maryland.

* * *

"Yeah, I thought about that," Jan answered Dr. Simmons' comment about Dan's booze breath being a turn-off. "But actually, I lost my sex drive before he started drinking so

heavily ... and actually, he really doesn't act that drunk."

"Well, which theory gets your guess?"

"Hum ... being Catholic and having the market cornered on guilt ... the guilt one sounds the best to me. Which theory do you buy?"

"Actually, it's most likely a combination of all of them. But I would add one hypothesis. If I had to guess ... and remember that's usually what a psychiatric diagnosis is ... I would say it all revolves around the strong-man issue we just discussed. You said you were always sexually stimulated by Dan's strength and manliness. But after Cole disappeared, he wasn't so strong and he has since retreated into a bottle. Maybe your sex drive went with his strength. Maybe you even blame his weakness for Cole's disappearance. Maybe you just now realize that Dan isn't as strong as you thought he was."

Jan thought about that one for a moment and suddenly realized that it was an idea she had had for quite some time, but which didn't clearly come into focus for her until Dr. Simmons put it into words.

"I think that may be it," she said softly, "in fact I dreamed the other night that instead of Dan sucking booze out of a bottle, the bottle was sucking something out of him. Maybe it was his strength. I guess the big question is what do I do about it?"

"Well, getting Dan off your back won't hurt and good sex might be good for you. I'm going to give you some meditation exercises, which will relax your mind and body. Do them to some soft music about an hour before you go to bed. Get fully relaxed. Then just lie back and daydream about the great sex you used to have with Dan. The meditation should put you in a receptive state and may revitalize your desire. But don't try to force it, just let it come naturally."

"O.K ... and what if it doesn't work?"

"Try it a few nights. If it doesn't work and you aren't bothered too much putting him off just continue to do it. If that gets to be too much though, I'd suggest relenting and getting it over with or possibly masturbating him. You'd then join the bedroom behavior of many women in America," Dr. Simmons chuckled with the first light-hearted grin of the afternoon.

"It doesn't sound very liberated."

"I know, but it's practical."

* * *

Doug Glassman hid his pedophilia quite well and he held true to his promise to Bobby Segal. But he made no such promise to Johnny Peyton. Like Bobby, Johnny was a product of a broken home. His black father had left his white mother at an age too early for John to remember. So, when Doug became his Big Brother at the age of eight he experienced his first real contact with a male role model. As with Bobby, Doug did not start the relationship with pedophilic sex in mind. In fact, he promised himself that he would not even think about it and that if at any time he had the slightest inclination toward it he would immediately pull out. But John was a special child and Doug saw in his eyes an attractive uniqueness of spirit from the first time they met. As the relationship progressed the oath he had taken slipped from his mind.

John seemed to overcome any difficulties he faced, not being fully accepted by either blacks or whites. He was an enthusiastic little fellow with a gleam in his eye who played ball and drew pictures and did everything else other little boys liked to do. When other kids made fun of him for his mixed race he just shrugged it off and told them that he was lucky because he got to have two cultures instead of just one. His mother had told him that one. But John wasn't really as Teflon-coated as he appeared and Doug knew it from the beginning. Once, after a ball game, they walked in the park when some kids John's age rode by on their bicycles and called him a half-breed along with several other racist names. Tears immediately welled up in the boy's eyes.

"What's the matter John?" Doug asked, "That stuff never bothered you before."

"I know," John choked back the tears, "but the one on the yellow bike was my ... my best friend, Ryan."

"Oh, I'm sorry Johnny. I'll bet he didn't mean it ... he was probably just going along with the crowd."

"Yeah, but he and I have talked about it before and he promised me he would never make fun of me 'cause we're best friends. He even said he would beat up anyone who did make fun of me. I thought he was different... but he's just the same as all the others and now I... I don't have any friends."

As his heart went out to John, Doug felt like crying himself. He thought about how unfair life can be sometimes and about what a big burden this was for such a little boy.

"Yes you do Johnny ... me. We'll always be best buddies," Doug said almost choking up.

* * *

Jan tried Dr. Simmon's ideas the next night and thought she might actually feel a little amorous. But when the moment of truth came, she suddenly became cold and numb and very anti-sexual. Having his hopes dashed Dan didn't understand or even try to understand why she couldn't just separate her mental condition from her biological urges, her "head from her crotch" as he so eloquently put it.

"Now, not only am I depressed," he grunted, "I'm sexually frustrated too."

"I'm sorry honey, but I just can't help it."

"I know you can't. I mean I understand that it's not your fault. But I can't seem to get by it and I've got to admit that it makes me feel bitter toward you. I know that's the last thing either one of us needs right now. I guess you were right all along when you accused me of thinking with my dick." And with that, Dan went back out to the living room for a drink. He certainly didn't need another reason to drink, but he had one and he took full advantage of it. He knew he was taking the weak way out, but he also knew that if he stopped drinking long enough to stare reality in its dismal face he might go stark-raving mad.

* * *

Big Brother Doug Glassman tentatively hugged Johnny and in spite of all the self-recrimination he had put himself through and all the meditations he practiced, his closeness to the boy aroused him. Then, it overwhelmed him and he repeated the sexual episode he had had with Bobby Segal.

Doug told John the same thing he told Bobby: that he shouldn't tell anyone, that it was their secret and no one else's business. He also said that it would never happen again, which it never did because he ended his relationship with the boy then and there. He knew it was a lousy thing to do since John had gotten so close to him and that he was just one more male role model being jerked out from under him. He also knew he had no choice. If he continued the relationship he knew he couldn't trust himself.

But now he had had a taste and his appetite was whetted.

CHAPTER 9

Unlike Dan, Jan immersed herself in the situation, which was also her way of escaping from it. Dan envied her strength but knew something she didn't. Each day that went by without finding Cole was only more evidence that he was no longer alive. The real horror that came to his mind was the unthinkable things that may have been done to his little boy. It was just those unspeakable horrors that Jan now confronted in her search for their son.

"Jack called about another tape that the Memphis police got and I have to go down to see it tomorrow ... do you want to come?" she asked her half-stewed husband one evening.

"No, if it's him I'll come," was his standard answer.

Child molesters, or pedophiles, sometimes make audio and videotapes of themselves raping their young victims. Some even record themselves torturing and killing the child. Whenever any police department in the U.S. confiscated such a tape in a pornographic book store raid or while searching a sex offender's home, police departments all over the country were notified. Then Officer Jack Adams would get a copy of the tape. If it was video he watched it himself to determine if the young victim was Cole Forester. If it was an audio tape, Jan or Dan had to listen to it to determine if the voice belonged to their son. Jan had been doing all the listening and so far no Cole.

"You know, this isn't easy. I could use your support," she said with no malice in her voice. They had had this conversation before and she knew what its outcome would be.

"Look, once again," he sighed, "you shouldn't have to do this. Jack has his picture and a tape of his voice. He should be able to tell if it's him or not."

"No, you look once again!" she said with unusual passion and anger.

"You know the audio quality of a lot of the tapes he gets isn't clear enough and sometimes the boy is wearing a mask. Besides, lots of times the kid is screaming and only you or I can tell if its Cole," Jan's throat swelled with nausea as she thought about the last tape she had heard. "Anyway, you know how great Jack has been in all this. He doesn't even have to get these tapes for us."

"I know," was all Dan could say at the mention of Jack's name.

Dan and Jack had begun drinking together about once a week and found that they enjoyed each other's company. Dan was especially struck with their intellectual and philosophical conversations, drunk as they were. But what they shared the most was a feeling of sadness and loss.

* * *

Jack Adams normally wouldn't have drunk so much at any bar, but his own happy family life had recently blown up in his face when his wife, Mia, had died in a car accident on the Capitol Beltway. He still found it hard to believe that the only woman he had ever loved was gone. She had been returning from a movie with their son Charles, when a drunk driver swerved into her car and sent it careening down an embankment. Mia died instantly as her side of the car slammed a utility pole. Charles survived but he suffered a brain concussion and a broken leg. Mia had put his seat belt on, but not her own. The drunk survived.

Jack was supposed to go with them that night, but he ended up having to work late. "If I'd only been there, I would've been driving and this might not have happened," he told Dan. His marriage to Mia had been a romantic one complete with flowers and candlelight dinners. The only person they loved as much as each other was their son Charlie and Jack reveled in fatherhood.

Inevitably, he blamed himself and his job for his wife's death and, like Dan, he now had second thoughts about his chosen career. His drinking had increased substantially since Mia's death and he found Dan an eager partner. They were tragic drinking buddies and their relationship was based on mutual misery, but they both enjoyed their long-winded philosophical discussions.

Jack had gotten close to both Dan and Jan, but he dealt with them separately. From the beginning, he had worked hard on their case, but when he lost his wife he worked even harder. He seemed to feel their pain even more intensely now than he had at first. Losing Mia had made him more keenly aware of his own child, and when he looked at Dan and Jan he could only think, there but for the grace of God, go I. Besides, as cop and crime reporter, Jack and Dan spoke the same language.

* * *

Jan had a busy and painful day ahead of her. First, she had to go to the police station to look at two videotapes Jack had for her. Then she had to go right from the station to give a speech to the P.T.A. in Rockville. Normally Jack would have looked at the tapes, but in these two the child-victims wore masks. He couldn't tell if one of them was Cole.

Jack was waiting for her at the front desk.

"Hi Jan," he said, trying to be casual. But both knew the circumstances were anything but casual.

"Hi Jack," she said trying to sound strong.

"These are bad ones. Do you think you're up to it?"

"I guess I have no choice, do I?" That is where she and Dan differed.

"I guess not," he said as he led her into the video tape room.

On the first tape two men forced a young boy wearing a black rubber mask into simultaneous anal and oral sex. Then they tied his hands and legs around a pole behind him and repeatedly whipped him with a cat-o-nine-tails. They even went to the trouble of spreading newspapers on the floor to catch his blood. It took two agonizing hours before the boy slumped into unconsciousness and every excruciating scream was caught on tape.

On the second tape one of the men strapped another, younger boy wearing a demonic-looking mask, spread-legged on a wooden contraption. Each time the man pulled a lever a projectile rammed up the boy's rectum and he let out a blood-curdling scream. After several assaults, he passed out. "Come on, you love it, don't ya'? Don't ya'?" the sadistic pedophile repeated with delight until Jan had to run to the bathroom and retch. She could tell by their bodies that neither boy was Cole.

In her campaign to find her son Jan had become a reluctant expert on pedophilia. Many of the things she learned sickened her. The wooden torture machine could be ordered along with similar devices from a magazine for pedophiles. The gag box, a balloon, which is forced into the child's mouth and held there by straps that fastened around his head, was also featured. The torturer inflated and deflated the balloon choking his young victim, sometimes to death. Also featured, of course, were a plethora of more traditional tools of torture like whips, spiked collars, and ropes and straps for bondage. But that wasn't all. In these magazines and on the Internet were classified ads selling audio and videotapes and pictures of men and women having sex with children and, in some cases, torturing them. In fact, whenever police arrested a pedophile it wasn't unusual for them to find literally thousands of kiddie porn pictures and a number of kiddie sex tapes in his home, although torture tapes were rare.

The pictures and tapes ranged from adults performing every kind of sexual act imaginable with children to kids having sex with other kids, to men, and occasionally women, sexually torturing and sometimes killing their young victims. Jan was sickened to notice that the children seemed to be doing what they did willingly. She had been told several possible reasons.

First, many of the kids were child prostitutes doing it for the money. Second, a pedophile who kidnaps a young boy often coerces him by convincing him that his parents don't want him anymore and that they gave him away. Third, the captor tells his victim he will kill him and his parents if he doesn't cooperate. Finally, abductors often keep their victims so drugged they are numb to what is going on.

But the worst things to Jan were the ads that contained camouflaged wording telling how to order a child to molest. Jan couldn't believe what a sick part of society this was, and, more than that, what a big part of society it appeared to be.

She was nauseated to learn that there were actually organized groups that advocated adult sex with children. The Child Love League, for example, claimed thousands of members all over the country and maintained that it is natural for both male and female children to have sex with adults. An organization called The Guild openly contended that boys want and need sex with adult men and advocated making such sex legal. The group argued that government had no place legislating people's sexual behavior. Both groups maintained that they were ardently against harming children or forcing them into sex in any way, and actually argued that it is their love for children that motivates their beliefs. Dan had heard a little about these groups while he was a crime reporter and was appalled.

* * *

While Jan learned about America's dirty little secret, Ross Huggins was at his FBI desk again, day dreaming. Now he drifted back to when he finished graduate school. After getting his Master's Degree he took the $7000 he had saved from six summers of work and backpacked across the United States ending up in New York City. From there he flew to England and toured Europe for six months. He slept outside and ate a diet of bread, cheese, and wine, so his expenses were minimal. He made it to Northern Africa, came back through Greece and then traveled cross-country to India on a Celestial Bus Company bus. The company sold the cheapest trips available and he found out why, when his bus broke down in Turkey. He had to wait three weeks in a village 400 miles from Istanbul for the spare parts to arrive. The Celestial Bus Company was serious when it advertised that its passengers traveled at their own risk with no guaranteed schedule or itinerary. From India Ross took trains through Asia, riding third class which at times meant on the roof. Running completely out of money in Japan he charged his way home on a credit card. "Ah, those were the days," he said to his dingy office.

* * *

Barely recovered from her ordeal at the police station, Jan Forester told a spellbound Rockville P.T.A. about the groups who advocate sex with children.

"These men say they don't believe in physically forcing boys to have sex with them. But they do believe that the sex is natural and good," she told the crowd. "Consequently, at every opportunity they will tell a boy about it and then give him the choice of whether or not he wants to try it. Of course, it's not a choice at all when we're talking about a 10, 11 or 12-year old boy who doesn't even know what sex is. A boy who is listening to an adult who he has been taught to obey." Jan looked around the packed lunchroom and realized that interest in her subject was growing.

"These men justify their actions by giving the child a choice. But the obvious flaw in this reasoning is that a child of this age is not capable of making an intelligent, informed choice about something like sex. Much of the time, because he's been taught to respect his elders and do what adults tell him to do, he will engage in sex with a man. Of course, any child is subject to sexual stimulation and he'll often believe he enjoys it, which often sets the course for his future homosexuality or sexual deviance. In other words these monsters get a boy before he knows what sex is and pervert it for him for the rest of his life, and they call it choice." The audience breathed a communal sigh of shocked dismay and you could feel the disgust in the air.

"But I tell you about these organizations only to demonstrate the sickness that's more prevalent in our society than you might think. These groups, however, should not be the main focus of your fear. They're relatively small when you consider the hundreds of thousands of men out there who belong to no organization and live otherwise normal lives, but who have pedophilic tendencies. They're your neighbor, your scout leader, your little league coach, your minister and your Uncle Bob … and they are the ones to be wary of. Teachers and doctors who are required to report any suspicions they have of a child being abused in any way, physically or sexually, reported about 3 million children last year. Of course, many of the cases were not actually abuse. But the sad reality is that today in our society one out of every four girls and one out of every seven boys will be sexually abused while growing up."

She could hear the metal seats creak as the parents in the audience shifted around uncomfortably. She knew she was making them uncomfortable and that's exactly what she wanted to do. Still, she wondered how these people could act like they had never heard this before, until she reminded herself that it was such a heinous subject most of them had probably tried to ignore it for much of their lives.

"How do you protect your children?" Jan was picking up steam. "By simply keeping close tabs on them. By knowing everyone involved in their lives and by not allowing them to be in a vulnerable position. That was the mistake I made. When you're at the mall or some other public place keep your eyes on your child every minute. A moment is all it'll take. Pedophiles go to places like this looking for a child who has strayed from his parent for just 30 seconds, long enough to grab him or her and run out the door. In one case a man put a 4-year old girl to sleep with a chloroform-soaked hanky, carried her into the store's bathroom, cut off her hair and put boys' clothes on her. Then he left the store carrying a child who looked like a boy and who appeared to be sleeping." She was building to a climax now like a fire and brimstone preacher. "How many times have you lost sight of your child for just a short time while shopping? We all have, and 99% of the time they are just in the next aisle, but do you want to risk that other 1% of the time?"

At this point all the parents in the audience seemed to exhale at the same time, each of them thinking of a time when they had lost sight of their own child. Jan was on a roll now and she knew it.

* * *

Still day dreaming, Ross Huggins sat at his computer recalling how he had gotten down to the serious business of job hunting when he returned home from travelling overseas. He had gotten straight A's in college and top scores on all the F.B.I. analytical tests, which made him a very attractive prospect for its analysis section. He jumped at the job when the Bureau promised it would seriously consider him for a field position in the future.

He met his wife Sara at the Library of Congress in Washington, D.C. where he sometimes went for resources not available at the Quantico headquarters. There she was, fumbling with a couple of books that were almost bigger than she was and a purse full of change trying to make copies at the duplicating machine. He couldn't help but laugh, but then he offered his help, which she gladly accepted, and four years later it was two kids and a house in the suburbs. Sara always told Ross that she hoped he would get the field agent's job. But secretly, she hoped he wouldn't because she knew the danger involved and the travel required. Their life was very happy and tranquil, but sometimes a bit too smooth for Ross. He loved Sara and his kids more than anything else in the world and although he had matured and mellowed substantially in the last few years, he still suffered from his chronic malady: boredom.

So, for now he paid his dues, doing research, and got his boredom-fighting kicks vicariously from the other agents. And now, he thought morosely, I have to profile scum of the earth child molesters. How thrilling.

* * *

Back in Rockville Jan felt like an inspired preacher on Sunday morning. She had the crowd in her grip and figured it was time to bring out the big guns.

"Law enforcement officials say that in the U. S. four to five thousand children a year are kidnapped and sexually molested by strangers, like for 30 minutes to an hour," she said. "Just long enough to ruin a child's life. According to some estimates, 300 kids a year are abducted and sexually molested for long periods of time ... say for months or even years ... and many of these children end up dead. I and many others believe the number is actually much higher since the vast majority of child sex abuse cases are never reported and most child molesters are never arrested. In one study the average sex offender had been arrested for only about one out of thirty crimes he committed. In a lot of the unreported cases the child knows his or her abuser and doesn't tell anyone about it. In fact, it is estimated that only about 10% of the child sex abuse cases are ever reported, which means that many of these figures could actually be ten times higher. Instead of four to five thousand children being abducted and abused for short periods of time, it may actually be forty to fifty thousand. Instead of 300 kids a year being kidnapped and sexually molested for long periods of time it may be closer to 3000." The audience murmured and stirred in unison as if it were one large creature.

"But even if the lower numbers are correct," Jan continued, "Do you want to risk your child being one of the four thousand or the 300? The most shocking figures of all, however, I've held until last. It involves the number of attempted but unsuccessful abductions by strangers in the U.S. One recent, unscientific study estimated that number to be 114,600 in one year. If you believe this study, that's 114,600 children who would have been abducted by a stranger and sexually molested if the abduction had been successful. Do you want to risk the abduction of your child being successful?" You could hear a scattering of "no's" from the audience.

"But besides all that, as I've said, thousands more children are routinely sexually molested each year by someone they know. They don't tell anyone, including their parents, because they're ashamed. We honestly don't know the exact numbers, but we do know that the main study on child sex abuse estimates that that the average pedophile molests 48 children in his lifetime. I say 'his' because most of them are men, but not all. When the audience gasped, Jan knew she was scaring them and that is exactly what she intended to do. It was time, she felt, for parents to wake up to these very real threats and stop treating pedophilia like America's dirty little secret and sweeping it under the rug.

"So, the average pedophile molests 48 children in his lifetime. That's probably low, but let's stay conservative to be as accurate as possible. And if you're even more conservative and say there are only 100,000 pedophiles in this country ... we know there are a lot more ... that means almost five million of our kids are being molested in one generation." Loud contempt went roiling through the audience as it could barely contain itself.

"The odds may be in your favor," Jan's voice was building. "But do you want to throw the dice with your child's life?" she finally exploded into a climax. This time the crowd answered with a collective and resounding "no" as everyone got to their feet with thundering applause.

As Jan's crusade gained momentum she got more and more invitations to speak. But her intentions were more than altruistic. An expert on missing children had told her shortly after Cole's disappearance that she had to do whatever she could to keep her son's name and face in the public eye. The biggest danger, he told her, was that the news coverage would decrease and ultimately end, and when Cole's name and face were out of the headlines and off the screen the chances of finding him would be almost non-existent. So, she called the local news media every time there was a possible clue to his fate, no matter how far-fetched it might be.

And far-fetched it often was. She got telephone calls from people who said they knew where Cole was. She heard from boys who said they were Cole. Even though she knew the calls were bogus she systematically told the authorities about them and reported them to the media, which usually took the bait and did another series of reports on the missing Cole Forester. She went on as many talk shows as she could and she spoke at numerous public gatherings where she collected donations for the Find Cole Forester Foundation.

All the while, Dan languished in his alcoholic fog, staying as numb as possible to the happenings around him. He was getting by at his job, doing the bare minimum. He felt like an unfeeling robot just going through the motions, subconsciously waiting for the clock to strike four-thirty so he could do some serious drinking with Jack instead of the maintenance drinking he did all day long. All the while, however, he knew in the back of his mind that Cole was dead. He also knew something else. Some voice from somewhere was trying to tell him something. But whatever it was, he had a feeling he didn't want to hear it.

CHAPTER 10

"Sit down Dan if you're not already. I ... I have something really rotten to tell you," came Officer Jack Adams's ominous call.

Dan's heart jumped into his throat. Suddenly everything around him stood still. Time froze and he knew what was coming.

"They arrested a pervert this morning and found ... a tape of Cole in his apartment and some of Cole's school books. He must've figured he was had, Dan...he confessed to Cole's murder."

Cole's murder. It was finally said. Cole was dead. Dan said nothing. He just involuntarily uttered the muffled wail of a wounded animal.

Jack went on, "Dan, the guy knows so much about Cole that it looks like the real thing. He's now telling us what he did with the body. I'm sorry Dan, but I thought I should tell you first and you'd want to tell Jan. We're going to go look for Cole now."

Jack's words burned like straight whisky on an empty stomach. Dan's heavy, alcohol-laden breathing coming through the receiver was just about more than his friend could bear. "Are you O.K. buddy?"

"I'll be there in thirty minutes," was his only answer. A sudden gust of reality blew away Dan's five month-long, alcoholic haze and somehow he clearly knew that he had to personally follow Cole's fate through to the end.

"Dan, I'm truly sorry, but you know you can't come. Besides, I don't think..."

"I don't give a fuck what you think, I'm coming. If it's my boy, I want to be there. Thirty minutes Jack. Give me thirty minutes." Dan was out the door before the receiver stopped rattling in its cradle.

He was beyond heartsick over the fact that he was probably about to see his little boy's mutilated remains, but at the same time an eerie excitement gripped him at the idea of a final resolution to his prolonged agony. Even Jan had once said that it was the not knowing that was the worst. Dan now subconsciously understood what she meant when she said she would almost rather know that Cole was dead than not know anything.

* * *

Doug Glassman was wracked with guilt over his pedophilia and from time to time he would sit and stare long and hard at the rifle his father had given him, now hidden in the back of his closet. He could almost smell the oiled muzzle and taste the polished barrel, and if it hadn't been for the effect it would have on his family he knew he would just blow his brains out. But that wasn't a realistic option so, instead, he just tried to numb himself to the world around him as much as possible and whenever a pedophilic thought entered his head he initiated his meditation exercises. Much of the time it worked, but when it didn't he simply ran for miles until he was too exhausted to have any erotic yearnings left. And on the rare occasions when that didn't work he just drowned his thoughts in a bottle of gin. But he wasn't really a drinker and it often made him sick.

* * *

Dan was greeted at the front door of the bustling police station by Jack Adams and two other police officers along with an assistant county coroner. Following close behind them, in handcuffs, and being led by a fourth police officer was Cole's alleged killer, Greg Dawson. Dan noticed that he didn't look like the neighbor or scout leader Jan had talked about. No, he looked about like what you would expect a child molester to look like with bulging eyes sunk into a lizard face. Dan, of course, knew instantly who he was, but didn't give him a second look.

"O.K. Dan. You know we're not supposed to do this, but I knew you would follow us anyway, so let's go. Follow us in your car," Jack said with resignation, pitying his friend.

"Thanks Jack," was the only reply. Jack could already see there was something different about Dan ... a new clarity in his gaze that suggested a sense of purpose, something which had been absent from those filmy, intoxicated eyes for a long time. Though he couldn't quite put his finger on it, Jack got the feeling that Dan was on the verge of something.

"Watch him closely," Jack muttered to his fellow officers when they got into the car, "if we find the body he may go off and have to be restrained." One of the policemen fidgeted with his taser. The cars drove off following Dawson's directions. Forty minutes later he led them into a wooded area just off the Beltway in western Silver Spring. He pointed to where he had buried the body. They smelled it before they saw it; the pungent odor of death and decay. Two officers dug carefully. As soon as the sheet Dawson had used as a shroud was pulled away Dan knew. It was Cole's face and Cole's body, though badly decomposed, and Cole's favorite shirt that his mother had chided him about wearing too much.

"But it makes me look cool," he had told Jan.

"I don't know how cool you look if your shirt is dirty," was his mother's inevitable reply. But Cole usually got his way, dirt and all.

Dan walked over to his son's decayed body and knelt down. He stared at what was left of his once lively, little boy for a full minute. All he could think was that it wasn't Cole.

* * *

"Tell me about your relationship with your mother and father when you were growing up," Dr. Johnson said after Douglas Glassman told her about molesting Johnny Peyton. He really didn't have much to tell on that score. He almost wished he could say that he had had a domineering mother and a wall flower for a father, a parenting combination he had heard cited as a reason for homosexuality in the past. But the fact was that he had had what would be considered a very normal upbringing. His mother and father were well balanced, loving parents and there really wasn't anything in his childhood that stood out as a possible reason for his deviant desires ... except maybe one thing. Between the ages of seven and ten he had been molested by his great uncle five times. The molesting was not violent and actually involved more fondling than anything else, so Doug didn't feel that it had left a big mark on his life. In fact, after the molesting stopped at the age of ten when his uncle died in a car accident Doug quite forgot the whole thing and never really gave it much thought ... until now.

* * *

That decomposed husk can't be my little buddy, Dan thought. But after gazing at the body a few more moments Dan couldn't help but say, "I love you, Cole," and a flood of tears forced their way out of his eyes. He turned away as the officers walked over to him, one carrying a body bag. He had known this scene was coming, but nothing could have prepared him for the pure agonizing grief of this moment. Everything around him crawled in slow motion, like a scene under water. One policeman stood taking notes while another outlined the shallow grave with lime chalk so that investigators would know exactly where the body had lain. But both moved in slow motion. Jack sluggishly and torpidly shook his head from right to left, hesitating a little too long at each swing. All three officers watched Dan closely, waiting for him to break and make a play for Greg Dawson. They knew and he knew that this would be his best chance.

* * *

"Uncle Bill just told me it was our special secret," Doug Glassman told Dr. Johnson, "That we couldn't tell anyone else and that if I told my folks they wouldn't understand and might not love me anymore. I guess I believed him because I never told anyone. In fact, you're the first person to ever hear about it out of my mouth."

"Uncle Bill sounds like the standard pedophile. He knew you were brought up to respect adults and do what they told you to do and he exploited that. He also knew that because of your respect for your elders you would believe him about your parents not understanding. After all, at that age you couldn't understand why he would lie."

"Yea, I believed it all and I really liked him. I just remember him as this great uncle who took me to ball games and bought me a lot of ice cream. The fondling really didn't mean much to me. I mean, I guess I got stimulated, but it wasn't like I hungered for it. I just did it because he said to do it."

"I don't have to tell you that Uncle Bill abused his position and responsibility as an adult by taking advantage of your youthful innocence."

The harsh words were like a knife in Doug's soul. In his reflections on his two lapses he had preferred not to use the words abuse and victims. But he knew Dr. Johnson was right and his feelings of deep guilt increased exponentially. After a long silence he simply said, "Yeah I guess so."

"It is possible that your biggest basic need in life, the thing you crave the most, consciously or unconsciously, is to be accepted and liked. This is, by the way, absolutely the most common and basic human need there is, so you are certainly not alone. Submitting to Uncle Bill's advances gained you acceptance and affection from him and that made you feel good. You may then have begun unconsciously equating adult-child sex with being accepted and liked and with that good feeling. But because you grew out of childhood you couldn't be the young one in the relationship anymore, so you had to assume the adult role in the relationship. In other words, it may be that your continued pedophilic desire is really just a mask for your desire to be loved and accepted."

"Wow, that's something I never would have thought of Doctor."

"Well, don't get too excited just yet. That's just one possibility. It could also be that you have an immense amount of repressed anger at your great uncle for defiling you and you are acting it out by feeling desires of your own for youngsters and then taking it out on them. It could be that unconsciously you are afraid of women and find the idea of sex with children a much safer and less threatening prospect."

If Dr. Johnson would have told Doug how she personally felt it might have come out something like, "Or it could be that you are one sick bastard."

Feeling his masculinity being bruised by her last comment Doug said, "But isn't it true that most child molesters were molested themselves as children?"

"Actually, many of them were, but possibly not most. One study suggested that a long time ago, but new evidence says that may not be true. Right now it looks like maybe about 30% of known pedophiles were molested as children. It could be a lot of things Doug and together we'll narrow it down to whatever the cause of your problem is."

"Hmmm ... oh well, old Uncle Bill. I guess maybe I might've felt more about that than I ever guessed huh?"

"It's possible. I guarantee you we'll find out."

The sessions with Dr. Johnson were really the only things helping Doug hold on at this point. He didn't know why, but for some reason his erotic thoughts of young boys had been increasing lately and he knew that without the good doctor he might have already acted them out on some other poor kid. What he had done, however, without telling Dr. Johnson, was subscribe to a number of kiddie sex magazines and videos containing every kind of child pornography imaginable. He avoided the porn dark Websites for fear that the police would track him down. Doug felt guilty about his love for pornography, but told himself that it was O. K. because he didn't go in for physical abuse and torture. After all, he genuinely liked children and was repulsed by the thought of hurting them.

* * *

All of a sudden Dan's life decelerated even further into a dream-like state offering him the hope that it was all a nightmare; that he would soon awake to find Cole alive and well. Maybe it's a dream and Cole isn't really dead, he thought. Unreal as it was, this train of thought kept him from going berserk.

But the zzzziping sound of the body bag being closed over Cole's face snapped him out of his hallucination and brought things back to their normal tempo. Still Dan did not fully comprehend Cole's death as the officers carried the corpse to the ambulance that had now arrived. In a misty haze he tried, but not very hard, to piece the real situation together. He was like a child putting together a jigsaw puzzle only to discover that some of the key pieces were missing.

Finally, his inescapable pragmatism no longer allowed him to wallow in this hopeful mire of unreality. The actuality of Cole's death hit him like a brick through a plate-glass window and abruptly his feelings shifted to a different mode of devastation. It wasn't anger. It wasn't even sadness. It was absolute, complete emptiness. What life Dan had kept over the last five months now completely seeped out of him. Probably, he thought, much like Cole's last breath. He felt vaguely like a virtual robot with no feelings.

"Dan," Jack's hand was on his shoulder, "I'm so sorry."

"I know you are," Dan said, and Jack noticed his cold, icy tone, something he didn't expect at this emotional moment.

Waiting until the other officers drove Greg Dawson away, Jack said, "Dawson admitted he called Cole over to his car that day pretending to ask for directions."

"Then he pointed a gun at him and made him get into the car. The rest you can guess."

At this moment Dan deeply regretted having taught Cole his extreme respect for guns. Instantly, he realized that if he hadn't taught him the seriousness of firearms he might have run away instead of fearing Dawson's gun enough to get into the car. Then, he dreamily pondered the parental ambiguity of teaching a child something for his own safety that backfires and hurts him instead. He knew Dawson never would have shot him. He just wished he had told Cole that.

"He's a pervert Dan, and he molested him," Jack said, jolting him out of his reverie, "But, if it's any consolation at all, it doesn't appear that Cole went through as much pain as you and I have seen in other cases ... and he died quickly."

"Thanks for everything you've done Jack. I'll never forget it," Dan said in a voice devoid of emotion.

"Dan..."

"I'll be fine Jack. We both knew this would come. Believe me I'm O.K. I'm just going to sit here a while and then go home and tell Jan." Dan turned toward Jack who saw a different person than he had known the last five months. There was a totally different look on Dan's tear-swollen face. It was almost a look of serene resolve. Jack had seen that look before when someone finally made up his mind to do something after a long deliberation.

"You're not going to do anything crazy are you Dan?"

"No, believe it or not I'm fine. As bad as this is, it's almost a relief to finally know."

"O.K.," Jack said reluctantly, "I'll come by your house tonight. Bye, Dan, and ... I'm just so sorry." Jack then did something out of character for both of them. He hugged Dan hard and left him standing there in the woods with the wind blowing through the trees, the distant sounds of the cars on the Capitol Beltway, the sickening, but savored odor of all that was left of his son and the odious hole in the ground at his feet; a hole he felt like crawling into and going to sleep ... forever. A light rain began to fall and Dan felt like wet crepe paper. He felt like the very life had been sucked out of him leaving only a hollow shell. The only thing that had ever given life meaning was now officially gone. The one person for whom he felt total love and devotion, gone. And why? "So some fairy cock-sucker could get his rocks off!" he screamed out loud. With that shout his melancholy began to dissolve slowly into anger, but, not passionate, furious, loss-of-temper anger. It was more like a cold and calculating fury gripping him, like the controlled anger he had used to his advantage in Iraq. He could still remember his sergeant's number one rule: "Kill, but stay in control!" Somehow, in some controlled way, he knew he was going to do something about the Greg Dawsons of the world. The thought gave his otherwise lifeless legs the motivation to get up and get into his car to drive home.

CHAPTER 11

"**J**an, sit down," Dan said somberly when she greeted him at the door. Looking at him told her the story. "They found him didn't they?" she burst.

"Yes. It's our worst fear."

The sound she made as she slumped back into the overstuffed living room chair was almost inhuman. It was the last gasp an animal caught in a trap might make just before it dies; it was the muted, eerie, piercing scream of a rabbit as the hunter's bullet takes its life away.

Dan told her the grim story and they sat in their living room lost in their own tortured thoughts. No hugging or consoling today. Just isolated sorrow. It turned out that Greg Dawson had a long record. He had been in mental institutions three times for molesting children. Because of overcrowding and an overworked legal system, he had also been released three times. In fact, he had been released from the last one just six months before he kidnapped Cole. His therapist had declared him 90% cured. By all rights, Dawson should be convicted of Cole's abduction and murder and put away for the rest of his life, and the crime reporter in Dan told him that was exactly what would happen.

Dan had decided that although he favored capital punishment in cases like this he could live with a life sentence. It wasn't that he didn't want Dawson to suffer for his crime; he very much did. It was just that many inmates have children of their own and consequently child molesters are considered the lowest of the low in prison and they often get violently raped and physically abused almost daily. Nothing's too good for Dawson, thought Dan. But there was one little problem with that scenario and his name was Wayne Larson, the Montgomery County District Attorney who had his eye on the Maryland Governor's mansion.

* * *

Because of his intimate familiarity with the circumstances Officer Jack Adams was temporarily assigned to the detective division to work on the Greg Dawson child molesting-murder case. As he told his partner, Pete Hansen, on the drive to the courthouse for a meeting with the prosecutors, "Dawson may be nuts, but he isn't stupid. He knows he's a three-time loser and headed for the joint ... and in stir you know how popular child molesters are. He'd be a dead man ... a dead man with a big butthole."

"Well, at least he'd never be constipated," was Pete's acidic reply.

"That's for sure. So, he says he'll drop a dime on a big kiddie porn asshole ... and I'd like to be in on that bust. But if they do a deal Dawson goes to the nut house and will probably convince the moron doctors that he's cured and will get out in seven or eight years ... to do it all over again."

"Yeah, didn't you say he had already done that a few times?"

"Yeah, he fooled the doctors at two other loony bins. You know how it is. If a psychiatrist is worth a shit, he ain't workin' in a state mental hospital."

"I know. In most of those creep joints you can't tell the patients from the doctors."

"That's about right and Dawson knows it. But the good thing for him is that the rest of the inmates are too far out in left field to know or care about what he's in for. Plus he'll have his pick of crazies to bugger, and who're they gonna' tell?"

"So, he gets a pervert's holiday complete with catatonic love slaves ... and then he gets out. Some justice eh?" Pete cracked as he pulled up to the curb to let Jack out.

"Yeah," Jack said as he hesitated before getting out of the car, "the district boys keep telling me to look at the big picture ... that we're putting away a big kiddie porn king and that will save a lot more kids' lives than Dawson will have a chance to ruin. I 'spose they're right, but you know that isn't the real reason they're going for the deal. It's really just to make a big name for Larson. I think he wants the big job. I just wonder what Dan will do if this deal goes through."

"It's a great life isn't it?"

"The best," said Jack as he shut the door and watched Pete drive away.

* * *

District Attorney Larson had made the plight of the American family his one-issue campaign and at the top of the list of threats to the American family was pornography, particularly child pornography.

Greg Dawson, meanwhile, had a very large collection of kiddie porn and a smart public defender. But best of all, he claimed to personally know a major supplier of child pornography who lived in the Washington, D.C. area. "Tell 'em I want to deal," he told his lawyer, "tell 'em I'll roll over on a very big fish in kiddie porn."

His attorney told police Dawson would help set up the smut dealer for a bust if they would recommend to the judge in his case a life sentence to be served in a mental institution for the criminally insane instead of the expected life prison term. Dawson knew his chances of staying alive in a mental institution were better than in a prison.

* * *

New York City Detective Derek Lindsay's meeting with Sam the informant was interesting to say the least. He had a wild story about a mysterious foreigner who ran a child prostitution ring out of Manhattan. The word was that he pimped young boy prostitutes to visiting foreign dignitaries and even sold them to some of the men to take back home with them as sex slaves.

"If Sammy isn't completely nuts this one could make me glad I'm a cop again," Derek told his partner Sean Casey as they drove toward the federal courthouse in Manhattan.

"Yeah," was all Sean said as he tried to mentally digest all the bizarre things Sam had told them.

Derek instantly realized what a case like this could do for him. Two precinct captains' positions were opening up in the next year and making a big bust could help him get one of them. He could still be a policeman, but not have to go out on the street as much and that could get him back into the lives of his wife and son. He also realized, however, that the case may involve some government officials of the pimp's home government which could mean international relations problems between the New York City Police Department and the

U. S. State Department. He knew he would have to be extra careful on this one.

But before he could do anything else he knew he had to wrap up the big case he was working on and he thought he was about to do just that by testifying against mob boss Anthony Arena. He had been chasing Arena for years and now it looked like he might actually have him. Arena was slick and had slid out of his hands several times during his career. But now he had been charged with a contract murder and prosecutors had a witness.

"I can't wait for this one," Derek told Sean as he got out of the car and walked toward the courthouse steps.

CHAPTER 12

The deal was struck and Greg Dawson pled guilty to second-degree murder. He was sentenced to the Morrisville Mental Health Institute, a maximum-security facility for the criminally insane, for 110 years. But before he went, he told the police where kiddie porn kingpin Martin Burger had a warehouse full of child pornography, "chicken pictures" as he referred to it, and a printing press to print it.

The problem, said Dawson, was that Burger seldom, if ever, visited the warehouse himself. So, while detectives began the painstaking process of tracing the ownership of the building back to him, through a myriad of subsidiary corporations, police officers started a 24-hour stakeout of the building hoping he would appear.

After only 10 days of surveillance they got a break. Burger himself entered the warehouse. Twenty-five policemen converged on the building, arresting him and six others who were actually operating the printing press at the time. Dawson hadn't lied. This was undoubtedly the biggest or one of the biggest child pornography manufacturers in the U.S.

Of course, police already knew this since Officer Jack Adams had broken into the warehouse undetected earlier in the week to confirm Dawson's story. What he saw made even this law enforcement veteran sick. Thousands of magazines, pictures and videotapes packed up and ready to ship all over the

U.S. as well as to 30 different countries. All contained graphic scenes of children being sexually abused by adults in every way imaginable, children having sex with each other, children being tortured by adults and on and on until Jack thought he would retch. Then, as he was climbing out the way he came in Jack caught a glint of light reflecting off of something shiny in the corner.

* * *

Dan had not had a drink since Cole's body was found. While Jan numbed out, as he called it, he seemed sharper than ever. When they were informed of the deal cut by the district attorney's office Jack figured Dan would go ballistic. But instead he calmly said, "Well, that's plea bargaining." Finally, everyone involved in the Cole Forester case considered it closed for good. Now maybe they could, as Jack Adams said, get on with life.

But before Jan could get on with her life she knew she had to work through her grief. So, she grieved ... and grieved ... and grieved until, although she never completely accepted it, she was finally able to bear the fact that Cole was gone forever.

Dan, on the other hand, could not quite come to grips with the fact. And as long as he didn't completely face it, he felt a little like Cole might still be alive out there somewhere. Jan had been to Cole's grave several times. Dan had never gone, not even at the funeral. Although he considered himself an ultra-realist, he retreated into a sort of fantasy world.

* * *

Officer Jack Adams went over to investigate the shiny object in the kiddie porn warehouse and stumbled onto something that Greg Dawson had described, but that he had doubted. The glint of light came from a camera lens. Burger had a video studio set up for making kiddie porn movies that he then sold and posted on the Dark Web. Dawson claimed that Burger paid him to bring children to the studio blindfolded and then rape them on camera.

"What I did with the kid afterward," Dawson told police, "Marty said was my business. But he made it pretty clear that if I ever ratted on the operation I was dead meat."

"What did you do with the children?" Jack had asked.

"I let them go. I got them so fucked up on downers they didn't know what was going on. Besides I always kept them blind-folded going to and from the studio."

"Did you take Cole Forester to the studio and make a tape?"

"Yeah."

"Why did you kill him instead of letting him go like the others?"

"Because he pulled his blindfold off as we were driving away from the warehouse and I didn't notice it until we'd gone a few blocks. I looked in my mirror and there he was looking out the window. He just didn't seem as downed out as the others, so I figured he might be able to identify the neighborhood. The dumb kid ... all he had to do was leave it on and he would be alive today. It was his fault, not mine."

Jack thought about that as he climbed out of the window. *His fault*, he thought, *I shoulda' fragged him right there and saved Dan the trouble.* He still wasn't buying Dan's acceptance of the whole thing.

* * *

So, there it was. Dan and Jan's worst fear. Cole had not only been sexually abused, but on videotape. Even his memory had been sickly perverted. The thought of degenerates all over the world watching their son being molested was just too much for both of them. Jan had given numerous speeches about the big business of child pornography, but now that it touched her so intimately she fell apart. Dr. Simmons could tell immediately that the deep pit of depression was at hand, so she did what she previously had been reluctant to do, and changed her prescription to a more powerful anti-depressant. This one brought back the initial anxiety but after that settled down it kept Jan from sinking into complete, abject despair. The only problem is that it also made her feel even more numb to the world around her ... a feeling she almost welcomed. She immediately took an indefinite leave of absence from the hospital and retreated to the sanctity of her home.

* * *

As Detective Derek Lindsay sat in the courtroom waiting his turn to testify against Crime Boss Anthony Arena his thoughts began to drift to his personal problems and that meant ex-wife Julie. He loved her but stewed about her unfairness. He felt she didn't try hard enough to understand what he had to go through at work. Julie, on the other hand, felt she had tried and tried hard. In the end, she asserted that understanding his job did not change the fact that it was hurting their marriage and she begged him to find another career.

"Doing what?" he had asked her, "driving a garbage truck? That's about all I'm qualified for."

"No, there've got to be other things that aren't so different from being a cop. How about a security guard?"

"Oh yeah, that would be great. Then I could make a whole $10 an hour."

"Well, how about just something safer, like insurance or selling something?"

"You know that I'd go crazy sitting in an office all day and I'm not a salesman. Besides, I'm forty-five years old. Companies don't want old guys like me who are set in their ways. They want young guys they can mold, not to mention pay less."

"Are you saying that being a cop is the only job you can get?"

"Not really. I guess I'm saying being a cop is the only thing I know and it's the only thing I want. What am I saying? It's not something I do ... it's what I am."

"Even if it means losing your wife and kid?"

"That's not fair Julie. You knew I was a cop when you married me. We talked about the implications of being married to a cop a bunch of times and you said that it was all fine because we loved each other. Now suddenly things are all different."

"I know, but I was young and in love back then. I'm older and in love now, but I'm a lot smarter. I hate to say this ... but it has to be your job or your family ... it can't be both."

"So now I've got to pay for your naivete back then. I knew you were heading for an ultimatum and now here it is. The thing is that I would be miserable as a sales-man or whatever and if I'm miserable I'm not going to be that great a husband and father anyway. So what have you accomplished?"

"Well, you may not be any better a mate, but at least I wouldn't be lying awake at night wondering if you're lying dead in an alley somewhere ... and at least you'd be home instead of working these crazy hours."

"Life is tenuous at best honey. I could become an insurance salesman and walk out of the office and get hit by a bus. I believe that when it's your time it's your time whether you're a cop or a garbage man. Besides, I have the reputation of being the smartest man on the

force ... the one who has survived the best. I have a feel for this work. I always seem to know what's next. I know this sounds corny, but it's true, so I really don't think I'm likely to die in the line of duty."

"Well, you may not think it, but I get cold sweats every time I hear a siren go by and I'm just not going to live that way anymore!"

Part of the problem was that Derek had tried hard to shield Julie from his real-life experiences on the force. When she accidentally heard about some of them from another cop's wife she was stunned. The clincher came when she found out why his nickname around the squad room was Daring Derek.

CHAPTER 13

Now that all hope was gone Jan sank deeper and deeper into a bottomless pit of despair. She spent weeks never leaving the house. Dr. Simmons was now concerned for the very life of her patient and friend. She knew that Jan had been so consumed with hope, slim as it was, that she hadn't actually grieved for Cole. Dr. Simmons knew she had to work her way through the grieving process. She just hoped it didn't kill her. She also knew that Jan needed another purpose, but what? Cole was gone and the Find Cole Forester Foundation was no more. The thin hope she had had was also gone. Then she hit on it.

* * *

"Susan," Bob Manson yelled at his star reporter from across the newsroom, "Can you come here for a second?" With natural grace Susan Jensen walked over to his office door. The office was a jumbled mess of files, papers, books and videotapes piled in every conceivable inch of open space. Whenever he was asked about his disorganization Bob would reply that he, and only he, knew exactly where every item was and then proceed to describe the woe that would come to anyone who ever dared to move anything in his office from its resting place. Directly in front of his desk three television sets constantly flickered KNOC-TV's programs as well as those of the competition. On one side of the room hung his rogue's gallery of journalistic awards he and his news staff had won. On the other hung a collection of epigrams, the most prominent of which said "Don't let the bastards scare you." It was an aphorism that referred to the many lofty-positioned people out there who routinely try to intimidate reporters out of doing strong and accurate reports.

"What's up Bob?" Susan asked as she shut the door and sat down.

* * *

"It's the children's issue itself," Dr. Simmons had an epiphany, "Not just Cole, but the whole cause of missing children. You need to fight for the cause," she said out loud. She had concluded that a higher purpose might give Jan something to live for.

"I can't do that," was Jan's initial reply to the doctor's proposition, "I can barely get out of bed in the morning."

"Right now, you can kill two birds with one stone. You can do something that will get your mind off of your problems and you can prevent other parents from going through the same misery you are going through."

It took several weeks of urging, but she finally convinced Jan that while she couldn't save Cole, she could save many children like him. On Dr. Simmon's urging Jan resumed her speech giving on exploited children. She believed it would be good for her to occupy her mind with a mission once again.

Dan, too, experienced a sort of new beginning. Since seeing Cole's body unearthed he had silently, subconsciously and almost involuntarily dedicated himself to a life-fulfilling mission: to save children from child molesters. He didn't know how, but he knew he must do something to save the thousands of children's lives that are ruined or ended each year by pedophiles. He also knew that no parent should have to go through what he and Jan had gone through. Although he didn't know specifically what he was going to do, just the fact that he had a clear vision of what his mission was gave him a strange sort of peace. He couldn't explain the feeling except to say that he had lost one purpose in life just to have it replaced by another, vague as it was. He knew he was on the verge of figuring out something, but what?

With the revelation that his son had been sexually abused on videotape, something insiders like Burger called tape rape, Dan's mission began a path toward clarity. As he leaned against the bookcase in their comfortable earth tone-decorated den, he thought about the sick perverts all over the world getting their kicks watching his little boy being molested. The rage within him built almost to sheer madness. The thought that his son's last few hours were spent in tortured anguish infuriated him. The fact that he hadn't been able to save Cole pushed him toward the abyss. And the realization that he was somewhat to blame for the whole thing by letting Cole walk to school shoved him over the edge. "But ... got to have control," he muttered, "Control."

* * *

"A letter from the Children's Protection Society came for you in the morning mail," KNOC-TV News Director Bob Manson told Susan barely hiding his excitement. The two just stared at each other for a moment and then both looked at the letter lying on his desk as if it were a sacred inscription stolen from a cursed Egyptian tomb that would cast an evil spell on whoever opened it.

"Well, I guess this is it. They said we would probably hear from them this week.

So, go for it, Bob. You do the honors." Susan's heart rate did triple time as she watched her boss, friend, and mentor pick up the letter.

* * *

A whirlpool of thoughts swirled around in Dan's head one night as he listened to the speech Jan gave so often about the world's pampered treatment of pedophiles with very little regard for their victims. In a packed school gymnasium that smelled of sweat and athletic games Jan was on a roll. He was surprised it had taken her only a couple of speeches to get back into the swing of things. He entered late and sat in the back so that she wouldn't see him.

"The legal system isn't doing it," she hammered at the audience, "but that's a moot point because most child sex abuse cases are never reported anyway. The child is told by the very adult who is abusing him or her that they will be killed if they tell. Or they're told their parents won't want them anymore or the child is just simply abused and killed leaving little or no evidence for a case."

Although he was listening intently, Dan couldn't help but visualize all the exciting basketball games that had undoubtedly been played here. While inhaling the sweat so deeply absorbed into the wrestling mats hanging on the walls, he reflected back to his own high school basketball-playing days. He had been quite an athlete back then and part of him yearned for those simpler times. At the same time he was subconsciously framing an idea.

"The courts aren't doing it," Jan went on. "Many of the cases that are reported never make it to court and of those that do, too many are plea-bargained down to a lesser charge meaning the child molester often serves little prison time. Of the cases that are not plea-bargained many do not result in a conviction, often because the defense is able to establish the child as an unreliable witness. Can you believe that? The child who was raped is an unreliable witness!"

Dan could almost hear the crowd yell and the basketball ricochet off the backboard. He could distinctly smell the years of sweat fermented into the wrestling mats lining the gymnasium walls. He was on the verge of something, but he didn't know what.

Jan continued, "But, at any rate, many of the pedophiles who are convicted are given light sentences. Because of prison over-crowding, the ones that get longer sentences often get out early on parole and so are right back on the street looking for another victim. Right now, according to Justice Department figures, 60% of the convicted sex offenders are out on parole or on probation. The problem, of course, is that the child molesters know this and they feel immune from prosecution and prison. And well they should, because so many of them are. And remember ... that's just the convicted sex offenders. There are hundreds of thousands more out there who are never even charged." Jan's voice was reaching a fevered pitch now and the crowd was right with her. "We're talking about millions of kids having their lives ruined while we do very little about it. We're talking about allowing a whole generation of children to be raped. It's madness! Let's stop the madness and let's stop it now before it's too late!"

For a second Dan thought he actually was playing basketball and the crowd was giving him a standing ovation. Then he realized it was Jan's crowd that was standing and applauding her last statement.

Jan continued campaigning for an overhaul of the entire set of laws dealing with child sex abuse cases. She wanted more manpower on police forces to deal with pedophile investigations. She wanted increased enforcement of laws dealing with the growing problem of Internet child pornography. She wanted defense lawyers to be prohibited from attacking the child-victim's testimony except in absolutely clear cases where the judge had strong evidence that the child was lying. She wanted drastically increased mandatory prison sentences with no parole for convicted child sex abusers. She wanted anyone sentenced to prison for child sex abuse chemically castrated upon release. "There is no such thing as the rehabilitation of a pedophile," she argued, although there was a lot of debate over this point. One study showed that many of the pedophiles who are caught and rehabilitated never molest another child. Jan had her doubts about this study and countered that even if it was accurate, by far and away most pedophiles are never caught.

Dan had heard it before and again his mind wandered back to all the basketball games that had been played in the gym. He daydreamed with a half-smile on his face about the school band that always played hip music at intermission. No matter how hip the music, it still sounded like a school band.

Jan wanted an end to plea-bargaining in all child-molesting cases. But most of all she wanted a federal law passed requiring missing children cases to be instantly reported to a central government office. She argued that such a requirement was necessary to demonstrate to lawmakers and the public just how huge the epidemic of abducted and sexually abused children really was. "With no reliable statistics hitting them in the face it's easier to just sweep this problem under the rug. Not until they see how far things have gotten out of hand will they do anything about it." Now slowly coming back to the present, Dan could unconsciously hear Jan approaching the end of her speech. But he was still caught somewhere between fantasy and reality.

If her position seemed harsh her logic was simple. "Although crimes committed against adults are morally wrong," she told her audience, "at least adults have the potential to protect themselves. Children have no way of protecting themselves, which makes crimes committed against them by adults more immoral. They are simply unconscionable and intolerable. We need more legal protection of our children than we do for adults even if it raises constitutional problems. Why? Because they need it. They simply can't protect themselves. If we don't protect our children with our laws who will?"

"I will," Dan blurted out, involuntarily rising to his feet and drawing some startled stares. Jan's question gave him an epiphany. The legal system was not working to protect society's children. If the system couldn't do it, he would. This was absolutely the right thing to do. He knew it. Suddenly, the word *prophecy* popped into his head and he didn't know why. But he dismissed it as a random thought and began thinking about how he was going to protect children like Cole.

* * *

"No ... I think you should open it." Even tough, old news veteran Bob Manson's gnarled hands were trembling.

"I can't. I'm too nervous. Would you do it, please?" said Susan Jensen, her heart leaping up into her throat.

With quivering hands Bob opened the envelope and unfolded the letter. It weighed heavy in his hands and he closed his eyes for a few seconds. Then he opened them slowly and read aloud, "Congratulations, you have been awarded the requested grant in full for the production of two one-hour documentaries on the subject of child sex abuse." Susan leaped up out of her chair, grabbed him, and they both danced around the office howling with delight. Hearing the unaccustomed commotion coming out of Manson's normally sedate office, the rest of the news staff stopped dead in its tracks and just gaped at his closed door. For a few seconds the only sound in the big room was the choppy chatter of the police scanner, like muffled machine gun fire. The staff knew something was up.

* * *

It was in the gymnasium that Dan came to another stark realization: except for Iraq, most of the decisions he had ever made in his life had been based on logic or reason instead of instinct or emotion. In Iraq he often had to act on pure instinct instead of intellect and he believed to this day that it made him a good soldier and, more importantly, it kept him alive. Since then, however, he realized most of his actions had been based on intellect rather than on instinct.

But the formation of our intellect, he reasoned, is limited by the reality we experience here on earth. Earth, though, is just one of millions of planets with their own realities and what's intellectually true here may not be true in another part of the universe. The intellect may not be a reliable judge of what is right and wrong. It may actually get in the way of our instinct of what's right and wrong and it may get in the way of the natural course of life. Dan chuckled at the thought of what his old war buddies would think of this line of bull shit. But he knew he had to follow through on this course of thinking now or he would lose the thread of his logic.

So, acting on how I think instead of on how I feel may not be the natural way of doing things, he thought. There may be a system of natural law in the universe which can be complied with only by following one's instinctive, natural emotions which are somehow tuned into that law better than one's intellect. Maybe we should observe that natural law by heeding our feelings rather than our intellect, especially when it concerns something we feel strongly about. And if there was anything Dan felt strongly about now it was the pedophile issue. He instinctively felt that it was now time to follow what he felt was natural law instead of man's law and convert his natural, intuitive feelings into action. But how?

With that, Dan suddenly became aware of the fact that only he and his wife remained in the gymnasium. The speech was long over and he was so lost in thought he didn't notice the audience leaving. Jan noticed him sitting all alone after the crowd cleared out and waited for him to show signs he was finished with his obviously heavy train of thought.

"Figure it out?" she yelled from her podium as she collected her papers.

"Figure what out?" he jumped. Seeing her across the gym floor, he feared that she had somehow read his mind.

"Whatever it was you were thinking so hard about."

"Oh … yeah. I was just thinking about all the things you said. You're quite a speaker Janny."

"Thanks," she said feeling something had changed about Dan, and they left together.

* * *

Susan immediately telephoned the Children's Protection Society in Washington, D.C. to confirm the grant. She was so excited it took three tries to dial the number. "Yes, it's true," they told her, and could she fly to Washington next week for a personal interview and to sign the necessary papers? After the telephone call Bob Manson and Susan went directly to George Abbott's office to explain the situation and ask for her leave of absence.

"It will be great publicity for the station, Susan doing a national documentary," Bob appealed to George's business sense.

"Absolutely not," was the answer they both half-expected. "How can you expect me to lose my top reporter for a year and hold her job open till she comes back? No way!" Then came the ultimatum that Abbott thought would keep Susan in her job, "if you want to do this thing, you have to quit." Abbott, the basically blind bureaucrat, had the odd notion that since KNOC-TV was his universe it must be the be-all and end-all for everyone else. He just couldn't imagine any of the station's staff getting better jobs anywhere else and took it as a personal affront when they did. Then he held out the big carrot. "If you stay," he said with a vacuously knowing look on his face, "there's a main anchor spot for you." George knew enough to know that most reporters drastically wanted to be anchors and he considered himself pretty crafty in his strategy.

"Here's my letter of resignation Georgie," Susan said instead with a wry, satisfied smile on her face as she shoved the letter onto his desk, "have a nice life." They both turned and walked out leaving a stunned George Abbott to stare after them in disbelief.

"Wait!" he belatedly sputtered, but she was gone and his inflated ego kept him from going after her. "You know ... you can never come back," he weakly yelled, trying to save a face that even he knew couldn't be saved.

"You know what this means Bob," Susan gushed as they walked down the hall, "no more insipid city council meetings to cover. No more putting my best effort into stories that I don't really give a damn about. No more running my blood pressure up and risking a heart attack just to make a deadline and get a lousy two-minute story on the air that no one gives a shit about anyway. Just creative journalism with the money and the tools to do it right." She realized with delight that once she got one successful documentary under her belt more would follow.

"You're free, Sue!" Bob said and impulsively they hugged each other. There had never been anything but a professional relationship between them, but this news inspired passionate joy, something neither was accustomed to.

The announcement to the news staff was difficult because Bob had managed to assemble a top-notch group of journalists who cared more about accuracy and ethics than about hairstyles and make-up. They had grown close in their rough and tumble world of hard news and deadline pressure and considered themselves to be among the last vestiges of good journalism in America. They loved Susan and knew the newsroom wouldn't be the same without her. That night the staff threw the wildest going away party in the history of the station.

CHAPTER 14

"Yup," Derek Lindsay muttered to himself as he sat in the courtroom, still waiting his turn to testify, "It was Daring Derek that did it." One of his fellow officers had pinned the name on him when he got involved in gang investigations and infiltrated a particularly brutal gang. One day the gang learned that he was the cop who busted one of their members and laid a trap for him. When he arrived at a meeting on an apartment building rooftop they grabbed him and tried to tie him to a post. What they planned to do wasn't clear and Derek didn't want to find out. In the scuffle he managed to pull his gun out and shoot two of his would-be captors. The only problem was that they all had guns. He quickly looked for an exit.

The roof door was closed and the only other way out was over the side of the building, a 25-story drop. Without a thought Derek ran as fast as he could, jumped over the side, and just barely caught the edge of the next roof. Two of the more brave or crazy gang members leaped right after him and he was again in trouble. This time there was no roof within jumping distance.

* * *

Dan was pensive. He had the seed of an idea of what he wanted to accomplish, but he didn't know how to do it. He knew it was going to take some time to figure it all out, and that was good because he needed to help Jan get through her grief.

"How has Dan taken all this?" Dr. Simmons asked Jan shortly after Porn King Marty Burger's arrest.

"That's the strange part. He has taken it extremely well ... too well if you ask me. I mean, for five months he did nothing but drink and now that we know Cole's dead he stops drinking completely and actually seems to have shaped up."

"It's possible that the resolution of Cole's fate ... just knowing, as opposed to not knowing, is a relief for him."

"That's what I figured, but there just seems to be more to it than that. It's almost like Dan now feels some purpose in his life, which ... believe me... he never had before."

"I wonder what that purpose is."

"I don't have the slightest idea, but he sure is being nice to me and that helps a lot. The thing is ... it seems like he hasn't really accepted that Cole's gone. He's never gone to the cemetery. I wonder if it's because he just doesn't want to face up to it."

"Could be. But it's good he's being nice. A lot of times in a crisis like this a person suddenly becomes more aware of the people he cares about. Maybe he has decided his purpose is to make you happy."

"I'd like to think that, but still there seems to be something else; something I just can't put my finger on."

"How's the sex life?" asked Dr. Simmons subconsciously hoping to get some juicy details.

"The same. Actually worse, if that's possible. At least before, I could get interested in it once every couple of months. It was like I really didn't want to do it, but I had this animal urge that needed to get out every so often. But now there's no urge at all and I don't really care if I ever have sex again."

"It's most likely the anti-depressant. It often kills the sex drive and that's one of the reasons I was reluctant to put you on it. But I don't see that we had much choice. It is obviously really helping you cope. Are you giving Dan some sexual relief?"

"No, I just can't. I know I should, but I just can't seem to give a damn."

"Again, it's probably the drug. It can numb your feelings which is its purpose, but sometimes it numbs feelings you would rather keep alive. But I would suggest that you force yourself on occasion to masturbate him or something like that because his sexual frustration could make him turn not-so-nice again and you don't need that."

"I know. I've thought about it a few times, but each time I just lie there and say to myself what's the use? I just can't get my motivation up to do it... or much of anything else for that matter. I feel like there's something ... something missing, but I don't know what it is. The only thing I halfway enjoy is the public speaking and I don't really like it."

"All the drug, Jan. I wish it didn't have these side effects, but it does. Once we get you through the worst part of this we'll slowly wean you off of it and you can go back to a normal life."

"Things will never be normal, but that would be nice," Jan said listlessly. She was terrified that if she went off the medication the horrific depression would return.

Dan, meanwhile, was sexually frustrated. But nothing creates energy like frustration and he was channeling his into planning his mission. Dusting off his library card he checked out every book he could find dealing with pedophilia and photocopied every article about child sex abuse cases he could get his hands on. He also read and re-read the materials Jan had assembled until he had created a solid profile of a pedophile. Then, one day in the middle of an article it hit him. Finally, the seed of an idea had germinated into a seedling of a plan.

* * *

Still daydreaming in the courtroom Derek Lindsay was mentally back on that apartment building roof. He looked around quickly for a way out and there it was: a long mast for a TV antenna. He grabbed it and ran for the edge of the roof at full speed. Just like pole vaulting in high school, he thought as the end of the pole hit the soft, warm tar roof ... and stuck, thank goodness. He went flying up and over to the next roof 20 feet away, spraining his ankle when he landed. His pursuers weren't that crazy and they hadn't pole vaulted in high school. In fact, they hadn't attended high school. They stopped dead in their tracks and tried to shoot him. In the darkness Derek zigzagged and limped to the roof door and down the stairs to safety.

Even some of Derek's fellow officers thought he was a bit crazy, but they admitted that the ensuing bust of the gang for drug-running, murder and a plethora of other serious charges was good police work. Julie, however, wasn't impressed. She was just plain shocked. The Derek Lindsay pole vaulting off 25 story buildings while being chased by vicious killers just didn't seem like the man with whom she shared her bed and her life. After hearing that story, she fretted and worried every day when he went to work.

* * *

Now the seedling needed watering. All that was left was to wait and scheme. Dan's plan needed a lot of refinements, but they would come with time. Jan would need him around for a while longer. He spent much of his day at work reading books and articles, careful not to bring them home lest Jan get suspicious of his sudden interest. And he began working out again every night at the health club.

* * *

There were other things Julie Lindsay didn't like about her husband's job. She knew that in the course of some of his undercover assignments Derek had associated with extremely rich drug lords. She also knew that their lifestyles included beautiful women. Her natural suspicion was, of course, that Derek might have had to have sex with some of these women so as not to blow his cover. The fact was that he had never been put in that position and he told her so. But he also knew that if he ever had been in that situation he would probably have had to bed the woman rather than risk raising the suspicions of the drug dealers he was trying to bust. He never mentioned that to Julie. What he did tell her was true. He had been completely faithful to her and never strayed, even in the line of duty. The fact was that he didn't need to play around for his thrills ... he got enough excitement from the job. She believed him, but still had lingering fears that it might happen sometime in the future.

All these considerations were just too much for her to cope with and after a year of separation she divorced him. They had stayed on good terms and occasionally even slept together. His son Gary blamed Derek for the divorce and, like many teenagers, didn't particularly care for his father. Derek, however, dearly loved his son and the one big regret he had in his life was not having spent more time with him. Still daydreaming in the court room, he hoped that he would soon be able to make up for that. Then the words "call Detective Derek Lindsay to the stand" snapped him out of his reverie.

CHAPTER 15

The deeper Ross Huggins delved into his FBI study on pedophiles the more intrigued he became. In the course of his research he was turning up information about child molesters that made the bureau's old information obsolete. One newly established fact was that many pedophiles are adult males who prefer to molest young boys rather than girls. The old study said the vast majority of them were men who raped little girls. Also, the old study set forth the common belief that the vast majority of pedophiles molested children because they had been molested in their youth. Ross found that a little under half of the pedophiles in the United States had been molested as children, which left a big question mark about the other half's motivation.

"What drives these creeps?" he asked friend and colleague Roy Bellizi one day at work.

"They're sick," came Roy's predictable reply. Roy, like most people Ross knew, always seemed to be satisfied with surface answers. If an adult molests a child he's sick, that's all there is to it. There's no need to look into it further. But Ross had to look into it further. That was his nature, that was his job, and that was one reason he was a good researcher.

"I know they're sick, but what made them sick? Is it environmental or physiological? A lot of these guys had normal upbringings which makes you wonder if they've got a bad chromosome or something."

"Who cares why they're sick, they're just sick. They're like a disease that society has and law enforcement is the cure. Of course, our law enforcement is pretty weak medicine right now."

"Yeah, you've got to wonder why the legal system seems to be the most lenient with the people who commit the worst crimes."

"Well, you know what they say, in the monopoly game of life the only way to get out of jail free is to be rich or a child molester."

"Who says that?"

"I did, just now. Didn't you hear it?"

"I swear Roy, you oughta' write your proverbs down and publish a book. You could call it Roy's Ramblings."

"Yeah, and if it didn't sell I could always use it for toilet paper."

"Well, with the shit you spread you probably need it."

In spite of the joking, the question of nature versus nurture loomed large in Ross's mind and he would have liked to research the environmental backgrounds of the thousands of pedophiles he had on file to get an answer. Unfortunately, there wasn't enough background information on most of them to get statistically significant results. He had discovered a few things, however, like the fact that many pedophiles had molested or had had the urge to molest children ever since they themselves were young. Some reported molesting four-year-old children when they were ten years old, but the average pedophile started when he was about fifteen.

The most commonly accepted psychological reason for pedophilia involved vulnerability and power. Many mental health experts believed pedophiles were attracted to their young victims precisely because they were young and vulnerable. In other words, pedophiles felt less threatened by younger kids than they did by someone their own age. The theory went on to say that the victim's vulnerability also gave the pedophile a feeling of power that he wouldn't have with someone his own age. In fact, it was thought that many pedophiles kill their victims as an ultimate expression of that power more than to keep them from telling. This seemed to make sense to Ross, but he still felt that there had to be a deep-seated physiological reason for the pedophilic behavior.

* * *

Finally, Jan gave up the speeches and public appearances. The medication that kept her from sliding into the pit of depression also made her increasingly numb and lethargic and gave her an incredibly dry mouth, which made her speeches difficult. She went into seclusion, watching television and reading fiction, going out only when she had to. Her home was now a refuge from the world's cruelties. Dan was there for her, but he didn't seem to need her to be there for him.

Months went by and Jan visited Dr. Simmons twice a week. One day, for no clear reason, she could honestly say she felt halfway good. It had been so long she wasn't sure if it was real or a dream. But it was real. The only problem was that the feeling only lasted half a day, then she was back in the dumps. A few days later the feeling returned and this time it lasted longer. She wasn't ready to put on her dancing shoes, but it was a big step up from the total worthlessness she had felt for quite some time.

"The feeling just came out of the blue," she told Dr. Simmons, "but I was so afraid that it would go away I couldn't really enjoy feeling good again."

"That's very common," Dr. Simmons said, "but the main thing is that you did get the feeling and I'm happy to tell you that that is the first sign of your recovery. You will most likely continue to experience these periods of normalcy and with any luck they'll last longer and longer. When they are constant for a good period of time we'll wean you off the medication, but that will be a while."

"Well, excuse me if I don't jump up and do a jig. But I'm still scared to death that this is just a fluke and I'll end up right back in the pits." The idea of going off of her medication terrified Jan more than staying on it.

"I won't lie to you. It could happen. But I will tell you that it is unlikely."

"Well, that's the best news I've had in months. I think I'll go home and tell Dan. He could probably use some encouraging news after putting up with my moods all this time."

Dan was encouraged by the news, but not for the reason Jan had thought. For him it meant the beginning of his mission was getting closer. He already had fifteen different identifications printed up by a forgery expert he had busted a few years earlier and with all the work-outs and weight lifting his body was returning to a fine-honed condition.

* * *

Detective Derek Lindsay testified about his involvement in the Anthony Arena investigation, giving the prosecutors what they wanted and playing verbal volleyball with the defense attorney. Arena controlled a big portion of the crack and heroin trade in Brooklyn and he was personally guilty of several murders. But he had somehow slipped out of the law's clutches time after time. This time, however, there was a witness willing to testify that he saw Arena order a killing. As Derek left the courthouse he thought maybe this time Arena's number was finally up. It wasn't.

"Your witness changed his tune Derek," Sean Casey said the next day at the station.

"What?" Derek asked, stunned.

"I just got a call from the courthouse. He suddenly knows nothin' about nothin'."

"The son-of-a-bitch got to him." Derek just sat and stared for a good 30 minutes, almost unable to believe that Anthony had done it again. But he was determined to get Arena one way or the other.

* * *

Dan toyed with the idea of killing his son's murderer, Greg Dawson. But he eventually decided he couldn't kill unless it was in war, in self-defense or in defense of another. In the end it didn't matter because Porn King Marty Burger made good on his promise and had Dawson stabbed to death by a fellow inmate serving a life sentence for serial murder.

* * *

Shortly after crime boss Anthony Arena was found not guilty, he held a meeting of the big shots in his family at a resort in the Catskills. Detective Derek Lindsay found out about it and decided to crash the party. The family bosses were gathered in one of the hotel meeting rooms with bodyguards at the doors when Derek arrived. Wasting no time, he knocked one of the guards out with a nose-crushing blow and slammed into the room, striding past a large Italian woman singing at a piano bar in the corner and right up to the podium which was vacant.

"Don't let me disturb your linguini slurping," he said coolly into the microphone as twenty surprised heads shot up from the lunch tables and the pianist stopped playing. "I just wanted to let you slime-balls know that it's not over till the fat whop sings. Arena," he said staring straight at Anthony, "I've got nothing better to do than to constantly hound you for the next few years and that's exactly what I'm going to do. Like the song says, every move you make, every step you take, I'll be watching you. I'm going to be there when you go to bed at night and when you get up in the morning and when you think you see your shadow, it's gonna' be me. Why? Because I'm crazy for one. But also because you and I both know that you will slip up one of these days and I'll be there to rub your face in the shit and to take the rest of your greasy friends along. O.K. big mama, finish your song." He nodded to the woman at the piano bar and walked briskly out with everyone too surprised to do anything about it. So stunned was everyone in the room that no one moved, not even Arena's body guards. But even that brazen exhibition of chutzpah wasn't enough for Derek. He had to do one more thing.

* * *

Six months after Cole's burial Jan felt she was returning to a more normal state. Dr. Simmons was right; her good moods continued to increase in length and number and she thought she might actually be feeling an intermittent sense of contentment.

"I've hesitated to tell you this Dan because I was afraid if I did ... I might go right back to being depressed, but I think it's for real now. I think I'm going to be O.K.," she told him one night.

"That's great, honey. I know you wouldn't say it if it weren't true. I'm just glad you've been able to work through it. Now maybe you can get on with your life."

"Yeah. I think I'm actually going to go back to work in a week. I talked to the hospital and they said they've really missed me and that made me feel good."

"I'll bet they did. You always did a good job. I think it'll be good for you to keep your mind occupied with something you like again."

"Yeah, now that I'm half-way sane I don't think I could sit around the house all day anymore."

"Right," was all Dan said as he decided that he would wait and see how Jan's first few weeks of work went before he told her he was leaving. In the meantime, he started reading mystery novels.

* * *

After driving away from the hotel Derek Lindsay circled back and parked behind the curved driveway's decorative trees. He then furtively entered the men's restroom outside of the family's meeting room. First, he emptied his bowels in the toilet and didn't flush it, and then he hung an out-of-order sign on the stall door. Climbing up into the ceiling and hiding in the crawl space between the ceiling tiles and the roof he then watched as several Arena men came and went. After a while, his patience paid off when Anthony entered. Derek leaped down upon him, dragged him to the stall toilet and pushed his face into the murky water, holding his head under until he ran out of breath and started aspirating. "Sorry Anthony, but I couldn't wait to rub your face in the shit," he said in a muffled voice. He held Arena by the hair and bobbed his head in and out of the toilet, "besides it gives me a thrill to see you eat my turds ... so eat 'em greaseball and like it! It's probably better tasting than that crap you've been eating for lunch." Then, he slammed the toilet seat down on the sputtering man's head and started for the door laughing, "see ya' around Anthony. Say, you look like hell ... you oughta' take better care of yourself. But then, I always knew you had a taste for shit."

"You're dead," Arena spit the words out along with bits of feces, "dead, Lindsay!"

By then, Derek was already out the door, out of the hotel and on his way to his car. Driving away, he thought briefly that Anthony Arena could and very possibly would put a contract out on his life, but the exhilaration of what he had just done quickly pushed that worry out of his head. He cranked up the car stereo and started laughing uproariously while careening down the twisting and turning mountain road.

CHAPTER 16

One week after her big going away party Susan Jensen flew to Washington to make the final arrangements for the grant money and to start her research for her documentary on child abuse. Her good-bye to her old friend and mentor News Director Bob Manson was a tearful one because they had grown so professionally close over the years. "I've been so excited about my good luck, Bob, that we haven't talked about you having to stay here," she said with genuine concern.

"That's O.K.," Bob replied, "I'm too old to do what you're doing and anyway, ten bucks says Abbott will get the ax in a year's time and I'll get to break-in another G.M."

"You're a rock Bob ... and ... I love you."

"I love you too Susan ... now get the hell out of here and make me proud."

Because the Children's Protection Society was a central clearing house for everything ever written about the child sex abuse issue and it kept tabs on all reports of missing kids and convicted child molesters nation-wide, Susan couldn't have asked for a better resource. She planned to organize abused children who appeared to have been sexually molested by a stranger into one group, children abused by someone they knew into another, and all convicted child molesters into a third. She would then set up interviews with the kids and their relatives in the first two groups. After that she planned to track down, catalog, and index the third group so she could find them when she was ready to interview them. Many of the third group's interviews would undoubtedly have to be done using a hidden camera without the subject's knowledge.

In her preliminary research Susan had discovered several recent child molestation cases in the Washington, D.C. area, which meant less distance to travel for interviews and a savings on production costs. She also came across a name she recognized of a boy in the area who had been killed by a pedophile. She figured she would give the parents a little more time to grieve while she conducted her preliminary research.

* * *

Dan continued to meet Officer Jack Adams at the corner bar occasionally. But he drank mineral water while Jack continued putting away the Scotch. One night, however, Dan fell off his self-imposed wagon and the two of them held one of their old-time drinking sessions, heavy-laden with philosophical discussion. "You know Dan, I was really kinda' surprised at how well you took everything," Jack's booze-loosened tongue allowed him to say, "I kinda' expected you to go after Dawson or something," he slurred out.

"Well, of course I thought about it. But hell, Marty and the nut-job with the knife saved me the trouble."

"Yeah, like Pete said the other day, what're they gonna' do to the crazy bastard, give him another life sentence? He already killed 13 people ... Dawson was just another notch on his belt. Except he was probably the only one that really deserved it."

"Yeah ... speaking of deserving it," Dan hesitated. He took a long drink of his beer to give himself time to decide whether or not he should continue. "Ya' know the statistic about one pervert molesting almost 50 kids in his lifetime?"

"Yeah."

"Well, we've both seen the way just one rape can ruin a kid's life for good. What do you think oughta' be done with the bastards?"

"I think they oughta' be hung up by their balls with piano wire and roasted over a hot bed of coals."

"You're holdin' back, Jack. How'dya really feel?" Dan said sarcastically.

"I'd take him naked out into a blizzard and set him down on a log. Then I'd nail his scrotum to the log and hand him a rusty knife. He'd have a choice ... freeze to death or cut off his own balls."

"Some choice," Dan said, laughing and actually considering the idea.

"Well, actually, you know I think the laws and sentences should be a lot tougher," Jack was serious now. "I think they should get the death penalty when they physically hurt a kid. But I also think anyone convicted of child molesting should be forced to be shot up with that drug that chemically castrates them."

"Oh yeah, the one that makes them impotent," Dan had read about this treatment which involved regular injections of female hormones into male sex offenders, "The only problem is the molesters have to keep getting the shots or their sex drive comes back. Anyway, I think a lot of these assholes don't do it for the sex. They just like the power and the control."

"Well, then I think they should be physically castrated. They've done it in other countries and it cut down on re-offenders big time."

"Not a bad idea, but I think the Civil Liberties Union might have something to say about that. It would never happen. But what if you could just push a button and suddenly ... say ... ten pedophiles would be put in prison for life right now? Say they've already molested half of the 50 victims they're gonna' molest in their lifetime so they've each got 25 to go. You'd be saving like 250 kids' lives. Would you do it?"

"You and your fucked-up questions," sloshed Jack. For as long as he had known him, Dan had had an odd and often comical tendency to ask this kind of question. Usually the questions involved money like, "Would you do this for a million dollars or that for ten thousand dollars?" The one he remembered the most was the proposition, "Say there's an empty swimming pool in a town of 100,000 people. Every time each one of them had to blow their nose, throw up, take a leak or a dump, bleed, ejaculate, pop a pimple, sweat, have their period or excrete any bodily discharge in any way, they did it in the pool until it was full to the top. For a million dollars would you jump in and swim around for five minutes?" Of course, there were many, many more. Some were funnier but few sicker, yet Jack had to admit that they were often entertaining.

"Well, would you?" Dan pushed.

"Damn right I would, but what a dumbass question. What're ya' drunk?"

"Simply hypothetical officer ... simply hypothetical."

CHAPTER 17

As his pedophile study continued, Ross Huggins didn't learn much that was new and interesting, until one day he came across a statement by a convicted pedophile alleging that there was an organized child-stealing ring operating in the U.S. The child molester claimed that the ring was a loosely connected group, some of whom kidnapped kids and others who acted as middlemen and brokered them to pedophiles. There was one organization, which allegedly did both; a Los Angeles motorcycle gang. The statement piqued Ross's interest. He began a computer search for similar reports from other child molesters.

Sure enough, he found them. The story was usually the same. The allegation was that the child-stealing ring kidnapped children and sold them to rich pedophiles. The Los Angeles motorcycle gang was called El Muerto or The Dead. They were reportedly into drug dealing and gun running in Mexico and Central America and also ran a child-stealing network on the side. According to the stories, several members of the gang scoured the country for young boys and girls who were good looking and vulnerable. They kidnapped the ones they found and sold them to child brokers who had pedophile clients waiting to buy them, or they sold them directly to their own millionaire clients at huge prices. One report claimed that the gang's favorite targets were newspaper boys because they were out on the street alone early in the morning and were easy to kidnap.

Another report maintained that a number of the rich pedophiles kept their child victims in homes in foreign countries and that a major buyer of the children lived on a big estate in Mexico where he had a virtual harem. When they got too old, said the report, he had them killed.

The reason the concept of a child-stealing network had never been given much credence by law enforcement authorities was that all these reports by pedophiles had never been collected and put together before. Now Ross felt he had more than enough evidence to declare what the FBI called a finding. The finding he made was that there was a very good chance the child-stealing network did exist. He took that finding to his superiors.

* * *

Jan went back to work at St. Christopher's Hospital where all of her old co-workers threw a welcome back party. Nursing is a profession in which close friendships are often made and Jan had her share of good friends at the hospital. Being both naturally friendly and the highly proficient nurse she was, most of the staff liked and respected her. It was surprising even to Jan how quickly she settled into her old work routine. Here, once again, was something she knew well and was comfortable with, something that gave life meaning. She genuinely needed to help other people and nursing was a way to do it. Jan knew she would never be whole or happy again, but at least now she felt she might be able to go on.

* * *

Ross Huggins' FBI bosses put the information he gave them out to all law enforcement agencies across the country with particular emphasis on Los Angeles, the home of El Muerto.

"Good work Hug," Don Westerhof said as he walked into Ross's office. "Your finding has put police departments on alert and may just lead to something really big."

"Thanks Don. Actually, the research has been interesting and this has turned out to be a good assignment," Ross didn't tell his boss about the days he had to stop his work because the graphic descriptions of the pedophiles' sexual abuse and torture of their victims made him physically ill. Every time he read one of these accounts he would get the image of his own two kids in his mind. The thought of them being sexually molested was more than he could bear.

"Well, it may turn out to be more than interesting research," Don said. "I probably shouldn't tell you this in case it doesn't work out, but you've done such a good job on this so far the boys upstairs are seriously talking about giving you your wish and putting you out in the field on a pedophile case."

"You're kiddin' me!"

"No, I'm not. But remember, I just heard them talking about it ... unofficially. Nothing has been decided and they don't have a specific case yet, so mum's the word O.K.?"

"O.K.! Thanks Don. Thanks a lot," Ross was so excited about the prospect of becoming a field agent that he forgot what his friend Roy had said earlier about not wanting to go undercover on a child sex abuse case. He also conveniently forgot about fellow agent Joe Carnahan's suicide after just such an assignment.

CHAPTER 18

"Oh, what a day," Jan said as she came in the door one night after she had been working for two months, "Andrea and Kelly both called in sick and we were already short-staffed, so I never sat down all day. What are you doing home so early?"

Dan looked at her with a serious expression and she knew something was wrong.

"What?" she asked.

"Now that you seem to be getting along O.K.," he began, "I need to do something for myself. I ... I'm going on a trip to get myself together."

"But, you seem so together already," Jan reacted. "I think you've handled this whole thing a heck of a lot better than I have."

"I know. That's what I wanted you to think so I could be strong for you and help you recover. But, honestly, I've been torn up the whole time too. We both know you need someone strong and since I'm the only one here, it had to be me. Besides, if we'd both fallen apart you'd probably still be watching soap operas and popping downers." The cruel words came out so fast he couldn't believe he had said them. What he knew, however, was that he always strove to be clever even if the only words available to him at the time were insensitive or inappropriate. Jan was too astounded by his news to be hurt.

"Where are you going? What're you going to do?" was all she could muster.

I'm going to Colorado first to spend some time in the mountains and collect my thoughts. After that, I just don't know. Don't worry, though, I'll keep in touch. I just have to go. In a weird way, it's my therapy."

"But, Dan I'm just coming out of my dark days. I can help you come out of yours. Stay here. We'll work it out," she pleaded, knowing that his decision was irreversible as all of his past decisions had been.

"I wish I could honey, but I can't. I have to do this alone. It's important that I get away where I don't know anyone and pull myself together ... by myself."

Jan had known from the first that Dan was different than other men she had known. One of the things that set him apart was that he never discussed his problems with anyone, not even with her. As long as she had known him, he worked out his problems completely on his own. He had often gone off on his own for a few days to do it. She knew that he was about to do it again, but in a larger way.

"How long will you be gone?"

"I know this is inconsiderate, but I don't honestly know. This thing's got me so bad it could be a couple months or it could be a year. I just don't know."

"A year! Dan, I can't live here without you for a whole year! How about if we go together. I could get another leave of absence ... they would understand.

"No honey. That would destroy the whole purpose. I really need to go alone. You'll be fine. You've got your friends. It will be just like when I was gone before," Dan said, referring to his past absences when on special undercover assignments. The difference was that it really wouldn't be the same, because then Jan had Cole ... now she had no one. "Besides, I didn't say it would absolutely be a year. I said it could be. It will probably be a lot shorter."

Jan knew at this point that there was nothing she could say to change her husband's mind so, as she had done so many times in the past, she accepted his decision and adapted to it the best she could. "Well, I guess if you have to you have to. But, I don't think this is going to be too great for our marriage," she said dejectedly.

When he heard this Dan knew that he was over the hump. He knew that Jan would be all right. "Our marriage is going to have problems if I'm not together," he told her, "getting my head together will make our marriage stronger and this is the only way I know how to do that. I feel it in my gut and I know that if I don't go my mental state is going to get worse until there won't be much of our marriage left anyway."

Jan reluctantly understood and when she considered her recent strides toward her recovery she realized that Dan deserved his healing, even if he
went about it in an unusual way.

"I guess you took a leave of absence from your job, but how are you going to pay for the trip?" she asked him resignedly.

"You're probably not gonna' like this, but I cashed in the IRA. I know I won't spend it all. But I wanted it just in case."

"That was supposed to be Cole's college money!" she blurted out, not thinking.

"Exactly."

They looked at each other for a few moments until Dan said, "Anyway you always said since I inherited it, it's my money and I always said whatever you got from your parents is your money."

"I know. I know. It is your money, but it would have been nice to have it for retirement."

"Yeah, well, after all this I think we both know that life is too uncertain to plan too far ahead."

"I guess so. Dr. Simmons said we all take different roads back to wholeness. I just didn't realize that in your case it's a real road."

"I love you, Jan."

"I love you too."

* * *

Douglas Glassman's life was a dichotomy ever since he began therapy. On one hand he and psychologist, Dr. Christine Johnson, were making clear progress in their search for the roots of his sexual desire for young boys. But, on the other, at the same time, those desires were intensifying and increasing. Up to now Doug had been able to have a semi-normal sex life with his wife Sandy, but faking sexual interest in her was getting harder and harder. In the past he had always gotten aroused by imagining her as a naked, young boy. But that wasn't working anymore. He wanted the real thing. After being repressed for so long, his true sexual desires were ready to burst out, and he was having a hard time faking desire for Sandy anymore. She, like many women her age, had gained a few pounds over the years and blamed herself. She went on a strict diet and exercise program and lost 30 pounds. When it had no effect, Doug tried to explain that it was his problem, not hers.

"I don't know why, but I'm impotent," he told her. He lied that he still desired her strongly in his mind, but it didn't seem to transfer to his body and he didn't know what was wrong. In reality, although her weight loss made her attractive, he had practically no erotic feelings left for her. It had been months since they had had sex and it was beginning to threaten their marriage.

Doug's sex drive hadn't actually abated. In fact, it had grown stronger, but for boys, not girls. The stronger it grew the less he felt for his wife. But sexual deprivation of any kind is like steam in a pressure cooker; it builds up and eventually comes out, sometimes savagely.

Doug was fantasizing about sex with boys twenty times a day, every day and none of the meditation exercises he learned from Dr. Johnson worked anymore. He hated being so passionately drawn to young boys, but it was the only passion in his life and it excited him immensely. At 40 he had also stepped back and looked at his life only to realize how boring it actually was.

* * *

Derek Lindsay sat at his desk deep in thought, pondering the best way to proceed in the investigation of a child prostitution ring allegedly run out of Manhattan by a rich foreign businessman. Sam the informant had told him Ali Ban Hashemi was the man many foreign leaders went to when they wanted something that they couldn't get through official channels and that they wanted kept quiet. According to the informant, if you wanted arms you went to Hashemi, if you wanted imports that were banned from your country you went to Hashemi, if you wanted women you went to Hashemi, and, most nefarious, if you wanted kids you went to Hashemi. The latter category was what interested Lieutenant Lindsay. "Let the federal boys tackle the guns and imports and the broads nobody cares about. But when it comes to selling little kids ... that's something else," he thought as he hatched a plan for the investigation.

* * *

After watching Jan for a week and making sure she was genuinely feeling better, Dan decided it was time to leave. "I'd like to leave tomorrow, but tonight I would like to fuck your brains out," he said, shattering any romantic mood that might have developed on their last night together. But Dan had never been a moonlight and roses kind of guy. Instead, he had always gotten right down to it. Though Jan yearned for romance herself, his directness and crudeness about sex always turned her on. In the back of her mind she knew his talk about sex appealed to her because it rebelled against her sheltered, orthodox background. It excited her. Even farther back in her mind she also knew that Dan's crude references to sex were probably a result of his own immaturity.

Nonetheless, knowing it was one of the last nights she might see him for a while, she got in the mood and with no comment walked to the bathroom. After showering she put on her red and black bustier, garter belt, thong, and black silk stockings. The straps felt good against her flesh again, reminding her of the steamy sex they used to have and making her feel sexy for the first time in months. As far as Dan was concerned the more straps the better and he liked her to keep the lingerie on while they made love. It had taken him years to get Jan to dress this way. She said she felt like a whore or a circus clown. Dan's stock answer would be that as long as she dressed up just for him it was O.K. Tonight she made no protests and when the bedroom door closed they experienced an explosion of long overdue, pent-up sexual passion and performed enough erotic acrobatics to make an X-rated movie star jealous.

Afterward, lying there in the dark smoking, Dan briefly and fancifully wondered if the night's spectacular sex might have broken the logjam of his wife's desire and if he might get more of the same if he stayed home. But, deep inside he knew that one night of acrobatic sex did not a complete reversal-of-desire make. Something told him that tonight was a special gift and that sex with Jan was never again going to be like it was before Cole's death. In fact, he knew, and Jan knew deep within herself, although she wouldn't admit it, that the once passionate, burning love between them had dwindled to smoldering embers. Cole's disappearance had sucked it out of them, and they both genuinely doubted whether they could really love each other or anyone else ever again as they had in the past. Their tragedy might have ended that chapter in their lives. As Dan drifted off to sleep he began dreaming about the new chapter in his life; his mission. As he dreamed he found himself flying toward the sun. Silhouetted against the ball of light was Cole's face. He was talking, trying to tell him something, but no words came out of his mouth. He thought he was saying something like *provenance* or *providence* but he couldn't be sure. Then he disappeared and all that remained was the incredibly bright light of the sun.

* * *

With nothing but an informant's word and the fact that suspected child pimp Ali Ban Hashemi had no prior record, Detective Derek Lindsay could not get a warrant to tap his apartment and telephone. That was really a minor problem. He tapped them both anyway with his own wire-tapping equipment, something that was commonly done by New York City Police Department detectives to gather unofficial information. Derek set up the monitoring and voice-activated recording equipment in a van in the basement-parking garage of Hashemi's apartment building. All he told the garage manager was that he needed to leave the van there for a couple of weeks as part of a police investigation and that was enough. Then, since he didn't have a family to go home to anyway, after each day's work he went to the van and played back Hashemi's home and phone conversations of the day. What he discovered was that Hashemi didn't have many visitors to his apartment and those he did have were either legitimate business associates or women that he dated. Derek noticed that all of his calls were answered by an answering machine; he never answered in person, even when he was in the apartment. Also, all of the messages left a number to call back. "Smart," thought Lindsay, "that way he'll always know who's calling and what it's about so that he's never caught unprepared. And he doesn't risk saying anything incriminating over the phone in case it's tapped." Derek knew Hashemi must be wary of a tap because he never used his own phone to return the calls. "He's got to be either using a cell phone from outside the apartment or pay phones," he thought. He started the tedious task of tracing the numbers the callers left on the machine to see just who he was dealing with.

CHAPTER 19

Dan slid the clumsy headphones over his ears and listened to some light rock music as he nestled back into his coach seat on the early morning Washington to San Diego flight. San Diego, California was the city Dan chose to begin operations for no particular reason other than that it was far away from Washington. He planned to work his way up the West Coast and then head east, zigzagging up and down the country on the way. Drifting off to sleep he thought about how ironic it was that he was beginning his mission in the state some of his Army buddies used to call the land of fruits and nuts.

After an uneventful flight Dan took a taxi to the El Ranchero, a cheap but clean motel on the city's north side. He and Jan had stayed there on their California vacation years ago and found it had everything they needed, including privacy. As soon as he checked in, he scanned the classified ads for a newer, used car. Finding the one he wanted, he arranged to buy it that day and drove it back to the motel. Now, all that remained was the call to the San Diego Police Department.

* * *

The more Susan Jensen researched child sex abuse, the more intrigued and horrified she became. Intrigued by the magnitude of the problem. Horrified at the lax attitude toward it. Her study turned up case after case in which an accused pedophile had either plea-bargained his way out of going to court or had gone to court and was not convicted. Of course, there were many who were convicted but given relatively light sentences. In one case she was stunned to read what a judge said about a man convicted of raping an eight-year-old girl. He stated that he was handing down a light sentence because the victim had dressed up like a much older

108

girl and enticed the defendant. He went on to say that while the defendant could not be excused for what he had done, it was understandable, since he thought the girl was older than she actually was. Just how old can an eight-year old girl make herself look? thought Susan.

In another case the judge sentenced a father to just five years in prison for molesting his 7- year old son. The reason? Because when he asked the boy on the witness stand if he liked or disliked the things his father did, things his mother considered sexual abuse, he simply said, "I don't mind it." All Susan could think of was, What's the kid supposed to say with his abusive father glaring at him from across the court room. Besides, a child doesn't know what to think when his own parent makes sexual advances toward him.

* * *

"Public information, Officer Bates speaking," said the voice at the other end.

"Hello. My name is David Anderson," Dan lied, "I'm a journalist in town doing research for a book on pedophilia and I'd like to make a request. I'd like access to any files you have on convicted child molesters in your jurisdiction. I'm trying to put together a comprehensive profile of a pedophile. The records would be very helpful."

The reply was what Dan had expected. "Well, that's an interesting request Mr. Anderson. We may be able to grant it, but I have to check with my captain. There are some confidentiality issues involved. Give me your telephone number and I'll get back to you."

Dan gave Officer Bates the El Ranchero's phone number and his room number. At 10 o'clock the next morning the telephone rang.

* * *

In her documentary research Susan Jensen was also discovering that the lenient attitude toward child sex abuse wasn't confined to the legal system. It was as much a parental problem as anything else. In one case, in a southeastern city, a young man started a children's choral group which grew very popular under his direction. In time it became clear that when the curtain fell more than singing was going on. The director was routinely sexually molesting the boys in the group. The horrifying thing about it was that although many parents suspected what was happening, they did nothing because the director was considered to be a great talent who had brought the group to national prominence and the children were getting such valuable training. Some parents warned their sons away from the director, but kept them in the group. Others looked the other way hoping the rumors weren't true or, if they were, that their sons would not become victims. Eventually, one father and mother chose not to ignore what was going on and the director was convicted of molesting their son. He received a two-year sentence in a minimum-security prison. He was paroled in eighteen months. He had molested an estimated 25 children.

* * *

"Mr. Anderson, this is Officer Bates with the San Diego Police Department," came the phone call. "Your request to see the pedophile records has been granted with two conditions. First, you have to read the files here. You can't take them with you ... and second, you can't photocopy anything ... you'll have to take notes."

"That's great Officer Bates," Dan said with reluctant excitement. "When can I come down and get started?"

"This afternoon, say about 1 o'clock?"

"Fine. I'll be there. Thank you." Dan hung up, leaned back in his chair and shivered. "I'm really going through with it," he shuddered. During the planning stage the mission wasn't entirely real to him because, while he intended to do it, he knew he could always back out. With the wheels now in motion, soon there would be no turning back.

CHAPTER 20

Opening one of his suitcases, Dan carefully got out his favorite undercover tool: a disguise kit. He had used it before and was very good at making himself look like someone else. First, he stuck two false, dark and bushy eyebrows over his own thin ones. Then he fastened a thick, black mustache under his nose. The next part was more difficult. He stretched flesh-like latex, which had been professionally fit, to his lower face over his chin. It changed the whole shape of his face by providing him with substantially bigger jowls than he actually had. He then applied olive-tone make-up over the edges of the latex to smooth them out and to the rest of his face and hands to make him look darker-skinned than he actually was. Finally, he glued a false beard onto the latex and put on a black curly-haired wig.

* * *

At the end of the day Ross Huggins could hardly wait to tell his wife Sara the news about his possible promotion at the FBI. But, instead of a joyful response he got an unhappy and scared look from her.

"What's the matter honey? Aren't you happy for me?" Ross asked, a little confused.

"Well, I guess I'm happy for you ... but not for me. The truth is I always supported you in wanting to be a field agent, but I never thought it would happen. Honey I'm scared. It's dangerous. With you down in research I know you'll be home every night, but out in the field you could be hurt or killed and it scares the hell out of me." Ross took her into his deceptively strong arms and held her tight.

* * *

George Dunphy was the name on the first file Dan examined at the San Diego police station. As he hoped Officer Bates gave him the files on every pedophile convicted of child molesting in the San Diego area over the last five years and then left him alone. He spent the afternoon doing nothing but copying down pedophiles' names and addresses and any other pertinent information about them. When he left he checked into another motel. This one was called the El Diablo and it was just off Mira Mesa Boulevard, which made him wonder if anything in San Diego had a North American name.

Dunphy lived in a sleazy efficiency apartment and worked as a short-order cook at a hamburger joint downtown. He had been convicted twice of molesting young boys. He had picked each of them up while they were hitchhiking in the San Diego metro area. God only knows how many other boys he raped and never got caught for, thought Dan.

* * *

"I guess I can't blame you for being scared," Ross Huggins told his wife, "but you know I'm conservative and won't take unnecessary chances. Field agents aren't like the freewheeling cowboy detectives you see on TV. They're deliberate and care-ful ... and, you know me, I'd be the most careful one of the bunch."

"Yeah, but no matter how careful you are, the bad guys aren't so careful… one of them might just put a bullet in you. Then where would your family be?"

"Well, I'd be lying if I told you that no FBI agent had ever been killed on the job, but the number is small and the chances are about one in a hundred thousand. I probably have a greater chance of getting hit by a car."

"I know. I know. But, I don't think a husband and father should be doing this job. It would affect too many people if you got killed. Let someone else do it."

"You really don't want me to take the job, do you?" Ross said, a bit stunned.

"No, I don't," was Sara's blunt reply. After a tense silence Ross spoke.

"Look, I understand your feelings, but you've got to understand mine. As long as we're being brutally honest, I've got to tell ya' I'm going out of my mind with boredom. I love you and the kids, but I can't go on like this. I'm missing something and I believe it's this job. I'm sorry, but I need more excitement than this place can offer." His gesture took in the house, the neighborhood and its occupants. "I can't take it. Be fair."

"Oh Ross, I want you to be alive."

"Well maybe just being alive and breathing is enough for you, but it's not for me."

"I know and I'm scared."

"But, if you spend your life being scared what've you got? Honey, I need this job, and if it's offered to me, I'm gonna' take it. But, let's not argue. It's just talk now and maybe will never be more than that. Maybe you won't have anything to worry about."

"But, what about you?" Sara asked half-sincere and half-sarcastic.

"I can live with never being given the chance, but not with being given the chance and then turning it down."

"Well, lover, I hope you're never given the chance. Now we really know where each other stands don't we?"

"We sure do. How about, if the kids are gone, we go in the bedroom and find out where each other lies."

"They are. Let's go." Sara led her husband into their room for a session of steamy passion. And as Ross confided to Roy later, nothing seemed to rev up her sex drive like the prospect of losing him. "I oughta' worry her more often," he said.

* * *

Though both of George Dunphy's convictions were open and shut cases Dan decided to watch him to make sure he was, indeed, a pedophile before carrying out his plan. He had seen too many innocent men convicted of crimes they didn't commit and he didn't want to take any chances. After he completed his research he followed Dunphy, knowing that a child molester wouldn't be long in succumbing to his urge to go after another victim.

His prey got off work at midnight. When he left the restaurant and got into his car, Dan was right behind him. Instead of going home he drove to a nearby bar called the Blue Flame and went in. Viewing the patrons going in and out of the place he realized the Blue Flame was a gay bar. *That puts George off to a great start,* he thought as he settled back into his seat and listened to rock music over a pair of headphones. He learned long ago that when you are on stake out by yourself you cannot read or watch a portable television, as you might like, because you have to keep your eyes on the subject all the time. Listening to music was about the only distraction he could risk.

At 2 o'clock in the morning Dunphy strolled out of the Blue Flame holding another man's hand and left in his car. Dan followed them to Dunphy's apartment and watched them go inside. *Consenting adults,* he thought, *no kid.* "Good night George," he said quietly, "See you tomorrow," and he went back to his motel to sleep.

* * *

"There has been no passion, no excitement in my life," Doug Glassman told Dr. Johnson in one of their therapy sessions, "Not like other people's lives. I look at some of the single men I know and at how exciting their lives have been and are and I think I've missed out."

"Doug, I know it seems that way now. Many men feel that way at forty. But, the passion and excitement you think you see in other men's' lives isn't as strong as you might think. In fact, I'd wager that many of the men you're talking about would give anything to change places with you. Many of them would rather have a devoted wife and two loving daughters than the occasionally interesting but lonely lives they have. Look at the great things you've got, like the love of your family, and accept that it's a lot."

"Well, I used to think so too, but, the plain fact is that, because I have lost all sexual feelings for Sandy, our marriage is a joke. It's pretty plain that my daughters think I'm an idiot. I used to have such a close relationship with Katy and Kelly when they were little. But, they're teen-agers and they never talk to me. When I talk to them they act like I'm imposing on them."

"Well, you know, that's just teen ... "

"Yeah, yeah, just teenagers. I've heard that so many times it makes me gag. I suppose it's true, but it doesn't make it any easier. So, what if kids act that way? I still have no parent-child relationship to speak of and it really depresses me ... whatever the reason. I'll tell you the truth, I'm beginning to wonder if someone like me wouldn't be a lot better off just having a loving relationship with a young boy."

* * *

Dan followed the same routine for eight days and nights. Sometimes Dunphy went straight home from work and sometimes he drove down to a local drug dealing area and bought heroin from a street pusher. Dan figured it had to be heroin because one night when he followed him home he looked in his window to see him put brown powder into a spoon, break it down in water and inject it into his arm. Mexican Mud they called it ... mediocre heroin smuggled in from Mexico. Yes, George was a junkie, but still no proof that he was a child molester ... until night number 9.

* * *

"We've talked about this many times," Dr. Johnson told her pedophile patient Douglas Glassman, "and you've agreed each time that while you might be better off in that kind of relationship, the boy wouldn't be."

"I know and I have thought about it, believe me, but, lately I've wondered if I just haven't found the right boy. I mean the two boys I ... uh ... molested ... uh

... weren't willing partners ... they didn't even know what was happening and that made it very wrong. But, aren't there boys out there who are positively homosexual and would genuinely enjoy a relationship with a man like me?"

At this point Dr. Johnson hesitated nervously. She felt that Doug could have a point. She believed some boys were naturally homosexual by the time they were twelve or thirteen years old. Some probably would enjoy and even benefit from a love relationship with an older man. But, she also knew that to condone this idea could ruin her patient's life. There was obviously no way for him to live out this fantasy in Fort Wayne without disgracing himself and losing his family and his job. She knew she had to be careful how she answered this genuinely nice man now looking at her with innocently probing eyes.

"Doug, you might find a homosexual boy who would seem to enjoy your relationship," she picked her way carefully, "but you can't really know if you are doing him harm or not. Let's say you didn't have a relationship with him and he finds out later that he isn't gay or that he's bisexual. If you had the relationship he may never find that out. Wouldn't that be doing him a terrible disservice?"

"Yeah, it could. But, isn't that really all life? I mean if you do this, this may happen or if you don't do this that may happen. I'm beginning to think you shouldn't live according to what might or might not happen ... you should just go out there and follow what feels natural ... something I've never done. I've always worried more about how my actions would affect others than about how they would affect me and I'm starting to think it's about time I did things the other way around. But, I mean do it responsibly ... only with a kid that I know is a consenting homosexual."

"How are you going to do that here in Fort Wayne?" asked Dr. Johnson.

"I probably can't. But, if I can't I don't know what the heck I'm going to do. These are new thoughts to me and I have to sort 'em out."

"Whatever you might do, remember it would most likely lose you your family, your reputation in the community, and probably your job."

"Oh, I know all that. But, look ... my family basically doesn't mean diddly to me now, my reputation has really never gotten me anything I want and my job bores the living crap out of me. Can you imagine selling insurance for twenty years? Anyway, could things get any worse? I really kinda' doubt it."

"Believe me, they can," the doctor assured him.

* * *

Late that night Dan followed George Dunphy to an area he had not been to before. It was one of San Diego's homeless areas, where street kids hung out. As he followed him at a long distance he saw him drive slowly through the area like he was looking for something. Suddenly he stopped the car and got out, leaving it running. He raced over to what appeared to be a human form wrapped in a blanket, next to an old, abandoned building. Dunphy raised something in his hand and brought it down hard on the form, then picked it up and hustled back to his car. He loaded the blanketed form into the back seat and drove home. Dan suspected the blanket contained a homeless child. When he got to Dunphy's apartment his suspicions were confirmed. The blanket partially fell off of an unconscious boy as he carried him inside.

Dunphy's small apartment had ground floor windows with tattered curtains, which made it easy for Dan to look in. When he did, he saw him put the still unconscious boy in the bathtub and wash him up. He then started performing oral sex on him and masturbating himself at the same time. Dan felt he had seen enough to figure out what was going to go on there next. He didn't really want to see it. Suddenly the boy's face turned into Cole and Dan wanted to smash through the window then and there and strangle the life out of George Dunphy with his bare hands. But, the face changed back and Dan regained control of himself. Besides, he knew doing that would be stupid and pretty much ruin his mission before it even got started. He also knew Dunphy's MO was not to kill his victims so this young boy would have to endure his molestation, but no one after him.

* * *

"You feel like things couldn't be any worse Doug ... but they could be," Dr. Johnson told Douglas Glassman. His file was marked "P" for Pedophile. "Remember," she said, "a person often doesn't appreciate what he's got until he loses it. I believe you have a lot more than you now know. Please don't do anything to lose it so that you realize just how valuable it was only when it's too late. Besides, I think that your increased yearnings for boys are clouding your judgment. The human sex drive is a very powerful mind-controller and I think you're letting it affect your rational thinking. I want you to step up the meditation exercises we've worked on and apply them whenever you get these pedophilic thoughts."

"But I told you they don't work anymore."

"You have to try harder. I think they don't work because you don't want them to work and you're really not applying yourself. Just concentrate twice as hard as you have been. Most likely you enjoy the thrill of these fantasies and therefore are subconsciously not trying as hard as you can to get them out of your mind through the meditation. No one ever said it would be easy, but if you want to control your urges you have to do it."

"That's just it! I'm not so sure I want to control them anymore," Doug said with newfound conviction.

The session was over and as Dr. Johnson watched her patient leave a feeling of foreboding came over her.

CHAPTER 21

Back at the El Diablo Motel Dan pulled out two packages and examined them. One contained a quarter-ounce of heroin laced with fentanyl, which is 50 times stronger than most street heroin. The other had a half-ounce of 80% pure cocaine. Jack Adams had skimmed the drugs off the top of a drug bust before he got sick and gave some to Dan after their conversation about killing pedophiles. "Just in case you need these," he had said. Dan figured he must have vaguely guessed what he was planning. Skimming drugs from a bust was a common practice among cops, not to keep for themselves, but for bargaining tender to get information from junky informants. "Nothing opens a junkie's sealed lips like a dime bag waved in his face," Jack used to say.

* * *

As Doug Glassman left his therapist's office he realized that he was about ready to cut and run, and he felt that something he read in a kiddie porn magazine might be his key to the highway. It was an invitation to pedophile men to join The Guild, an organization which believed it is natural for many young boys to have a sexual relationship with adult men. The ad read "Feeling guilty about your natural urges? Well, feel guilty no more! They are quite normal and there are many of us out there." The ad then said that if a reader wanted to know more he should write to a blind P.O. Box for information. Doug wrote and received a full packet of information on the organization and its contention that pedophilic sex was normal and good. It was based in Chicago and it invited Doug for a visit to get a feel for the group.

"Maybe I've been looking at child sex through the eyes of the rest of society for too long," he muttered to himself, "maybe it's time I looked at it another way." He wrote back to The Guild telling them what day he would be there. He told his family that he would be driving to Chicago the following week on insurance business. He was so excited, he could hardly contain himself, but all the years of living what he considered a wasted and boring life had trained him to act normal and sedate. He gave nothing away.

* * *

Dan packaged five bags worth of the powder into a tiny, square plastic bag like those used by many drug dealers. He then put on a curly haired wig, a fake mustache, sunglasses and a hat that drooped over his forehead and headed for the street where he had seen Dunphy buy his drugs. It didn't take long to find the same pusher he had seen sell heroin to George.

* * *

Suspected kiddie pimp Ali Ban Hashemi was a large man, tipping the scale at about 275 pounds, with close-cropped, coal black hair and a flowing, black mustache. He had grown up in another country. No one knew exactly where. He had friends in high places and some said his contacts went all the way up to one country's royal family. His father was one of the few ministers in the government who was not a member of the royal family and this gave him many advantages. It also gave him a taste for the rich life and he had decided at a young age that he would someday be rich like his friends, whatever it took. He went to law school in the United States and practiced in New York City, specializing in international trade. He quickly became known as the "deal maker." If a leader wanted to skirt U.S. trade laws he saw Ali Ban Hashemi. If he wanted to speed up arms or other types of negotiations with the U.S. he saw Ali Ban Hashemi. If he just needed someone to squire visiting dignitaries around New York or the U.S. he saw Hashemi. It was the latter service that involved Hashemi in the child prostitution business. Personally, he was interested only in women, but some of his countrymen had a taste for boys, especially fair-skinned boys, which they could not get at home. So, when a visiting delegation came to the United States some of them looked forward to more than the business at hand. They depended on Hashemi to provide them with extra-curricular sexual recreation with what to them were exotic young boys. A little-known adage Hashemi had heard one of them say once was "Women are for babies, boys are for pleasure."

* * *

"Don't move mother fucker!" Dan said with practiced authority as he silently moved up behind the dealer and shoved a .38 caliber pistol into his back. The gun was one of several weapons he had shipped to San Diego before he left Washington. "I'm a cop and you and I are gonna' have a little chat," he scowled as he flashed a fake badge in front of the man's face simultaneously checking him for a weapon.

"Shit," was the only reply.

"You're not busted, home boy," Dan assured him, "Yet, that is. Yer' gonna' do me a little favor and then I'm going to do you a little favor and not take you in for what we both know you have in your pocket."

"I ain't singin' on nobody, so you'se can forget that."

"I don't wanna' hear no singing, besides you don't look like you could carry a tune. See this picture," Dan said pulling out a photograph of George Dunphy he had shot a couple of days earlier. "This is one of your customers and he'll probably be by here looking to make a buy sometime in the next few days." Still jamming the gun into his spine, Dan handed him the bag of pure heroin. "You sell him this bag instead of your usual shit and tell him it's the same strength, but cleaner and you'll have a friend in the police department. But, if you don't sell him this stuff yer' gonna' have a very nasty enemy in the department who's gonna' make sure you spend the next five years getting butt-rammed by a big meth-head named Bubba in the state pen. Got it?"

"Yeah man, I got it."

And with that Dan was gone. The whole episode had taken less than three minutes.

* * *

Ali Ban Hashemi wasn't exactly crazy about the pimping he had taken on, but it went part and parcel with the other deals he put together, and it was, by itself, quite lucrative. Unlike members of the royal family, Hashemi had to be concerned with money. He didn't stand to inherit billions of dollars like his childhood friends. Rather, he stood to inherit exactly nothing and he knew that whatever wealth he accumulated he would have to make on his own. So, he set up a network of nefarious contacts who dealt in children, mainly young boys. Now, the "deal maker" made deals out of his expensive Manhattan apartment, preferring not to rent a costly office.

* * *

Two days later George Dunphy died in his apartment of a drug overdose. Dan was there, parked across the street when the ambulance pulled up. When Dunphy hadn't shown up for work a co-worker went to check on him and found him lying on the floor with the needle still stuck in his arm. As Dan expected, the police classified it as a simple drug overdose and there was no investigation.

It had been easy, maybe too easy. Dan knew it can be a jinx when the first mission goes that easy and he wasn't taking it lightly. Then, as he sat in his car, it seemed like a dark cloud was suddenly descending over him. He sat in the cloud for two hours contemplating what he had just done. He, who had once been sworn to protect the rights of others, had just committed murder. The feeling could not be described as good. In fact, something very bad gnawed at him as he pulled away, watching Dunphy's crumbling neighborhood fade away in his rear-view mirror. Heading back to the El Diablo for some aspirin and a nap to kick a fast-growing headache, he kept reminding himself that he had probably just saved about 24 kids.

As he drove down the street the sun was shining brightly, but Dan felt the dark cloud surrounding him. When he lay down for a nap, a slightly familiar dream came to him. He was drowning, going down and down and down through the water when all of a sudden, he saw his son Cole's face swirling around him. Once again, Cole was trying to tell him something, but no words were getting out. This time, he was sure Cole was saying *prophecy*, but he didn't know why. He was also saying another word that seemed to start with a *P* but he couldn't quite make it out.

* * *

Ali Ban Hashemi soon discovered that getting young prostitutes in New York City was not difficult. By carefully weeding out the lower scale street pimps he managed to assemble a collection of reliable and discrete child pimps. He called them "child providers," as if the term sanitized the operation in some way. Most of his business was local, providing a child for sex for the night to a visiting client. But every now and then one of these clients wanted to buy a child outright and take him back to his home country, and that was quite difficult as well as very profitable. It usually involved buying a boy from one of his providers for fifty to a hundred thousand dollars or more and then selling him to a client for at least three times that amount with a guarantee that no one would come looking for him. It was rare for a client to request a little girl, but it did happen. It never ceased to amaze Hashemi that someone would pay up to a half-a-million dollars for a little blonde-haired, blue-eyed American child when he could get a local, swarthy boy for nothing. But, then, he reminded himself that half-a-million dollars to these men was like ten dollars to many people.

What further amazed Hashemi was the large number of children on the street that no one seemed to care about. In many countries, poverty was so widespread that homeless children were not unusual. He had expected something better in the U.S., the richest country in the world. The reality, however, was that there was no shortage of willing grist for his human mill. They were hungry and they often had no other way to live. He had actually talked himself into believing he was doing his victims a favor because they would get very good treatment in whichever country they were sent to. But Ali Ban Hashemi's talent for rationalizing was nothing compared to his cloak-and-dagger stealth abilities. He was wily and Detective Derek Lindsay was not going to have an easy time nailing him.

CHAPTER 22

"How can people treat the rape of children like this?" Susan Jensen asked her old KNOC-TV boss Bob Manson over the phone one day.

"I think it's such a vile, disgusting concept that the mind shuts it out, even if it means ignoring the obvious," Bob replied.

"That could be part of it, but I'm beginning to think it's more sexist. It seems too coincidental that most child molesters are male and so are 98% of the judges in this country. It seems to me that a lot of judges almost condone this behavior. That's sad."

"Well, before you trash all male adjudicators, remember that the reason for a lot of the leniency is that a lot of judges really believe pedophiles can be rehabilitated. They believe they're not really deliberate criminals, but instead helpless victims too."

"I know, and I believe that's an example of how far society has gone to protect the criminal's rights at the expense of the rights of the victim. You said it yourself, molesters are considered victims, victims of their own sickness. But, tell that to the little boy whose life is now ruined. Tell him that his abuser is the victim. Or tell the little girl who'll never have a normal love relationship that her abuser was the victim. Somehow, I don't think it's gonna' wash."

"Yeah, I know. But still, a lot of judges think pedophiles can be rehabilitated."

"That's such bullshit. I'll tell ya', the statistics I'm finding on rehabilitation are lousy; the recidivism rate is pretty high."

"They want to do it and they're going to do it."

"That's right. It's not a bad habit ... it's a natural, driving urge. One they can't control. It's easy enough to fool their psychiatrists, but then---BAM ... they're back on the street molesting more kids."

"I know what you're saying is true, Sue. But are you feeling this thing too much? Are ya' sure you're keeping a professional distance?"

Susan stopped for a moment, but she knew the answer. "Yeah, I'm professional enough to do an objective, unbiased piece. It's just that I'm disgusted by what I'm finding out about the attitudes toward child sex abuse in this country. It's like what you said earlier: the subject is so abhorrent that people would rather ignore it and sweep it under the carpet than deal with it."

"Yup. That's why you're bringing it out in the open."

* * *

George Dunphy was easy. He had a vice that Dan turned into his demise. The next one on the list, however, appeared to have no such vice. In fact, all that Dan had learned about Don Baker after following him for several days was that he was a mailman who lived alone and usually went home after work. His rap sheet said that he was convicted of molesting a 7-year-old boy on the little league baseball team he coached. He had served an 18-month prison term and received psychiatric treatment for pedophilic tendencies while on parole. The Postal Service had given him a job under a special government rehabilitation program.

Dan picked the lock on his door and searched his apartment. He wasn't surprised to find a collection of child pornography hidden under Baker's bed, but this really didn't prove that he was a child molester. However, when he felt something taped up under the dresser he ripped it out with certainty. It was a large envelope filled with photographs of men and boys having sex. Nauseous, Dan flipped through them. He was about to put them back when he came upon several photos of Baker forcibly sodomizing what appeared to be an 8 or 9-year old boy who was screaming in obvious pain and anguish. Another showed Baker whipping a boy who had blood streaming out of his wounds. But the clincher was a photo of a boy tied and restrained in a guillotine-like contraption being forced to perform fellatio on Baker while another man sodomized him.

"O.K. you sick bastard," Dan said out loud as he carefully put the pictures back the way he found them, "you're history." He needed no more proof of Baker's pedophilia. He began looking around the apartment for some clues to his everyday habits. He knew that the best way to kill someone was to use one of his routine habits against them. Then he noticed the portable television in the bathroom.

* * *

Susan Jensen was on a roll in her conversation with her old news director, Bob Manson. "I've come across dozens of cases where a kid told his parents he had been molested," she told him, "and they did nothing. They don't believe it. They say they don't want to put the child through the embarrassment that would come with filing charges and a trial. But, you've got to wonder who they're trying to protect, their child or themselves? Besides, when they refuse to do anything, it must make the kid feel like the abuse is acceptable. I'll tell ya' ... I'm beginning to see that child sex abuse is a lot more common than even I thought. More than ever I know I chose the right subject."

"Me too. And I'll tell you something," Bob came back, "I'm glad you're doing it and not me. When I read this shit and see all this child pornography I just keep thinking 'what if that were one of my kids?' And, boy, when you think about it in terms of your own child it's scary."

"Scary! It's horrifying! Ya' know, the local police and the feds have given me a bunch of child pornography and just looking at it makes me physically ill. I can't get one picture out of my head of a little boy with an anus the size of a coffee cup from being sodomized so many times. I wonder where he is now or whether he's even alive."

"Man, like I said, I'm just glad I'm not the one having to go through all this stuff because I'd think too much of my own son as a victim." Bob wound it up, "When do you think you'll be ready to start shooting?"

"Actually, we can start the day after tomorrow. I want to begin with a local case here where a boy was sexually molested and killed."

* * *

He watches TV while he takes a bath, Dan suddenly realized as he looked in Don Baker's bathroom, *I guess the dumb shit hasn't heard about electrocution.* Then it came to him. A simple plan that would eliminate his second target. "But he's sure gonna' hear about it now," he whispered to himself as he silently crept out of the apartment.

He didn't have to wait long for Baker to come home from work. Then he sat back and waited until nightfall. Every night around nine o'clock Baker's bathroom window fogged up, obviously by hot running bath water. The rest should be easy, he thought.

At nine o'clock the bathroom window misted over. "That's my cue," Dan said out loud as he got out of his car carrying an industrial-strength hair dryer and a long extension cord. *Toss the hair dryer into the tub with Baker before he knows* what's going on and you get parboiled pervert, Dan thought. He then planned to pull the hair dryer out and knock the TV in. It would look like Baker was just another dummy who knocked an electrical appliance, which shouldn't have been in the bathroom in the first place, into the bathtub.

He didn't have to pick the door lock because Baker had left it unlocked. Dan crept into the apartment silently, plugged the hair dryer into one end of the extension cord and the other end of the cord into a wall socket near the bathroom door. He could hear a sitcom's laugh track coming out of the bathroom as his left hand fingered the hair dryer's "on" button and he turned the doorknob ever so slightly with his right.

* * *

"His parents went through pure hell during the time he was missing," Susan went on, "and his mother became an activist. It's the Cole Forester case, remember?"

"Oh yeah. Pretty sad," said Bob Manson, "I remember the mother went public and the father didn't say much."

"Right. Well, now that they know their son's fate I think they'll make good interviews. They won't be your standard parents at home pining away for their child. As it turns out Dan Forester just left on a long trip to try and get his head together. Mrs. Forester told me that's his therapy. She said he might agree to us flying there and interviewing him. Or, he may come back to Washington and we can get him here. Either way, the travelling part gives it a unique twist, don't ya' think?"

"Absolutely, that's what you need; something different than the ordinary profile of grieving parents. Good work Sue."

After hanging up, Susan got to work setting up the shoot with Jan Forester. She had decided to use free-lance camera crews for each shoot instead of hiring one crew. One reason was cost, but another big consideration was that local crews knew their areas and could help with logistics and information. Nevertheless, Susan was always apprehensive about using a new camera crew.

She rented the services of a free-lance crew for three days and wanted to get as much footage of Jan at home and at work as she could. She knew there were a lot of incompetent video photographers in Washington, D.C. and most of them were free-lancing only because they couldn't hold a regular job. In other words, in Washington, free-lancing was often a synonym for unemployed. But this crew had come highly recommended and Susan was hopeful.

* * *

Suddenly the doorknob stopped turning. Dan couldn't believe it. *The dumb bastard leaves his apartment door unlocked, but locks his bathroom door,* he realized. Standing there, frozen in time, he thought about breaking the door down and going through with his original plan. Then he knew a broken-down door would make Baker's death look suspicious. Besides, he thought to himself, the oldest rule in the book is that if the first plan goes wrong, retreat and make a second plan. So, slowly and quietly he returned the knob to its original position, unplugged the hair dryer and swiftly left as silently as he had entered. The sound from the television had helped him go in and stay for five minutes undetected by Baker, but, he hadn't succeeded and he was angry that he wasted so much time. On his way out the door, he noticed that the telephone in Baker's kitchen hung on the wall right next to the stove.

* * *

Ross Huggins' FBI study continued until he had a complete profile of the average American pedophile. Generally speaking he was a white male, between 20 and 40 years of age, homosexual or bisexual, and in a lower to middle income bracket. He lived alone, was a drug or alcohol user, and usually molested children he knew. He found that abductions and sexual abuse by strangers occurred 4000 to 5000 times a year in the U.S. and that in most situations the abductor let the child go shortly after the abuse occurred. Of course, in some cases the abductor tortured and/or killed his victim. Reviewing recorded interviews with pedophiles he found that because most victims never report the crime, many feel more or less free to repeat it. In addition, he learned that many pedophiles believed adult male sex with a young child is natural and right and that children actually desire it. Even so, the interviews showed that many pedophiles felt genuine remorse for molesting their victims. Finally, Ross discovered that true rehabilitation of pedophiles was pretty rare; it appeared that. But, at the same time he found that many child molesters who are caught do not repeat the offense.

"Pretty bleak picture, isn't it?" Ross asked Don Westerhof after giving him his preliminary results.

"Yeah, they're a bunch of sick mothers all right. It's pretty obvious that there's really no way to spot a child molester from any outward appearances or behavior, which is what the top brass hoped for."

"What?"

"Oh, I know they said they wanted an updated profile, but, they really wanted a lot more. Believe it or not, they were hoping that you'd come up with a common denominator that would help cops identify and keep track of 'em before they molested children. Then, when a kid was molested, they'd know exactly where to go for a suspect."

"Yeah, right ... like that would be possible. Sounds a little big-brotherish doesn't it?"

"Well, you know the great minds. Anyway, this stuff is more current than what we have and it'll be valuable just the same."

"Valuable enough to get me outta' here?"

"We'll see. We'll see."

"Yeah," Ross mused, "most of them look and act like John Q. Public. But, you're right ... this data can't help but be helpful to local police departments. What do ya' think of the part about the recidivism rate?"

"Well, I must admit I thought some child molesters could be cured, but I see that's probably a fantasy. I think the sentence for child molesting oughta' be the same as for murder: life in prison."

"I can't disagree with you there, but the prisons are full and there's just no room." Ross could see that Don was gearing up for one of their social/ legal discussions and he was glad. Don was strongly opinionated and Ross enjoyed their occasional deep talks.

"Well, we've got to build more prisons. The problem with the American public is that they want everything both ways. In this case they want more law breakers like child molesters in prison and serving longer sentences, but they don't want to shell out the tax money to build the prisons. Do they think the prisons just magically spring up out of the ground? Well, they don't."

"No. But, cut the tax payers a little slack ... we're all over-taxed and a lot of the tax money is going for some real idiotic pork barrel things."

"I know. I know. I don't blame the average taxpayer. I just blame them for unrealistically screaming for more prisons without thinking how we're going to pay for them."

"Well, how about chemical castration? They don't have to go to prison. All you have to do is give them regular shots that reduce their testosterone level. It's a hell of a lot cheaper than keeping them in prison."

"Personally, I'm for it, but again, you have the problem of this country wanting its cake and eatin' it too. The public wants the perverts stopped, but it doesn't want controlled chemical castration, just like it didn't want forced sterilization of welfare mothers with twelve kids. It's a violation of their constitutional rights, they scream. Well, I'd ask, what rights? Rights to rape children? What about the children's rights? Don't they have the right to grow up without the threat of sexual abuse?"

"It's a tough one. I think Civil Liberty Union thinkers view the law as black and white, as if it actually protects everybody's rights. But it doesn't. Like you said, if we protect the rights of the child molester we may violate the rights of the victims. There are just some things constitutional law can't address, but common sense can. The laws deal adequately with about 95% of our life situations, but not with the other 5% ... and child molesting falls into that 5%. In the 5% of the cases where the law is not absolute or black and white let's use common sense and castrate the bastards."

"Yeah, but, playing devil's advocate, if you willingly violate the rights of one segment of society where does it stop? Doesn't that open the door for you to violate the rights of others? That's the Civil Liberty Union argument."

"Well, first of all, that argument is based on the view that the law is omnipotent, sovereign and absolute and I say it's not. Not only can it not apply to every life situation, but look at the changes it goes through. Look at all the things that were legal years ago and are illegal now or at all the things that were illegal before and are legal now. Besides, what is the law? It's what the public says it is, so if we really want to deal effectively with this 5% of cases the law misses why don't we have a national referendum vote on them? Let's put it to the American public ... do you want child molesters to be chemically castrated? I have a feeling the answer would be a big yes."

"That's really not a bad idea. You could do it with all of the legal gray areas and it would be truly democratic. But, with all your great arguments you still haven't addressed the morality or legality of deliberately violating the pedophile's rights."

"I can answer that one easily. When he raped the kid, he gave up his constitutional rights. With rights come responsibility ... the responsibility to respect others' rights. When you violate those rights, especially in a heinous way, you lose your own. How does that sound?"

"Pretty good. But, of course the civil libertarians would out-slick you in debate."

"I know. That's why I'm not a lawyer. I'm just a cop on the beat. And that's why everything I've said is my personal opinion which I'll deny if I have to."

"Hmmm. Well, I'm glad we figured out the world's problems, but I better get my big butt back upstairs before they think the crypt down here swallowed me up."

"Yea, I've got to get back to work too. I'm starting on the health and causes of death now. See ya' later, Don," Ross said as he turned toward the mountain of papers on his desk.

* * *

The next morning Dan entered Postman Baker's apartment again, this time picking the lock. He went straight to the telephone and unscrewed the mouthpiece. Disconnecting its two wires he pulled out a pocketknife and stripped the insulation off of each. He hooked a long bare wire to them and ran it along the wall to a burner on the stove. At the end of the wire he attached a tiny device. He raised the cover on the stove and extinguished the pilot lights on the burners and the oven. After checking to make sure all the apartment's windows were closed he turned all four burners and the oven on high, leaving the oven door open just an inch.

* * *

The week dragged by slowly until the day Doug Glassman made the trip to Chicago that he hoped would change his life. He had been instructed to go to the Chez Chicago French restaurant to meet a representative of The Guild child sex group. Sitting at a table, waiting and sweating, his heart was pounding a nervous rhythm. After an hour and a half, Douglas decided he had made a mistake on the meeting arrangements or was the victim of a cruel hoax. Crestfallen and on the verge of tears, he got up to leave.

* * *

At exactly 5:05PM Don Baker drove up to his apartment building, got out of his car and headed for his apartment. At 5:06PM he unlocked his door and upon entering his apartment immediately smelled something odd.

* * *

Suddenly, a slight, balding man put a hand on Doug Glassman's shoulder and said, "Hi, I'm Barry Anderson with The Guild. You must be Doug."

"Yes ... yes I am," Doug said, a little unnerved.

"I'm sorry about the wait, but we have to be careful about new members and I had to check you out." He had been watching Doug the whole time. The Guild was a legal organization but was constantly on the lookout for an undercover policeman trying to infiltrate their ranks.

* * *

At 5:06PM and 2 seconds Dan Forester dialed Baker's telephone number from a cellular telephone in his car. A tiny electric current coursed through the telephone and through the attached wire to the tiny device at the end. It set off a spark much like the automatic lighter on a barbecue grill. The spark ignited the gas and blew Don Baker into little bits. "Another one bites the dust," Dan sang as he drove away thinking about the 48 kids he had now saved. He had to think about them to keep from thinking about the fact that he was now a double murderer ... and the fact that the now-familiar black cloud was back and descending around his head. He couldn't admit to himself what it really was; a cloud of growing guilt.

CHAPTER 23

The third name on Dan's hit parade was very different from the first two. Harold Stanton was a respected and well-to-do real estate developer in San Diego. According to police records he had been arrested and charged with molesting a 10-year-old foster child that he and his wife had taken in several years earlier. They had a boy and girl of their own, but sometimes took in foster children. He was found innocent of the charges because the jury in the case believed that the child made the story up.

Since Stanton hadn't been convicted, Dan wondered why Officer Bates had let him see the file. But, then he remembered that the records also contained a note from the investigating officer claiming this wasn't the first time Stanton had been accused of being a pedophile. So, Dan began his painstaking surveillance. He followed Stanton everywhere. He watched his house at night until the family went to bed. Because the house had many large windows Dan had a good view of the living room and the stairs going from the ground level to the second story so he was even able to keep tabs on much of the movement inside the house through binoculars.

But Harold Stanton presented a picture of normalcy and after two weeks when absolutely nothing out of the ordinary had occurred, Dan was beginning to wonder if the foster boy really had made up the story. The only even remotely odd thing he noticed about Stanton's behavior was that on several nights after he and his family had gone to bed he got up and walked upstairs from his and his wife's downstairs bedroom. He then returned to his own bedroom about 30 minutes later.

* * *

Relieved and excited that he had made his contact, Doug Glassman sat back down and he and his new friend ordered dinner. While they ate, Guild President

Barry Anderson told him that while the group's beliefs seemed deviant they were actually steeped in historical tradition. He described how sexual relationships between men and boys had been an accepted part of many civilizations, including the ancient Greeks, one of the most civilized societies ever studied. He explained that America's present-day homophobic society had given man/boy sex an ugly image.

"Well, obviously I'm attracted to boys or I wouldn't be here," admitted Doug, "but I need some answers and I need to ask you some hard questions."

"Of course, Doug. Ask away"

* * *

On night number 15, after the Stantons were in bed, Dan was parked outside of their house watching the windows. He periodically glanced over at the blinking lights of a television tower in the distance. The tower seemed to wait until he looked at it to blink its red lights since they blinked the second after he turned his eyes toward it. He had always found slight humor in the games one plays to pass the time while on stakeout. He had just about decided to call this one off when he saw Harold again head upstairs. Curiosity more than anything else made Dan get out of his car and climb up the Stanton house's trellis to peer into the 8-year-old son's bedroom through his infra-red goggles. As his eyes slowly adjusted themselves he began to see movement in the area of the boy's bed in the corner of the room. It then suddenly became nauseatingly clear what that movement was. Harold Stanton was naked, lying on top of his face-down, naked son. He was so shocked he almost fell off of the trellis. The son-of-a-bitch is screwing his own kid, he realized, of course he doesn't have to go out and find one to molest 'cause he's got one right at home! As he climbed down the trellis his head filled with disgust to think of how much he had loved his own son, and then to see a father do this to his own boy. "This bastard's goin' down," he said out loud as he drove away.

Stanton wasn't going to be as easy as his first two victims because of his lack of outward vices and seemingly normal family life. After two days of concentration Dan came up with a plan. Once again, he would use one of his intended victim's routine habits. He had to wait three more nights outside Stanton's house before Harold made another depraved visit to his son's room.

* * *

"Well, your critics would say that anatomically the male and female are naturally made for each other," Doug Glassman went on with his questions for Guild President Barry Anderson, "that the male genitals are naturally made to fit into the female genitalia. But male genitalia are not naturally made to fit together, so homosexuality between consenting men or between a man and a boy is unnatural. They would say that what you're advocating as natural is actually against the laws of nature. How do you answer that?"

"Very simply. Where is the book listing the laws of nature? In other words, who really knows what's natural and what's not? Just because the male genitalia fits into the female genitalia doesn't mean that's the only natural way to have sex. It probably really means that it's the only natural way to have children. But, that doesn't mean that two males engaging in sex is unnatural. The two are mutually exclusive. We think it's superficial to say that just because two sets of genitalia fit together to produce a fetus, all other same-sex relations are unnatural. Besides, physically the male genitalia fits the mouth just as well as it does the female genitalia. Isn't that just as natural?"

"Well put, Barry," said Douglas aroused by his last point, "Now for the hard part. What about the critics who charge that although you say you're giving the boy a choice of whether or not to have sex, he really doesn't have the ability to make an intelligent, informed choice because of his young age?"

"That's a tough one and it's really at the crux of our beliefs. Again, we believe there is historical evidence suggesting that these sexual relations are normal and that many boys not only choose the sex but want it badly. But our critics say the boys in historical eras were being abused too. All I can say is that emotionally we believe many boys want these types of relationships and that they're good for them. It's something we feel and feel so strongly that we know we're right. We also believe that only a gay person can understand it. Let me ask you something. How old were you when you knew you were gay or attracted to younger boys?"

"I was 12."

"Well, I rest my case. You knew then that you had different sexual instincts than your peers. We argue that many boys are like you. They're absolute homosexuals or bisexuals at a young age. We do not make them that way. Remember, we only advocate sexual relationships with boys who are admitted homosexuals. We're against adult male sex with straight boys who don't know or are confused about their sexuality."

"Yeah, but how many admitted homosexuals are out there?"

"Too many for you to handle my friend, and right here in Chicago."

* * *

As soon as Harold Stanton was out of sight, Dan silently entered the living room through an unlocked front window, closing it behind him, and crept to the top of the stairs. He waited there, occasionally hearing muffled sounds from behind the young Stanton's door. True to form, after about 45 minutes Stanton Senior emerged from the bedroom and headed for the stairs. Hiding in the bathroom directly across from the top of the stairs, Dan readied himself. He planned to push Harold down the stairs and then just to make sure, rush down and break his neck with a special martial-arts move. He would then quickly leave through the front door, locking it behind him, before anyone got to his victim. It was a big house and the nearest bedroom was quite a distance from the living room, so Dan calculated that he would have just enough time to escape before he would be seen; especially since Mrs. Stanton and one of the children would be roused out of sleep. The plan was good and Stanton's death would look like an accident, but timing was everything. If he hesitated just a second or one of the Stanton family members was quicker to respond than he expected he would be seen leaving.

It was time. Stanton turned toward the stairs. Dan started his lunge, but stopped in mid-leap because Harold abruptly turned around, probably to go to the bathroom, and suddenly he was face-to-face with the man he was about to murder. The encounter only lasted a split second, but that's all it took for him to see two things on Stanton's face: surprise, of course, but also guilt. He would never forget that look. It was almost as if he knew that what he had just done in his son's room was heinous and unconsciously wanted or needed to be punished for it. Dan almost hesitated, but Stanton's face suddenly turned into the face of his own son's murderer, Greg Dawson, so he swiftly shoved him down the stairs backward. He sprang after him, grabbed him around the head and with one instantaneous motion twisted until his neck snapped audibly. Hearing footsteps, he quickly and silently slipped out of the door. Mrs. Stanton came into the room with a gasp. It was so close that part of her consciousness actually noticed some slight movement at the front door as she entered the room. But the perception never registered and was lost forever as she focused totally on her husband's body lying prone at the foot of the stairs.

That was too close, thought Dan as he crawled out of sight of the house's windows and headed toward his car. He would never cut things that close again. As he drove away he felt that now-familiar dark cloud surrounding him and waited for the inevitable intense headache that always followed.

Back inside the Stanton house Harold's wife was calling 911 and his daughter was standing over him weeping. His, son Jonathon, however, just sat at the top of the stairs with an uncomprehending look on his face. It wasn't grief. It wasn't fear. It wasn't even sadness. What neither mother nor daughter knew at the time was that it was relief.

Two days later the local newspapers' obituary column listed Harold Stanton's death due to an accidental fall at his home.

* * *

"Really?" Doug Glassman asked Guild President Barry Anderson incredulously, his appetite suddenly whetted. You could almost see the drool.

"Really. But I don't want you to get the wrong idea about our group. Sex is really a minor part of the whole thing. The love of the boys is really the focus of The Guild. We feel that society has gone the wrong direction in its man/boy relationship and that adult males are not there, as they should be, to lead the boys through their growing up stage. Who better to lead them than a male who has already been there and who loves them? Like you, we love boys and want only the best for them. We don't believe in doing anything that would hurt them and believe that a relationship with an older man can be very beneficial to their development. Let's face it ... growing up gay in America is no easy task and an older man can help a kid through it with love and affection. Sex is a natural outgrowth of that, but it's certainly not our main concern. We're an organization of men who live in our own places and hold down normal jobs. We meet once a week at my house. Sometimes a member will bring a young lover or one will refer another to a boy who is looking for a lover. Of course, the rest of the world thinks we're queer, sex-starved child molesters. You must know that's a hard label to live with."

Doug was amazed by what he was hearing. It was unlike anything he had ever heard before. It was being presented to him by a very articulate, professional looking, and likable man. But, above all, it just made sense.

"Barry, I feel all my life I've been hiding who I really am and that it's turned me into a zombie."

"You're not alone, my friend. Many members came to the same conclusion at about your age and are now living the lives they know they were meant to live and enjoying it."

"Yeah, the only problem is that I have a wife and two kids, so living that life would be kinda' difficult."

"That, Doug, is entirely up to you. Obviously the two are incompatible and you have to make a choice. Your choice will depend to a large extent on how happy your family life is. I won't give you any advice, but I will tell you that many members also had families and were terribly unhappy because they were denying their natural instincts. They chose The Guild and several actually moved here to Chicago to follow their hearts."

"And are they glad they did?"

"All of them are, as far as I know."

"Well, I've got a lot of thinking to do and, by gosh, I'm gonna' come to some decision. I've got to or I just can't go on."

"Doug, you have a lot of soul searching to do. I hope you decide what's right for you. Certainly, no one else can decide it for you. Here's my phone number in case you have any questions. Please memorize it and throw it away. Whatever I believe about everything we've talked about, the rest of the world thinks I'm a pervert who oughta' be in jail. I have to be careful."

"I understand. Thank you so much, Barry. You've opened my eyes to a whole new way of thinking. I guess I'm still learning at forty."

"Well, hopefully, we never stop learning. Good-bye Doug."

On the drive home Doug mulled over what Barry had told him. Mainly, he thought about how good it would feel to actually be who he was without having to hide his real self from everyone around him. He felt that life was rapidly slipping away from him and he didn't want to live the rest of it as a lie. Only three things kept him from coming out of the closet, his concern for his family, his fear of being a social leper and his fear of hurting the young boys he desired. If he moved to Chicago and joined The Guild he would have a whole new social life, one which didn't condemn his lifestyle. His wife and daughters would also not have to face ridicule from their Fort Wayne friends. Furthermore, if what Barry said was true, he wouldn't be hurting the kids he had relationships with. Doug spent the next two weeks weighing his options.

CHAPTER 24

"Steve Gardner, come on down," Dan said out loud as he looked over his notes on the next pedophile. Gardner had been convicted of child molesting four years earlier when he was a bus driver for a San Diego school for special-needs children. His file said that he had been rehabilitated by psychoanalysis. Dan laughed at that one. His crime was particularly ugly because his victim was a disabled 7-year-old girl. The address in the police file was wrong and it took some good detective work to track Gardner down. But when he did, Dan was amazed to see that he worked at a large day care center in a San Diego suburb.

Dan thought about Jan's campaign to change the laws so that any facility that deals with children would be required to run a thorough background check on all of their employees so that a child molester could never get hired. If she had been successful, he thought, maybe this asshole wouldn't have gotten the job. To Dan it was just one more argument for the premise that when a society neglects the protection of a large part of its population, and a particularly vulnerable one at that, it's up to the individual to provide that protection. Besides, Dan mused, the individual can do what society cannot. My justice is swift and final. Even if pedophile laws were tougher the courts would take forever and many child molesters would slip through the cracks in the process. Not so in Judge Forester's court.

But even though Dan believed his own ruminations, there was something nagging at the back of his conscience; an inner voice that asked the question: "Who made you supreme judge and jury? What gives you the right to play God with anyone's life, pedophile or not?" Dan was able to tune out the voice with the argument that doing what is right, especially when you're bucking the system, is never easy and there are always going to be lingering doubts. Still, the black cloud was always close at hand and the headaches were increasing.

Enough philosophy, thought Dan. He wasted no time starting his new case. Putting on a blonde, straight-hair wig, light eyebrows and a latex chin, he decided this time to be a light-skinned, beardless Aryan-looking fellow. He applied light make-up until he looked like his name might be Larson. He drove to the day care center where Gardner worked, parked across the street and waited. At about 5:00PM he saw what he was looking for: the center's janitor, Milton Barnes, shaking out some rugs at the side door. He waited until Milton got off work at 6 o'clock and then approached him as he headed for his car.

* * *

After four weeks of Detective Derek Lindsay's unauthorized tap on Ali Ban Hashemi's telephone all of the messages simply asked Hashemi to call them back at a given number. None stated what they were calling for and none indicated that anything other than legitimate business was going on. Derek knew different. He figured that at least some of the calls were from clients who wanted to buy the services of a young boy or girl. He had a gut feeling that he was getting close to something big. The only problem was that all of the numbers left in the messages traced back to legitimate foreign government officials and businessmen.

When he explained the situation to his boss, Captain Mark Lewis, he didn't get a very enthusiastic response. "You tapped the guy for four weeks on your own and got nothing! And now you want me to authorize you to tail him full-time. That's a tall order for something that'll probably turn out to be nothing but a junkie informant's con isn't it?" he said.

"Well, Cap, you could look at it like that. But, you could also look at it like this: if I crack this case it'll be great publicity for you and the department, not to mention … save a lot of kids." Derek could be very persuasive when he had to be, as well as very tenacious. When he had wanted something from Captain Lewis in the past he had just badgered him until he got it.

"Yeah," Captain Lewis said obviously taking to the publicity angle, "But the fact is that with all the budget cut-backs we're short-handed and I really can't afford to put even one detective full-time on a maybe."

At this point Derek knew the captain well enough to see that he was about to lose his argument. So, he tried another tactic. "O.K. … how about a few months, but part-time, and if I don't get anything by then I promise to drop it completely and work overtime without pay on other cases. Give me the time and I guarantee you I'll bust this operation. I can feel it. I'm close."

Lewis looked him straight in the eye and said nothing for several seconds. *Well, that's a good sign*, thought Derek, *At least he didn't say 'no' right off the bat, so he must be considering it.* Captain Lewis was weighing the rewards of a possible bust of this magnitude against the loss of the services of his top detective for a few weeks. He knew Derek was right about how good the publicity of busting such an operation would be for him and the department. Derek, however, didn't really know just how great, since Captain Lewis was thinking of making a run at the Police Commissioner's job down the road, and needed a higher profile than he had to help him win the appointment. Lewis also knew how persistent Detective Lindsay could be when he wanted something and he really wanted him off his back. So, he compromised.

"Ten weeks ... and you still do your regular cases. If you don't turn it in ten weeks it's over, and I never want to hear about this bastard again. You got it?"

"Yeah. Thanks Cap," Derek walked out of the office a happy man because ten weeks was a lot more than he thought he would get when he went in. Now he would have to call in some favors to get some of his fellow detectives to help him with his other cases. He also knew that he would need some luck to get anything concrete on Hashemi in such a short time. Still, something told him he was very close. But, close to what, he didn't know.

* * *

"Hi. This is going to sound pretty strange," Dan said to day care janitor Milton Barnes as he unlocked his car door, "but I need your job for a couple of weeks and I want to give you $3000 to take a leave of absence and recommend me as your replacement while you're gone."

"You're right. It sounds strange ... now get the hell away from me!" was Barnes' frightened and angry reply as he opened his car door and started to get inside.

"Well, nothing talks like the real thing," Dan said as he flashed a packet stuffed with one hundred and fifty $20 bills.

Milton's impulse was to get in his car and drive away, but the sight of the money, more money than he made in three months at his part time janitor's job, transfixed him. "O.K.," he said slowly, "let's say you've got my attention. What's the gimmick?"

"You know how they say there's no free lunch? Well, in this case they're wrong. There actually is no gimmick. I need your job for two weeks for reasons I can't tell you about. But, I can guarantee you that you won't get in any trouble because it's for nothing immoral or illegal," Dan fibbed.

"And all I have to do is take two weeks off?"

"That's right. Just ask your boss for a two-week leave of absence ... say your mother is sick or whatever you want ... and recommend me, an old friend, as your replacement while you're gone. What do you say?"

"I say give me the dough."

"Half now and half after I get the job."

"No ... all now."

"Deal," Dan agreed and handed over the money.

Dan got the two-week job and began working a noon to six shift two days later. His plan was to catch Steve Gardner molesting one of the center's kids and then, if he did, mete out his own personal justice. For several days wherever Gardner went, Dan, or Bud Larson, as he was going by, watched him, unnoticed behind a broom or a mop. *No one ever notices the janitor*, he mused. For the first time the black cloud made its presence felt *before* he killed anyone.

* * *

There was definite chemistry in the air when Susan Jensen and Jan Forester met. It was one of those rare, undefinable feelings of genuine liking and friendship. Although they came from very different backgrounds, Jan from the farm and now married, and Susan from the big city and single, their personalities seemed to fall instantly into sync. Of course, one thing they did have in common was the issue that brought them together in the first place; child sex abuse. Susan probably understood Jan's pain more than most people since she had had her own bad experience with her sister's abuse, and Jan undoubtedly sensed her genuine empathy, something that was presently in short supply from those around her.

"The fact that people just don't know what to say so they usually end up saying just the wrong thing," Jan said to Susan's interview question of what bothers her the most these days.   "I know they're uncomfortable about it...I mean, who wouldn't be? After all what do you say to a mother whose son has been raped and killed? But because it's such a delicate subject they usually overcompensate and say things that hurt."

"What would you prefer people do and say?" Susan asked.

"Well, although I loved Cole more than anything else in the world, he's... he's gone, and if I'm not going to go insane I have to try and put this whole thing behind me. So, I guess what I really want from people is for them not to talk about it at all, unless I bring it up. I really want them to act like they did before any of this happened. A lot of my friends feel that talking about it is healthy for me, but it's not. The present theory is that you must grieve for your loss before you can start to get over it. But, with my background and my outlook on life I could literally grieve for years and I just don't think that it's gonna' help me deal with it. You can only go through the misery and pain so many times, and then it's time to try and forget."

"You said 'with your background' ... what do you mean by that?"

"I mean that people back home really know how to grieve. In fact, I think they invented grief. Basically, it was the land that time forgot ... mental attitudes haven't changed much there in the last hundred years. Those people are still the best people in the world. They're certainly the hardest working and, believe it or not, they really know how to have good clean fun and a lot of it. But, at the same time I have always felt that there's something dark and brooding about them and that characteristic really comes to light when someone dies. I mean first there's the viewing of the body. Then there's the wake. Then there's the funeral. And then the real grieving process begins and that can last for years."

"Excuse me for saying so, Jan, but you sound almost removed from all this. Do you think your own tragedy may have hardened your heart when it comes to death?"

* * *

Dan began to think he'd wasted his time, not to mention $3000, when the two weeks were almost up at the day care center with no evidence of Steve Gardner's pedophilia. Maybe he really was rehabilitated, mused Dan for a moment, a thought which would pretty much blow his belief that rehabilitation was impossible out of the water. But then, he realized, that's

why I investigate these guys before I hand out the sentence, to make sure I don't execute an innocent man.

His prey, however, was not destined to disappoint him. On the very last day of Dan's janitorial stint he saw Gardner lead a young girl who had scraped her knee, off the playground and into the building to get a band-aid. Out of sight around the corner from where Gardner was applying the bandage, he heard him tell the girl to come with him to the storeroom so he could check the rest of her body for cuts and scrapes. "Bingo," he whispered to himself as he heard how natural and easy the words came to Gardner's mouth.

Following the two to the storeroom undetected, Dan saw the door close behind them and heard it lock. The asshole probably thinks he's safe behind a locked door. The only thing he forgot is that I have a pass-key, was Dan's only thought. Just to be sure, he waited five minutes and then quickly opened the door to see Gardner on top of the girl. Gardner couldn't have been more shocked. He jerked himself to his feet, his face turning as red as a beet.

"Sorry," Dan said, "I didn't know anyone was in here. Don't worry man, I didn't see nothin'. Besides, this is my last day here and..." he gestured toward the girl still lying on the floor, "we've all had a little a' that." With that he closed the door and left the building and his career as a janitor. He peeled off his disguise as he drove back to his motel.

* * *

"Do I think it hardened my heart?" Jan repeated Susan Jensen's question, "That's a good question, but the answer is no, because I felt this way before Cole died. The fact is that I think one can grieve too much. At some point a person has to try and get on with life and put the sadness behind them, and if they are deliberately continuing to grieve because that is their cultural tradition or because their psychiatrist advises them to, they're never going to get over it. At least, it's going to take a long time, and in the meantime, they may sink into a deep depression they can't climb out of. I mean life really is for the living and death is for the dead." Jan amazed herself with her own words.

"Do you think to some that may sound cold?"

"Probably. But, when you think about it we're all going to be dead soon enough … why rush it?" Again, Jan surprised herself. It was as if she had been thinking these thoughts all along, but didn't realize it until she put them into words in this interview. Strange, she thought, that she had never said these things to Dr. Simmons. But, then, Susan often coaxed feelings out of people, which they didn't even know they had. That was what made her the good interviewer she was.

"Some have called you the iron maiden because of your strength. What do you think about that?"

"I'm sure they've called me more than that. But, one thing I should say is that I wasn't always this logical and strong about it. I was a mess for a long time after Cole's disappearance. I was desperately depressed and at times suicidal. So, before you think of me as this hard-nosed, stoic realist, know that it took me awhile to get here."

By the end of this final interview Susan did something she had never done before and would probably never do again; she reached over and hugged her interview subject and they both cried. Perhaps it was because Jan was verbalizing feelings similar to those she had experienced after her sister's ordeal. Perhaps it was because Jan's feminine strength of character in the face of devastating adversity was a trait Susan aspired to and hoped she possessed. But whatever the reason, in that moment of intense emotion a strong bond was formed between them.

CHAPTER 25

With his faith restored in the depravity of child molesters Dan began planning Steve Gardner's demise. This one normally wouldn't have been easy because Gardner lived with his mother and didn't go out much. However, while surveying his bedroom window with long range, night vision binoculars, Dan had seen Gardner practice auto-eroticism by playing with himself while hanging from the ceiling by a rope. He lifted his feet off a stool and hung by his neck, reducing the oxygen supply to his brain, which provided him with a sort of high. All the while he masturbated. Then, just before he blacked out, he put his feet back on the stool and removed the noose from his neck. Part of the thrill was seeing how long he could hang without blacking out.

"What are you doing Saturday night, Steve?" Dan said out loud. "Oh, just hanging around," he answered himself. Wearing a garter belt and fishnet stockings he made quite a sight swinging back and forth in front of the window and Dan thought he would laugh himself sick. Steve's hobby was probably going to provide the perfect vehicle for his end and enable Dan to help some of the children Gardner had molested at the day care center. It might even raise their parents' consciousness about the pedophile issue.

He only had to watch the window for three nights from his hiding place in some nearby bushes before Steve obliged him. Placing his silenced Sturm-Ruger Mini 14 Rifle on a tripod, which he had shipped to himself from Washington, he adjusted the night scope and aimed at one leg of the stool from which Steve was getting ready to jump. It was a hot, summer evening so the bedroom window was open, meaning the only evidence of a bullet passing through would be a small hole in the screen, which Dan was pretty sure no one would notice.

"Three, two, one," said Dan to himself as he counted down the jump to ecstasy, and then, "We have lift off." He let Gardner swing for about 30 seconds until his feet started fishing for the stool. He then fired once, hitting the top of the stool and knocking it over, leaving one panicked pedophile swinging back and forth, frantically thrashing in the air like a fish out of water. Gardner then reached his trembling hands up to try and pull his neck out of the hangmen's loop, but it was too late. The last bit of oxygen to his brain was choked off, his hands dropped to his sides and his body went limp. Dan took one last look at the swaying figure clad in a bra and crotch-less panties, packed up his tools of execution and left, heading not back to his hotel, but rather to his and Gardner's former place of employment. The black cloud had now fully descended upon him and the headache was beyond most human endurance. But, he forced himself to finish what he had started.

* * *

The final decision Douglas Glassman came up with was the one that he had suspected he would reach from the beginning. He decided to leave his family, move to Chicago and join The Guild. His boss arranged another insurance job for him in Chicago and now all that remained was to tell Sandy and the girls, which was going to be the hardest part. He decided to tell Sandy the truth but asked her to tell Katy and Kelly only that they were getting a divorce because they were no longer in love.

"You mean you've had sexual desire for boys ever since we were married?" Sandy asked him incredulously.

"Yes," was his sober reply.

"And you've actually molested two boys right here in Fort Wayne?"

"Well, not really. I had sexual encounters with them ... and I am deeply ashamed of it." Confession was good for the soul.

"Oh this is too much," she said as she collapsed into a living room chair, "I can't believe you've been this way all along and I never had a clue. I guess that's why you haven't been interested in sex for a while huh?"

"Yes, my feelings for boys have been growing so strong that I can hardly think of anything else ... especially not about sex with a woman ... even my wife."

After a long pause and a disdainful stare, Sandy simply said, "You're sick. You need help."

"But, I have been getting help for years from Dr. Johnson. You know that."

"Yeah, but I didn't know it was for this. Besides, she must not have done you any good because she didn't cure you."

"Sandy, it has taken me a long time to understand it but I think I finally do. It's not a disease. It's a sexual preference. If you approach it right there's nothing wrong with it."

"What about the two boys? You said you were ashamed of it."

"I am because they weren't confirmed homosexuals and weren't really voluntary, willing partners. Now I believe there are a lot of young boys out there who are definitely gay or bisexual. My relationships with them will help rather than hurt them."

"Well, if they're gay they're gay because some pervert like you made them that way and you having a relationship with them will just make the problem worse. It's not natural Doug. It's sick and you're sick ... and I can't stay married to you anymore either. You've got your divorce and I won't tell the kids a thing. I don't want them to know their own father is a child molester. Of course, you can visit them, but I would prefer that you don't."

"I understand Sandy. To be honest I don't think they're going to care too much about that anyway. I'm ... I'm really and truly sorry that things turned out this way. I wish I was normal and that we could live out our lives normally, but I'm not and I just can't deny who I am anymore. Whatever you think of me now, I do love you." Doug moved toward Sandy to hug her good-bye but she was so repulsed by his revelation that she quickly moved away. With head hanging and a sour feeling in his gut Doug went upstairs and told his two daughters the news. As he expected he didn't get much reaction. They were stunned and surprised, but accepted the situation without argument. Of course, over half of their friends' parents were divorced, so it wasn't that unusual. He hugged Katy and Kelly good-bye and felt for a moment that maybe he had been wrong; that maybe they really did love him. But, it was too late. He had laid his course and now he had to follow it. He left, shutting the door on sixteen years of marriage and leaving behind the only adult life he had ever known. Sadness lingered in his soul, but the excitement of an uncertain future rose in him. He was sorrowful over what he was losing, but pleased with his newfound freedom. Most of all, he was thrilled and filled with excited anticipation over the possibility of future, guiltless sex with young boys. "Next stop, Chicago," he said out loud as he drove away, all the while thinking of turning back.

* * *

Having made a copy of the key to the main door of the day care center, Dan entered the day care easily, went straight to the big bulletin board in the lobby and pinned up a typed note that read:

I, Steve Gardner, cannot live with the shame and guilt of what I have done. I have sexually molested many children here at the day care center, mostly girls, but some boys. I am very sorry for what I have done, but I just could not seem to help myself. The only way for it to stop is for me to kill myself and that is what I have done. Parents and day care teachers, I have one thing to say to you: you make it too easy for people like me. You seem to think we don't exist and that your precious little kids are not in any danger, but they are and I am living proof of that danger.

What you don't seem to realize is that any group activity your child becomes involved in, be it day care, little league baseball or boy scouts, is where you will find pedophiles. They are drawn to positions associated with kids, like day care workers, baseball coaches and Boy Scout leaders.

Parents seem to take it for granted that all the men who hold these positions are normal and because many of them have never been convicted of abuse, their background checks find nothing. Although we all wish it were so, we just don't live in a world anymore where you can trust everyone. Many parents also are reluctant to warn their kids about pedophiles for fear of scaring them. Well, folks, SCARE THEM! It's better to scare them by repeatedly telling them to run, scream and tell if anyone ever tries to touch their bodies in any way than to have them submit to abuse because their molester is an adult authority figure, as many of my victims have done. I believe that if any one of the kids I have molested had had this drilled into them I wouldn't have been able to molest them and would have been fired from my job and maybe even kept in jail. You just make it too easy.

If you want to keep your children safe from monsters like me watch them a lot more closely, keep strict track of their whereabouts, and carefully check out the background of anyone who has the slightest contact with them, including and especially their day care workers. I know this is often difficult to do on your own and that is why you should lobby for tougher background checks that will show if someone was ever even accused, but never convicted of child abuse. Many will say this is a violation of privacy, and it may be. Liberals will argue that if you start requiring these kinds of checks on people working with kids what's to stop you from requiring them on anyone and everyone else thereby invading peoples' privacy? Well, I say that privacy laws dealing with the relationships between adults should remain basically the same as they are now because adults at least have the potential for defending themselves. But, laws dealing with children should be subject to a different standard because children are defenseless. When it comes to protection laws you just can't treat adults and children the same because they are not the same. What are you more concerned about anyway, an adult's privacy or your child's very life? Besides, if more stringent background checks were required many pedophiles would just avoid these child-oriented jobs and activities for fear of being found out, and wouldn't that accomplish a lot by itself? Why are you more concerned with a possible criminal's rights than with your own child's safety? After all, they are your most valuable possession and deserve your full protection.

I will leave you all with this: society, in general, makes it much too easy for those of us with a sexual appetite for children. We are ruining the lives of much of your future generation and you seem not to care. Laws against child molesting need to be toughened up, sentences need to be increased, and the court system needs to believe all children when they say they have been molested. I have seen too many pedophiles like myself go free because a sharp defense attorney convinces the judge or jury that the child victim made up the charge. Believe me, they never make them up. If children say they were molested they were. I, myself, have molested several children just in the 3 years I have worked here at the center and none of them told on me because I convinced them that they were now "spoiled goods" and that their parents wouldn't want them anymore. It's too late for me, but it is not too late for the many children who may have become my victims had I continued my life. Don't let them become someone else's.

Steve Gardner

As Dan expected, Steve Gardner's death was officially ruled a suicide. No one found the bullet hole in the stool because no one looked for it and the small hole in the window screen went unnoticed. Milton Barnes, the day care janitor, had a fleeting thought that his newfound wealth and two-week vacation might somehow be related to Gardner's suicide, but he couldn't figure out how. So, not wanting to get in any trouble himself, he just kept mum about it. All this, Dan had anticipated, but one thing he didn't foresee was the intense, nationwide media exposure the case received. He had anticipated that the local San Diego news media would carry a story as juicy as this one, but not the national news media. Must've been a slow news day, was all he could think because all the television networks and most of the country's major newspapers gave the story extensive attention. One network and several newspapers even used it as the focal point for multi-part series reports on child sex abuse.

On the one hand Dan was glad to see the issue receive so much coverage and believed that he may have helped spark a movement to do some of the things that should be done with child sex abuse. But, on the other hand the high profile of the story bothered him immensely. The last thing he wanted to do was to draw a lot of attention to any of these deaths. The success of his mission depended on giving law enforcement officials no reason to investigate them or tie them together in any way. He fervently hoped that the attention the suicide note drew had not inspired some intuitive detective with a hunch to investigate recent pedophile deaths in San Diego.

CHAPTER 26

It was hot and the air-conditioner rattled its dying fan as Dan lay on an iron-hard motel bed, reading notes on his next target. Tyrone Palmer was particularly interesting. According to police records he'd been convicted twice of child molesting, but had served only one year of two five-year sentences. The salient fact about Tyrone, however, was that he was strongly suspected of running a prostitution ring using young boys. "Tyrone, it's time to boogie," mumbled Dan dreamily as he dropped his notes and drifted off to sleep. He was wolfing down aspirins like candy these days, trying to rid himself of increasingly frequent headaches.

Four days later Dan thought business must be good as he sat in his car down the street from Tyrone Palmer's upscale home on the outskirts of San Diego. Beside him a receiver picked up tiny microphones he had hidden throughout the house when he had broken in. The receiver also picked up the bug in Palmer's telephone.

For three days, Dan heard Tyrone make coded drug deals over the phone, but nothing had been said about child prostitution. Other than the television and an unremarkable conversation between Palmer, another man who apparently lived there and a young boy, the microphones in the house hadn't turned up anything. Then it happened.

* * *

Not wanting to waste any time after getting the green light from Captain Lewis, Detective Derek Lindsay went directly from the station to the office building facing suspected kiddie-pimp Ali Ban Hashemi's high-rise. He had found a vacant office and arranged to rent it. From its window he could see the apartment building's front door and the parking garage exit. He could see when Hashemi drove his own car, when he was picked up by a chauffeur-driven limousine he occasionally used, or when he walked a few blocks and hailed a cab. Once he signed the lease in the name of the department, Derek settled in for a long, tedious stakeout since he had to constantly keep a vigil on the garage exit and the front door. He knew that he was going to be living in the office for weeks. He hoped what he found would be worth the effort.

* * *

"It's chicken time," said the man's voice on the phone using the slang word for sex with young boys. The boys who provided sex were often called chickens and the pedophiles were called chicken hawks.

"Same place, two o'clock," was all Tyrone Palmer said. As Dan listened to the phone tap, he noticed the routine sound of Palmer's voice. He had clearly done this before.

"Fine. I want Rodney."

"You got 'em."

"Bye."

Dan thought that Rodney must be the kid whose voice he had heard and that Palmer must pimp him out. He wondered how much money he got for a kid as he drove to the end of the street and parked where Tyrone's car would come out onto the main drag.

At noon Palmer drove past with a young, blonde boy of about ten or twelve in the passenger seat. Palmer's bronze Cadillac pulled out heading southeast. Dan followed a few cars back. After an hour and a few twists and turns the car headed into the rugged wasteland east of the city. Finally, it pulled off the road into an abandoned rock quarry site and parked in among several large, empty warehouses. Dan drove on and pulled onto a road just past the warehouses reaching for his long-range binoculars as he came to a stop.

At 2 o'clock another car pulled into the quarry and parked near Palmer. Through his binoculars Dan saw the blonde lad get out and climb into the other car. Then something clinched Palmer's guilt and sealed his fate. The man in the other car leaned over and gave the boy a long, sloppy kiss on the mouth as they drove away. Palmer left a few minutes later.

Two for the price of one, thought Dan. He headed for his motel to plan the end of both Palmer and his customer. But then a new idea hit him like a thunderbolt.

* * *

Ali Ban Hashemi's main concern at this moment was contacting one of his regular pimps by telephone to arrange a boy for a visiting dignitary due to arrive in New York in two days. He had found that the easiest way to avoid detection was to use a different type of communication for each transaction and then to send the payment money to the pimp by courier. Most of the time, he used a burner phone that was hard to trace. But sometimes he would use a pay phone, if he could find one of the last few pay phones left in New York City. Sometimes he walked or drove his Mercedes to the phone. Sometimes he took a cab or a chauffeured limousine. Since the police could not know which pay phone he was going to use, and consequently, couldn't tap it beforehand, he figured he was safest that way. His only real, nagging fear was that one of the pimp's phones might be tapped and he could be implicated, especially if the pimp were busted and decided to testify against him. For protection, he used a code word instead of his name every time and even disguised his voice, figuring that if it ever got to court it would be his word against the pimp and he would come out on top.

* * *

More bang for the buck, Dan reasoned as he sat in his hotel room. "Why not make it more than two?" he asked out loud. He was aware that his one-at-a-time method was inefficient and he wished he had a more effective way. Now he realized he may have found it.

* * *

One night, after 72 hours of Detective Derek Lindsay's stakeout, Ali Ban Hashemi chose to take the taxi route. He got into a cab that the apartment building doorman called for him. The taxi driver drove him to the 21st Century Nightclub with Lindsay close behind. Hashemi got out and went into the club like any other patron. Derek, on the other hand, had to do some quick illegal parking and jump out of his car carrying a long-range listening device the police department had recently purchased. When aimed at the person doing the talking, the parabolic microphone clearly picked up and recorded a conversation from up to 40 yards away. The receiver and recorder Derek hid under his jacket. But the tiny dish had to be exposed, as he had to aim it at the subject to get any sound.

* * *

That night after Tyrone Palmer and his housemate left their driveway, Dan broke in and searched the house thoroughly. After two hours he was ready to give up. Then, hidden above the false ceiling he found what he was looking for. Not too smart, he thought, paging through Palmer's address book. All the pedophile clients' telephone numbers were in it. Dan copied names and numbers, noticing that each one had a different code word. He correctly guessed that Palmer used the code words in his transactions so that his clients would know it was him. What the book didn't say was that only three of its thirty-seven names had ever been charged with child molesting. The number was close to the national percentage that Jan used in her speeches. Dan sat back in an easy chair and relaxed, waiting for Palmer and his housemate. At about 2:00AM the Cadillac pulled into the driveway.

* * *

Figuring that Ali Ban Hashemi came to the 21ˢᵗ Century Nightclub for the phone and not the nightlife, Detective Derek Lindsay found out from the coat check girl where the pay telephones were. As he rounded a corner he saw what he expected, Hashemi dialing a pay telephone. Leaning against a wall he quickly, yet carefully slipped the dish out of his jacket and aimed it at Hashemi. The dim lighting and hustle and bustle of the crowd made it easy for Derek to avoid attention even though he was holding what resembled a miniature satellite dish. But then, this was New York City where not much of anything drew inordinate attention.

Not wanting to look too suspicious by adding headphones to his get-up, Derek couldn't hear Hashemi's conversation while it was being recorded. He fervently hoped that everything was working properly. His subject spoke for only a minute and then hung up and went into the nightclub's bar. Derek slid the tiny dish back inside of his coat and followed. Watching from the corner of the bar he saw Hashemi sit down and order a drink. After taking a few sips of his whisky highball, he got up and walked to the restroom. Ten minutes went by and Hashemi had not returned. Suspicious, Derek went to the men's restroom.

* * *

"Hello," was all Dan said as Tyrone Palmer and another man entered the living room and turned on the lights. For a moment they stumbled against each other looking for a way out until Dan gestured with the .357 Magnum pointed at their bellies. "Sit down." They did at once.

"Take anything, just don't hurt us," whined Palmer's companion. Palmer, more reserved, guessed this was more than just a robbery.

"All I want and all you're gonna' give me," Dan said evenly looking straight into Tyrone's eyes, "is the full story of how you run your chicken business ... don't bother to waste my time denying it ... I saw you deliver Rodney this afternoon. Just pretend I'm franchising your operation. Tell me how you work."

Glaring at him with disdain and fear, Palmer thought of lying and telling the intruder he didn't know what he was talking about. But Dan's steely stare told him that this guy was no one to fool around with. It was a seasoned, steady look that told Tyrone he'd better play it straight if he wanted to live.

"Well, it's pretty easy," Palmer started slowly, "I pick up kids, mostly boys, at the bus station or on the street and give 'em a place to live and food to eat. They work for me."

"How do you get them to do it?"

"It ain't hard. By the time I get 'em they're hungry and dirty and sometimes cold or sick. They'll do about anything for room and board." He shrugged, "After a while a lot of 'em get to like it. Oh, I pays 'em too."

"How much?"

"Ten bucks here ... twenty there."

"And how much do you get for one rendezvous?"

Palmer hesitated on this one.

"How much asshole?" demanded Dan, moving the .357 slightly.

"Two-grand."

"You must deal with rich people."

"Only rich folks. But look here," Tyrone pleaded, "these kids would starve if it wasn't for me. I gives 'em a warm place to live, food to eat and clothes to wear. I think I should get somethin' for it."

"Oh, what a great humanitarian you are Tyrone. If you believe the shit that just came outta' your mouth you're dumber than you look. How many kids do you have working?"

"Usually about three."

"Why is there only one now?"

"Two are out on lease and one ... was sold." The word didn't immediately register with Dan.

"You mean you rent these kids out for days at a time?"

"Yeah ... and for weeks and months," Palmer said, actually beginning to brag about his business.

"How much is a kid for a month?"

"Twenty-grand."

"How much for a week?"

"Seven-grand."

"How long did you rent Rodney out for?"

"Three days."

"When does the other one come back?"

"Same day as Rodney."

Then it hit Dan. "Whaddya' mean ... sold?"

"I sold him."

"For good?"

"For good."

"What do ya' get for him?"

"A hundred-thousand."

"Why would someone pay $100,000 for a kid?"

"Because he's safe. They knows I made sure he don't have no family that will come lookin' for him. I'm reliable, man. Also, they're extra pretty. This last kid was as pretty as a child movie star."

"What does the client do with him when he's through?"

"That's his business."

"No, right now it's your business! 'Cause if you don't tell me in two seconds I'm gonna' blow your fucking head off."

"Aight! Aight! Easy man. He'll probably just let him go."

"Wrong! You got one second," said Dan raising the gun toward Tyrone's face.

"O.K! O.K!" he shouted covering his face, "he'll probably kill the kid and bury him out in the sticks somewhere. At least that's what I know one dude did."

"That's what I figured."

"But I ain't responsible for what these guys do with the kid once I sell him to 'em," Tyrone pleaded. "They don't tell me. And I don't ask. Once I saw on the news that they dug up a kid. I'd sold him about two years before. So, I figured that must be what some of 'em do, at least in this country."

Dan's icy stare hid his inner rage as the scene of Cole's body being dug up replayed in his mind. His finger tightened on the trigger, but at the last instant his tug-of-war logic made him stick to the plan. "What do you mean, in this country?"

"Well, a couple 'a times I sold boys to this foreign dude and I think he may re-sell 'em to someone in another country."

This new wrinkle sickened Dan but intrigued him at the same time. "Where's this guy from and where does he live?"

"I dunno'. I only talked to him on the phone"

"Wrong again," Dan said as he once again leveled the gun at Palmer's head and tightened his finger on the trigger.

"I don't know where he's from!" he blurted as he raised his hands to his face.

"And he lives where?" Dan asked

"New York," Palmer sobbed hiding his face in his hands.

* * *

"Shit!" Detective Derek Lindsay said out loud rushing out of the 21ˢᵗ Century Nightclub's restroom to see that the club's back door was right next to the men's room. "He's smarter than I thought," he said, almost admiringly. Obviously, Ali Ban Hashemi had slipped out and Derek knew he had no chance of catching up with him. What interested him now was the tape. Back at his apartment he set up the recorder and played it. The nightclub had been loud and there was a lot of traffic so he wasn't sure of what he would get. What he got was a lot of ambient noise with just bits and pieces of understandable conversation from Hashemi.

So garbled was the audio that the next day Derek took the tape to the police department's forensic lab and had a lab technician analyze it. By electronically taking out much of the background noise the technician was able to produce an audible voice, disjointed and broken up as it was. Then, feeding the tape through a computer program, which completed bits and pieces of broken words, the tape was ready. What Derek heard was Hashemi giving directions. After playing the tape back thirty times, he barely made out what Hashemi said, "I need ... a cab at the ... back of the 21st Century Night ... Club on 181st street. Make sure the driver comes to the back of the club please and I'll be waiting."

CHAPTER 27

"What makes you think this guy sells the kids in another country?" Dan asked kiddie pimp Tyrone Palmer, still sitting in his living room.

Still very much afraid he answered simply, "A dude I know said the guy probably buys 'em for some rich foreigners. They want white kids. But he says they probably don't kill 'em when they're done with 'em. When they're too old or worn out he says they probably make 'em slaves," Tyrone said this as if it vindicated him in some way.

"I want his name and address and I want it now."

"Come on, man," whined Tyrone, "these guys play for keeps. He said if I ever ratted him out I wouldn't live to see the sunrise."

"Well, if you don't get me the name and address in exactly 5 seconds, you won't have to worry about the sunset! I'd just as soon waste you right now as look at you. It's your choice."

As the watchful, dark eye of the .357 Magnum followed him he got the number from a hiding place in his bedroom and gave it to Dan.

"The only name I have is Mr. G. No address, just a number. He won't talk to nobody but me. I have to call the number and leave a message," Tyrone said with a sigh of doomed resignation. "He calls back."

"Thanks, Tyrone. Now, at least you'll live to see tomorrow's sunrise. By the way, you guys both screw the kids yourselves, don't you?"

Neither man spoke.

"You do, don't you? If you don't talk truth in two seconds they'll be scrubbing what's left of your skulls and brains off the wall behind you."

"Yeah," grunted Tyrone. His companion, Andy said nothing.

"Well, boys, we're gonna' spend a few days together. Frankly, you're not gonna' enjoy it as much as I am," said Dan.

* * *

So, the fat bastard stuck it to me, thought a frustrated Detective Derek Lindsay. He knew now that kiddie pimp Ali Ban Hashemi only went to the club to call another cab to go where he really wanted to go in case he was being followed. He beat his fists on the desk as he painfully realized that by underestimating Hashemi's guile he had committed a rookie mistake. "Idiot," he roared. He was so good at his job that whenever he made a mistake he beat himself up over it for days. One thing he knew was that he would not make this kind of mistake again with Ali Ban Hashemi.

* * *

"Come on boys ... this way to your accommodations," Dan said waving his gun in the air as he led kiddie pimps Tyrone Palmer and Andy to the basement and handcuffed them together to a floor-to-ceiling pillar. Dan settled down on the upstairs couch for a few hours of sleep. When he drifted off his familiar dream began. This time he was walking on a frozen lake, slipping and falling down. Looking down he saw Cole under the ice beckoning to him. There seemed to be a bright light behind him and he was trying to say something important, but no words came.

The next morning Dan threw the address book into Tyrone's lap. "Make the calls," he said matter-of-factly.

Palmer began dialing almost with a sense of resignation. "Chicken special," he said into the receiver, "half-price going out of business sale but it's gotta' be now."

Tyrone made 37 calls and reached 14 of his clients setting up appointments for them one hour apart over the next two days at the quarry. He told them that he was leaving town for good and needed the money. He also told them that if they were one minute late for their meeting time he would leave.

"So you want in on the money," Tyrone breathed with almost a sigh of relief after his last call. This was something he could finally understand.

"Something like that," Dan said.

"You gonna' shake 'em down, aren't ya'?" appealed Tyrone.

"Something like that."

Andy slept handcuffed to the bathroom plumbing that night, while Tyrone hugged the basement pole.

* * *

Besides the female bonding and feelings of sisterhood they were experiencing Jan Forester and Susan Jensen found they genuinely enjoyed each other's company. Jan found engaging and fun conversations with Susan. It was refreshing to have a friend who hadn't known her before her tragedy. Sue, who knew no one else in Washington, found Jan to be intelligent and interesting, qualities she always believed to be her own but which were sadly lacking in many of her co-workers. But then, Sue was a television journalist, a field many enter for egotistical rather than journalistic reasons. After shooting for three days in Jan's home and at St. Christopher's Hospital Susan bid farewell to the camera crew, which had done a great job, and went back to her research at the Children's Protection Society, the Library of Congress and the U.S. Justice Department. Sue's interest in missing children breathed new life into Jan's concern for the issue and she proved to be a big help. She supplied Susan with sources of information that were obscure, but accurate.

The biggest obstacle Sue faced was that most cases of child sex abuse are never reported, so the figures she was able to get were usually low. Consequently, aside from statistics on sex abuse convictions, she had to search social service files from every state, tabulating suspicions as well as accusations. The problem was that most states kept these files confidential.

She was able to get around this obstacle by conducting the largest survey on child sex abuse ever done. She mailed out 500,000 questionnaires asking a random sampling of anonymous respondents if they had ever been sexually abused as children and if so what the circumstances were. She estimated that about 15,000 surveys would be returned and many were already coming in. Once they were in she planned to have a professional polling company tabulate them. The pollster's statisticians would then work up the percentage of respondents who had been molested and how they were molested. From those statistics they could then infer the number of people in society at large who had been sexually molested. Between the survey and the legal records, they would make the most accurate estimate ever made of how widespread child sex abuse was in America. From preliminary figures Susan estimated that one out of five children had been sexually abused in some way in their lifetimes. That meant 20% of the population.

* * *

"Rise and shine," yelled Dan the next morning, as he uncuffed Tyrone, leaving Andy cuffed to the sink. "It's show time."

With an odd half-smile on his face, he forced Tyrone to drive his Cadillac to the quarry. After handcuffing him to the wheel he told him, "See that water tower?

That's where I'll be with this," he pointed to his 30.06 rifle, another of the guns he had shipped to himself. "You said this was a shake-down and you're right ... sort of. You're gonna' sit here and motion to your customer when he pulls in to come over to the car. If you do anything else I'll put a bullet in your head. If you follow my directions I'm only going to put a bullet in his head and you'll live. Got it?"

"Oh, man, you're gonna' ice these guys!" Tyrone screamed.

"Ice is such a cold word. I prefer ... rid the world of vermin. Anyway, you've got your instructions. Follow 'em and you live. Don't and you die. Simple, huh? Even for a tiny brain like yours."

Tyrone whimpered as Dan climbed the water tower ladder, got in a prone position and waited. As the first pedophile pulled in at nine o'clock and stopped next to the Cadillac, Tyrone motioned to the driver to come over to his car. He did, and "pop," a silenced shot to the head brought him to the ground. Dan climbed down the tower, uncuffed Tyrone and ordered him to stuff the body into the car's trunk and drive it into the empty warehouse. Walking beside the car as it moved slowly into the warehouse and pointing the gun directly at his head, Dan reminded Tyrone that his chances of escape by hitting the accelerator were next to none. He then made him take the money from the dead man's wallet and give it to him.

The scene was repeated twice more, with the successful assassination of two more pedophiles.   But right from the beginning Tyrone had been working out an escape plan and on pedophile number four he put it into action. As he drove into the warehouse with Dan walking next to him he gunned the car and laid down in the front seat at the same time, hoping to crash through the wall at the other end of the building and drive to freedom. Dan fired at the car several times, but the bullets just buried themselves in the metal. "Shit!" he screamed as he realized his scheme was over. But then, something happened that neither of them had counted on. On the other side of the wall was a huge, old crane, which was rusted into place. The car made it through the wall, but smashed into the crane with an ear-splitting, metal-grinding thunder. Dan raced over and pulled a bleeding Tyrone from the wreckage. "Dumb move, Chief," he said as he wiped the blood from his face. Next time I'll just shoot you if you go over one mile an hour.

Things then went pretty much according to plan with pedophiles 5 and 6. But then 7 and 8 didn't show and Dan got worried. Probably too short 'a notice, he thought, trying to put the best face on it. But he was clearly concerned that something was amiss and pedophile number 9 confirmed his fears.

* * *

The next phase of Ross Huggins' pedophile study was pretty routine. The results showed about what he had expected; that generally, pedophiles had about the same health picture and died from about the same things as the rest of society. He did find a slightly higher incidence of AIDS among them, which he attributed to the fact that most were homosexual or bisexual and some injected themselves with drugs sharing used hypodermic needles.

After eight weeks of collecting and analyzing data from state records offices and law enforcement and social service agencies all over the country Ross was approaching the end of the project. He was disappointed that he had not found a definite trend for his superiors. He knew that even though his research was accurate, the fact that he didn't come up with the kind of dramatic trends they were looking for could mean he wouldn't get the field promotion. You have to stand out if you're going to get promoted, he thought to himself.

Then, just as he was putting the finishing touches on his final report some new cause-of-death data came in from four states, including California. He debated with himself whether or not even to look at the new information because he was sure it wouldn't alter his conclusions, but his sense of duty won out and he analyzed it. It was, as he expected, routine, except for one thing. The information from San Diego, California showed some peculiarities that another researcher might have missed. Ross caught them because of his extreme attention to detail.

What he read raised his curiosity to say the least. In the last two months four known or suspected pedophiles living in San Diego had died under not-so-normal circumstances.

One had died of a heroin overdose, one from a gas explosion, one from suicide, and one from a fall down the stairs.

* * *

"What the hell?" Dan said out loud as he saw a Mercedes pull into the quarry. He was getting ready to pack it in and was standing in plain sight holding his rifle. The driver saw it and immediately tried to turn the car around to beat a hasty retreat leaving Dan with an instantaneous decision to make. Was this a pedophile early for his appointment or was it just someone out for a drive? "Yes or no," he screamed at Tyrone, "Is that a client?"

Nothing but silence from Palmer and the car was spinning its wheels in the loose gravel.

"Now or you die!" Dan shouted as he leveled the gun at Tyrone's head.

"Yeah ... it's him," he said just as Dan's finger tightened on the trigger. The Mercedes was now out of the gravel and speeding away.

Quickly but deliberately Dan wheeled around and took careful aim. "Pop," went the 30.06. Unfortunately for pedophile number 9, Dan's marksmanship was exceptionally keen that day and he ended his life with one shot through the rear window. Along with the physical conditioning he had done in Washington, Dan had perfected his marksmanship as well as his martial arts and knife-throwing skills. The Mercedes skidded off the road into the ditch and the driver slumped over the wheel honking the horn in a long, shrill squeal. Dan quickly ran to the car and pulled the dead man off of the steering wheel.

"I guess," said Dan with an eerie calm, "the early bird doesn't really get the worm." Tyrone just grunted with disappointment. For a brief instant he thought the early arrival of pedophile number 9 might be a way out. But for Dan it was an even worse omen than numbers 7 and 8 not showing. He immediately ordered Tyrone to call the rest of the scheduled pedophiles on his cell phone and cancel their appointments.

* * *

Detective Derek Lindsay's assessment of how and why kiddie pimp Ali Ban Hashemi had given him the slip was mostly correct, but not entirely. After leaving the nightclub Hashemi had taken a cab to another pay telephone to call a pimp who had proven to be reliable in the past. Identifying himself as "Mr. Z," the conversation was brief, as he told the pimp the date, time and hotel room where the boy prostitute should go. Two days later Hashemi would send the payment by courier. The only physical involvement he ever had with the operation was the phone call, and he was always careful about that. Derek spent the next two and a half weeks on a constant, but futile vigil of Hashemi's apartment building.

* * *

Dan weighed the risks of waiting the extra day for the return of Rodney and the other leased boy and, in spite of the risk, decided to chance it. It was then back to business as usual as they repeated the scene twice without a hitch. Their pedophile customers never knew what hit them. The tricky part was shooting the pedophile without hitting the child he was returning, and then Tyrone had to shout to the kid that he was safe and not to run away. Dan left Tyrone uncuffed and instructed him to get out of the Cadillac, go over to the stunned boy and explain to him that he had to get out of there fast and forget what he had just seen or that he ever knew Tyrone Palmer. Tyrone then handed each kid some of the money taken from the dead pedophiles, and pointed down the road to San Diego. Dan knew he took the chance that Tyrone might run, but he also knew that Tyrone was a coward, and was scared to death of his marksmanship. Besides, he had hurt his leg in the crash into the crane.

The two boys were shocked, but happy to leave with more money than they had ever seen. They left quickly without a second glance at the slumped body of their abuser. At least, Dan figured, there was a better-than-even chance they wouldn't report it. After the last boy Dan climbed down from the water tower and looked at Tyrone.

"Well, that's it huh? That's all of em'. I hope ya' enjoy the coin. Now you're gonna' let me go right?" Tyrone said, not at all convinced.

"That's right. There's just one more thing we've got to do," Dan said as opened the car trunk and took out two packages.

* * *

For seventeen days under Detective Derek Lindsay's surveillance, Ali Ban Hashemi conducted what seemed like routine business and social activities-a few dates with good looking women here, several meetings and social outings with visiting clients there-nothing unusual or suggestive of anything illegal. Hashemi had not touched a pay telephone in all that time and Derek hadn't seen him buy a burner.

* * *

Dan handed Tyrone and Andy each a package. "Hold these a minute," was all he said.

"What's going on? I thought you were gonna' let us go!" blurted Andy, suddenly very frightened.

"I am. I am, but first I'm going to let you Andy, my man, go up that water tower." Wearing gloves as always, he took back the packages and put them in the Cadillac. Then he handcuffed Tyrone to the car door. Confused and scared Andy started the climb.

Dan climbed up behind Andy, carrying the rifle that had done so much killing. He forced him down on his stomach on the platform and handcuffed him to the railing. He then swung around quickly and yelled, "Bye, Tyrone, you tycoon you," as he snap-shot one round through Tyrone's head with the 30.06.

Andy screamed as he suddenly realized Dan's plan. "You can't do this! You're gonna' make it look like I killed Tyrone!" That's when Dan realized the two were probably lovers.

"You catch on quick," Dan said climbing down the tower ladder.

"How are you gonna' explain the hand cuffs?"

"I'm not," Dan called back from the ground. He walked to Tyrone's body, turned and shot Andy with his .357 Magnum. He then climbed back up the tower, uncuffed Andy's dead body, and placed the 30.06 in his limp arms, making sure to press his finger tips to the barrel and stock. He then pulled Andy's index finger on the trigger, shooting the gun once and getting powder residue on the dead man's hands. On the ground again, he put the .357 in Tyrone's hand and shot it a couple of times to get powder burns on his fingers. Both guns' serial numbers had been filed off and they were untraceable. He stuffed the remaining money into Tyrone's coat pocket.

The two packages, each containing a kilo of 49% pure heroin, lay on the front seat of the Cadillac. Dan had cut his kilo of 98% pure junk in half and mixed it with milk sugar to make two kilos. He had kept about 1/2 of an ounce of the 98% stuff for any possible future needs. He hoped the police would think Tyrone lured the dead men to the spot on the pretense of a big dope deal so Andy could shoot them and they could steal their money. With Andy on the tower and Tyrone on the ground it would look as though after they finished, they had their own shoot-out, possibly over the drugs or the money, and killed each other. Tyrone and Andy's finger prints were the only ones on the dope packages. Dan had worn gloves during the entire operation.

He calmly walked out of the quarry and down the road to his own car, got in and drove back to his motel. He packed up, checked out, and drove out of San Diego. Along with the black cloud hanging over his head he had a nagging fear that the dead men in the warehouse might soon be discovered and that some might have child-molesting records which the police would discover. He also hoped no enterprising investigator would make a connection between their deaths and the other pedophile deaths.

"That's eleven more," he said aloud as he drove up Highway 5 toward Los Angeles, his next target. According to Jan's math, if all the pedophiles he just killed had already molested half their lifetime victims, he just saved about 264 more kids. "Not bad," he muttered, calculating the overall tally so far at about 360. He was trying hard to couch the increasing guilt he felt about his mission and ignore the excruciating pain in his head, which had been surrounded by the black cloud for several days. He knew he had to find a way to keep the pain and the cloud at bay if he was to finish what he had started.

CHAPTER 28

With the sound of an old favorite, the Rolling Stones' "Midnight Rambler" ringing in his ears, Dan drove up Highway 5 to Los Angeles. As Mick Jagger bellowed "Well, you heard about the Boston Strangler" and as he listened to the song's smooth harmonica, the San Diego murders began to collapse inward on him. Up to this point he had thwarted off the guilt for taking human lives, no matter how admirable the reason. Now he was leaving the first phase of his mission behind and his only hope of fending off the dark cloud of remorse was to concentrate on the centerline of the highway. It was hypnotic, but he couldn't help but think hard about what he was doing as the black cloud again descended upon him.

"I'm talkin' 'bout the midnight rambler," the song went on as Dan lost himself in a whirlpool of guilt. He believed his mission was right, but he couldn't get rid of the feelings of remorse. He also knew that the people he killed were the worst of the worst and that he was saving many lives, but maybe ... just maybe, killing is wrong, no matter what. Maybe he didn't have the right to play God. After all, God created the men he killed. *So, I've destroyed something God created*, he thought. *What was that line from the Bible? What God has created, let no man put asunder.*

With that reflection, he promptly decided not to do something he had been contemplating since he left Washington, kill pedophile priests. It was painfully clear that thousands of Catholic priests had been sexually abusing thousands more kids all over the world for many years while the church stood by and often ignored it. It almost appeared that molesting children had long-been an institutionally-accepted practice with one church official maliciously remarking that, "It's been going on for 2000 years and the church is still here."

That kind of wicked arrogance made him livid with rage, but there were several reasons he decided not to go after them. For one thing, there were too many of them. For another, many of the abusers were either dead or too senile to do any more molesting. Besides, he wanted to believe that since the scandal had gotten so much media attention, fewer priests will be likely to abuse children in the future. And then there was Jan. Such a devoted Catholic was she, that she wouldn't be able to forgive him if she ever found out. But most of all, he was afraid that God might severely punish him if he killed his holy representatives, no matter how evil and unholy they may be, and he didn't want to take that chance.

"I'm talking 'bout the midnight gambler," droned the stereo.

Then again, Dan reflected, *if God created everything … he created killing and that's what I'm doing. He created mass killing in the animal kingdom … hell, the killing done by many animals would make the killing done by humans look like nothing, and aren't we just a higher form of animal? Besides, lots of animals kill to protect their young and isn't that exactly what I'm doing?*

By the time Mick Jagger sang "I'll shove my knife right down your throat and baby that hurts," Dan had decided that what he was doing was right, cloud or no cloud. He further resolved that his guilty feelings were just a natural reaction to the disdainful business of murder and that they were distracting him from his quest. He then remembered his old sergeant's words, "never question your instincts … when you do, you lose them." His instincts had kept him alive in Iraq and they would make him successful now if he could just follow them. He vowed to himself to consciously control his guilt and not let it interfere with the most important mission of his life. Still, he knew he wouldn't go after the priests. *Better to be safe than sorry*, he thought as the cloud swirled around him.

He was soon in L.A. and he headed into town looking for a motel to use as his base of operations. He found one, checked in, and immediately booked a flight to Denver under a different name. He would stay in the Rockies for a week and send a letter to Jan to establish an alibi.

A week later he returned to Los Angeles, called the main L.A. police station and asked about access to its pedophile records. To his amazement, it was even easier than San Diego. The switchboard connected him with the police information officer right off the bat and he gave him the needed permission on the spot. After the first good night's sleep he had had since he left Washington, Dan got up and put on another disguise. This time he had brown hair and eyebrows and a fat double chin. He wore an inflatable body suit, which made him look 60 pounds heavier. He drove to the station and sifted through the records.

* * *

It had been 5 days and Ross Huggins hadn't gotten a response to his request from the San Diego Police Department for updated information for his FBI pedophile study. He was about ready to call the new pedophile deaths a fluke when they called and told him about a bizarre mass murder where eleven men were killed in what police were calling a drug deal gone bad. Some teen-agers found the bodies while having a beer bust at a local gravel pit. "Yeah," said Ross, "so?"

"So," said the voice at the other end of the phone, "you might be interested to know that two of the dead guys were convicted pedophiles."

"Gotta' be more than coincidence," Ross told his boss Don Westerhoff as he asked for more time to analyze some new data.

"Take all the time you want on this one," was Don's reply and Ross requested another round of updated death statistics from around the country, beginning with California.

* * *

As Dan leafed through the Los Angeles Police records he realized that all police records look about the same.

Most of the child molesters in Los Angeles had similar records to those in San Diego, until Dan came across something unexpected and unique. In the file was a report from the FBI on an L.A. based motorcycle gang called El Muerto that was suspected of kidnapping children and selling them. "Shades of Tyrone Palmer," he lamented.

The report detailed the gang's mode of operation, listed the places it hung out, and recorded the names and addresses of its leaders. Dan was disgusted and pleased. Disgusted that child stealing was more organized than he had ever before dreamed, but pleased that he had a chance to wipe part of it out entirely. He impulsively wanted to make El Muerto his first L. A. case, but knew that it could get very messy. If he targeted them first he might not be able to hit the rest of his list. He put the gang on the back burner and concentrated instead on Damien Howard, the first on his list.

His thought was that he couldn't let guilt interfere with justice as the cloud descended and he returned to his motel to plan Mr. Howard's demise.

"This is a tough one," Dan said out loud as he sat in his car keeping an eye on Damien Howard two-and-a-half weeks later, "19 straight days and nothing to show for it." Cops often talk to themselves when they are alone on a long stakeout.

Howard had been convicted of molesting a 7-year-old boy who lived in his neighborhood two years earlier and had actually served a year in prison. He was now a dishwasher in a cheap L.A. diner. Dan watched his every move and saw no evidence of pedophilia. A search of his apartment turned up nothing.

He had been convicted on solid charges and Dan thought maybe he should kill him anyway. But he knew he couldn't risk killing an innocent man. So, he gave up on Damien Howard after three weeks and went on to the next name.

"Brian Armstrong, come on down," he said out loud as he sat in his motel room studying the information. Brian Armstrong had been convicted three times of child molesting and had served two years in prison. He was unemployed and living with his mother in a small house in the L.A. suburb, El Segundo. After watching him for several days Dan discovered his one regular habit; taking long evening walks to a park about three miles from his house which was a meeting place for homosexuals. Once there, he made contact with another gay man and they had sex in a nearby wooded area. The interesting thing about Armstrong's frequent sojourns to the park was that he took a different route each time and always seemed to be looking for something.

* * *

Detective Derek Lindsay discovered that kiddie pimp Ali Ban Hashemi conducted his legitimate business over his cellular phone whether in his apartment or his Mercedes. Since tapping the cellular phone would be too difficult, Lindsay went to the telephone company for copies of Hashemi's long distance bills. Lacking a valid warrant for the bills he simply altered the dates and phone number on an old warrant he had used two years earlier to get the bills of a drug dealer. The phone company accepted the forged document and turned over copies of the bills he requested. Unfortunately, most of the cellular phone calls were to numbers that had been left on the answering machine, and to other genuine, foreign business contacts. None were made to anyone Derek could tie to a child prostitution ring.

"All this tells me," Derek told his partner Sean, "is that he never sets up the kiddie deals on the cellular in his apartment. Either he hasn't done one in the last few weeks or he's leaving the apartment to call from another phone in the building and I'll never catch him doing that."

So, frustrated, he was right back where he started; with absolutely nothing on Hashemi. Sitting in the food wrapper strewn, rented office across the street, he gradually accepted the harsh reality that the clock was ticking on his ten-week authorization, and things didn't look at all promising. Daydreaming about the wasted time and hours of overtime, his attention suddenly focused on Hashemi's Mercedes pulling out of the parking garage and into traffic. He immediately followed it mumbling, "please go to a pay phone. I promise I won't lose you this time."

* * *

As Armstrong walked through a secluded area he saw a boy about eight or nine years old sitting on the sidewalk playing with toy army figures. "Hi," Armstrong said, "I see you like army men. You know what, I sell army men to toy stores and I've got a hundred of them that were left over from the last sale. I don't need them and if you want them I'll give them to you." Dan suddenly knew that Armstrong found what he had been looking for.

"Really?" the boy asked.

"Really," Armstrong assured him. "They're in my car," he motioned down the street toward a small wooded area, "come on and I'll give them to you."

The boy hesitated a moment reflecting on his mother's warnings about strangers. But, this guy is going to give me a hundred army guys, he thought and his fears abated. He followed Armstrong down the street.

As Dan watched through his binoculars, Armstrong grabbed the boy, clamped his hand over his mouth, and quickly carried him into the woods. His impulse was to run to the boy's aid and kill Armstrong, but he restrained himself, knowing that such an action could blow his whole operation. Instead, he got closer to the patch of woods to see if Armstrong tried to kill the boy. If he did, Dan planned to intervene no matter what the risk to his mission. But sickening as it was to watch, the boy only stood at knifepoint masturbating the man. When he finished with a shudder, Armstrong told the sobbing child to stay where he was for ten minutes. He said if he moved before that he would come back and kill him. Armstrong fled into the night leaving the lad shivering with fear and confusion.

"What about my army guys?" he whimpered pathetically after Armstrong left.

"That's your last one, Brian Baby," Dan whispered as he walked back to his car. The next night would be Armstrong's last on earth.

At 6 o'clock sharp the next evening Brian Armstrong walked out the front door of his mother's house and headed for his favorite park, deliberately taking a route far from the one he took the night before. Dan followed, absent-mindedly patting a slight bulge in his jacket sleeve.

It was dark when Armstrong made his sexual rendezvous among the trees. When they were done, they kissed and left in opposite directions. As he walked out of the trees, Armstrong saw someone standing in the middle of the path. It was Dan and he said, "Did you think you could get away with raping little kids forever, Brian?"

"Wha…?" was all that came from Brian's mouth as he tried to figure out who it was.

"I'll make it easy for you … you can't."

The two were fifteen feet apart when Armstrong did the last thing Dan expected him to do. He deftly pulled a .38 caliber handgun from a shoulder holster under his jacket and leveled it at him.

"Son-of-a-bitch!" was all he had time to sputter as he dove behind a nearby bush feeling the first bullet whiz by his head. He knew the bush wouldn't stop the next few bullets and desperately hoped Armstrong was not a good shot. Instantly jumping to his feet while pulling his knife out of a sleeve holster he heard two more shots as he drew back his arm and threw it with blinding speed for a bull's eye in the heart. Still holding the gun Armstrong dropped where he stood, gasped once, and died instantly. Dan rushed over and checked for a pulse. There was none. He then pulled his knife out, whipped a note from his jacket pocket and pinned it to the dead man's shirt. The note read:

"This public service brought to you by the Anti-Fag Coalition of Greater Los Angeles."

Dan beat a retreat to his car four blocks away, asking himself how he had missed the gun.

The L.A. Police Department recorded it as another gay-bashing incident by one of the anti-gay groups that had cropped up in Southern California recently. Dan watched it on the local news.

Back in his room he examined his information on his next target. The scene of his bloody knife sliding out of Brian Armstrong's bloody chest kept overpowering him. He couldn't concentrate and he could feel the black cloud coming back. This had been more up close and personal than the others. It bothered him. Little by little, the view that taking a human life for any reason was immoral crept back into his consciousness, and the dark cloud plagued him more and more. All he had to do to get this bothersome idea out of his head was to think of what his commander had drilled into him in Iraq. "These people are the enemy," he had said so many times, "They need to be killed. If you hesitate to kill them because of any moral question, they will kill you or your fellow soldiers and none of you will be alive to even ask that moral question. When in doubt … kill."

Like the good, disciplined soldier he still was, Dan forced the nagging doubts out of his mind. They were natural obstacles to his mission; obstacles he must overcome. More and more he began to see little difference between his present life and his life in Iraq. Again, he felt he was a front-line soldier in a war of us against them. But just starting to seep into his consciousness was the awareness that both were losing wars. Iraq didn't accomplish anything, and it became more and more apparent to Dan that his crusade was only putting a slight dent in the number of pedophiles waging war on the nation's children.

CHAPTER 29

Once again Dan woke with an incredibly painful headache. He wondered if the headaches were trying to tell him something. But he quickly put an end to this train of thought. After taking twice the recommended dose of extra-strength aspirins he went to the address of the next name on his list and found it to be a building that had been torn down six months earlier. He figured urban renewal saved this one's life.

He also had trouble with the next three names on the list; they were not at the addresses listed in the police records and none of their neighbors knew where they had moved. "Man, I guess I just got lucky in San Diego," he muttered as he walked down the steps of the last apartment building. But the next name on the list wasn't so fortunate.

Roger Buckman had been convicted of molesting his seven-year-old niece a few years earlier and had served four years in prison. His file said he had been rehabilitated and had a clean record since prison. He was now self-employed as an electrician in Covina. It was stakeout time.

As with all the others Dan followed Buckman's every move, which mostly consisted of driving from the apartment where he lived alone to and from his electrician jobs around the Covina area. Dan didn't have to wait long on this one. A search of Buckman's house turned up a large collection of kiddie sex videotapes and magazines with pictures of adult men having sex with young girls ranging in age from 4 to 12.

Roger was into little girls instead of boys. "What a refreshing change," he muttered to himself. The thought stunned him. He suddenly realized that while he was horrified at the idea of an adult having sex with any child, he was a little less instinctively repulsed by the idea of a man having sex with a little girl than by the thought of a man having sex with a young boy. He realized that both crimes were equally hideous, but that while they both were pedophilia, homosexual pedophilia seemed more vile and unnatural to him. "Maybe Jan was right," he grumbled to himself, "Maybe I am homophobic."

Searching further and putting each item back where he found it one-at-a-time, Dan found a note containing a date, time, place, and the name Sexy Sissy. He instantly memorized it, which wasn't that difficult because the date was that day, the time was nine o'clock that night and the place was a sleazy bar called The Roost in nearby Chino. Remembering that some kiddie sex magazines offered children for rent, Dan thumbed through the magazines on a hunch. It didn't take long to find what he was looking for. In the classified ad section of a magazine called Young and Beautiful, under the video tape heading was an advertisement that read "Sexy Sissy! A thrill ride you'll never forget!" and a post office box address.

Either Roger is going to this bar tonight to pick up a kiddie videotape or this is a code for actually renting Sexy Sissy herself, reasoned Dan. Then, looking at the rest of the videotape ads, he saw that you could order them by mail. *Why would he pick one up in person*, he wondered. He examined the Sexy Sissy ad closely to see how it might differ from the other ads and found one distinguishing mark. In the lower right-hand corner of the small advertisement was a single black dot that wasn't present in any of the others. "This has got to be a code," he murmured.

But he didn't have time to ponder his discovery because just then his trained ear heard the sound of Buckman's pick-up truck pulling into the driveway. He was home early. This was the earliest he had returned during the week-long stakeout. It did help that the truck had a loud exhaust system. Dan was in a cool panic, but like the professional he was, the first thing he had done upon entering the house was to find a suitable escape route in case something went wrong. He quickly but methodically put the magazines he had been looking at back where they were and without a sound stole out of the back door, silently shutting it just as Roger Buckman came in the front.

* * *

Driving into Chicago, Doug Glassman felt he was entering a new city, even though he had been there several times. The outlying suburbs and the city skyline all seemed new as he anticipated his new life of finally being who he really was. Fumbling with the directions he had been given he drove to the city's west side and found Guild President Barry Anderson's house.

"Douglas!" Barry seemed genuinely glad to see him, "Come in, Come in."

"Thanks," Doug said feeling ill at ease and excited at the same time.

"Did you have any trouble finding the place?"

"No ... no. Your directions were right on the money," Doug answered appreciating Barry's ice-breaking small talk.

"Here let me help you with your things. I'll show you your room. You know you're welcome to stay here until you get on your feet."

"I appreciate it Barry. By the way ... it looks like I may already have that job I told you about."

"Oh great! In insurance?"

"Yeah. Still in insurance ... I guess I can't expect to make too many changes all at once, but it pays the bills. So, I'll probably only need to stay here a couple a weeks, until I find an apartment."

"Well, whatever ... I just want you to know you're welcome as long as you want to stay."

"Thanks so much, Barry ... with everything I'm going through right now it really makes me feel better knowing I've got a friend like you," Doug surprised himself with his honesty, but he felt good saying it.

Barry helped carry Doug's suitcases into his room, gave him some time to rest, then yelled from the living room, "Doug, could you come out here a minute?"

"Sure," Doug said as he entered the living room, "What's up?"

* * *

At 7:30 that evening Dan watched Roger Buckman back his pick-up truck out of his driveway and drive down the street to the Chino Highway. Dan followed, knowing the destination. When the truck pulled into a parking lot with The Roost on one end and a construction site on the other, he stopped at the building site and watched Buckman through his binoculars. In ten minutes, he realized his suspicions were correct. The door to the bar's back room swung open and a middle-aged man with a girl who looked to be about 12 years old came out. She had pigtails and wore a navy-blue school girl's uniform that looked like it had come from a private girl's school. Her male companion opened the door of the pick-up and said something to Buckman as she climbed in. He closed the door and drove off with Dan on his tail thinking sadly, *That's gotta' be Sexy Sissy.* Following a couple of car lengths behind, he saw the girl's head go down on the driver's side of the truck as it pulled out of The Roost's parking lot. "I guess the horny bastard couldn't wait," he groaned. Although it was clear what was going on, he still wanted to be absolutely sure. So, he followed them to a cheap motel a few miles away and checked into the room next to theirs.

Listening through the wall with a stethoscope he heard the unmistakable sounds of sex, and rough sex at that. Convinced he was right, he was about to quit listening and leave when he heard a slap and a shriek. He heard Buckman shout, "You've been a bad girl and I have to punish you," followed by another slap and shriek. Then he heard the girl plead, "Hurt me daddy, Sissy wants it bad." That was enough for Dan. He was out the door and in his car in ten seconds flat, not wanting anything more to do with this warped world of pedophilia. Suddenly this whole affair had turned his stomach into a seething, sour stew and he felt sick to his soul.

Figuring that Buckman would return the girl to The Roost the next day, Dan drove to the bar early the next morning and waited by the nearby building site. At 12 noon Buckman pulled into the lot and Sissy got out to be greeted by the same man who had led her to the truck.

After the Sexy Sissy session Dan followed Buckman for three days watching him do electrical work at three different houses. The first two houses were occupied so there was no chance to get to him. The third house was vacant and Buckman was rewiring it. The plan was simple.

* * *

"There's someone I'd like you to meet Doug," said Guild President Barry Anderson. Douglas Glassman looked behind him to see a brown-haired boy, who looked to be about 13 years old, "Jim this is Doug, a new friend of ours. Doug, meet Jim."

"Hi, I'm Doug Glass ... "

"No, no, no Doug ... we only use first names here."

"Oh ... O.K ... I'm Doug," he said with a nervous chuckle.

"And I'm just plain old Jim," the boy said with an easy friendliness.

"I've got to go to the store," said Barry, "so why don't you two get acquainted. There's beer in the fridge and I'll bring back some steaks."

"Sounds great," said Jim as he turned to Douglas who was already taking a liking to him.

Doug was stunned that he may already be meeting someone who he could have a relationship with. The thought made him so excited he could hardly contain himself, but he realized that he was jumping the gun. Besides, he didn't even know if Jim was involved in the Guild's activities. But when Barry got home he put his mind to rest.

"What do you think of Jim?" Barry asked him when they were alone in the kitchen.

"Nice kid," was all Doug said hoping he was going to hear exactly what he wanted to hear.

"He's yours if you want him."

Doug's brain did a cartwheel and he felt like a kid on Christmas morning. "You mean I could be with him?" he asked incredulously.

"Yes Doug, you can be ... with ... him, if that's how you want to put it. Jim has had relationships with several of our members and is truly a fine boy. You'll find him delightful."

"Oh gosh ... I'm so flustered I can hardly think. I feel like a teen-age boy on his first date."

"I can imagine how you feel after hiding yourself for so long ... so go out there and enjoy yourself and start really living. Frankly, I asked Jim over as a sort of welcome home present for you...'cause you are home now Doug...and I think you two will be good for each other."

"Well, I guess there's no time like the present. Thanks again Barry ... and now, if you don't mind, I think I will start really living." With that Doug walked back out to the living room with two beers, one for him and one for his new friend Jim, or Jimmy as he soon began affectionately calling him.

* * *

In the darkness of night, Dan slipped into the house Roger Buckman was wiring and found the main electric power switch, which was turned off. Dan disassembled the switch and reversed it so that it looked like the power was turned off when it was actually on. He went back to his motel room and slept his usual fitful sleep. Again, he saw Cole in his dreams. This time he dreamed he was outnumbered in a big firefight in an Iraqi desert when Cole appeared up in the sky barely blocking out an unusually bright sun. But there was something different about the sun in this dream. It was warm and loving instead of bright and blinding. His son beckoned to him, trying to tell him something, but he couldn't understand what he was saying. Then, in a sudden burst of clarity, he was sure he heard the words *prophecy* and *providence*.

Rising early the next day Dan drove to the house and parked nearby. Shortly, when Roger Buckman arrived he carried his tools inside. Dan waited ... and waited ... and waited. All day and into the night he waited and Buckman did not come out. When darkness fell Dan entered the house and found him lying on the bedroom floor, still clutching a pair of pliers whose rubber insulation had partially worn off of the handle. He had been up on a ladder working on the ceiling wiring when his pliers came into contact with a live wire. Dan calmly went down to the basement junction box and re-wired the main power switch back to its original configuration. He walked out of the house whispering to himself, "That's one parboiled pervert."

The silly reference did nothing to dispel his oppressive mood and he drove to The Roost where he waited at the construction site near the bar's parking lot with his binoculars. He could feel the black cloud close behind, almost chasing him.

* * *

Jan and Susan Jensen developed a friendship that went beyond their journalist-subject relationship. They met two times a week for dinner and occasionally had drinks at downtown Washington, D.C. bars. Susan liked Jan's strength and Jan loved their intellectual conversations, something she didn't get enough of these days.

"If this one works, I plan to make a full-time career out of making documentaries," Susan said one night, "Once you get a good track-record, the grant money starts to flow."

"What are some of your other ideas for subjects?" asked Jan.

"Population growth, for one," answered Susan, "To insure a surviving son or two, many Africans have six or so children, knowing that several of them will die. If you could show 'em that their kids will live and give them enough birth control pills, they'll naturally have fewer children. That should make the pro-choicers happy and achieve more population control without massive abortions and make the pro-lifers happy in the process."

"So, both sides are happy. That would be quite a feat. What else?"

"Well, there's always climate change, but it's such a huge subject, I would have to narrow it down to one part of the overall issue."

"Anything in mind?"

"Yes, the economics involved."

"Like what?"

"Well, how do you explain the fact that the U. S. contributes about 25% of the world's pollution, but yet pulled out of the Paris Climate Accords because it's too expensive for American businesses?"

"Maybe it is."

"But, it's not. According to one respectable study, if we do nothing, climate change will cost the world $1 billion a day by 2027. That's *a day*. So, in reality, doing nothing will cost us more than doing something."

"Yeah, we do think too short-term, don't we?"

"Always have. Corporate America is so short-sighted with its eyes on short-term profits that it can't see that it stands to make more money with the development of alternative energy systems than it makes with oil."

"Can you back that up with real data?"

"O.K. how 'bout this? Last year more jobs were created in the alternative energy industry than in the oil business. But let's forget these little tid-bits of information and look at the bigger picture. If the planet doesn't survive the pollution, it won't matter who did the polluting or who's right or who's wrong because we're all dead." Susan was on a roll now and feeling more and more enthusiastic about her arguments.

"Sounds like a doomsday scenario," Jan said.

"Well, it could be, if we don't wise up soon. But there's another part of climate change that would probably make an even better documentary."

"What's that?"

"It's wiping out our water supply and right now 750 million people around the world have no access to clean water. Oh, it's also starting wars."

That was something Jan remembered Dan saying and she asked, "How's it doing that?"

"Higher temperatures 'cause increased evaporation and that can produce droughts. Right now, a lot of Africa's fertile land is turning into barren desert and people are fighting over the scarcity of good farmland leaving tens of thousands dead and millions more displaced. By 2050 estimates are that 25 million to 1 billion people will be forced to migrate."

"What countries are we talking about right now?"

"Oh, Mali, South Sudan, and the Central African Republic to name a few ... but it's not just lower Africa. Droughts led to civil wars in Syria and Yemen and in Yemen, alone, 8.5 million people are on the verge of starvation."

"That's a lot of people."

"It sure is, but the real crime is that 85,000 children have already died there of starvation."

"And Syria?"

"That's an interesting place. Climate change was actually one of the causes of the war there in the first place."

"How's that?"

"It can make storms stronger, cold spells longer, and water supplies drier."

"So?"

"So," Susan went on, "That added to all the other social stressors there and helped kick it into high gear. Syria had the worst drought on record between 2006 and 2011 and it destroyed agriculture there causing many farm families to move to the cities. That added to the ethnic and cultural conflicts already created by refugees pouring in from the war in Iraq. But it wasn't just that. The drought also pushed up food prices, which aggravated the poverty that was already there and that was it. Voila! Civil war."

"What about the rest of the Middle-East?" asked Jan, now enthralled by the conversation.

"The news isn't much better there. The entire region is facing a drier, hotter climate because climate change is doing two things. Higher temperatures are increasing evaporation and that makes for more dried-up dirt. Then weaker winds bring less rain from the Mediterranean during the wet season. Heck, the Tigris and Euphrates rivers are even starting to dry up."

"So, all these never-ending wars are all because of climate change?"

"Not all, of course, but certainly some. There're also a lot of economics involved. For instance, there's nothing more expensive than being poor in the third world."

"How's that?"

"Well, did you know that in many water-deprived countries poor people get their water from water trucks and pay more for it than people with money?"

"I did not know that."

"And that's what causes populist uprisings and starts wars. Anyway, it does look like the areas with the biggest water problems seem to be the ones with the most security problems. Just look at Africa and Southeast Asia. One study says that over the past 30 years in Sub-Saharan Africa, the rise in temperatures correlated with an increase in the likelihood of civil war. After all, when you're starving, you go to war."

"Yeah, but you know those studies," Jan said, "They can say anything they want."

"True," Susan answered back, "But another one showed that climate change pushed up food prices in Egypt and that started the revolution there."

"Again," Jan said, "Another study that reaches the conclusion it wants."

"Could be, but I just think that from all the evidence, it's pretty clear that drought is stressing water resources all over the world and it makes sense that it would hit hardest in the deserts of places like the Middle-East that are already dried up."

"And cause more wars I suppose."

"Yup, that's what the evidence points to."

"I suppose," Jan said, "But how do we know it's all caused by climate change and how do we know we're causin' it?"

"We don't," Susan answered, "But apparently the rest of the world does."

"Huh?"

"Yeah, 95% of the world's scientists from 80 different countries agree that it is and that we're causin' it."

"How about world health for a subject?" As a nurse, Jan had always been interested in the health problems in other countries.

"That's a good one too. Fifteen hundred people die every hour from diseases like AIDS and malaria and tuberculosis. One million people will die of malaria alone this year and TB killed eight-and-a-half-million people last year. Do you realize that the number of kids who die from malaria each year would fill seven jumbo jets a day."

"What is it with you lefties and the airplane analogies?" Jan joked, "I also heard that two jumbo jets full of people die each day from cigarettes."

"It's true," Susan said laughingly, "1200 people die every day from lung cancer."

"But I thought TB and Malaria were cured a long time ago."

"They were supposed to be and they could be. But tuberculosis is still big in South America, Asia, and the former Soviet Union, and there's a new strain going around Africa that regular medicine doesn't work on."

"No kiddin."

"No kidding. It's called XDR for 'extensively drug resistant' and it's probably spreading from South Africa to Lesotho, Swaziland, Mozambique, and Zimbabwe. Actually, it may explode in Africa because of HIV."

"How so?"

"TB thrives when the immune system is weak and millions of people in Africa have weak immune systems from AIDS. If it gains a foothold in the HIV population it could spread to tens of millions in sub-Saharan Africa and then we have a real pandemic on our hands."

"Why don't we do something about it?" Jan asked innocently.

"Good question. We're the richest country in the world and we don't bother to spend the few dollars it would take to save millions of lives. We would rather spend it saving our oil and kill people in the process."

"You mean like in the Middle-East?"

"Among others," Susan answered, "In many countries, especially in Africa, the poverty is so bad that the only way a man can support his family is to become a soldier. So, men are joining the military and fighting their own people who are, of course, considered rebels. If we could provide these people with education and jobs they wouldn't have to join the military and might even rise up and fight for their rights."

"Yeah, I 'spose the big problem is that the education and jobs you're talking about don't go over real big with the ruling junta. And even if we could give them both, most of the countries don't have the infrastructure to support a growing economy."

"True. That's why we would first have to build their infrastructures."

"Sounds good, but I'm not so sure they would know what to do with it."

"That's where the education comes in."

"Maybe. But, again, the dictators in these countries don't want their people to be educated because they might realize how bad they've got it and revolt."

"You're right there."

Their heavy conversation was interrupted by two drinks arriving at their table bought by two men across the bar. "We'll take 'em," Jan said, "I just hope they're not too disappointed when we leave after we drink 'em."

"Screw them," said Susan said with half-a-smile, "They should know better. Besides, they're too young for us."

They often attracted young men's advances and got a big kick out of it. In Washington, men were often judged by the jobs they held and the cars they drove, not necessarily in that order. The fact was that both women were more interested in each other's company than in one-night stands with good-looking, sexy, over-confident Washington executives, lawyers or politicos driving Porsches. Nevertheless, each still harbored occasional primal urges.

* * *

For five nights Dan saw nothing out of the ordinary. On the sixth night Sexy Sissy appeared again with her middle-aged companion. They came out of the same back room and headed for a car in the parking lot. Her escort guided her to the car, watched her get in, turned around, and headed back to The Roost. But this time Dan intercepted him before he could walk through the door.

"What's your name, Partner?" Dan asked nonchalantly.

"Peter Pan," was the flippant reply, "Who wants to know?"

"My little friend," Dan answered as he jammed his .357 magnum into his spine, "And he gets very jumpy when he doesn't get an answer ... fast!"

"Paul Politzki!"

"Uh. Uh. Now tell me your real name or they're going to have to scrape what's left of your head off the parking lot," Dan said cocking the gun.

"O.K. O.K. My first name really is Paul. My last name is Deats."

"What do your friends call you?"

"Pauli."

"Just wondered Pauli, good bye," and with that Dan pulled the trigger once and Paul Deats fell like a rock. Dan dumped the corpse in his car trunk and drove to the construction site where a radio tower was being put up. He got out of the car and carried it to a deep hole in the center of the site. In talking to one of the construction workers that day he learned that the tower would be sunk into this hole which would then be filled with concrete the next day. As soon as the crew got off work Dan had climbed down into the hole and dug it four feet deeper. He put Pauli's body in the hole and covered it up with dirt, smoothing the area down so that no one could tell there had been more digging. "Just think Pauli," he said to the soft night air, "You're now in the communication industry." His humor did nothing to dispel the now ever-present black cloud surrounding his aching head. Dan then drove back to his motel, got cleaned up and climbed into bed for another restless night's sleep.

The next day at 11:00AM he went back to the bar and hung an envelope containing two thousand dollars and a note on the door through which Sissy and her escort had come. The envelope was addressed to Sissy and the note said "I'm getting out of here fast and getting away from this life. You do the same. Do not go into the bar. It is very dangerous for you here now. Take this money and go home." Dan signed the note "Pauli" hoping Sissy would think it was from her pimp. He got back in his car and waited for Sissy's return.

While he was waiting he watched as a crane lifted the radio tower up into the air preparing to lower it into the big hole that would become its permanent home. His body tensed as he saw the crew foreman signal to the crane to stop and began peering down into the abyss intently. Both hands gripped the steering wheel tightly as he saw the foreman climb down to the edge of the hole. His knuckles were white and his body was like an overly-taut bowstring. He was just about to ease the car out of the parking lot when the foreman came back out of the chasm and motioned for the crane to continue. His sweaty hands slid off the steering wheel and every muscle in his body relaxed as he saw the workers lower the tower and pour in several tons of concrete. "I'd say you got a better tombstone than you deserve," he said absent-mindedly, looking at the tower, "At least you got a bigger one than most." Dan figured someone who was so low as to be pimping for little girls probably wasn't going to be missed by anyone and probably wouldn't even be reported as a missing person.

At 12:15PM Sissy and her client, pulled into the parking lot. She got out and started walking toward the bar's back room looking around for Pauli. Her client drove away with Dan behind him. As he drove by her, Dan saw Sissy open the envelope and begin reading the note. Getting his first good look at her in daylight, he noticed her face showed a tragic loss of innocence. Like many child sex abuse victims, she looked numb and worn. He hoped she would take the note's advice.

Now he had other things to think about, such as how to eliminate her date who was driving down the road in front of him. His prey pulled onto the freeway with

Dan keeping a safe distance behind him. But Dan hadn't anticipated one thing. L.A. drivers get so few opportunities to drive uncongested freeways that when they do get the chance they drive like it's the Indianapolis 500. This guy was no exception. Dan made the mistake of staying too far back and lost sight of his target. By the time he accelerated to catch up, he had gotten off on an exit and was gone for good.

"Damn, what an idiot I am!" He beat his hands on the steering wheel and screamed, "I can't even keep a dumb pervert in sight! I must be losing it!" Deep inside Dan was almost glad this one had gotten away. He didn't really feel up to another murder so soon. At this point the guilt gnawed at him like maggots on a dead dog. He felt the cloud's presence constantly. He went back to his motel and stared at the flickering TV for hours. Drifting in and out of sleep at times he almost thought he saw a familiar face on the screen trying to tell him something. The pain was getting unbearable and he was almost ready to give up. But something told him that it was not yet time.

CHAPTER 30

The next name on the list was Alan Demerest. He had been convicted of sexually molesting a six-year-old boy a year ago and had received a five-year prison sentence of which he served three-and-a-half years. Alan was married with a daughter, and worked as a computer programmer. He appeared to be fairly well off, living in a nice house near a canyon. The fact that he was married and a father bothered Dan a little, but not enough to deter him from his mission.

In what had by now become routine, Dan followed Demerest's every move, staying especially close whenever he drove on the freeway. In three weeks of surveillance he saw only a model husband and father. If it had been any other case Dan might have given up. But with this one he felt an obsession he couldn't explain. Something told him the subject was guilty as sin and he decided to hold on for the long run. Besides, because of the problems he had run into earlier, he was behind on the number of pedophiles he had set as a goal and he didn't want this one to add to the deficit.

Then it happened. The lucky break. On day 20, Alan Demerest deviated from his regular home-to-work-to-home routine and drove to Santa Monica Boulevard in Hollywood. The boulevard was notorious, to anyone who was interested, as a big chicken hawk area. Kids from all across the United States managed to scrounge up enough money for a bus ticket to L.A., as if it were the solution to all of their problems; as if it were Mecca or paradise where everything was good. Then, after days and weeks of hunger and desperation, many of them ended up on Santa Monica Boulevard, selling the only commodity they had ... themselves. It was an American tragedy.

Men like Alan Demerest didn't see it that way. What they saw was an opportunity to satisfy an uncontrollable, burning desire of which many of them were ashamed, but which raged in their hearts. Dan followed as Alan drove slowly down the Boulevard, making eye contact with every young boy on the sidewalks that he could. Finally, he pulled over and a boy about 12 or 13 years old walked over to his car. Dan eased to the curb and watched as the boy got into Demerest's car and it drove away. Following at a distance, he knew what was coming and he really didn't want to watch. Yet, because he felt a strong urge to verify his target's guilt, he followed the car and what he saw did not surprise him.

Demerest and his new acquaintance checked into a nearby cheap motel. Dan didn't have to check in next to them to figure out what was going on. Santa Monica Boulevard was probably the most famous chicken hawk district in the country and a man picked up a boy there for only one reason. Dan waited outside of the motel for several hours until Demerest and the boy came out. Alan drove his young friend back to Santa Monica Boulevard, let him out, and then drove off as if nothing had happened. Dan followed, planning Demerest's execution. He followed him back to his suburban home and then returned to his motel for some sleep. He would deal with this target the next day.

* * *

"How long has it been for you?" Susan asked Jan one night after several White Russians.

"Well," Jan reflected, "It hasn't been that long. Danny and I had quite a session before he left. But before that it had been almost half-a-year ... I basically lost my sex drive when Cole disappeared," she admitted looking down at her drink and pondering the phenomenal sex she and Dan used to have.

"I can understand that."

"I wish Dan could have."

"Well, you know men. It's the BBB syndrome."

"The what?"

"The BBB syndrome. You know ... brains below belt."

"Oh yeah ... my therapist says the same thing. No matter how sensitive or liberal a guy is, he still thinks with his lower half."

"I know. But I don't really see the big attraction. I mean ... I can take it or leave it. There are times, though, that I need it and I just wish I could have a sex prince for one night and he would disappear in the morning. Unfortunately, there's always the next morning and that generally keeps me celibate."

"You mean you aren't ... involved with anyone?"

"I mean I make it a point to never get involved ... but I still have a sex drive that rears its ugly head once in a while. That's what it is ... a sex drive and nothing more. Not a desire for love and affection ... just a desire for simple, rock hard sex. Sometimes I just want a man

to ... excuse my French ... fuck me. Not make love to me, just fuck me. I just don't like the things that go along with it, like having to see the guy again."

"Well, I'd be lying if I said I never felt that way. There are certainly times I would rather

be ... you know ... than made love to. But ... it sounds so cynical."

"It does and I'm not real crazy about the way I feel. I really would prefer to be in your shoes when it comes to romance. I wish I had a guy I loved and had been married to for a while ... but that just doesn't seem to be me."

"Why do you suppose you feel that way? Are you afraid of the 'C' word?"

"Commitment? Yea, a little. But I think it has a lot to do with my sister. After seeing what an unbridled sex drive did to her I kind of got soured on sex. Unfortunately, for women, when you get soured on sex you often also get soured on love and affection."

"Well, that I can relate to. I would say Danny and I had one of the best marriages around before Cole disappeared. We loved each other very much and our sex life was truly phenomenal. But when Cole went, so did my desire for sex and from then on it was downhill."

"But ... I thought..."

"I know. I told you about the good parts of my marriage, but I left out the bad. When I first lost my sex drive I still loved Dan and really felt that we could have a good marriage without it. Dan disagreed and as time went on he grew more and more distant. I know I was a walking loony tune and then a zombie from my medication, but we grew so far apart I really wonder if we can ever get back together. It all started because of something as stupid as sex."

"Oh, I didn't realize. What about him being gone ... isn't that making things worse?"

"Probably, but I didn't have much choice. By the time he told me I knew he had already made up his mind and I couldn't stop him unless I did something like threaten suicide. That just isn't me. I wouldn't threaten it unless I was going to do it. But, I really wasn't all that sorry to see him go. I mean our feelings for each other were at a low ebb and if he had stayed I think they may have just gotten lower. Besides, I've got all I can handle right now maintaining my own sanity without dealing with his problems too. Does that sound callous?"

"No, it sounds strong. A lot like me. I don't care what the situation is, I believe you owe yourself more than you do others. I mean, compassion for others and treating people fairly is fine, but start with yourself. . . make yourself right ... then you can go on to the people around you. I don't think you can be right with the rest of the world until you're right with yourself and that's all you were trying to do."

"Well, I'd like to believe that."

"Where is Dan these days?"

"I'm not sure. I think he's in Colorado because that's where I got the last letter from. But he could be anywhere."

"Doesn't he keep in regular touch with you?"

"No, but that's not that unusual. He has gone on several trips, some on undercover assignments and some just for fun or to get his head straight. Most of the time he never kept in close touch. He's like that and we both got used to it. In our own ways we have both been pretty independent and I'm not really the worry-wart type."

"I think that's great. It sounds like you had something good going for a while ... something I could envy. I'm sorry for the way things have turned out, Jan."

"I know, Sue. Other people have told me the same thing, but with you, for some reason, I can tell you really mean it. You know, you have been good for me. I never would have thought that this late in life I would have made a friend like you, but I consider you a really good friend and I want you to know it."

"I feel the same way Jan. I know this sounds crazy, but I almost feel like you are the sister that I lost. Because of what happened to her we could never have the kind of sister to sister relationship I would have liked and now, with you, I feel like I'm making up for it."

"That doesn't sound crazy. I'm flattered you feel that way."

"Well, we're lucky that we haven't had a few more high-balls or we might be hugging and slobbering all over each other and making a big spectacle of ourselves."

"Yeah, lucky," Jan chuckled and they both laughed easily, knowing comfort with each other that neither had felt before.

* * *

The morning after he confirmed that Alan Demerest was a pedophile Dan bought several pieces of equipment. Among the purchases were a high-power car battery, two car headlights, and some wiring. After having the battery charged he wired the headlights to it and was pleased to see them light. All he had to do now was wait for nightfall.

At 9:30PM Dan took his homemade light show to the bottom of the steep, winding road which led down from Demerest's neighborhood and ended in a sharp curve to the left. In his surveillance he had found that Demerest liked to drive his sporty Audi fast. He figured that Alan had driven this one-way road so many times, he knew it by heart and was sure that nothing could cause him any problems. Picking up his cell phone, Dan dialed Demerest's number and was relieved when he answered.

"Hi Alan," Dan greeted him, "This is a friend, so listen and listen carefully. I have proof of your pedophilia and I want you to get professional help. I am not interested in blackmailing you for money or anything else, but I will show this proof to your family and employer if you do not meet me right away so we can discuss getting you the help you need. Meet me in 20 minutes in the parking lot of the Express Store on Canyon Drive. Do you know it?"

"Uh ... yes," came the stunned reply.

"I'm in a blue station wagon. Come over and get in my car and I'll explain everything. But if I don't see you in exactly twenty minutes I blow the whistle. Understand?"

"I ... uh ... understand. I'll be there."

Then Dan heard the dial tone whining in his ear and felt like just sitting there and letting it absorb him. But, he knew he had better get to work. First, he set up a sawhorse with the headlights attached to it on the road at the curve, close to the inside. He connected the headlights to one of the battery posts. The other post he left disconnected. Then, he waited.

Five minutes later he heard a car. His night-vision binoculars told him that it was Demerest's Audi. Crouching down in the ditch by the battery he waited. Just as Demerest's car got to the curve Dan connected the remaining headlight cable to the other battery post creating a blinding light that Alan could only have perceived to be an on-coming car. He reacted instinctively, swerving to the right to avoid a head-on collision. The road was narrow and there wasn't much of a right lane to swerve to. Demerest must have realized this at the last minute because he quickly whipped the wheel back to the left and headed right for where Dan was crouched on the side of the road. Dan lurched to the side, the car's bumper scraping a substantial portion of flesh from his arm. A split second later he heard the sound of screeching brakes and the squealing, smashing of metal as the car struck the roadside guardrail. Then, a curious silence, which lasted only a couple of seconds, but seemed like an hour. Finally, an ear-splitting crash as the car veered back to the right, went over the canyon wall, and struck the rocks below where the gas tank exploded.

With blood flowing and an intense, throbbing pain in his arm Dan had only a few minutes to find what was left of his materials. Incredibly most of it was spread out on the road. Driving away he mumbled to himself, "Alan, I guess I saved you the price of a cremation." Deep, down inside he knew he wasn't as callous as he sounded. But he also knew that this callous facade helped him cope with the guilt that was slowly, but surely, building up inside of him. Somehow, acting as if he were a ruthless killer with absolutely no feelings about his victims or his actions helped him bury those feelings.

He sped away with the sound of sirens behind him saying to himself, "I'm getting too old for this shit." But at the same time, he knew that it was now time for possibly the most challenging part of his mission; El Muerto. "With any luck," he mused aloud as the pain increased ten-fold, "I may be able to help the gang live up to its name." He was almost grateful for the stinging pain because it temporarily overwhelmed the black cloud. But he knew it would return as he drove back to his lonely motel room to bandage his wound. He figured he would take a little break to give himself time to heal up and make plans.

CHAPTER 31

The notes spread out in front of Dan said the El Muerto motorcycle gang members spend much of their time at a bar called the Pig's Eye on Highland Avenue in Orange County's Redondo Beach. There wasn't any hard evidence of child stealing, just the statement of a former member who had been arrested on unrelated charges and who told police that while he was in the group he heard talk of such a thing. Detectives staked out the Pig's Eye repeatedly, but turned up nothing. There were too many gang members and the police were too short-handed. Dan knew the only way to crack this one was from the inside. With that he started checking the classified ads for a used Harley Davidson. He had ridden many dirt bikes in his youth, but not many large street bikes. As soon as he bought the 1200cc hog he began practicing his riding skills on the L.A. freeways and highways, all the while giving his arm time to heal.

On a bright, sunny day with the sun showing unusually clear through the smog, Dan pulled into the parking lot of the Pig's Eye. His arm was mostly healed. He had outfitted himself in second hand motorcycle leathers. He hadn't shaved or had a hair cut in over a month. He looked every bit the part of a greasy biker. There were only two cars in the parking lot and about 20 Harleys. Well, it's now or never, he thought as he walked confidently into the loud, blasting music of Guns 'N Roses blaring out of the oversized stereo system.

* * *

Following kiddie pimp Ali Ban Hashemi more closely this time, Detective Derek Lindsay saw him pull into a grocery store parking lot. On a hunch he drove around to the back of the store and there it was: a pay telephone. He knew he had to act fast as he aimed the long-range camera and shotgun microphone directly at the telephone from his car window. With the lens zoomed all the way in he could clearly see the phone's buttons. Then his hunch paid off as Hashemi came strolling out the back door of the store nonchalantly looking in all directions. Dan froze as he looked right at him, but he was too far away to see that there was someone in the car looking back at him. He walked to the phone and dialed a number. The camera got it on tape and everything he said came in clearly over the long-range microphone. "This is Mr. K," Hashemi said, "Tomorrow night, eight o'clock, Hotel Fontainbleu on 165th and Madison, room 138." Derek shook with excitement and satisfaction after Hashemi hung up the phone and walked back into the store. He had no reason to follow his prey any further and drove straight to the police station to run the phone number he had recorded him dialing through the computer. It turned out to belong to Vincent Slazak, a convicted felon who had served time for armed robbery when he was a kid and extortion later as an adult.

* * *

Looking neither right nor left Dan walked right up to the bar in the Pig's Eye, seemingly oblivious to the surprised stares he was getting, and ordered two shots of whisky with a beer chaser. He wondered how the booze would affect him. He hadn't drunk since he arrived in California. He had barely finished ordering when a grunting voice behind him asked, "You lost, motha' fucka'?" The voice belonged to the biggest and meanest member of El Muerto, a man appropriately named Hog.

"No, just slumming," was Dan's instant reply without turning around.

"No, you must be lost," contradicted the guttural voice, "or you wouldn't be here." Dan glanced up at the big mirror in back of the bar to see the reflection of a six foot six, 280-pound behemoth with a beard and a long black, greasy ponytail.

"Well, you look like you'd need a road map to find your ass, let alone where here is," Dan mocked as he discretely gripped the underside of the bar with both hands. The big man's lunge forward was faster than Dan had anticipated, but not fast enough to prevent him from making a move he'd learned while studying Tae Kwon Do. His movement was so quick it was almost imperceptible. Focusing every ounce of energy into one action, Dan kicked his leg backward and connected with his assailant's kneecap while at the same time slamming his right elbow back hard into his nose. Stunned by the blows the giant was slowed only for a moment. "Shit eating fuck!" he spit through the blood streaming down his face. He made another clumsy grab for Dan who still faced the back-bar mirror, drinking a shot of whisky as if nothing had happened.

Dan's quickness again beat his opponent's strength as he gracefully slipped aside and let the big, clumsy fellow's momentum carry him to the bar. Dan administered two quick, hard kidney punches and a knife-hand strike to the back of the neck that sent him head down onto the top of the bar.

"Motherfucker," was all the big guy could muster as he spit out several globules of blood.

"First of all, Gargantua," he said calmly as he broke a beer bottle over his head, grabbed him by the hair with both hands and began bashing his face on the bar, "you must be the one who eats shit since your breath smells like you've had your head up a dog's asshole. Secondly, my parents were married, unlike yours who were undoubtedly brother and sister."

In just a few seconds Dan had stunned the crowd into inaction by seeing the biggest, meanest member of the gang beaten by a stranger. No one had yet moved to help Hog. Then the surprise wore off and as the big man lost consciousness two others charged Dan who, anticipating their move, bounded over to the nearby pool table to grab the best weapon a bar brawler could ask for: a cue stick. Grasping the cue in the middle he smashed the thick, blunt end into the face of the first one to reach him. He then jabbed the small, pointed end into the other's eye and brought the thick end back again into the first man's neck, choking him and putting him out of commission. He kicked the second attacker squarely in the groin, which brought him to his knees and swung the cue like a baseball bat, knocking him out cold.

By then three more El Muerto thugs had jumped out of their chairs and were heading for Dan. Throwing the cue stick like a spear, blunt end first, he hit the one with the knife squarely in the forehead eliminating him from the fray. He leaped up onto the pool table just as the remaining two reached him and started kicking their faces one at a time, in succession, like a Russian step dancer gone wild. In fact, Dan put his hands on his sides and after each kick turned his head aside and yelled, "hey!"

Taking a cue from Dan one of the pool players threw a pool stick at him, heavy end first. But Dan saw it coming and in one lightning-fast motion he caught it and broke it in two over his knee. Now swinging the two sticks in all different directions at the same time he leaped from the table into the middle of the four gang members nearest him and knocked all of them to the floor shrieking in pain.

At this point the gang had had enough. The shock of Dan's performance had worn off and now the entire bar rushed him. But Dan had saved the best for last. He pulled a .38 revolver from his jacket and fired it over their heads twice, stopping them cold. A hush came over the crowd immediately as everyone gaped at this crazy man with a gun. Most of them were undoubtedly armed, but after Dan's exhibition they were more than a little leery of pulling a gun on him. Even the stereo fell silent. Dan's cocky and calm commentary rang through the stillness, "No, no, don't bother to get up. I hate to be rude, but as much fun as this has been I've really got to run." He inched his way to the door smiling and steadily waving the gun back and forth at the crowd. Keeping all of the angry bikers in front of him necessitated keeping his back to the bar, which he considered a calculated risk. But his calculation was wrong. The bartender who had been crouched on the floor throughout the fight suddenly rose up and bashed him on the head with a small baseball bat. He fell like a rock.

"Let's dump him in the canal," yelled someone from the crowd and two men bent down to pick Dan up.

* * *

"Well, here it is, Cap. The pay-off," Detective Derek Lindsay told Police Captain Mark Lewis as he laid everything out, "This is just the tip of the iceberg."

"Whaddya' mean?" Lewis asked already knowing, but wanting to savor the answer.

"I mean if we keep on this we're bound to round up not only Hashemi, but a bunch of kiddie pimps too. We should get our pictures in the paper."

This was what Captain Lewis wanted to hear, hoping that someday it would be Commissioner Lewis. "Good job, Lindsay," was all he said, "You've got all the time you need now. Use whatever resources necessary, but clear the manpower with me."

"Yes sir, Captain sir," Derek said as he left, using the mocking military address he had used as an Army officer.

* * *

"No," came a uniquely strong voice from the back of the Pig's Eye, "The canal will wait." The leader of El Muerto, Lee Santucci had watched Dan kick the crap out of ten of his men without a word. Now he walked toward them and said, "Get his billfold, Hog, and let's see who this crazy mother is." Dan lay on the floor unconscious.

For an instant, with sweat pouring down his face and spitting out a tooth, Hog glared at his leader with disdainful defiance. Then he did as he was told. He always did. The glare, Lee correctly figured, was Hog's way of proving he wasn't a lackey, but he actually was. Everyone in El Muerto did what Santucci ordered out of respect and admiration for him, but also out of fear. Ever since Hog had seen him kill three men armed with knives with his bare hands he had decided to steer clear of conflict with him. "I may be stupid," he had once said to another gang member,

"But I ain't crazy." Lee Santucci, on the other hand, was considered by his gang to be completely crazy and dangerous. That was one reason they all feared him. He had shown on a number of occasions that he was not afraid to push the envelope, to stretch and go beyond all normal limits.

What his gang didn't know and probably wouldn't have understood anyway, was that Lee Santucci had absolutely no morals. Most of the gang had very low moral standards, but all maintained a sliver of an idea of right and wrong. Lee didn't believe there was such a thing. He was an atheist who believed that people made up their own morals. Some of this turpitude was undoubtedly due to his upbringing by an alcoholic uncle after his parents were both killed in a car accident when he was 5 years old. He had basically raised himself. The rest of his moral void was probably formed by the Iraq war. He spent the years during which many people form their ideals and principles in the deserts of Iraq as a member of an Army Special Forces unit. His group called themselves the Death Eaters and its motto was *if it moves kill it*. He did more than his share of killing, finding that he actually enjoyed war. When a combat buddy asked him once on patrol what he believed in he answered, *action*.

"No, I mean what are your moral beliefs?" asked his friend.

After thinking about it for a while Lee had answered, "I don't have any… they shot 'em out of me." He had been wounded and yet signed up for a second tour. The only thing that brought him back home to the United States was a second, more serious wound during his second tour.

"My money says crazy vet," Lee said absent-mindedly, "You ever see a guy fight like

that ... with so much style? Kinda' reminds me of me."

"He just got lucky," grunted Hog.

"Yeah, and if he'd gotten any luckier some of you guys would be dead," said Lee as he looked around at the bleeding members of his gang nursing their wounds.

"Yup, he's a vet alright. He's got a Marine I.D. card in his wallet. His name's Garret Taylor and it looks like he's from Seattle. O.K. now we know who he is. Can we throw his ass in the canal?" asked Hog sarcastically.

"No, just throw some water on him. I want to talk to this suicidal freak." The first thing Dan saw when the cold water brought him out of his coma was Hog's big, ugly face staring at him, "Don't tell me," he said, "I'm in Hell and you're the devil."

"You'll wish I was just the devil before I get through with you, you fucking ... ."

"That's enough Hog. Get Mr. Taylor a couple shots of whisky," said Lee, ignoring the defiant look again. Grumbling, Hog went to get the drinks.

"Hog, huh?" said Dan, "Why doesn't that surprise me. Make it a handful of Percocets too pig ... I mean Hog." His head was pounding like a jackhammer and his arm felt like it was on fire.

"Sit up here Mr. Taylor. I'm Lee Santucci, head of these animals. Tell me just why you came in here. You had to know that this place was not going to welcome you with open arms."

"O.K. O.K. You got me. I'm a member of the Jehovah's Witness Church and I've come to save all you lost souls," Dan said as he painfully pulled himself up onto a chair.

"Uh huh," said Lee with a half-smile, "Now why are you really here?"

"Well, to tell you the truth, I'm with the state bureau of names and I've come to investigate a complaint that there are entirely too many barnyard animals' names being used here. I mean Pig's Eye and Hog ... what is this, Animal Farm?"

Santucci was immediately impressed that a crazy grunt who had just been knocked unconscious would make a casual reference to the George Orwell novel, especially in what could be a tense situation. It showed the guy might actually have a brain and be a reader and a thinker unlike most of the bikers he had associated with over the years, including his fellow El Muerto members.

"O.K. we know you're funny, but you got one more chance to give me a straight answer or I'm gonna' let some of those barnyard animals have you for evening slop."

"Well, since you put it that way, I just got bored and needed a little excrement ... uh, excitement."

"You certainly got that," Santucci looked at Dan long and hard and decided that he almost believed him ... almost. "Actually, I know what you mean. I get a little bored myself. But suicide isn't exactly the answer."

"What ... these guys?" Dan said motioning to the crowd that had gathered around him, "Naw."

"I guess these guys aren't as exciting as Al Qaida ... huh?"

Dan gave him a *how-did-you-know* look.

Lee handed him his wallet and said, "The military I.D. I'm gonna' go out on a limb here and bet you were one of those guys who kinda' liked the action."

"Sorta."

Hog brought the drinks and Santucci offered a toast, "To one crazy motherfucker who reminds me of someone who I admire very much ... me." They swallowed the first of many shots of whisky and Dan was grateful as the pain in his head and arm was growing exponentially.

"Remember," someone from the crowd shouted, "He don't like bein' called a motherfucker." The crowd roared, Hog grunted, the stereo started blaring again, and everyone went back to their own business while Dan and Lee continued their conversation.

* * *

Detective Derek Lindsay took all of the information to a judge who had been helpful to the police department in the past and who was known to be harsh on crimes against juveniles. He got a warrant to put a microphone and surveillance camera in room 138 of the Hotel Fountainbleu the following night, over the loud objections of the hotel manager.

The next evening at six o'clock a middle aged foreign-looking gentleman checked into room 138. At 6:30 he ordered dinner from room service. At seven o'clock he served himself several whisky highballs from the room's honor bar. At eight o'clock the man answered a knock on the door and greeted a young sandy-haired boy of 13. "Come in, come in," he said huskily, escorting the boy into the room while sizing him up with lust. The pedophilic sex act that followed was predictable and captured entirely on videotape.

With another camera Derek had recorded the bronze BMW that drove up to the hotel and dropped the boy off. He had radioed in the car's license plate number and gotten the owner's name and address from the police dispatcher. "What was the phone number on that?" he asked dispatch. "496-3310," was the answer. "Bingo," he almost shouted.

It matched Vincent Slazak's phone number, which he had videotaped Hashemi dialing the day before. This was a solid connection of the kind he so fervently wanted. "Ya' might've slipped up big time ya' creep," he said out loud as he hung up the phone. All he had to do was wait for the boy to come out. At 9:45 the BMW arrived just as the boy came out of the hotel. He got in and the car left with two unmarked police cars following it. At the address Derek had gotten from dispatch, a luxury apartment building on Manhattan's west side, the car pulled into the building's parking garage with one of the police cars not far behind. Officer Jim Waxman, a good friend of Derek's, videotaped the boy walking to the garage's elevator accompanied by a man who appeared to be in his mid-thirties to early forties. It was Vincent Slazak. The investigation was on.

CHAPTER 32

"Who've ya' ridden with?" Lee Santucci asked Dan. He was the president of El Muerto.

"The Angels up in Seattle and a little bit down here in L.A. But that got old."

"Yeah, they're not what they used to be are they?"

"No, and I don't even know what they used to be."

"Well, I rode with 'em for several years, but they got too careful on me, so I quit and started El Muerto. A bunch of guys left the Angels and went with me so I'm not too popular with those assholes."

"That makes two of us. Before I left I played out a scene with them similar to what you just saw here."

"Man, you like it don't ya'?"

"What?"

"The blood and guts and ... excrement?"

"Yeah, I do ... every now and then ... or else I feel like I'm gonna' be bored into a straight-Jacket."

"Me too. That's the big reason I'm running with these Neanderthals. Whenever I feel the need for action it's not too hard to find." Lee didn't know why he was telling this total stranger all this since normally he never discussed his feelings with anyone. But for some reason, it felt right with Dan. "Besides, I realized a long time ago that I'm a leader and who else am I gonna' lead in civilian life?" he finished.

"Makes sense."

Sensing a serious conversation getting started, the rest of the gang left the two men to themselves.

"Besides, this is my place and I call it home."

"I haven't had a place to call home for so long I don't remember it, but that's the way I like it."

"I did too, for a long time, but you might find that your tastes change as you get older."

"Well, that's true. I've sure as hell changed that," Dan motioned over to two scruffy-looking gang members sitting at a table shooting up meth.

"Dope?"

"Yea. I was into smack and blow for a long time. Now I wouldn't give you a dime for either of 'em. Just give me the old reliable," Dan said as he held up a shot of whisky and downed it. He had a hunch that was the conclusion Lee had reached.

"That's funny ... me too." Dan's hunch was right. "My arms used to look like road maps and man I must've spent several fortunes on the shit. But now, like you said, just give me expensive whisky ... and cheap women, of course."

"Of course."

"When I got home from Iraq things were so damn boring that I got into it."

"Yeah, I should be a freakin' millionaire right now with all the shit I sold in Seattle, but as you might guess, it all went in my arm and up my nose."

"I know the feeling. No matter how much coke you have it's never enough. After a while I just made a game out of doing bigger and bigger shots to see if I would die or not. I think if I hadn't stopped when I did I probably wouldn't be here now."

"Yeah, with blow especially, no amount was enough. No matter how much you do you always want more, so it's like a never-ending cycle and that just seems unnatural."

"Not natural like this stuff huh?" Lee chuckled while downing his fifth straight shot of whisky."

"Yeah ... of course, you know what they say ... cocaine is God's way of telling you ya' have too much money."

"Right. A lot of times the only thing that kept me from overdosing was that I ran outta' money to buy more. It makes you so stupid you just keep doing it, if you can afford it, until you die."

"At least with this," Dan said as he held up a shot of whisky, "It takes longer to kill you."

"A little longer than ten seconds anyway. With the other shit you're gonna' buy the farm. That reminds me. You mentioned Animal Farm earlier ... did you actually read it?"

"Didn't everyone ... back in grade school?" Dan answered.

"Yeah," said Lee, "But most of 'em probably don't remember it."

"Apparently, you do, huh?"

"Yup, along with a few others. But you sound like you might be well-read. Who's yer' favorite author?" Lee asked with growing interest, feeling glad that the rest of the bar couldn't hear what he was saying.

"Kurt Vonnegut, Tom Robbins," said Dan.

"Oh, man they're two of my favorites too. Existential and hilarious."

"Thus spake Zarathustra."

"Nietzsche huh! I take it you read the heavy shit too," Lee asked intrigued.

"I've read the cock suckers ... Descarte, Huxley, Sartre and all the other existentialist assholes."

Santucci loved the way his new friend mixed intelligent conversation with crude colloquialisms just as he himself liked to do. It was almost as if neither of them wanted to sound too intelligent, although each was. "I've read 'em too," he said and what followed was a very long and increasingly drunken discussion of the differences in the philosophies of some of the world's great thinkers. Luckily Dan had read his philosophy and could actually discuss it intelligently even while drinking heavily. Thank God for U.V. and long nights with Jack Adams, he thought. Lee often longed for this type of conversation, but had no one to talk to. Dan reluctantly found himself enjoying it also, and even more reluctantly found himself liking this man who may be responsible for untold child abuse.

Finally, late into the night Dan felt he shouldn't over-stay his welcome and got up to leave, his head still aching. "I hate to drink and run, but I've got a rendezvous with a rich young lady who just thinks I'm so excitingly dangerous. I gotta' go, but, um, I enjoyed talking to you Lee and thanks for not killing me."

"Any time Garret."

As he left Dan waved to the crowd and said, "See y'all later and don't think it hasn't been fun, 'cause it hasn't." A few murmured epithets came from the crowd with a "fuck you" from Hog and the rest just ignored him.

"Don't be a stranger man. In fact, bring in your bitch so we can show her some real excitement," Lee yelled after him.

"O.K., but I can't guarantee the bitch. She'll probably find out the kinda' guy I really am and ditch me after I spend all her money. See you guys and let's do this again real soon."

When Dan got out to his Harley he realized just how drunk he was. He also had a splitting headache from the bartender's baseball bat but at least it made him forget about his stinging arm. I'm definitely too old for this shit, he thought as he carefully negotiated the road back to his motel. "But what a surprise," he said to the night wind as he cruised down the freeway, "an intellectual, criminal motorcycle bum."

As for Lee Santucci, it had been a long time since he had met anyone he genuinely liked. Sure, he was the leader of 40 men, all of whom admired and respected him, but he couldn't really say he had a true friend he could relate to among them. The rank and file of El Muerto were tough soldiers who followed his orders to the letter. But none of them were very intelligent and most were just plain crude, and he did feel a void of someone to talk to on his own intellectual terms. Maybe Dan would fill that void and maybe he wouldn't. It wasn't really a big concern of his, but it would be nice if he did.

* * *

"I know it sounds crazy," Ross Huggins told his FBI boss Don Westerhof one morning, "but I'm telling you someone may be systematically killing pedophiles. Whoever it is started in San Diego and moved on to L.A."

"Are you absolutely sure Hug, because we have to be before we take this upstairs?" Don said.

"Am I absolutely sure? No. But there have been just too many deaths of pedophiles in San Diego and Los Angeles to be naturally occurring. Some of them were classified as accidents, some as murders over drugs and one as a possible suicide. But, the fact is that in a two month period there was a 700% increase in pedophile deaths in the two cities and it looks too suspicious to be a coincidence."

"Couldn't it be just a fluke?"

"Yeah, but the odds of that are about two million to one."

"O.K. O.K. You're the statistician. I'll take your report upstairs. And don't tell me, let me guess. If they want this investigated you want the job, right?"

"You read my mind."

"Well, it's probably about time. They've been talking for a while about giving you a field assignment and since you've done the legwork on this one I'd say you've got a good shot at it. But boy you could have picked a better assignment to get your feet wet on."

"Believe me ... I know."

Ross' heart skipped a beat with excitement. "I'll be waiting," was all he said as he anxiously watched Westerhof carry his report out the door.

Since he started his investigation Ross had had to familiarize himself with the whole issue of child sex abuse. He had become physically ill a number of times while watching FBI confiscated kiddie porn films and looking at child pornographic pictures. The children in both were obviously coerced into doing what they did and the men coercing them were obviously inhuman monsters. He often thought of his own young son during the investigation and felt the rage that only a father can feel when he sees how other children were abused. What would he do if someone molested and killed his son? The answer, as much as he hated to admit it, came back that he might take the law into his own hands and kill the molester, just as someone may be doing now. He quickly pushed that realization out of his head, however, for fear that he might sympathize too much with the killer and it might interfere with his research. Besides he didn't want to blow his first field assignment, if he got it, by identifying too much with the criminal he might have to catch.

* * *

Not wanting to appear too anxious and nursing his slight concussion from the bartender's blow and his skinned-up arm, Dan waited three days before returning to the Pig's Eye. When he did he didn't come empty handed.

"Here boys," he said as he entered the bar throwing a plastic bag containing white powder on a table in the center of the room, "Christmas came a little early this year. Help yourselves." In the bag was the rest of the cocaine he had brought with him from Washington.

"Hey man," Santucci said from the back of the room as a surprised number of El Muerto members swarmed around the cocaine like pigs around slop, "You musta' missed us."

"Well, Lee, actually I missed Hog. I think we had a meaningful encounter last time I was here." Hog characteristically grunted in the background as he snorted several lines of Dan's cocaine up his nose. Others had already gotten their spoons and needles out and were shooting it into their veins. Obviously, Dan's generosity had endeared him to several of the gang members.

"Yeah, Hog thought so too," Lee said laughing, "Come on over here and meet someone."

Dan walked through the smoke-filled room over to Lee's table and saw that a very shapely young woman with long, fiery red hair was sitting on his lap. His heart skipped a beat as her hair reminded him of Jan and a life that now seemed so far away. You could say she was beautiful, but you would also have to add that she was a bit sleazy looking, which actually made her more appealing.

"Garret meet Rita. Rita meet Garret. Rita why don't you make old Garret feel at home." And with that the lovely Rita went over and sat on his lap, immediately laying a long, wet kiss on him while gently and very sensuously massaging his genitals at the same time.

"Glad to meet you Rita," Dan said without missing a beat once she pulled her slippery tongue out of his mouth, "in fact I just remembered it was you I missed, not Hog."

"But we haven't met," Rita cooed in a deep, sultry voice breathing her hot breath into his ear and then filling it with her tongue.

"Oh yea, I'm sure I have … in one of my dreams," was Dan's turned-on reply.

"Garret, why don't you and Rita go in my private office back there and get better acquainted," said Lee with a big grin creeping onto his face.

Dan was now faced with a tough decision. In spite of Jan's sexual problems he had never cheated on her, mostly out of a sense of honor, but also out of love for her. And as sexy as this girl was he didn't really want to start now. But if he refused Lee's offer he might very well draw suspicion on himself and blow his whole mission.

* * *

"You got it Hug," Don Westerhoff said stepping into Ross Huggins' office later that afternoon and bringing him out of his reverie. "You're the point man in this pervert killer investigation."

"Alright!" whooped a stunned Ross, "my own case! Thanks Don."

"You deserve it, buddy. Now what do you want to do first."

"Well, I want to fly to California as soon as possible to look into the deaths in San Diego and L. A. I hope to establish a pattern in the killer's M.O. and maybe even get a description." Ross sounded like a kid anticipating his first trip to Disneyland. "Go for it. You can fly out tomorrow."

"Thanks again Don."

"No problem, I know you won't let us down on this one."

Don Westerhof walked out of the office leaving Ross to celebrate the fact that after a long and frustrating wait, he finally got what he wanted. It was up to him now and him alone. The fact that the person he was going after may be saving a lot of kids bothered him a little, but not a lot. What irritated him, however, was the letdown he now felt. Now that he finally had the opportunity, he had craved for so long it seemed anticlimactic. Now that his own investigation was a reality he was also a little frightened.

Yesterday he could only dream about how great it would be to be a field agent; today he would have to do it and deal with the challenges and dangers the position carried with it. He silently hoped he was up to it. He also hoped that the pedophile deaths really were murders instead of accidents, as they appeared to be.

CHAPTER 33

Dan realized he had no choice. If he didn't take Lee Santucci up on his offer to have sex with Rita the leader of El Muerto would be suspicious or even worse, think he might be gay. Besides, it would give him a chance to get a look at the office, where any child sex abuse evidence, if it exists, would probably be hidden.

"Works for me Lee," he said taking Rita by the hand and heading toward the office at the back of the bar, "thanks for the use of the office, this might take awhile."

"The longer the better honey, and I mean that in more ways than one," whispered Rita as she slithered into Santucci's office just ahead of Dan. Her jeans were so tight you could almost read the tag on her scanty underwear. They were like a second layer of skin and when she walked her buttocks looked like two baby cougars fighting each other in a tight burlap bag.

"Take as long as you want Garret," Lee yelled after them with the bar's music blaring out its hard rock music in the background.

The room was more of a plush hideaway than an office, with a large bed against the wall, expensive Persian rugs on the floor and what looked like fine art hanging on the walls. Before Dan had even shut the door behind them Rita was doing a sensuous strip tease out of her blue jeans and T-shirt to reveal a perfect body clad in a black lace bra and thong panties. Dan sidled over to her pulling off his own shirt as he went and she immediately began kissing his face, chest, and waist and loosening his belt as she went on working her way down to give him oral sex that he would not soon forget. Watching her red-haired head bob up and down not only intensely turned him on, but also profoundly reminded him of the last night he had spent with Jan. In fact, even though here was a young and incredibly sexy girl going absolutely wild on him, he was almost more turned on by pretending it was his wife than relishing this youthful, voluptuous creature that most men would flip over. "It's a dirty job," he said out loud, "but somebody's gotta' do it," as they both fell on the bed in a steamy spectacle of undulating bodies. All the while, Dan scoured the room with his eyes looking for security cameras and an alarm system. He saw neither.

Forty minutes later Dan walked back into the bar and sat down across the table from Santucci. "You sure know how to treat your guests Lee," he said just starting to regain his normal breathing.

"Well, we aims to please. Now how about gettin' into some of my 20-year-old scotch?"

"Might as well ... I just got into some of your 20-year-old Rita."

"Is she that old?" asked Lee and Dan thought he was serious.

The waitress brought drinks to the table and the two men began what turned out to be a long and very enjoyable night of drinking and revelry for both of them. Dan noticed there were several good-looking women with a hard edge in the bar that night and most were being passed around like sacks of potatoes. He also noticed a lot of drugs being used with some gang members not being shy about shooting up out in the open.

Lee had never found anyone who could keep up with him drinking whisky, until now. Dan was obviously his match. Some members of the gang could match his intake of booze by taking stimulants like amphetamine or cocaine, which made them thirsty and kept them from passing out, but the drugs just made them dumber than they already were and numb drinking companions. It didn't take Dan long to get back into the swing of controlled, heavy drinking and it was clear to Lee that Dan was the real thing. By the early hours of the morning Santucci had invited him to join the gang on a probationary basis.

"I'd rather not," Dan said, "I just don't work well with others."

But Lee made it clear that if he didn't join he couldn't hang out at the Pig's Eye.

So, Dan reluctantly accepted, but with the understanding that he was also putting El Muerto on probation. Lee loved it.

He was in. But now the problem was that he really liked Santucci and he almost hoped he wasn't a kiddie pimp.

* * *

"Honey, I got it!" now Ross Huggins exploded with joy as soon as he got home that night.

"Got what?" Sara said apprehensively, knowing but hoping she was wrong.

"I got the field assignment!"

"Oh ... congratulations," she said downheartedly. She had been dreading this day, hoping it would never come.

"I fly to California tomorrow to head up a murder investigation." That was about all he would tell Sara and she knew better than to ask for details.

"Tomorrow already?"

"Yup. You can't keep the wheels of justice waiting ya' know."

"Yeah, I guess. It's just kind of sudden." Her growing anxiety was showing. She knew that she would never be able to relax again because she would be constantly worrying about Ross's safety.

Ross, on the other hand, recognized her growing apprehension and while he sympathized, he also anticipated the great sex he knew he was going to get that night. He remembered Roy Belizzi saying that nothing turns a woman on like the smell of danger.

He must have been right. They spent a night reminiscent of their early years together when their relationship was more sexually charged.

"Did the kids tell you about the creepy guy hanging around the park yesterday?" Sara asked over coffee the next morning.

Ross dropped his spoon. "No, what about it?" he asked.

"Oh, some guy was watching the kids at the park and tried to give Johnny Hansen candy. His sister grabbed him and dragged him away and the guy drove off real fast. Anyway that's according to the kids."

Ross felt like he'd been punched in the pit of his stomach. Here I am, he thought, trying to stop someone from killing a creep like that ... a creep that may molest my own son.

"What's the matter?" Sara asked, "you look funny."

"Oh ... nothing. I was just thinking about child molesters. Make sure you tell the kids to run home whenever they see someone like that and tell you so you can call the police."

"I already did and I gave them the old don't talk to strangers speech too."

"Good. I'd rather scare the crap out of them and keep them safe than not scare 'em and risk them getting grabbed."

"Me too," was all Sara said.

Just then the taxicab's horn blared outside.

"Well, gotta' go," Ross said as he picked up his suitcases and headed for the door. After a long kiss he went on, "I'll call you from San Diego."

"You do that, mister. And you be careful. Remember what you've got here."

"I will," was all Ross said. He walked to the cab trying to clear his mind of his doubts about what he was doing that were already beginning to sprout.

* * *

"What's G-F-E-M-D stand for," Dan asked Lee looking up at a big sign on the wall containing just those letters.

"God forgives, El Muerto doesn't," Lee answered.

"Clever."

"It just means if you fuck with El Muerto, you die ... slowly."

"Remind me never to fuck with you guys," Dan joked half-mockingly.

"Well, we can be the best friend you ever had or the worst enemy. It's your choice."

"Uh. Huh. Right now I'll take the friendship," Dan said as he clinked glasses with his new friend.

Over the next few weeks Dan partied heavily with Santucci and El Muerto and rode with them on their weekend outings into the mountains. The two men's friendship grew stronger and stronger with Lee taking Dan into his confidence more and more. El Muerto, he explained to him, was involved in smuggling cocaine and heroin through Mexico. The gang also sometimes smuggled guns to several revolutionary, guerrilla groups in Central America. Often times they would trade the guns for drugs. The gang members would then sell the drugs in large quantities to dealers in the Los Angeles area and in several large cities across the country. By doing the smuggling themselves, thereby cutting out the middlemen, they made huge profits on the drugs. It was big business and business had never been better. Dan correctly figured that somewhere there was a huge stash of cash and he guessed that Lee Santucci was the only man who knew where it was. He also figured that each member of the gang could end up a millionaire if he didn't spend all his money on getting high, which most of them seemed to do.

"You oughta' invest your cash resources in stock mutual funds Lee," Dan said during one of their frequent drinking bouts.

"Naw, I want it instantly liquid so that we can leave with it at the drop of a hat. Remember, this is a dangerous business and I'm sure that out there somewhere there's a cop trying to nail us. Besides, investing the money would leave a trail for the IRS to follow."

"Yeah, I suppose so. I just hate to see money sit and not make more money."

"I know, but with any luck, one of these days we'll all have so much cash there won't be any need for it to make more in an investment or whatever. That's what we're looking for in the long run and it could happen in a couple of years if we stay outta' jail,"

"Is that what you plan, to retire wealthy in a couple of years?"

"Yup. Wealthy enough to swim in my money, live in a mountain mansion, bang only the highest of the high-class broads, drink only vintage booze and do whatever the fuck I please whenever I please. I might even write a book."

"Works for me," said Dan, thinking that Lee would probably never make it to that point.

CHAPTER 34

In the two months he had spent riding with El Muerto Dan had taken part in several gun and drug smuggling runs, but had not seen or heard a thing about any child stealing operation. In fact, the only strange thing he had noticed about Lee Santucci was that two times he and six of his gang members had just disappeared for a few days. Both times it was the same El Muerto members and they would just pop back in the Pig's Eye and say nothing to anyone about where they had been. Dan was suspicious, but he didn't have an inkling of proof that their absences may have been connected with child stealing, so he decided to get more aggressive in his search for evidence.

One night, long after the Pig's Eye had closed and everyone had gone home, he broke into Lee's office and looked for clues. After searching for a long time, he had turned up nothing but a few notes on some drug transactions ... which he didn't really care about. Frustrated, he sat in Lee's chair behind his desk and just looked around the room trying to decide where he would hide things if it were his office. Unfortunately, every place he chose he had already searched. He was about ready to give up. Then, as he scooted the wheeled office chair forward he heard a slight squeak from a floorboard underneath it. He promptly moved the chair and the hard, plastic sheet it sat on aside and inspected the floor. After testing each individual board he found one that was slightly loose and removed it. There beneath it, in a small plastic box was one lone computer disc. "Bingo," said Dan to himself thinking that if Lee had gone to this much trouble to hide something it may very well be related to the kiddie operation. Quickly he placed the disc in the computer sitting on the desk and booted it up. The menu held only three items, which were named Specifications, Orders and Network. He immediately accessed the first item, thinking how uncharacteristically careless it was of Santucci not to have installed a password into the computer that would deny access to anyone without it. But then he thought that maybe Lee wasn't as smart as he seemed.

The first heading, *Specifications,* appeared at first to be a list of male names and addresses in various parts of the U.S. and in Mexico. But upon closer examination Dan sadly realized that this was what he was looking for. Beside each name were different descriptions of children; descriptions like male, white, between 9 and 12, black hair, pretty face, small boned and one particularly bothersome category of experienced or inexperienced. His heart sank with the discovery.

Dan was sure that experienced meant a kid who had had sex before, probably a child prostitute, and that inexperienced meant just a normal kid from a normal family in the U.S. who was growing up fresh and innocent. These, he figured, were the various types of children preferred by the names on the list, and he noticed that most of them were listed as inexperienced. He figured that a sick pervert would prefer a clean-cut kid who has never even thought about sex before, to a pro. He also noticed that one name read Mr. M and wondered if there was a correlation between this guy and Tyrone Palmer's client, Mr. G.

Then he saw it; Mr. M's telephone number was the same number as Mr. G's, which he had memorized in San Diego. Same guy, different name. Dan reasoned he probably had twenty different names listed with twenty different pimps like Tyrone and Lee, all with different letters of the alphabet. His suspicions were confirmed when he accessed the second heading, *Orders.* It was just what it sounded like; actual orders, which had been placed and filled for some of these types of kids, complete with prices and dates of delivery. The prices immediately shocked Dan. The highest was listed at $200,000 and most of the rest were in the $20,000 to $100,000 range. Dan figured that all of the customers were rich and that Lee charged them different prices based on how much he thought they would pay.

There was only one order that apparently hadn't been filled yet. It called for an inexperienced, white, blonde boy between the ages of 9 and 12 to be delivered to an address in Acapulco, Mexico 10 days hence. Then, following the order was the name *Donnie Stevenson,* the words *newspaper drop,* and a street address of an inter-section in Oklahoma City, Oklahoma. It all came together now. Dan remembered that Santucci had said the day before that he was going out of town on business the following week. Donnie Stevenson must be the target. He must be a paper boy and the street intersection must be where he picks up his papers early in the morning and Lee or one of the gang must've already picked him out to kidnap from there. He figured that they would then take him to the Acapulco address and sell him to some rich pervert.

Now Dan accessed the Network heading not having any idea of what he would find. It took about ten seconds for the screen to fill with a list of the nicknames and ages of children and the sexual services they would perform. There were names like B.J., A. Passion, Large Lips, and S/M Princess. Sick bastards, he thought as he began to realize what the program was. It was a network of pimps selling kids and kids selling themselves. It was a two-way program so that you could send a message by electronic mail to anyone on the list using their specified computer code telling them to call you at a given telephone number. Dan figured correctly that Santucci must sometimes set up meetings with a kid from the list who meets the experienced specifications of an order, then kidnap and sell him or her. Dan dolefully realized that with this list Lee doesn't even have to go out and look for kids. He now knew what a sick, completely immoral monster his new friend was.

Suddenly Dan realized that he had probably been in the office too long so he copied the disc, put everything back the way it was and went back to his motel. All he could do now was wait for Lee to leave and follow him to see if he did actually kidnap a child and deliver him to the address in Mexico. He wanted to make absolutely sure this was what he thought it was. Besides, he had genuinely grown fond of Lee and wanted to give him every benefit of the doubt, even though he knew in his heart how things were going to turn out.

In the meantime, Dan went to sleep only to dream once more about Cole. This time he was stranded in the desert with the hot sun beating down on him while he staggered across the sand dunes. Then, in the rippling heat waves off in the distance, he saw Cole's shimmering face. He was saying something, but it was unintelligible. "What are you trying to tell me?" he silently shouted. Once again, he thought he heard, the words *prophecy and providence*, but he wasn't sure.

* * *

When Ross Huggins got to San Diego the first thing he did after checking into his hotel was visit the downtown police precinct captain to ask for his help.

"No problem Agent Huggins," said Captain Henry Morales, "I'll tell my staff to give you

all the help you need."

Agent Huggins. It sounded so good to Ross. "Thanks Captain," he said, "What I need first is access to the death records of several men who died in San Diego in the last few months."

"You got it." Captain Morales buzzed the records department and instructed the officer there to give Ross what he wanted. Ross went to the records office and began wading through the coroner's reports and other documents, starting with George Dunphy.

The only factor that stood out in the Dunphy case was that after using heroin for a long time why would he not know the potency of this particular batch? But junkies do die of overdoses and this was too inconclusive. So, Ross went on to the Don Baker, Harold Stanton and Steve Gardner cases, all of which proved equally inconclusive. But the Tyrone Palmer case was intriguing. Here was a convicted child sex pimp who was shot and killed along with 10 other men and two of them had been convicted of their own kiddie sex crimes. Ross felt there had to be a connection, but he couldn't figure it out.

The Los Angeles cases also perplexed him. Roger Buckman's electrocution seemed accidental enough on the surface, but Ross wondered how an experienced electrician would leave the electricity on while working. Alan Demerest mystified him too. How could a man who drove the same road every day of his life suddenly forget a sharp curve and drive off a cliff? But first things first and Ross got down to work on the San Diego cases.

CHAPTER 35

The next week racked Dan because he had to keep up a good front to Lee and act as if nothing had happened while his disgust for him swelled. He managed to pull it off by forgetting about the whole thing while he genuinely enjoyed his company. Lee mentioned that he was leaving town Friday so Dan knew he had to move on Thursday.

"It looks like we're going to be gone at the same time," he told Santucci, "I'm going to see my cousin up in Grants Pass."

"Have a good one Garret," was all Lee said, suspecting nothing.

But on Thursday, instead of heading for Grant's Pass on his motorcycle, Dan boarded a plane for Oklahoma City under one of his several phony names. Renting a car at the airport he bought a map of the city and went searching for the intersection listed on the computer disc he had found in Santucci's office. Once he found it he drove to a nearby motel and checked in for the night. Setting his alarm for 3 o'clock in the morning he got up and drove to the intersection, parking two blocks away with his long range, night vision binoculars. At 4:30AM a truck pulled up and threw several bails of newspapers on the ground at the intersection. At five o'clock the first of several young boys rode up on his bicycle, put two of the newspaper bundles in his bike's saddlebags, and rode off. At 5:10 a blonde boy, about 12 years old rode up and picked up his newspapers. Dan figured it had to be Donnie Stevenson. He followed him on his route figuring that it would be somewhere along the way that they would snatch him. Once he felt reasonably familiar with the area he returned to his motel and waited for the next morning. He figured Lee and his men would make their move then.

3:30AM came quickly and Dan drove to the position he had picked out the day before. Crouching down with his head slightly above the dashboard he trained the binoculars on the newspaper pick-up spot. Then, almost on-cue, a blue van with one car in front of it and one behind drove through the intersection and on up the street heading along the blonde boy's newspaper route. Dan recognized the driver and passenger in the first car as members of El Muerto who always disappeared at the same time Lee did. He couldn't get a good look at the occupants of the van or the second car.

At 5:15 the blonde boy rode up to the newspapers, loaded two bundles in his bike baskets, and started up the road on his route. Dan got out of his car and walked up the road the boy was on, staying a block away to keep him in sight most of the time. Two blocks into the route he saw what he was expecting. The first car drove slowly up the street past the boy with the van and second car not far behind. Dan could clearly see now that the occupants of the second car were El Muerto members. When the van was right beside the boy its side door slid open and two men that Dan recognized jumped out while it was still moving and grabbed him and his bike. Clamping their hands over his mouth to stifle his screams, they carried him, bicycle and all into the van, slammed the door and drove off. In less than ten seconds there was no clue that a boy, a bike, and his newspapers had ever been there. All six of the gang members were those who always disappeared with Santucci. As for Santucci himself, Dan figured he was probably driving the van. With that he drove straight to the Oklahoma City airport and boarded a plane to Acapulco. He guessed that the kidnappers wouldn't risk taking Donnie to Acapulco by commercial transportation. They would drive him instead. He would beat them there by almost two days and would have time to set up surveillance of the house where they would deliver the boy.

* * *

Several messages greeted Susan Jensen when she got home from her night out with Jan. Most of them were about her documentary, but one of them was from her father and she instantly thought of her sister, Jenna. Jenna had been sick lately and doctors couldn't figure out what was wrong with her ... other than her HIV status. Her dad had said that he didn't think she was taking her meds and Susan was worried that she might be getting full-blown AIDS. Dialing her father's number with trembling fingers, she listened to the ringing phone on the other end almost hoping he wouldn't answer. But he did.

"Dad," she said, "it's me."

"Hi Sue ... you got my message."

"Yeah ... is it Jenna?"

"Uh ... I'm afraid it is." Susan's heart skipped more than a beat.

* * *

Acapulco was every bit as beautiful a seaside resort as depicted on calendars Dan had seen, although it was a bit over-commercialized. But he didn't have time to enjoy the sights or bask in the sun like everyone else. Instead he rented a car and found the address. "Whew!" was his only response when he drove past the handsome mansion built right into the cliffs overlooking the Pacific Ocean, and surrounded by a high security fence, armed guards and dogs. Obviously, money wasn't a problem for this guy. He found an elevated spot about a quarter of a mile from the house from which he could watch without being detected, and as he had done so many times in the last few months, he settled down to wait. He figured the kidnappers would drive straight through and would arrive late in the afternoon or evening of the next day.

He wasn't disappointed. Toward sunset a different van than the one he had seen in Oklahoma City pulled up to the house's front gate followed by an unfamiliar car. Two guards spoke to the driver and then telephoned the house from the guard station. The gates opened and the two vehicles drove in the driveway. The van's side door opened and two El Muerto members escorted Donnie Stevenson to the front door of the house. Dan recognized the sixth gang member who was always gone when Lee was. That left only Lee himself. At that moment Lee Santucci stepped out of the car and headed for the house.

The two men that led Donnie to the house came back out five minutes later and got into the van. Santucci followed in another ten minutes carrying a brief case and they all drove off, one behind the other. Dan, however, didn't follow. He knew where they were going and he had other business.

* * *

"Is she...?" Susan Jensen started.

"No ... no ... but Jenna's very sick. She has pneumonia," said her father.

"What do the doctors say?"

"They just say her lungs are filling up with fluid and it's real serious," his voice started to break up, "she ... could recover or ... not ... they don't know."

Both Susan and her father knew that Jenna had never been very healthy overall and that she had had several STD's. She also had not taken her medication regularly and the chances of her fighting off pneumonia with the HIV virus in her system were dicey.

"I'll be there tomorrow," was all she could say.

"I think that's a good idea Sue. Call me with your flight and I'll pick you up."

"O. K. dad. I'll talk to you later."

"Susan."

"What?"

"I love you."

"I ... love you too dad."

"Bye."

Hanging up the phone, Susan sat and stared at the wall trying to mentally digest the danger her sister was in. "It's not fair," she sobbed, "Jenna's dying because of that sick bastard. I could kill the son-of-a-bitch right now and not regret it a minute."

* * *

Dan realized immediately that the Acapulco mansion was unapproachable from the north, east, or south because of the guards and dogs. To enter from the west, the ocean side, meant climbing 500 feet up a sheer cliff with death at every foothold. It appeared difficult, if not impossible, but he actually welcomed the challenge. It reminded him of one of his missions in the war when he had gone into the mountains between Pakistan and Afghanistan to assassinate two high ranking Al Qaida officials. He had been successful then and he hoped he would be now.

At 4 o'clock in the morning, clad in a wet suit and infrared, night-vision goggles he had bought at an army surplus store, Dan paddled a rubber raft up to the foot of the cliff and began the bare-knuckled climb. Inch by inch he scaled the cliff, slipping twice and nearly falling to his death on the rocks. Finally, he reached the top. As he poked his head over the peak he saw the back courtyard and swimming pool of the mansion. Pulling a plastic bag containing a .38 pistol from his pocket he crept silently across the courtyard to one of the mansion's back doors. Naturally it was locked and alarmed. But Dan was prepared.

The security alarm was pretty basic. A wire crossed the door's threshold. If the door were opened it would break the wire and set off the alarm. Using his wire-cutters he stripped the insulation off of two sections of the wire about four feet apart. He then attached each end of a five-foot length of electric cable to the two bare spots. Then, the moment of truth. He cut the wire in two halfway between the two connections. No alarm went off and he knew it had worked. It was then a simple matter of opening the door about three feet moving the now elongated wire with it and sliding through.

Searching each room with a small penlight, he found two rooms with two sleeping young boys in each and a third room with Donnie Stevenson, also asleep.

At the far end of the house he found another far larger and more elegantly furnished bedroom. There in a round bed were two naked, sleeping figures, a man who appeared to be in his fifties and a young boy. With only a little twinge of conscience Dan covered his already silenced gun with a pillow and fired it twice at the sleeping man's head. The two bullets made a softened pop and the dead man's sleeping companion only stirred, but did not wake up. Then he found his way to the control center for the mansion's video surveillance system. After turning it off he left through the same door he had come in and made his way to the yard south of the house. He knew, as does any experienced rock climber, that climbing down is exceedingly more difficult than climbing up. He preferred his chances of survival against the mansion's armed guards to the hard rocks of the seacoast.

Scanning the estate with the night-vision goggles Dan reckoned he had a good chance of seeing the guards before they saw him. When he found them he relaxed a bit. The only two guards for the night squatted together near the front guard station smoking a joint. Dan slipped to the fence and found a large tree whose branches hung over it. He started his climb up thinking he was almost home free when from behind him he heard a crack of gunfire. "Esta' aqui!" shouted an undetected third guard who had been making his rounds when he saw Dan climbing the tree. The tree's thick branches obscured the guard's view and he was armed with a less-than-accurate Uzi. He missed his target. Dan still had a long way to go before he cleared the fence and he was a sitting duck in the tree, so he dropped to the ground in a prone position and shot back. His trained eye, with the aid of the night-vision goggles, spotted the shooter and he pumped four quick shots into him from his .38. The guard dropped like a bag of cement and hearing the other two guards running toward him, he calmly, but calculatingly, started climbing the tree again. The other two guards saw or heard him and started shooting. Hearing the branches cracking around him, he dropped to the other side and started running. By the time the guards realized he was gone, he was already halfway to his rental car.

As he drove away, he called the Acapulco Police Department's version of 911. In broken Spanish he identified himself as an official with the American Embassy in Mexico City. He told the Policia on the other end that there had just been a mass shooting at the mansion south of Acapulco, which was being used as a prison for kidnapped American boys. Next, he telephoned the American Embassy and told the receptionist to get an embassy official out of bed. After telling him his story Dan said, "If you want to find several young American boys who have been kidnapped, including Donnie Stevenson who was taken from Oklahoma City just two days ago, you'd better get someone over there now. The local police are already on their way.

The man holding them captive is an American so you don't have to worry about starting an international incident." Then he hung up and drove off into the night.

Ditching the car on an Acapulco back street the next day, Dan took a cab to the airport and flew back to Los Angeles. He drove his Harley from the airport straight to the Pig's Eye, only to find that Santucci and the six gang members weren't there. He relaxed, drank his now-standard 12 shots of whisky, and left. The next afternoon he returned to see Lee Santucci and all six of the missing gang members whooping it up.

"What's the celebration?" he asked innocently.

"Oh, just the fact that we don't have to work for a living," an unusually drunk Santucci answered.

"Amen to that," said Dan rather dispassionately.

"Amen Brother Taylor."

"Hallelujah Brother Lee."

Dan and Lee looked each other squarely in the eye and for just a moment each thought the other might know something that he shouldn't. But then, that moment gave way to drunken celebration on both of their parts. Lee celebrating his latest, secret but lucrative business deal and Dan celebrating his discovery, trying to forget for the moment his next mission, which was bound to boil down to killing his best friend.

But Lee Santucci's drunken revelry wasn't as innocent as it appeared. Smarter than Dan had given him credit for, Lee had programmed a warning system into his computer which informed him if anyone used it. The system allowed others to use the computer without a coded password, but informed him of the use. Luckily for Dan, Lee hadn't checked the disc before the latest kidnapping or he might have postponed it. But he did access the computer upon his return from Oklahoma to enter that the order was filled, and when he did he saw that someone had hacked into it. Lee now knew that someone was onto his child stealing operation. It made him more than a little nervous. Beyond all his other illegal activities this was the one that he wished to keep secret. In fact, the six El Muerto members who periodically helped him locate and kidnap children were the only ones who knew of the operation's existence. Someone else now knew, and as reluctant as he was to accept it, the most likely candidate was the newest member of El Muerto, Garret Taylor.

CHAPTER 36

Just as Dan had wanted to make sure Lee was guilty, Lee wanted to make absolutely sure the man he knew as Garret Taylor was the one who hacked into his computer. After the Pig's Eye closed one night he installed a remote surveillance videotape camera in a ceiling vent in his office. He figured correctly that whoever had broken in had already checked for cameras. Now he figured he would just wait and see who was so interested in his sideline.

Dan, meanwhile, had a tactical and a personal problem. The tactical problem was how to eliminate seven members of El Muerto without drawing down the wrath of the rest of the gang. The personal difficulty was that he couldn't help but like Lee Santucci and he was one of the seven. Dan knew that if anyone had to go, it was Lee since he was obviously the leader of the child-stealing ring, but emotionally that was hard for him to swallow. Because he had never gotten to know his other victims, let alone like them, they were easier to kill.

Even as he pondered his personal dilemma, Dan developed a seed of an idea for getting rid of Santucci and his six henchmen. Although he hadn't followed them to Oklahoma City, it was obvious that they had flown there. Add to that the fact that Lee had a pilot's license and often rented a twin-engine Cessna for recreational flying, and it was a good bet he had flown the plane. Dan figured they took a commercial airliner back from Mexico to Oklahoma City, picked up the Cessna, and then flew back to L. A. That is why they didn't get back until the day after he did.

Dan knew that the only way he was going to get the seven men at the same time was to get them in the middle of another child kidnapping. That would be the only time they would be together with no one else around. His plan was simply to find out when their next job was and plant a bomb on the plane to go off in mid-air. The problem was that Dan had no way of knowing how long it would be until the next job. According to the computer disc he had found in Lee's office, another order was going to be made by the end of the month, which was only one week away. He had noticed that in the past the requested delivery date was soon after the order had been placed. He hoped this one was no exception. He decided to wait a week to break into Lee's office again and check the computer disc. He hoped that by then the order would be placed.

Lee, meanwhile, checked his surveillance tapes daily to see who was interested in the business that he found safer and more lucrative than dealing drugs. "It's a good thing I don't have a conscience," he sometimes boasted to his six fellow kidnappers, "because if I did I would sure as hell feel guilty about this." Actually, at times, he did feel a twinge of guilt over the kidnappings, but whenever that happened he pushed it out of his mind by reaffirming to himself his belief that there is no God and no right and wrong.

"Therefore, nothing I do is wrong ... or right for that matter," Lee told Dan on this night of heavy drinking, even for him.

"Let's just say you're right for a moment," Dan answered back, "that there is no right and no wrong. Then that would mean that there are no rules or laws for society to live by. It would mean total and complete anarchy with people constantly killing each other and violating each other's rights."

"That's right," replied Lee, "survival of the fittest, just like the cave-man days."

"But then a lot more people would suffer because there would be no laws to protect them, and wouldn't that be wrong?" Dan couldn't help but feel a drunken philosophical discussion coming on much like the ones he used to have with Jack Adams. He suddenly remembered how much he missed them.

"There's that dirty word again Garret. With that line of reasoning you forget that in the world we're talking about there is no right and wrong. So, the answer to your question is no, it wouldn't be wrong. It couldn't be wrong because there is no wrong."

"But if there are no rules ... no laws to protect people, then anyone could just kill you or violate your rights, and are you going to tell me that's not wrong?"

"Yeah, I'm going to tell you that. If someone hurts me it's not wrong; it just means that I wasn't strong enough or smart enough to prevent them from doing it. Remember it's survival of the fittest just like in the animal kingdom.

After all, we're all just a higher form of animal with a bigger brain and the ability to reason. But we're still animals with all the animal instincts, the instinct for survival being one of the strongest. We humans find a lot of things that many animals do revolting, but they're just living by their law, which is really no law or the law of the jungle." Dan recognized something vaguely familiar in that line of reasoning.

Lee went on, "We believe that we have advanced far beyond their savage stage to a more civilized and refined level of existence. But I maintain that we have gone too far in that direction, making laws to regulate practically every human action ... and all due to religion as we know it. Again, without religion there'd be no right and wrong. So, if you don't believe in a deity, as I don't, you don't have to live by what the world around you tells you is right and wrong."

"O.K. Let me put it another way," said Dan, "Remember the innocent people you saw shot to death in Iraq?" He knew he was getting dangerously close to the issue that was on both of their minds right now, but he wanted to figure out how someone as intelligent as Lee could justify such repugnant actions.

"Uh. Huh."

"Didn't you feel sorry for them?"

"Yea, I did. You could hardly help it."

"Well, you must have felt sorry for them because you felt that their agony and deaths were wrong."

"No. I felt sorry for them because, like you and everyone else in this world, while growing up, it was ingrained in my mind that this type of misery is wrong. But it was actually in Afghanistan that I opened my eyes to see that it's really just the law of the jungle; the weak die and the strong survive. It's not what's right or what's wrong, it's just what is."

"So, you don't think torturing and killing an innocent person who did nothing to deserve it is wrong?"

"Again, how can I, when I don't even believe there is such a thing as wrong? I think there is happiness at one end of the spectrum of life and sadness at the other end. But I don't think they are synonymous with right and wrong. I think most people see them that way because of the religious values that are drilled into them from the moment of birth."

"O.K. One more time. If you believe there is no right and wrong, then you must believe there is no good and bad. Now, without a good and a bad… a positive and a negative…isn't life meaningless?"

"Well, shit, I think we both decided life was pretty meaningless a long time ago. But that's another issue. Your premise here is wrong. There is good and bad ... they're what we say they are. I decide what is good or bad for me, but not on the basis of what society tells me is right and wrong ... only on the basis of what I want or don't want."

"Well, I want another round," Dan said, giving up on the conversation and motioning for the bartender to bring more whisky.

"Well, then that's good for you Garret, but not necessarily right."

"O.K. O.K. I get your point," and they both laughed.

* * *

Susan Jensen took a night flight to Tampa and her father picked her up at the airport. Without a word they hugged each other tight until a little of the pain they both felt abated. "Let's get something to eat and we'll go over to the hospital in the morning," her father finally said.

"No ... let's go now. I'm afraid to wait."

"Well ... I asked her doctor and he said he doesn't know much, but he's fairly sure she'll make it through the night."

"Is she talking?" Sue asked as they walked through the airport.

"Yeah ... but she's very weak."

"I've got to go tonight, even if it's just to sit by her while she sleeps."

"O. K. Sue ... I learned a long time ago not to argue with you ... besides I think I would feel the same way."

An hour later, standing by Jenna's bed, Susan was deeply saddened looking at her sister's sleeping, emaciated, bony face with tubes running out of her nose. Then Jenna opened her eyes.

"I knew it was you," she choked, "what do you think of my new look?" Even through all her strife she had not lost her sense of humor.

"A little on the thin side," Susan joked back half-heartedly, "how are you feeling?"

"About like I look."

"You're going to snap out of it and when you do we're going to take a sisters vacation to St. Thomas ... on me."

"Whoa ... my rich sister the filmmaker." Even though Jenna loved Susan dearly she had always been a bit jealous of her career success.

"Documentary producer," Susan corrected, "and yes I've got a little extra money that will give us a good time on the beach."

"Sounds great ... I think I'll just have to get better so I can show you up in a swim suit."

The conversation went on like this for a few minutes with both Susan and Jenna trying to keep it as light as possible. But eventually Jenna couldn't hold her eyes open any longer and drifted off to sleep.

"I love you Jenna," Susan whispered as she bent down to kiss her sister.

Jenna died in her sleep that night.

"Well, I had two daughters and now I only have one," Susan's father said while pouring himself a drink after the funeral. "So, you better take good care of yourself or I'll have none."

"I will Daddy," she said, never quite able to shake the feeling that she would always be daddy's little girl.

Susan spent the week at home with her father and then both of them had to get back to work. On the plane back to Washington Susan had a mixed bag of feelings. On the one hand she was severely depressed about her sister's tragic life and death. But on the other the whole experience reinforced her strong desire to produce a documentary that might prevent something similar from happening to other kids. She rode this roller coaster of emotions back to Washington and to her apartment until she was too tired to think anymore and collapsed on her bed into a fitful sleep.

* * *

With a killer hangover from the previous night's drinking bout, Dan broke into Lee's office to look at the computer disc. Unfortunately, he saw that it read the same as before; that a future order was expected, but that it hadn't been made yet. Even more unfortunately for him, however, his entire visit to the office was captured on videotape. Also, although Santucci had actually received the firm order two days before, he had deliberately not entered it onto the disc, knowing that someone would be looking for it. Frustrated, Dan left the office figuring that he would just have to wait until the order was placed to take any action.

The next day Lee saw on the surveillance tape what he expected, but hoped wouldn't be there. "It really was him," he said half out loud seeing Dan walk into his office and access the computer. "Well, he must be a cop," he thought deeply disappointed, "He sure fooled me and now I gotta' waste him." With that he called the six members of his kidnapping team to the Pig's Eye early in the day, before it opened.

"We've got a problem," he told them, "It looks like Garret's a cop and we've gotta' take him out."

"No shit!" one of them said astounded, "Man I never would've figured him for a cop. He always seemed too cool."

"No kidding. How do ya' think I feel ... I took him in as a friend. Well, I guess he actually took me in." Lee's genuine sadness at losing Dan as a friend was outweighed only by his anger at him for playing him for a dupe. "Anyway, he's gotta' go and we're the ones who've gotta' do it because it looks like he was investigating our side operation."

Silence fell over the group at this revelation. They were outlaws, but none of them wanted to be labeled a child abuser. Lee was the only one who didn't care what label was put on him; he just didn't want to get caught before he made his millions. "So, we've gotta' do it and not tell the rest of the boys," he said nonchalantly.

"Yeah," another one said, "They'll just think he split. How're we gonna' do it?"

"I'll call him at eight o'clock tonight and tell him I've got to do some business at Kendley Park and that I want him to come along to help. Then, when he gets here we'll drive over to the park, to that little clearing where we've done deals before, and five of you guys will be waiting there with silencers on your guns. Beano, you stay here at the bar because if you're all gone he may get suspicious. About ten minutes after we leave, you come to the park too, to give us some help if we need it. Anyway, two of you will be lookouts guarding the entrances. Hide when you see us coming and then guard it after we pass. I'll walk in first and hit the dirt just as we enter. The other three will whack him as soon as I go down. Jackson, you bring your car so we can load the body in it. Just don't shoot me by mistake you crazy fucks. O.K. You all got it?"

"Got it Lee. See you at Kendley."

* * *

FBI Agent Ross Huggins spent the week interviewing everyone in San Diego who was even remotely connected to the victims and went over the death scenes painstakingly. People who knew George Dunphy agreed he was too experienced a junkie to make that kind of mistake, but those who knew Don Baker and Harold Stanton accepted their deaths as unfortunate accidents. Steve Gardner's death was called a suicide. The few people Ross found who knew Tyrone Palmer bought the theory that he and his companion Andy had killed each other in a dispute over money following a sting operation they had perpetrated on a number of wealthy drug customers. But they doubted that the two were smart enough to come up with the plan on their own.

Ross's first break came in an interview with the director of the day care center where Steve Gardner had worked. When he asked her if anything out of the ordinary had happened at the center prior to Gardner's death she remembered that Milton Barnes, the janitor, had taken a two week leave of absence and furnished his own substitute. Barnes knew he was in trouble when he heard the FBI was talking to people at the center. He figured it would just be a matter of time before they got around to him. "I knew that money would come back to haunt me," he mumbled to himself as he mopped the center's floor.

At first, he told Ross that the man who filled in for him was an old friend. When Ross asked for his name Milton had trouble remembering it. When Ross asked how he knew him he lost control and blurted the truth. "O.K.

O.K. I don't know why, but this crazy guy gave me $3000 to take my place for two weeks," he said in a shaky, scared voice, "he said it wasn't for anything immoral or illegal, but I 'spose that was a lie, wasn't it?"

"That's what we're here to find out," Ross said, getting a little excited about his first possible break in the case. He then made Barnes repeat everything the fill-in janitor had said and done several times. Ross confiscated the seventy-five dollars that remained of the payoff to have it analyzed. Maybe the bills' serial numbers would yield clues to its origin. "You're probably not in any trouble," Ross told Milton, "But tomorrow I'd like you to come down to the police station to describe the guy to a police artist who'll put together a composite drawing of him." Milton readily agreed, relieved to hear that he was not in trouble.

Ross went to his hotel that night feeling he was onto something. He sat down in the room's one easy chair and reviewed every last detail of what he had found so far to try and figure out what, if anything, he had left out. "The best method of investigation is the Socratic method," his favorite FBI Academy instructor had said. "When you're stumped ask yourself basic questions about the case." So, Ross did.

"Why is this person killing pedophiles?" he asked himself out loud. He suspected someone who had either been sexually abused as a child or someone whose son or daughter had been abused and who was trying to rid the world of pedophiles. If it was the former he had no chance of identifying a possible suspect; there were just too many. If it was the latter, an FBI computer search could turn up a list of names of people who had reported their child being kidnapped or molested. But since most abuse goes unreported there was a very good chance that this one wouldn't be either. Besides, Ross didn't want to ask his FBI superiors to go to the trouble of conducting this search until he could show them some hard evidence to collaborate his theory. It was his first investigation and he wanted to look good.

"How did the killer get information about his victims?" he said, again out loud. The only place, he realized, was the police. He wondered if a renegade San Diego cop might be doing the killing. But he quickly dismissed that idea since other murders had occurred in Los Angeles. On a hunch he quickly got up and called Captain Henry Morales at home and asked him if anyone outside the department had had access to the pedophile records in the last three months.

* * *

When Dan got the call from El Muerto Head Lee Santucci at his motel room he was instantly suspicious. One thing he didn't believe in was coincidence. He didn't believe it was a coincidence that he had just broken into Santucci's office for the second time and now all of a sudden, he wanted him to come on a dope deal with him when he had never asked him anything like that before. But Dan also knew he had to go or risk blowing his cover. He hoped that it really was the coincidence that he didn't believe in, but just in case it wasn't, he put on his kevlar bulletproof vest under his shirt and jacket and stuck his small Ingram Mac-10 machine gun into his under-arm shoulder holster.

"Hey Garret," Santucci said as Dan entered the Pig's Eye, "Glad you could make it. I figure it's about time you get in on some of the side cash we all get on private deals. All you have to do is stand there and look mean while I do the deal and you'll make yourself two thousand dollars. Sound good?"

"Sounds great man. Let's do it," answered Dan.

"Just follow me. We're going to a park we do some business in." Darkness was approaching as they got on their Harleys and Dan had a very strong feeling that something was very, very wrong.

He figured he must have found out he was in his office. But he knew if he cut and ran now, all of the time he had put into this case would be for nothing. So, he decided he had to play it out, no matter what happened. The two motorcycles roared down the highway.

It was pitch dark as they pulled into the park's parking lot and Lee said, "Follow me, it's this way." He led him down a path about three-quarters of a mile into an area thinly wooded with large bushes and palm trees. Fortunately, the path was narrow enough that Lee had to go first. Seeing the clearing up ahead, Dan figured that it had to be an ambush and casually began to finger his Mac-10 hidden under his jacket. As soon as they reached the clearing, before Lee had a chance to duck down, Dan shoved him hard into the opening and darted off the path running to a pile of rocks about thirty yards away.

"Where'd he go?" he heard one of the ambushers say as he ran. Then, there was a mumble of excited voices as the two lookouts joined the rest of the gang and all six came running in Dan's direction.

"Think fast Dan old boy," he said to himself. Then he realized there really was nothing to think about, that all he could do was run and fast, which he did. Lee and the others were smart enough that they didn't want to draw attention to themselves by firing indiscriminately at Dan, especially when they couldn't see him very well in the darkness.

"Spread out!" Lee shouted, and they spread out and all ran as fast as they could, hoping at least one of them would get a good shot at him. Being outnumbered by pursuers who knew the area a lot better than he did, Dan knew his chances of getting out alive were slim. He also knew he had no choice but to play it by ear and use his instincts to find an unorthodox way out of this predicament. When he reached the park's playground he went directly to the merry-go-round and began pushing it around in circles as fast as he could.

Off in the distance he could see several dark figures coming toward him. As he expected, the six men had spread out in a half moon formation. They were closing a half-circle around him. It was vintage strategy from Iraq that Lee had undoubtedly taught them. When you've got someone cornered, surround him so that he has to shoot in too many different directions to be accurate.

"What the hell's he doing?" one of the men shouted at Lee who really wondered if his friend-turned-foe had lost his mind.

"Just close in," he said, "and don't shoot until I do."

Dan realized that timing was going to be everything as he continued spinning the merry-go-round faster and faster, wanting to blast away at all of them then and there, but knowing that the Mac-10 was not known for its long-distance accuracy.

Then, just as the gang got within range, Santucci suddenly realized what Dan was up to. But it was too late. Dan quickly leaped onto the merry-go-round while simultaneously pulling the Mac-10 out of its holster and fired it continuously as he went around and around and around. Moving that fast, he was a hard target to hit, especially in the darkness. All he had to do to hit his six targets was aim about four feet above the ground and keep the trigger squeezed. The merry-go-round did the rest, rotating him and his blasting gun from man to man. All six dropped like pins in a bowling alley with two of them actually hitting Dan in the chest with one shot each. Thank God for the vest, he thought as he was violently jolted by the hard punch of the slugs.

As Dan jumped off the merry-go-round he realized how dizzy he'd become and weaved toward the closest man like a drunken rodeo clown. He knew he didn't have much time, but he wanted to make sure all six were dead. They were, all except Lee, who lay on his back looking up as Dan approached. "Looks like you're the fittest," he gurgled.

Seeing Lee's gun lying on the ground ten feet from him, Dan relaxed a bit. "Not the fittest, Lee," he said sadly, "maybe the rightest."

Coughing and with a sickly half-smile creeping onto his face, Lee choked, "No right, no wrong. But I gotta' know ... are you a cop?"

"No. My boy was kidnapped by a fuck like you and I just wanted to make sure it doesn't happen to a lot of others."

"Oh shit … a pissed off father … always thought about that. We coulda' been a … great team Garret," Lee struggled to get the words out.

"No, we couldn't. You just took your no right and wrong shit too far." Dan knew he should finish Lee off and get out of there but he could plainly see the life was fast flowing out of him and besides, he really didn't want to shoot his friend again.

"Bullshit…" was all that choked out of the dying man's mouth in a death rattle as he breathed his last breath, and then, "you're no better … than me." Dan reached down and checked for a pulse. There was none.

Angry to the end, he thought as he took one last look at his friend, a tear coursing down his cheek "Well, Lee I guess you're about to find out if you were right or wrong," he lamented. Then Santucci's dying words hit him like a bulldozer. He was a murderer and maybe no better than the men he just killed. The black cloud was at hand but Dan knew he had no time to ponder any of this. He snapped himself out of his reverie and quickly ran back in the direction of his motorcycle, disappearing into the night. But he couldn't disappear quite as fast as he needed to because he met Beano running toward him. He had heard the shooting and had his gun pulled, not knowing what to expect. Beano recognized the running figure as Dan first and squeezed off several rounds grazing his left arm. Ignoring the pain, Dan raised the Mac-10 and blasted him with his last five bullets as he tried to duck for cover. After a quick check to make sure he was dead Dan continued his dash for his Harley, hearing sirens in the distance.

He drove the bike straight to his motel and took just enough time to clean and bandage his wound. He threw all of his belongings into his car and drove out of town going east on Highway 91, pulling the trailer he had rented with the Harley inside. He planned to dump it somewhere out of state. Mission accomplished, he thought as he drove into the desert night. He had originally planned to work his way up the coast to Portland, Oregon and Seattle, Washington. But with all the commotion he had raised in California, he now figured he had better continue his mission farther away from the West Coast just in case some smart investigator was starting to put two and two together. "Gonna' miss my Harley," he said out loud as he crossed the state line into Arizona, "and gonna' miss my friend."

As the miles flew by Dan knew it was there. It was inescapable and no matter how hard he tried to ignore it, it was still there. Like he did with fear in Iraq he had even tried numerous times to make it his friend. He couldn't. It was the cloud and it was darker and blacker than ever. He kept telling himself that by shutting down

El Muerto's operation he had probably just prevented at least ten pedophiles from molesting their 24 victims each and the tally now stood at about 696 kids saved. But it wasn't working and with a pounding headache and Lee Santucci's dying words ringing in his head, he struggled to get the words out, "Next stop Chicago."

CHAPTER 37

U.S. Interstate 80 brought Dan into Chicago where he stayed at the Interstate Motel. His plan was to play author again to gain access to Chicago Police records. After checking in, he bought a newspaper to read while relaxing in a hot bath. As he skimmed the paper's back section a list of upcoming events caught his eye. In it he noticed the Gay Pride Day Parade would march through downtown Chicago four days later. Something clicked. Jan had told him that a group advocating the legalization of sex with children marched in the Gay Pride Parade in Washington, D.C. He wondered if it might also march in this one. He had given up on the idea of getting to this group before because of the difficulty of finding any members. But now opportunity seemed to be staring him right in the face and he knew he had to figure a way to infiltrate the group.

* * *

"I don't know if anyone has been given access to pedophile records," San Diego Police Captain Henry Morales told FBI Agent Ross Huggins, "I've only been here for two months. I'll check and call you back."

Ross anxiously awaited the captain's call berating himself for not thinking of this earlier. He knew an experienced investigator would have thought of the police records right from the start. By missing it he may have put his investigation behind by a week. Feeling insecure, the thought suddenly hit him that he may not be ready to be a field agent. But before he could sink any further into his crisis of self-confidence the phone rang. "Yes," he said grabbing the receiver before the end of the first ring.

"You might be on the right track, Mr. Huggins," Captain Morales said, "my records clerk tells me an author writing a book on pedophiles examined the records a couple of months back."

"Bingo!" Ross blurted

* * *

"The cops can wait," Dan thought. The only problem was that he couldn't remember the name of the kiddie sex organization that marched in the Washington, D.C. Gay Pride parade. So, after being gone for two and a half months, he decided to call Jan for the third time and find out.

"Hi," was all Dan had to say before Jan started in.

"Dan! You sure wait long enough between calls. I thought you might be dead or something."

"Well, I'm not ... at least I think I'm not," he said thinking of her beautiful, crimson hair cascading over her slim shoulders and supple breasts. He suddenly realized that he missed her.   "Didn't you get my letter?"

Dan had sent her two letters from Colorado and Arizona. Not wanting her to know where he was and wanting to set up an alibi for future use, he had flown from Los Angeles to Denver. He stayed in the Blue Star Motel for a week, making himself known to the motel proprietor and mailing Jan a letter that would be post-marked Denver. He also mailed her a letter from Phoenix as he passed through on his way to Chicago. To further establish a presence in the southwest he stayed a few days at a motel in Flagstaff, making sure he was quite visible to the motel staff. If anyone checked later it would appear he had traveled from Colorado to Arizona and on west instead of flying to California and working his way back east.

"Yeah, but I would have liked to hear from you sooner." Jan interrupted his thoughts.

"Well, you'll be glad to know that I just sent you another letter, so you'll be getting it soon."

"Good. Anyway, it's good to hear your voice now. How are you?"

"Oh, I'm doing O.K. I think I'm working some things out. The time alone has been good."

"Where are you now?"

"Phoenix," he lied.

"How was Colorado?"

"Beautiful. Sometimes I really think we should've moved there a long time ago. Who knows? Maybe none of this would've happened." Dan had always felt a special passion for the mountains and their peaceful stillness. Above the din of everyday life they provided an escape into a unique, meditative silence you can't find anywhere else.

"Oh well, honey, you never know. Something worse might've happened." Jan bit her lip as the words came out, wishing she had never said them. After all, what could be worse?

But Dan just passed the remark off. "Well, how are you? What's new?"

"Oh, work is going good ... I'm working in pediatrics now and I really like it."

"How about your social life ... have you got one?"

"Actually, I do. You know what a recluse I was before, but I had to snap out of it or I'd have gone completely off the deep end. Believe it or not I've become good friends with Susan, the journalist I told you about who's working on the documentary on child sex abuse. We go out once or twice a week."

"Journalist huh?" Dan said with a cynical chuckle. He didn't know exactly why, but this piece of news made his stomach tighten. For one thing, as a former journalist himself, he had never been fond of TV reporters. They always seemed to sensationalize their stories and were more concerned with how they looked than with accuracy. Dan also felt that Jan's new friend's investigation of child sex abuse might be just a little too close for comfort.

"No, Susan's different. She's really a smart reporter..."

"Isn't that an oxymoron?" he broke in.

"Well ... she's a serious journalist."

"There's another one. O.K., so she's Edward R. Murrow come back from the dead. Why's she still in D.C.?" Jan had told him earlier that Susan wanted to interview him and he had tentatively agreed. But he planned to put it off hoping she would give up and go on with the rest of her documentary. The last thing he wanted was to appear in a nationally televised report on child sex abuse.

"She's using Washington as a base. Right now, she's doing a lot of research. By the way, she wants to know when she can interview you."

"How about never? I've thought about it and decided I don't want to do it. It's too personal. I just don't want to make my feelings public."

"Oh, honey, I know what you mean. I felt the same way, but I decided that I should help get this story out. It might prevent someone else from going through the same hell."

"I'm glad, Jan, because now that you've done it, I don't have to."

"Well ... Susan says the story needs both of us to drive the point home."

"Yeah, what she really means is that it needs both of us to get the tears going. I don't think my not doing an interview is going to hurt her documentary ... especially since you already did one."

"O.K.," Jan said, dejectedly. She really wanted to help Susan out, but could tell from his voice that Dan would not change his mind. "I know she'll be disappointed. I think you would have done a great interview with your police experience with ... uh, child molesters."

"Uh huh, that reminds me," Dan said, seeing an opening, "What was the name of that group of perverts you told me about once who advocates sex with children and marched in the gay parade in Washington?"

"Uh ... the Guild. Why?"

"Oh, I thought I read something in the paper about them a while ago and I just wondered if it was the same group."

"It probably was," said Jan, "They're based in Chicago and are pretty open about their beliefs."

Dan's heart raced. They were right here in Chicago! "Uh Huh," was all he said and then, wanting to quickly steer the conversation in another direction asked, "How's Jack? Do you ever see him?"

"Uh ... things aren't so good."

"What's the matter?"

"He's ... he's got a brain tumor and it's malignant."

The silence was deafening. Dan couldn't believe his ears. He had seen Jack just a few months earlier and he was fine.

"Dan?" Jan said wondering if they had been disconnected.

"Is he gonna' make it?"

"Well, he's just starting chemotherapy and radiation treatments."

"But is he gonna' make it?"

"The doctors are hopeful, but I've seen this kind of cancer before and I don't think things look too good."

"How long do you think he's got?" Dan was getting more and more upset thinking that he had just killed one friend only to find out his only other friend may be dying. It now occurred to him that he might have to go back to Washington earlier than he had planned.

"There's really no way to tell. But a doctor at work told me that no one with this kind of cancer has lived over five years past the diagnosis."

Dan relaxed a little. "Well ... tell him I'm thinking about him."

"I will."

"How're you doing?"

"Not bad. I'm coping, but I miss you. When are you coming home?"

"Not for a while. I'm making progress, but I feel like I still have a few kinks to work out and you know how being on the road helps me." The words unconsciously streamed out as Dan pondered Jack's tragedy and thought about his son Charlie.

"Why don't you come home, honey. Let me help you?"

"I would if you could, but you can't. I know I'm an odd ball, but this is the only thing that works for me."

"I know Dan. I know. I just want you to get over all this and be happy, so do whatever it takes. I'm here for you when you're ready. Maybe we can even make a fresh start." Lately Jan had been toying with the idea of having another child. What she didn't know was whether Dan would consider it. Dan felt all the love he had for Jan and could have had for a second child had dried up inside of him with Cole's death. Besides, he thought he would be so concerned for the safety of another child that he couldn't really enjoy fatherhood like he did the first time around.

"I appreciate that Jan. It may be another couple of months ... I just have to see how it goes. I'd better go now. Bye honey, I'll call again in a couple of weeks."

"O.K. I love you Danny."

"I love you too. Bye." Dan hung up the phone wondering if he really did love his wife. He liked to believe he did, but he didn't know if he could ever actually love anyone again. His son's tragic death had sucked all the love out of him. What he was doing now might make it impossible to replenish that love because guilt and doubts about his mission were eating away at his soul more and more. No matter how hard he concentrated on the children's lives he was saving, his doubts and guilt were growing. Once again, however, he shook off the foreboding by adding up the number of kids he had saved from ruined lives. That thought stifled the pain gnawing at his gut and chased the cloud away, at least temporarily.

He went to bed thinking about the parade and how to approach the Guild if they were there. In his sleep, the familiar dream came to him. But this time he was talking to Jack Adams.

"Poor Jack," he said in his dream, "You're dying."

"Poor Dan," Jack answered back, "You're killing yourself."

Then, all of a sudden in the ceiling's bright light was Cole's face trying to tell him something, and again, he thought he could make out the word *prophecy* and maybe *providence*.

* * *

"Did you get any background on the guy," FBI Agent Ross Huggins asked Captain Morales anxiously, "Like where he lives or works?"

"That's the bad news ... no one bothered. I'm going to be kicking some butt over this one."

Ross went instantly from self-recrimination for his own incompetence to accusation. He had to control his urge to scream about the utter ineptitude of the San Diego Police for letting someone see confidential police files without checking him out. "Can you have your sketch artist draw a picture of the guy from your record clerk's memory tomorrow?" he asked through clenched teeth with the veins in his neck straining against his skin.

"Certainly," Morales said, embarrassed.

"Good. Thanks Captain ... I'll be in early tomorrow."

He was angry about the police department's laxity but ecstatic that he may have just gotten his second big break. With any luck at all, he thought, Janitor Barnes will identify the artist's picture of the author as the same guy who gave him the $3000 for his job at the day care. Wouldn't that be tidy? After all, if Gardner was murdered instead of killing himself the killer has to be the one who put the suicide note up on the day care's bulletin board. That means he had the key to the building because he was the substitute janitor and the rest of the center's staff would recognize the picture too."

He went to bed, not to sleep, but to dreamily contemplate the case. He had found that he often got some of his best ideas while half-asleep. It was as if when he was awake his mind worked like a computer, placing all the elements of a case into different categories and then mixing and matching them using inductive reasoning but leaving no room for intuitive thinking. But when he drifted off into a dreamy state he left himself open to more instinctive and intuitive thoughts. One such thought caused him to suddenly rise up in bed. What made Gardner's death look like a suicide or an accident was that he deliberately or accidentally kicked over the stool he was standing on. "What if someone else was in the room and knocked it away so that he couldn't regain his footing?" he asked the dark room. Instantly he made plans to check out Gardner's room, paying particular attention to the stool.

* * *

Dan went to a local library early in the morning to look for newspaper articles about the Guild. The only one he found was a short story about a landlord who refused to let the New York branch of the Guild meet in his apartment building's activity room.

Limited as it was, it was what he needed.

After three days of rest and relaxation he headed for the downtown intersection where the newspaper said the Gay Pride Day Parade would start. When he arrived he saw several groups preparing for the march, including the Guild. Four exceedingly normal-looking men battled a strong Chicago wind, trying to unfurl their large banner. The wind comes off Lake Michigan with a powerful blast and the Chicago skyscrapers form a kind of wind tunnel for it to blow through. The banner read simply, The Guild.

Dan wondered if anyone would know what the Guild was. He also wondered why Gay Pride Day organizers allowed the Guild in their parade. After all, the gay movement says it supports only homosexual sex between consulting adults, not adults and children. They also argue that being gay does not make one a child molester. Some parents feel, for example, that gay teachers are a danger to their children because they might seduce or molest them. The gay movement's chief argument against this belief is that the gay teachers prefer only consenting adult members of their own sex like heterosexuals prefer adult members of the opposite sex. They don't have any desire to molest children. *If that's the case*, thought Dan, *why in the hell is a group that openly advocates adult sex with children marching in a gay rights parade?* That certainly makes it look like gays do support adult sex with kids. At least they should be more selective of who they let into their parades, but then maybe they would be guilty of the same kind of discrimination they accuse the straight world of. It was all so confusing and these thoughts plagued him as he walked the parade route to where the procession would end.

When he saw the lead marchers come into view he reviewed his story. He would tell the Guild members that he was a gay teacher from Washington, D.C. He had been fired for his sexual orientation and moved to Chicago looking for another position. He yearned for sexual relationships with young boys. He used Washington, D.C. because he knew the area and could answer questions about it.

As each wave of marchers reached the end point they disbanded. As the four Guild members passed Dan he called to one of them, "Excuse me, can you tell me a little about the Guild?"

* * *

The next day's high point for FBI Agent Ross Huggins was when the San Diego police record clerk's memory of the author was sharp enough for the artist to draw a fairly detailed picture of the man. The sketch was of an olive-skinned man with black, curly hair, bushy eyebrows, mustache and beard. The low point came when day care janitor Milton Barnes said this was positively not the man who had paid him $3000 to fill in for him. Ross's instantaneous thought was that there can't be two guys doing the killing. He then had the artist draw the man Barnes remembered, hoping he could tell if it was the same guy in disguise. So different were the sketches, however, that Ross concluded they were two different people. "This certainly complicates things," he said.

Another high point came when Ross carefully went over the room where Steve Gardner died. What he found amazed him. A close examination of the metal stool Gardner had been standing on revealed a tiny dent and groove in one of its legs. Further investigation turned up a bullet from a Sturm-Ruger long-range rifle lodged in the wall and hidden by a tapestry hanging from the ceiling. It looked as if the bullet might have struck the stool, glanced off, and went into the wall behind the hanging tapestry. Finally, a close look at the window showed a small hole in the screen. His first thought as he dug the bullet out of the wall was how ingenious, he shot the stool out from under him. His second thought was this guy's going to be hard to catch.

As much as he hated to admit it, his respect for the pedophile killer was growing and so far it appeared to him that all the victims were vile creatures who were ruining the lives of a lot of children, children like his own. But again he had to put these thoughts aside because it was his first case and he desperately wanted to solve it. The stool evidence gave him some proof, but it still wasn't enough. After eight days in San Diego it was time to move on to Los Angeles.

CHAPTER 38

Douglas Glassman, the newest member of the Guild, turned to look at Dan and answered, "Well, I'd be delighted to, but our president is the one you should ask. Barry, this gentleman would like some information about the Guild."

"O.K. Hi, my name is Barry Anderson, what's yours?" the Guild President asked like a politician canvassing for votes.

"Dennis Hanson," Dan lied.

"Dennis, what have you heard about our organization?"

"Just that it advocates making adult male intimate relationships with adolescent boys legal."

"That's basically correct. How do you feel about such relationships?"

"I think they're natural and that history proves it from the early Greek times. But I think modern society has tabooed them with a stigma to the point that they're now looked at as unnatural and deviant." Dan squeezed out the practiced words in as convincing a manner as he could without choking on them.

"Well, Dennis Hanson, it looks like we may have something to talk about. Let's you and I and the newest member of our group, Doug, go to lunch and talk about it."

Lunch was at the same restaurant where Doug and Barry had first met. "We're a fairly large organization," Barry told Dan, "with branches in many major cities and we're always glad to welcome a new member. Why are you interested in the Guild?"

"Well," Dan started out slowly, hiding his disgust, "I've always been sexually attracted to boys and I feel that male adult sex with them is natural ... that deep down inside, the boys want and need the intimate relationship as much as I do." He felt his skin crawling as he went on, "But society has made me feel like a sick pervert and I've spent my life basically alone. A few months ago though, I read something in the paper about the Guild and wondered if maybe I wasn't so sick. If there might be a lot more guys like me out there. Then, I saw your banner today at the parade."

"Are you bi-sexual?" Barry asked since many pedophiles also carried on sexual relationships with women, often their wives. The question caught Dan a little off guard.

"No ... I'm gay, but as I said I have special feelings for young boys."

"Have you ever been arrested for boy sex?"

"No, I guess I've been lucky."

"Or smart. Approximately how many boys have you had intimate relations with?"

Thinking that Anderson's use of the word *approximately* must mean that some pedophiles have molested so many boys they can't even remember how many, Dan answered, fourteen.

The interview went on for two hours with Barry and Douglas telling true stories about their own pedophile experiences and Dan making his up. Finally, seemingly satisfied that Dan was not an undercover policeman, Anderson gave him his card and invited him to attend the next Guild meeting at his house in five days. "You can meet some of the other members and get to know what we're all about," he told Dan.

They parted at the restaurant door with Barry and Doug going one way and Dan going another. "What do you think?" Barry asked Doug.

"About Dennis? I think he's O.K. What do you think?"

"I think ... he's probably O.K. too. But there's something about him ... I'm not sure."

* * *

The Ali Ban Hashemi child prostitution ring was Detective Derek Lindsay's only case and he devoted every hour to it. He had amassed a lot of evidence against the pimps that Hashemi used, but nothing concrete against Hashemi himself. He had taped telephone conversations between the man and known child molesters and pimps and he had videotaped the encounters that followed. He even videotaped a courier delivering money to one of the kiddie pimps; money apparently sent by Hashemi to pay for a child's services.

The problem was that Hashemi never said anything incriminating on the telephone and he sent his payments anonymously by leaving them in a package for the courier to pick up with a note and fee attached.

It was painfully obvious that Hashemi was too smart to get close to the people who actually dealt in child sex and it was frustrating Derek. It was also beginning to irritate his boss, Captain Lewis. They had had Hashemi under 24-hour surveillance for several months, but since he never did anything between 2:00 and 9 o'clock in the morning Lewis had recently stopped the overnight shift.

"The clock's tickin' Lindsay," Lewis told Dan, his eyes boring into him over the desk in his office, "time for some results."

"I know Captain, I'm getting close ... I can feel it."

"Well, what I'm getting close to is telling you to haul in the pimps and forget Hashemi."

"Ah, Cap ... if we do that he'll just shut down for a while and start up again later with new pimps ... you know there's enough of 'em out there." Derek knew the real reason for Lewis' impatience was that a new police commissioner would soon be named and he wanted the job.

"Yeah, yeah ... I know, but I'm just putting you on notice that something better break soon or we go after the pimps."

Derek knew this wasn't an idle threat. He also knew that Captain Lewis might be getting a little nervous about the political implications of charging a foreign national like Hashemi with such a hideous crime. "He's probably worried about losing the immigrant vote," he laughed to his partner Sean.

"And in this city," Sean said, "he might have a point. He might be getting cold feet and thinking it might be better to settle for the American pimps."

Derek knew what he had to do.

* * *

"I pride myself on being able to spot an infiltrator," Guild President Barry Anderson told Doug Glassman confidently as they walked down the street, "that's why I ask a lot of questions at first. And that's why I let you sit at the table for an hour before I spoke to you when we first met. I wanted to see what you would do if you thought I wasn't going to show ... if you would call your police contacts or whatever. I've had undercover police detectives try to infiltrate the group before, but I spotted them right away and wouldn't let them join."

"How do you spot them?" asked Doug innocently as they walked down the street with the Chicago wind whizzing around their heads.

"Well, first of all when they talk about sex with boys they often can't help but cringe just a little and betray their repulsion. But secondly, I just seem to have a sixth sense for a phony. Mr. Hanson didn't show any repulsion, but he also didn't show much of anything else ... no emotion at all when he talked about what must've been the most emotional and traumatic experiences of his life. That just didn't seem right."

"Maybe he's not an emotional person," threw in Doug.

"Maybe. I'm probably just getting suspicious in my old age. Anyway, we'll get to know him better and we can go from there. The thing is, even if a cop slipped into our group, it wouldn't be a great tragedy because we don't do anything illegal at our meetings. We just exercise our right of free speech and we can't be arrested for that." The Guild had a strict rule of no sex with boys at Barry's house. Occasionally one of the members brought a new young consort to meet the other members and sometimes begin a relationship with one or more of them, but it couldn't take place at the house. Douglas had had to take Jimmy to a motel. Now, of course, Doug had his own apartment and regularly had intimate relations with Jimmy and others. Barry's house was only for meetings, which were legal, and made it difficult, if not impossible, for authorities to prosecute.

* * *

On the verge of nausea Dan left Barry Anderson and Doug Glassman at the restaurant and went to his motel to pack. He took a taxi to O'Hare Airport and flew stand-by to Phoenix where he checked into the Sun Goddess Motel. During his four days at the Sun Goddess he made sure he got to know both the day and night clerks so that they would remember him. He was going to make sure that when a bunch of pedophiles were killed in Chicago there would be people to swear he was in Phoenix. Then he flew back to Chicago just in time to attend the Guild meeting Anderson had invited him to.

"Come in. Come in," Barry welcomed him, "I'm glad you could make it. Did you have any problem finding us?"

"No," Dan said, noticing several Guild members had already arrived and were drinking at the bar, "You gave good directions."

"Good. Let me introduce you to some of our other members. Guys, this is Dennis. He's thinking about joining."

The men gave Dan a few hellos and two of them came over to talk as his skin began to crawl knowing that some of these men were undoubtedly cut from the same cloth as Greg Dawson, the man who had raped and killed his son. He knew he had to repress that kind of thinking if he were going to be convincing, so he did.

"How did you find out about us?" one of the men asked.

"Well, I read in the paper about a Guild group out east that wasn't allowed to meet in a public meeting room. They were suing for discrimination. Then I met Barry and Doug at the Gay Pride Parade."

"Oh, yeah," said the second man, "that was the apartment building thing in New York. They had actually been meeting there for several years without complaint. But some local parents found out and pressured the landlord."

"Yeah, that was it. Anyway, that was the first I ever heard about the Guild. It sounded like my kind of group."

The conversation went on with several other members of the group who arrived later. By 11:00PM there were seventeen men present. The meeting consisted of Barry updating the group on the Guild's efforts to enlighten society to the merits of intimate relationships between men and boys. Most of those efforts involved literature that it circulated. For obvious reasons the group couldn't openly lobby, but rather, had to proceed clandestinely through mailings and articles or advertisements in offbeat publications. Except for the subject matter, thought Dan, this could be a Jaycee's or Shriner's meeting. After the official business, several Guild members stood up and related stories about their pedophile experiences and the meeting turned into an encounter group.

"Dennis, would you like to share anything?" Barry asked Dan.

"Well," he said as he got to his feet, "I have been sexually attracted to younger boys ever since I can remember having sexual feelings. For me it's as natural as mom's apple pie. As I told Barry, the rest of society has made me feel I'm a total deviant and I have had to have therapy to cope with the ostracism. I believe that it's natural and right for young boys to have intimate relationships with adult men and I believe it is highly educational and emotionally valuable to them. And I'm just glad to have finally found others who feel the same way I do."

The room erupted into theatrical applause and Dan felt that he must have sounded believable. Barry turned to Douglas and said, "I guess he's O.K.," but secretly he still felt a little uneasy about Dan although he couldn't say why. He decided to keep a close eye on him. Then the meeting broke up into a party with everyone drinking and talking informally.

What struck Dan most was that many of the men present looked and acted like ordinary people he might run into every day. They were well-dressed and well-spoken and their actions didn't betray any deep-seated perversion. A few, though, looked every bit the part of the child molester. But he noticed that they seemed somewhat unpopular with the rest of the group as if they were viewed as really being perverted.

Toward one o'clock in the morning, when the men started to leave, Barry asked Dan, "Well, what do you think?"

"I like what I've seen tonight, Barry, and I want to join."

"Great. We'll put it to a vote next week. I'm sure you're in. You really hit a chord with your little statement. We've all felt what you said."

"Yeah, the applause kinda' surprised me. Was everyone here tonight?"

"Most of the group was. There are three who didn't make it. They should be here next week, though, especially since we're gonna' vote on a new member."

Dan left knowing that a week from that night he would have to strike. He would also have to determine how. Taking out twenty people all at once was not going to be easy. Driving back to his motel, however, he had a seed of an idea. With some mental watering the seed began to sprout into a bona-fide plan. He lay down on his motel bed to give it some more thought, but fell asleep. Then came the dream. In this one, he jumped out of an airplane without a parachute, shouting, "I forgot my chute." As he fell, he looked up to see Cole's face looking out of the pilot's cockpit window. His lips were moving, but once again, Dan couldn't hear what he was saying. Then, all of a sudden, Lee Santucci's face appeared, suspended in the clouds. Dan could hear him saying simply, "No right, no wrong, no better than me." Looking back up to Cole, Dan saw him just shake his head.

CHAPTER 39

The week went by quickly. Barry Anderson worked the day shift so Dan just broke into the house the day of the scheduled Guild meeting and set things up. The house sat on a large lot a long way from the nearest neighbor. Barry couldn't have made a better choice.

That night Dan attended the meeting. He stopped briefly and slid a piece of paper into Barry's mailbox, which was about 80 yards from the house. Then he went in. A full turnout of all twenty Guild members appeared. After the regular meeting and drinks Barry asked Dan to leave while they voted on his membership. "Come on back in Dan," came Doug Glassman's voice a little later, "Congratulations, you're a full-fledged member of the Guild." Everyone applauded. Several shook Dan's hand and patted him on the back. At 11:45 he left the group on the pretense of going to the bathroom.

"What are you up to?" a voice came from the hallway and startled Dan as he crouched down in the closet of a central bedroom. It was Guild President Barry Anderson who had come to look for him after noticing his absence.

"Oh, just admiring your house," said Dan lamely as he stood up.

"From the closet?" a suspicious Anderson walked over to him.

"Well, I've learned that you can tell a lot of things about a person from their closet."

"Uh Huh," Barry said as he bent down to see what Dan had been hunched over when he entered. His eyes got big and he instantly rose up to confront Dan, but his quick reaction wasn't quick enough. He brought his .38 down hard on Anderson's head sprawling him out on the floor. "Say goodnight, Gracie," said Dan as he pushed him into the closet, covered him up with clothes, and shut the door.

When he rejoined the group in the living room no one had seemed to notice his or Barry's absence. "There you are," came Doug Glassman's voice, "I've been looking for you."

"You have," Dan said, slightly concerned, "Why?"

"Oh, I just wanted to see how everything was going for you and how you feel now that you're officially a member of the group. I know that joining the Guild was the best thing that ever happened to me."

"How's that?" asked Dan glancing at his watch. Just then he glanced across the living room and noticed that a teen-age boy had come in while he was gone. An alarm went off in his head.

"Well, my life before I joined was a living hell," Douglas bubbled, "it was just one long denial of who I am. Who I am is who you and the rest of the guys are. We love boys and now, finally, I know there's nothing wrong with that."

"How long have you been with the group?" Dan asked politely, trying desperately to figure out an instant plan for this unexpected turn of events.

"Just a few months and, you know, I've already had three lovers. The latest one I want you to meet. He's so cute you'll die. I'll tell ya', finally I'm living the life I was meant to live ... I feel so free. It's just not right denying who we are. I've never been so happy and I know you'll feel the same way."

"I think you're right and it may happen sooner than you think. But right now, what will make me happy is to meet that handsome lad over there, if you'll excuse me," Dan got to his feet.

"Of course," said Doug, "but don't be gone too long, I want to talk to you some more." Doug was enjoying his new social life and newfound sense of acceptance. Finally, he felt like he belonged.

"Me too," Dan mumbled as he walked toward the boy. "Hi I'm Dennis Hanson," he said reaching out his hand, "I'm new and Barry said to ask you to show me around the house. Would you mind?"

"Sure," said the boy looking a little confused.

"Barry said you should show me his lovely garden out back," Dan said as he took the boy's arm and ushered him toward the back of the house. He looked at his watch to see it was 11:57.

"I didn't know Barry had a garden," came the slightly suspicious response.

When they stepped off the back-porch Dan whirled around and punched the kid squarely in the nose, knocking him cold. He then swung him over his shoulder in a fireman's carry and ran through the back yard. He dropped the unconscious boy a half-block away from the house and ran another block to his rented car. At just about the same time Barry Anderson regained consciousness in the bedroom closet. At 11:59:30 he stumbled out of the closet and staggered to the living room.

"What the…?" Doug Glassman said as he and several of the men dashed toward their president who had blood streaming down his face.

"Dennis … Hanson…" was all Barry could muster. At that instant Douglas began to sense that the bleeding man's suspicions might have been right. But the realization came too late.

Dan saw it before he heard it. Just as he unlocked his car door he saw a blinding flash and heard a deafening explosion. He was glad to see that the batch of C-4 explosives he had saved from his days as a demolitions expert was still good. The way he placed the charges made the house implode upon itself and not disturb much around it. He hesitated only a moment to make sure the house was totally destroyed. Then, he got into the car and looked pensively at the distant glow of the fire and said out loud, "I'll bet I just won the world record for being a member of a club for the shortest time." He was still trying to use humor to ease the growing guilt gnawing at his insides. Even so, the cloud was back and giving him a humdinger of a headache. "Anyway, that makes about 1176 kids I've saved," he told himself as he drove off into the night listening to the approaching sirens and cranking up Mick Jagger screaming "I'm talkin' bout the midnight rambler" on the car stereo.

The note he had stuck in the house's mailbox read, "This is for what you filthy scum did to my boy." Dan figured the local police knew Anderson's house was the headquarters for the Guild and that after they found the note, they would conclude that the explosives had been planted by the parent of a boy who had been molested by a member or members of the group. He further figured that the police department would look at this mass murder as an act of law enforcement that did what it couldn't do. He banked on the investigation being swift and cursory. After all, who was going to loudly call for a more in-depth investigation, the kids that the Guild had molested? Dan didn't think so. But there was the boy.

* * *

In addition to the taps on kiddie pimp Ali Ban Hashemi's telephone and the hidden microphones in his apartment detectives were watching him from a vacant office in a building across the street. Derek had been on the early evening watch since that was when Hashemi seemed to be most active, but now he also took on the overnight shift that Captain Lewis had canceled. Besides, feeling the need for complete surveillance, Derek's instincts told him that Hashemi might be about to make a move during the early hours of the morning. After all, the only consistent thing he had done so far was to be inconsistent. When making his kiddie deals he never used the same pay phone twice, he never hailed a cab from the same location, and he never used the same pimp twice in a row. In other words, the fact that he had done nothing during the overnight shift so far meant he probably soon would. So Derek started watching his prey on the overnight shift in addition to his early evening shift and grabbing a few hours of sleep whenever he could. The only problem was that his new schedule interfered with the inroads he was trying to make with his estranged wife and son.

"Geez, do you look beat!" Julie said to him the morning after his fifth overnight shift. He had come to the house to take his wife and son to Coney Island as part of their reconciliation. He really wanted to cancel the outing so he could get some sleep, but knew if he did, he risked wiping out the little progress he had made. It was a giant step for Julie to agree to see him, and his son, who had previously been as cold as ice to him, now seemed to be warming up. He was trying hard. He was even playing ball with Gary, something he had rarely done in the past.

"Oh, I had to work late last night," Derek answered not wanting to admit that he was working the crazy hours she had always detested, and wanting desperately to avoid the old argument over which was more important, his job or his family, "Are we ready to go?"

"You bet! It's all Gary's been talking about." Just then Gary walked into the room.

"Hi Dad. Ready for a wild roller coaster?"

"Absolutely. Ya' ready for one of Nathan's finest?"

"You betcha', the hottest dogs on the planet."

Unlike most New York kids Gary had never been to Coney Island, another testament to Derek's past absences as a father. But that was changing and this trip was a first step.

The day started out grand with Derek winning several stuffed animals at the shooting gallery and Gary showing surprising skill at the baseball throw. There was cotton candy and pretzels followed by Nathan's conies and fresh-squeezed lemonade. They hit the midway and by the fourth exciting ride Derek felt like a walking dead man. He was trying hard, but his conversation was lagging and both Julie and Gary noticed it.

When they came out of the tunnel on the river raft ride he was asleep in his seat.

"Well," Julie said to Gary with disappointment, "I guess some things never really change."

"I guess not mom," was all Gary could say as he gazed from his sleeping father off into the distance.

* * *

Ross Huggins investigated the Los Angeles pedophile deaths in the order they occurred. The first was Brian Armstrong, the gay man who appeared to have been killed by an anti-gay organization. The glaring thing about the Armstrong murder was that it was the first time an anti-homosexual group in the area had ever killed anyone. Usually they just beat up a gay man here and there, but they never killed, at least not until now. Ross wasn't buying it. It was too much of a coincidence that gay bashers would commit their first murder at the same time a mad man was systematically killing pedophiles, especially since Armstrong was a convicted pedophile. This has got to be my man's work, he thought. Unfortunately, he could find no proof.

When he investigated Roger Buckman's electrocution he stumbled onto something interesting. A neighbor across the street from the house Buckman was wiring told Ross she had seen someone other than Buckman enter the house the night of his accident. It was too dark to see what he looked like, but she said he went in for just a few minutes, came back out and drove away in a blue sedan. She didn't know what kind of car it was and had not gotten the license number, so there was no way to trace the man. But it all contributed to Ross's slowly growing body of evidence that these deaths were not accidents.

The El Muerto Motorcycle Gang had no idea who shot their comrades or why. In reality El Muerto gang members were fairly dismayed at losing their confederates, but they weren't unanimously unhappy about it. Most of them knew they were involved in something other than their normal drug and gun business and that they were making a lot of money at it. They were jealous and silently angry at being left out.

CHAPTER 40

an's initial inclination was to get out of Chicago, and fast. But a gut instinct made him stay and follow the news coverage of the Guild House bombing for three days to see if the boy he had saved went to the police. He concluded that the kid would probably stay quiet and considered the fact that he had been wearing a disguise when he met him anyway. Consequently, he saw no reason not to stay in Chicago and proceed with his original plan to gain access to police records on local pedophiles. He also realized he could use the Guild house bombing as an excuse for his visit to the city, which might make his story more believable. Besides, he liked living on the edge. Four days after the explosion he was on the telephone to the Chicago Police Department's Public Information Office.

"My name is Eric Summers and I'm writing a book on pedophilia," he told the female police officer. "I've been doing research on the subject and I've come to Chicago because of the recent incident involving the Guild. What I'd like to request is access to the department's files on convicted child molesters for a pedophile profile."

"You mean you want to read the case files on anyone convicted of child molesting?" came the somewhat surprised response.

"Yes. That's exactly what I need."

"Well, I'll have to check on that sir. There may be some legal reasons we can't grant your request. Can you give me your phone number? I'll call you when I have an answer." Dan gave her his motel number and waited while he reflected on how easy the San Diego and Los Angeles Police had been. The thought occurred to him that the further east you go, the more uptight people are. He realized that now he may be in for less cooperation and it worried him. Several hours later another police officer called his room and asked Dan to come to the department in person to discuss his request with Chief Public Affairs Officer Randy Gibbs. He immediately stiffened up at the request.

Now he was at a fork in the road. If they're onto him, he knew that he had to skip town immediately. If not, he may be missing a good opportunity for the midwestern version of his mission. He had a somewhat compulsive notion of hitting pedophiles on both coasts and in the middle of the country, as if geography made any difference.

Then he realized that if they were onto him they would be beating down his door right now to arrest him.

After some anxious contemplation he concluded that after the explosion they're probably just being extra careful and the odds were with him. He didn't think about his long-standing proclivity for pushing his luck. But he did realize that they would be taking a closer look at him and that meant wearing an especially convincing disguise. This time he didn't use extra synthetic skin, but he dyed his hair, eyebrows, mustache and beard sandy blonde. A pair of blue-tinted contact lenses turned his dark-brown eyes blue and he was ready to go.

* * *

Two days earlier and 700 miles away Susan Jensen lay in bed figuring out how to re-work her documentary segment on the Foresters since Jan told her it didn't look like Dan would do an interview. The telephone rang.

"Did you hear about Chicago?" Her old News Director Bob Manson asked as she picked up the receiver.

"No, what?" she asked sleepily.

"Someone blew up the Guild headquarters."

"The what?" Susan woke up fast.

"The Guild ... that kiddie sex group. It killed 20 of them."

"You gotta' be kidding!"

"No. It happened yesterday. A friend of mine at The Times told me a note was found in the mailbox from a guy whose kid was molested by The Guild. I'm working on getting video of it from a Chicago station."

"Wow, Bob! I've gotta' get there right away. What great timing!"

"No kidding. This is gonna' play great ... angry father kills twenty child molesters. You couldn't have scripted it any better. Anyway, I'm one step ahead of you. I've already lined up a crew for you. If you can catch a flight there tomorrow you can start some interviews with the cops and the neighbors and go from there. Hell, if you get real lucky they might catch the guy who did it while you're there and you can get some tape of him being hauled in."

"Oh, that would be too good to be true," she said with a reporter's fervor, "I'll get out tomorrow and call you as soon as I get there. Thanks so much Bob."

"No problem. Bye Sue and good luck."

Susan hung up the phone flushed with excitement. What a break this could be, she thought. It was every reporter's dream to have something of this magnitude happen in the middle of a production. It gave the documentary immediacy and more than made up for the disappointment over Dan Forester backing out. She quickly booked a flight to Chicago for the next day and went about tying up some loose ends of her research. The Chicago incident had come at a good time since she was pretty much done with her work in Washington and was preparing to start a full schedule of shooting around the country anyway.

* * *

Things were not going well for Detective Derek Lindsay. He practically lived at the Ali Ban Hashemi stakeout now, eating and sleeping there. He had slept through another get-together with his wife and son. Worst of all was that Hashemi's kiddie operation had gone quiet and Captain Lewis was getting more impatient by the day.

"Here I am," he told his partner Sean at the stake-out, "killing myself ... and about to lose my wife and son ... again ... before I even get them back ... and for what?"

"To make a gigantic bust and get you to captain," was Sean's ever-encouraging response.

"No, I mean this shit isn't paying off and Lewis is about to shut it down. So far, all I've got is weak circumstantial evidence against Hashemi ... and Lewis is afraid that if we charge him and don't get a conviction we'll have a big lawsuit on our hands."

"Yeah, I know ... but things could break any minute."

"Yeah and it may rain beer any minute." Derek's frustration and sleep-deficit were beginning to show. He was trying to work 18 hours a day and get back in the good graces of his family at the same time, and it wasn't working.

He was taking amphetamines to stay awake. The only problem was that the speed made him irritable and cranky when he was awake, which didn't do much for his relationship with his wife and son.

Derek was about to admit that he wasn't going to get the big bust he had hoped for when Sean, looking through the high-power binoculars, blurted, "he's moving."

* * *

It was a cool October afternoon when Susan Jensen walked out of O'Hare International Airport and got in the taxicab line. The air was crisp and she could instantly understand why it was called the Windy City. She took a cab to the Shore Drive Hotel and immediately called her old News Director, Bob Manson.

"Hi. I just got in. What's the latest?"

"Not much new." Bob didn't have much more information than before, other than the fact that the news media would be carrying the full story of the Guild connection and the note the next day. The police had not wanted to release that information initially, but had to, now that it had been leaked.

"I guess I'll try to get some police interviews tomorrow."

"Yea, and so will everyone else, so I'm sure they'll end up holding a press conference."

"Great, that will give it immediacy."

"Yea and it should get the cops going."

"What do you mean?"

"Well, when bad guys get blown away the cops aren't gonna' work that hard at finding out who did it. When the bad guys are scum-of-the-earth child molesters they look at it like the killer did them a favor. In this case I'd have to agree with them. But we want them to find this one so you can have him. I mean can you imagine getting an interview with this guy?"

"Right," said Susan, almost salivating over the prospect, "Let's hope the Chicago cops are on the ball."

"Well, they will be, at first. But I'll wager if they don't find the guy right away, when the media attention dies down, so will the investigation."

Bob was right on all counts. There were so many requests for interviews once the newspaper stories hit the street that the Chicago Police Department had no choice but to call a press conference. Using a freelance camera crew Susan shot the news conference and then combed the neighborhood where Barry Anderson's house once stood for interviews with neighbors.

"Did you notice anything strange about the house?" went the routine questions. She got answers like, "Yes, there seemed to be a lot of men going in and out and a few times I saw young boys go in too." For the most part, although he had lived there for 5 years, no one in the neighborhood really knew Barry.

Now, all Susan had to do was wait and follow the police investigation. She scheduled interviews with several police officials and got the Chicago Fire Department's chief arson inspector to agree to an interview as soon as the arson investigation was complete.

The only thing she had to do was interview Chief Public Affairs Officer Randall Gibbs once more. She conducted the interview in the morning, finding out from Gibbs that the police were narrowing down a list of possible suspects. The camera crew took down its equipment as Susan made small talk with Officer Gibbs when his intercom buzzed.

"There's an Eric Summers here to see you, sir," the secretary's voice announced.

"Oh yeah," said Officer Gibbs, "Send him in. You know, you might want to meet this guy," he told Susan, "He's writing a book on child molesting and wants to research some of our files."

"Hmmm." she answered, "Sure."

* * *

"Let's roll," said Detective Derek Lindsay snapping into action and hoping this was the big one. Through the binoculars Sean had seen Hashemi come out the front door of his apartment building and walk down the street. He hadn't made it 100 yards before the two were following him, Derek walking on one side of the street and Sean following in the car. Predictably, Hashemi hailed a cab. Sean gunned the car up the street, Derek jumped in and they were off, after the cab.

"It's gotten routine," said Derek resignedly, "he'll make a call from a pay phone, we'll get the pictures, and that's all we'll get."

But this time Hashemi had something far different in mind. Instead of going to a phone the cab driver dropped him at a park on the city's west side. There was no pay phone in sight.

"What do we have here?" was all Derek could say.

* * *

Officer Gibbs' office door opened and Dan walked in. Immediately Susan Jensen had the strange sensation that she had seen him before. The only picture she had ever seen of him was one Jan had shown her of Dan and Cole fishing. The picture focused on Cole in the foreground and left Dan, who was wearing a hat and sunglasses, slightly out of focus in the background. She just marked it up to a false deja vu.

"Miss Jensen, this is Eric Summers, a journalist writing a book on pedophilia. Mr. Summers, meet Susan Jensen, a journalist doing a documentary on the same subject."

A bit taken aback, Dan shook hands with Susan while admiring her beauty.

"It's nice to meet you," said Susan holding out her hand.

"You too. Are you with a local station?" Dan asked.

"No, I'm an independent producer doing this documentary for PBS."

Electric currents instantly shot through Dan's brain. It can't be, he thought, but it has to

be ... her! Luckily his trained mind enabled him to instantly cover his shock.

"Oh, then I suppose you're here for the same reason I am ... the Guild incident."

"Right." Both felt something foreign and strange in each other. A preliminary seed of unexplainable attraction, of instant infatuation, or chemistry. Whatever it was, it slowly turned into a magnetic feeling, one which each tried to ignore to pursue their own agendas. "So, you're writing about pedophilia."

"Yes ... yes I am, and I'm putting together a profile of the classic pedophile. I'm here to look over the department's files on local cases."

"Well, perhaps we should interview you. You never know, the publication of your book might coincide with the broadcast of this documentary and it could be good for both of us." Susan was not in the least concerned with either her documentary or Dan's fabricated book. She was caught by unconscious animal instincts she couldn't explain. Instincts of attraction which forced her to make sure she saw this man again. Just then the telephone rang and Officer Gibbs answered it, missing the rest of their conversation.

"Yeah, it could be," Dan said in a low tone, "How about dinner tonight to talk about it?" he found himself saying, surprised at his own perilous words. He just knew he found her incredibly attractive. He also found her incredibly dangerous considering her relationship to his wife. But then there was his affinity for living on the edge, for pushing the envelope. Inexplicably and feverishly attracted to this man, Susan accepted the dinner invitation.

CHAPTER 41

Susan was radiant as she walked into the La Boheme restaurant. As he met her in the lobby Dan hoped her radiance would burn off the dark cloud that was now his near-constant companion. He showed up wearing glasses as a further disguise. She wore the only sexy evening gown she owned and was turned on by the idea that he was self-confident enough to wear glasses on a first date. They proceeded to get to know each other over drinks in the lounge.

In his dating days Dan had been so in love with Jan that he couldn't believe the intensity of his feelings. When Susan experienced her first and only love she was surprised at how powerful the emotion was. Now, what each felt was a step up from those passions. Each had once felt young, wild lust and love for another person. This was more grown-up and mature, but at the same time spontaneous and impetuous, which was substantially more dangerous.

As Dan listened to Susan, the stereotype he had held of her disappeared. She was immediately impressed that he was an author. Most TV journalists with any intelligence question at one time or another if what they are doing is serious journalism or just entertainment. A reality-based author, however, is the most serious journalist of all, something many reporters wish to be. Not only was Susan passionately captivated by Dan, but she felt instant respect for him as well.

"Is this your first book?" she asked, never taking her eyes from his.

"Yes, it is. I've written free-lance magazine articles under another name and before that I was a reporter at the St. Louis Tribune, but this is my first crack at a book," he easily lied. He figured no one would be able to check on his St. Louis Tribune story since the paper had closed down several years earlier. He told Sergeant Gibbs the same thing in case he did some checking. Right now, however, he was more interested in looking into Susan's eyes, but really concentrating about 12 inches lower where a sexy, low-cut evening gown barely hid a very substantial bosom.

"I've always wanted to take a year off and write a book, but I never felt I could afford it," Susan recited the lament of many journalists.

"Yeah, that's a problem. I probably wouldn't be doing this now if I hadn't inherited a small amount of money from a rich aunt. It's enough to keep me going while I finish the book, but after that, if it doesn't get published it's going to be back to real work."

"Why child sex abuse?"

"Well, I first got interested in the issue when a boy disappeared in St. Louis who was later found sexually abused and dead."

"Mathew Rogers, right?" blurted Susan since her research had turned up many names and stories of kidnapped kids.

"Right," said Dan, glad that he had done his homework on the Rogers case, "anyway in covering the Rogers story I talked to missing children experts who told me horror stories that turned my stomach. I was amazed at the size of the kiddie porn industry and that there are actually organized groups out there buying and selling children. I figured if I was that ignorant of the issue most of America probably was too. So, the book."

"Yea, it does seem to be America's dirty little secret. I've been amazed to find how lenient the courts are. It's like the legal system would rather just sweep the dirt under the rug than bring it out in the open and face it head-on."

"I know. That's one of the reasons I want to see several cities' police records on their local pedophiles."

"Is Gibbs gonna' let you?"

"I don't know. Today he told me he has to talk to the police chief and the district attorney."

"Yeah, they're really playing it close to the vest after the Guild deal. Normally, they'd probably let you do it, but I think they're afraid that some of the files are on members of the Guild and they don't want to risk jeopardizing the case."

It hit Dan in the face how utterly logical this was and he wondered why he hadn't thought of it himself. "How could that jeopardize the case?" he asked innocently.

"Well, I don't know exactly. But you know lawyers. If they catch a guy and he finds out the police have been showing his confidential records to a reporter, he might try to use it in his defense. It doesn't sound likely, but the cops don't want to take any chances."

"Do you get the impression this is one they would just as soon sweep under the rug?"

"Absolutely. It's pretty obvious that finding whoever planted that bomb is already becoming less and less a priority."

"Yeah."

"Gibbs told me off-camera that they interviewed several suspects ... all fathers of boys who were molested by members of the Guild ... but that all had iron-clad alibis. That's why they haven't charged anyone."

"Hmmm. They may never get anyone, especially if their interest in the case declines."

"It's not exactly like the public is crying out for the police to find the mad bomber. I think most people secretly feel he's a bit of a hero instead of a criminal. They're not gonna' put a lot of pressure on the cops to find him."

"What do you think? Is he a hero?" Dan asked.

Susan had to think about that one. "Well ... on the one hand, *yes*, because in one fell swoop he probably saved several hundred kids from being molested by these Guild guys. But on the other hand, it was murder and murder is wrong no matter who you kill." Susan was enjoying the conversation and realized she found Dan intellectually as well as physically stimulating.

As the talk and the drinks progressed both of them were feeling more and more amorous toward each other. On a very pragmatic, if unromantic basis both had practical reasons for feeling this way. Dan hadn't been with a woman other than El Muerto's Rita in several months and he was sensually hungry. For Susan, an affair with a man whom she found extremely attractive and who would be going in a different direction in a few days would allow her to safely quench her erotic thirst while avoiding the dreaded C word.

Dan felt a genuinely strong attraction like nothing he had felt since his early days with Jan. This was a lot like those early feelings for Jan, but different because Susan seemed to have a lot of qualities Jan didn't have; independence and a strong identity for starters, both of which he found intriguing. Taking all of this into consideration he made his move first. "I'm going to go out on a limb here," he said carefully, "and tell you that even though we just met, I feel something very unusual and intense for you. I just want to know if you feel it, too, or if I'm losing it."

Susan was tempted to take the easy way out and tell Dan she didn't share his feelings. But she couldn't resist because her own feelings were too strong. "You're not losing it."

"Well, I've got to admit this is a new one for me."

"Me too. In fact, you wouldn't believe how out of character this is for me."

"Well, what are we going to do about it?"

The two sat looking deep into each other's eyes for several awkward seconds until Susan finally said, "Well, as long as I'm out of character I might as well go all the way. We're not star-crossed kids anymore. We've both been around the block and know we don't have the time to date and build a relationship. So ... how about if we skip dinner and go back to my hotel?"

Dan stared at her in disbelief for a few seconds and then said simply, "Works for me. Let's go." As they got up to leave they were both flushed with sexual excitement. Susan felt like a young girl again. Dan was intrigued, but already feeling guilty.

* * *

"Quick," Detective Derek Lindsay sputtered to his partner Sean, "Pull over here. You tape and I'll get sound."

Kiddie pimp Ali Ban Hashemi got out of the cab and walked into a wooded area. Sean went one way and Derek the other, both trying to outflank him to get a straight shot. Sean carried the camera and Derek had the long-range, wireless parabolic microphone. Hashemi met another man on the path in the middle of the woods and they walked off into a thick patch of trees. "No way am I losing this one," Derek said under his breath as he desperately looked for a way to get a straight, unimpeded line of sight between him and the two men. Then it hit him. The only way was up, so he climbed a nearby tree. When he got above the lower branches he could see them clearly. He instantly recognized the man as Kenneth Jacobsen, one of Hashemi's regular pimps. From his vantage point he could see Sean on the other side of the trees, lying on his stomach and shooting video under the lower branches. "Gold!" was all he could whisper to himself as he turned on the microphone and started recording in the middle of the two men's conversation, just in time to hear Jacobsen say, "listen man ... this is serious shit."

"I know that, but you could've told me that on the phone. You know I don't like meeting like this."

"I know ... I know, but I thought this was something we should talk about in person

'cause ... if I go down you go down."

"Yeah, well" said Hashemi disdainfully, "if you would've done your job right in the first place we wouldn't have this problem."

"How in the hell was I supposed to know Lundquist would get away?"

"It's your job to pick just the right kid ... one who won't get away."

"Well, whatever ... the point is I need dough and I need it now to get out of town before the kid is singing all over the place about me ... and then I have to sing about you."

"O.K ... O.K ... I get the point. I'll send you the money the regular way tonight. Just go home and wait for it ... and I never, ever want to see your face again in this city."

"Don't worry ... you won't." The two men parted.

Derek climbed down from the tree in an excited sweat and met Sean at the car. They followed Hashemi's cab back to his apartment building.

"Tell me you got everything on tape," Derek said with excitement building in his voice.

"I got everything on tape," was Sean's simple answer.

"Well, so did I and I'm tellin' ya' this could be it. Apparently, Jacobsen sold some kid named Lundquist to one of Hashemi's clients and the kid got away. It sounds like they're worried that the kid will go to the cops. So, Hashemi's giving Jacobsen money to leave town."

"Well that explains why he broke with tradition and actually met with a pimp."

"Yea ... I figure Jacobsen told him either he meets with him or he goes to the cops and Hashemi had no choice."

"Lucky break, huh?"

"Could be just the break we need. We've got Hashemi on tape talking to a convicted child molester about a missing kid and we even got the kid's name."

"Yea, that's a little more than circumstantial. Now if we can find the kid it'll be like icing on the cake."

"Right, I'll get Sharon to do a computer search for a missing kid named Lundquist and see what we come up with."

"Yup ... in the meantime do we take Jacobsen in and put him on ice?"

"No. If we do that he may not squeal on Hashemi and we'll probably have to let him go. So, we videotape him getting the money ... then we follow him wherever he goes so we know where he is and can pick him up when we're ready."

"Ummm ... kinda' risky. We may lose him for good."

"I know, but it's a gamble we're gonna' have to take. He'll probably fly somewhere and wherever it is we'll have a man with him to see where he ends up."

"Things are cookin' my man," Sean said as he gave Derek a high five, "why don't you let me take care of the money drop and you get someone on Jacobsen."

"You read my mind. After that would you mind taking the watch? I don't think Mr. H. is going to be up to much tonight other than sending the money and I kinda' wanted to go see my kid."

"No problem. Say hi to Gary for me. Things goin' good in that department?"

"Well, they would be if I could stay awake long enough and stop standing him and his mom up."

"But I saw you guys a couple a weeks ago and you looked like the All-American family."

"Oh we're getting there. Actually, I shouldn't say this because I'll probably jinx it, but I think we might be getting back together soon.

"All right!"

"Yeah, I think this separation gave Julie time to see what her alternatives are in the man department and she doesn't like them."

"Well, good luck man."

"Thanks ... and thanks for taking the shift. I appreciate it. See ya' later," and Derek was out the door, having shared about as much confidence as he was capable of sharing.

CHAPTER 42

The mood in the cab on the way back to the hotel was electrified with erotic tension as both Susan and Dan fantasized about the things they were about to do to and for each other. As soon as the door to Susan's room closed behind them their mutual animal magnetism exploded. Dan grabbed her and kissed her long and hard. She melted in his strong accessible arms and slid instinctively into a posture of sweet surrender. Her gown fell to the floor with a soft rustle as she clung to his shoulders. With their lips locked together, she began unbuttoning his shirt, finally just ripping it off in one frustrated motion, absent-mindedly noticing that the hair on his chest was strangely black while the rest of his hair was blonde. They both chuckled slightly at her impatient passion as she clumsily started fumbling with his belt. He helped her now, taking only a second to strip off his pants. Resuming their clench, he picked her up and carried her to the bed with their eyes burning into each other. There they fell into several of the most fiery and torrid sexual experiences either could ever recall.

Both had a significant build-up of sexual tension from not having had a fulfilling sexual relationship for quite some time, and they spent the next ten hours massaging that tension out. Susan had never known sex like this and Dan had to admit that, though it wasn't quite as acrobatic, it was every bit as good as the marathon sex he had had with Jan early in their relationship. But he was younger then and the two experiences really couldn't be compared. At five o'clock in the morning they ended up in the hotel's hot tub, thinking that would be a good way to top off their sexual escapades. But instead of sedating them, the hot water re-stimulated both of them into another sexual frenzy and they made passionate love right there in the hot tub and on a nearby pool chair. It was so early that there was no one around to watch as they twisted and turned for forty-five minutes.

After a final dip they went back to Susan's room and slipped into bed to try and get some sleep. But sleep wasn't to be and ten minutes later, they were at it again. At last, sheer exhaustion drove them to the sandman and both drifted off into the most peaceful slumber either had had in a long time. Even so, Dan's sleep brought the inevitable dreams he had not been able to figure out. This time he dreamed he was being chased by gigantic birds and when he looked up to the sky Cole's face was silhouetted against an incredibly bright sun. He was motioning to him and trying to tell him something, but once again nothing came out of his mouth.

Upon awaking the next afternoon, they went at it again. Instead of taking showers to wash the fermenting sweet and sour passion from their bodies, they both lingered in bed for another hour in varying stages of embrace, hungrily breathing in each other's essence. "Well, as much as I'd like to," Susan finally murmured with sensual satisfaction, "We can't stay in bed all day."

"Right," replied Dan sliding out of bed, "There are cops to irritate, books to write and documentaries to produce." Dan jumped into the shower only to be joined by Susan for yet another session behind the thick, steamy glass of the shower door.

Then, as they sat having breakfast in their room he had a half-true confession to make. "Last night was pretty unusual for me and I know I feel something special for you," he began, "but I have to tell you something so that we don't start out on the wrong foot..."

"You're married!" Susan gasped, "I knew it was too good to be true!"

"No, now don't get all excited ... you didn't let me finish. I have an estranged wife. We lost something along the way and I don't know if we'll ever get back together, but for now we're separated."

"Well, that makes me feel a little better. Do you love her?"

"I don't really know. I did at one time ... now I don't know. But even if I decide that I do, there are just things that make us incompatible and actually I don't give it much hope." Dan was telling the truth.

At her age Susan had gotten used to the fact that most men she met were either married, separated, or divorced and so this revelation didn't shock as much as it disappointed her. Besides, after reflecting on the unbelievable sensual experiences she had just shared with Dan, his marital separation bothered her less and less. "O.K.," she said calmly, "I can live with that."

* * *

Derek Lindsay had come to genuinely hate Ali Ban Hashemi. Watching him live his lavish lifestyle on the misery of the children he sold while he could barely make ends meet made him want to kill the man. He and his fellow officers had videotaped six pedophile/child prostitute encounters, all of which were circumstantially tied to Hashemi. But circumstantially was the key word. Hashemi had never been careless enough to let himself be in any way directly connected with the transactions, and the Manhattan District Attorney told Derek it was quite possible that a sharp defense lawyer would get him off. He had the videotape of Hashemi's meeting with Ken Jacobsen, which was incriminating but he had not been able to find the Lundquist boy who had escaped from his pedophile captor. Unfortunately, the district attorney told him the tape alone would not guarantee a conviction. They knew where Jacobsen was now living and could pick him up at any time, but there wasn't much satisfaction in that. In the meantime, all Derek could do was sit, watch, and wait.

* * *

The night's sexual adventures set the pace for what was to come as Susan and Dan repeated the scene many times, both day and night, over the next week. Susan remained in Chicago waiting for the conclusion of the police investigation of what was now being referred to as the Guild House Bombing. Just as Bob Manson and Dan had predicted, when the media attention died down the investigation lost steam fast and went nowhere with no suspect being arrested. Susan was secretly glad the investigation was taking so long. The longer it took, the longer she could enjoy her newfound lover.

Dan, meanwhile, was still waiting for permission to go over the police pedophile records. The police department had put him off for over a week, until all the bodies in the explosion had been positively identified and the records removed. He didn't mind the wait since he had other things on his mind, like Susan.

"I've got a confession to make," Susan said on her 9th day in Chicago, as they lay in bed after a particularly steamy session.

"You're married!" Dan said.

"No!" Susan said laughing and playfully slapping his shoulder, "nothing that drastic. It's that I'm only staying here because of you. If I hadn't met you I would've packed up and left by now."

"Don't feel like the Lone Ranger, honey, because that's the only reason I'm still here. If I was just concerned with the book I'd be working somewhere else while the cops made up their minds about letting me see the files. But I'm concerned with a lot more than that and it's all lying right next to me." Dan was telling the truth.

Susan had given him a welcome respite from his mission and the headaches and dark cloud of guilt that went with it.

"Well, I guess we can't stay here forever, can we?"

"Who cares about forever ... that's such an obscure concept. Let's just be concerned about the here and now and appreciate our good luck in finding each other."

"I do and I've never felt this way with anyone else in my life. But we're going to have to leave some time, and what then?"

"Woman, thy question is reasonable. Why don't we cross that bridge when we come to it?"

Her reporter's instincts sensed that Dan wanted to avoid the issue of parting. Susan asked point blank, "Why don't you want to talk about it?"

"O.K. I guess it's because I've already thought about it and I'm not sure you'll like my thoughts on the matter. First of all, I feel things for you I never thought I would feel for anyone and I definitely want to continue our relationship. But right now, we're both in the middle of the most important career work of our lives and our attention to each other could interfere with that work. I think when we leave Chicago we should both concentrate on finishing our jobs and see each other when we can. When we're done, we can take up where we left off and who knows after that."

Most of what Dan said was true. He did feel strongly for Susan and he was in the middle of the most important work of his life. He also wanted to continue the relationship, but he knew that his future was so uncertain it would be unfair to Susan, not to mention the fact that she was his wife's best friend. So, he bought himself some time, hoping that the situation would resolve itself, as often happened.

"But that could take a year. I want more than occasional visits," said Susan dejectedly.

"What do you want?"

"Well, I'm not sure. I guess I would like to see you more than that."

"I'd love to too, but that's the problem. If I do it will take me five years to write this book. Baby, you're addicting. I can tell already that if I try to divide my attention between you and the book the book is going to lose out, and while you're suddenly very important to me ... so is the book. Besides, I have a feeling it's the same with you. If we see each other a bunch it will inevitably take your attention away from the documentary, and we both know how important it is to you." In reality, Dan knew that carrying on a steady, long distance, relationship with Susan would hurt his mission and might even unfairly drag her into it. He also knew that her relationship with Jan made any future for them impossible.

"Why do you have to make so much damn sense," Susan pouted, realizing he was probably right.

"It's something I was born with."

"O.K., I give. We'll do it occasionally," she said nuzzling against him, working her tongue along his chin to his ear lobe while simultaneously rubbing her soft and supple breasts against his chest, "but right now make me glad I'm a woman again will you?"

"You don't have to ask twice," Dan breathed his response as his lips found hers. He was relieved that she had agreed to his plans. What would really transpire between them, he couldn't guess.

Two days later they said good-bye. The investigation had stalled and Susan couldn't justify staying any longer. Besides, she had to get back to Washington for an important interview with an FBI agent who specialized in child molesting cases. Dan said it was also time for him to get back to his research. They were resigned to the fact that, for now, their exciting liaison was over. He promised to call her in Washington and they agreed to get together soon for a weekend.

After putting Susan on a plane back to Washington in an almost tearful farewell Dan drove back to his motel. Instead of leaving town, he got back to work. Susan had provided him with a respite from the deep, almost uncontrollable guilt that had plagued him since he blew up the Guild House and replaced it with a different kind of guilt for cheating on Jan.

Before Susan, the dam holding back his river of remorse had broken and nearly drowned him as he began to realize the gravity of what he had done. But before he had too much time to brood over this flood of self-reproach he had met her and their torrid affair had begun, giving him a needed break. Now he returned to his mission realizing that he had to limit the number of his intended Chicago victims in light of the attention the Guild House explosion had brought. He felt he could get away with a few more, but didn't want to push his luck.

Meanwhile, Susan sat back in her airplane seat with her eyes closed, bathed in the afterglow of the most intense love affair of her life. It almost seemed like a dream to her. She felt like Dan had untied every uptight, hung-up sexual knot in her being. Then, of course, reality set in and she began to wonder if she would really ever see him again.

CHAPTER 43

"I'm sorry, Mr. Summers," Officer Gibbs told Dan the day after Susan left, "The district attorney has determined we can't allow you access to the records you want."

"Why not?" Dan asked, genuinely surprised.

"There are some confidentiality statutes in Illinois law that make it questionable. Besides we still haven't identified all the bodies in the Guild House explosion and the district attorney is worried that some of them may be in those files."

"What would be wrong with that?"

"Well, he says if we show you confidential files and then you write about the people in them, their relatives could sue us for defamation of character. But there is one thing you can do. You can file your own lawsuit and try to get a court order for the files." He said it as if he wanted Dan to file the suit.

Dan then realized he had hoisted himself on his own petard by blowing up the Guild House. The police were now too skittish to let him see the files and he wasn't about to draw more attention to himself by filing a lawsuit. The only thing to do was to leave town and fast.

* * *

Having done everything he could do in California, FBI Agent Ross Huggins flew to Chicago to investigate the pedophile deaths in the Guild House Bombing. The first thing he did was to ask Chicago Police Officer Randall Gibbs if a journalist had been allowed to read the department's pedophile records. Gibbs answered, "No, but it's funny you should ask because one asking to see the records just left an hour ago." Ross literally jumped out of his chair. "Do you have an address on him?" he nearly yelled.

"Yeah," answered Gibbs, "He's staying at the Budgetmaster Motel on 64th."

Ross asked for and got two police officers to take him to the motel. When they got there the desk clerk told them Dan had just checked out 5 minutes earlier.

"Damn!" was all Ross could say.

Dan had registered under the name Erik Summers and a search of his room turned up nothing. Ross had the policemen dust the room for prints, but knew instinctively that the guest had worn gloves. He sat down in a lobby chair and breathed a sigh of disappointed resignation. "I had him! I had him right here!" he growled pounding his fist on the chair arm.

Back at the police station he had a sketch artist draw a composite of the journalist, Erik Summers, from Sergeant Gibbs' and the motel clerk's memories. He was intensely hoping that the picture would be of one of the two men whose pictures he had had drawn in San Diego. But instead, it was of an entirely different person, a man with blond hair. Then Ross had an epiphany. There can't be three men committing these murders. It's got to be one guy with several disguises. Alas, Ross still had no idea what he looked like.

The Guild House bombing was a crime of such magnitude that it alone should have yielded some significant leads. The only problem was that the men with the needed information had blown up with the house and none of their relatives could shed any light on their deaths. The only clue came from the U.S. Military C-4 explosives, which meant the bomber might have had a military background or was still in the service.

It was the bombing that capped off enough circumstantial evidence to convince Ross's superiors that his conclusions about a pedophile killer were valid and that they warranted a continued investigation. Feeling disappointed, but partially successful, Ross flew back to Washington, D.C. to do a massive computer search for an angry parent with a military demolitions background.

* * *

Dan had no idea how close he just came to getting caught and the black cloud of guilt had returned with full force. It was as if his affair with Susan had held it at bay for so long that it was now bursting at the seams and coming at him harder than ever. He had to fight it off and the only way he knew how to do that was to drink it away. It had been a long time and he hated to break his sobriety run but, on his way east he stopped in Indianapolis and went on a three-day drunk. A half bottle of aspirin later he was again heading east on Interstate 80 intending to proceed to New York City and continue his mission.

* * *

When Ross got back to FBI Headquarters he began an immediate computer search for the parents of any child kidnapped and/or sexually abused in the last five years. He knew that sorting the possibles from the maybes from the no's was going to be a long and arduous task, though cross-checking them with anyone with a military background would streamline the process and narrow it down. But something else was quietly nagging at him. While he knew killing of any kind was wrong, after going over the files on the victims he felt that the assassin had done a lot of kids a big favor by killing the pedophiles who would have undoubtedly molested them had they been allowed to live. He thought of his own two children and knew he could easily go off the deep end mentally if anyone sexually abused them. He knew how lenient the law was with pedophiles and could see himself killing the man who hurt his kids, although going on a nationwide hunt would not occur to him. He had begun to identify with the man he was looking for and knew that that could affect his investigation. When he returned to the FBI office in Quantico his boss, Don Westerhof, was waiting for him. "You're about to be a celebrity Hug my boy," he said.

"What da' ya' mean?" Ross asked.

"A TV reporter is doing a documentary on pedophiles and wants to interview you."

"Oh man, that's all I need right now. Why me?"

"She called, asking if the bureau had a profile on pedophiles. 'Do we ever,' said the boys upstairs. They think it'll be good P.R. and want you to do the interview. Just remember, you can't talk about any specific cases, just about the profile study. If she asks you anything at all about any case just explain that you can't talk about it."

Ross could tell that he didn't have any choice in this one, but he gave it a feeble try anyway, "Do I have to do this, Don?"

"I'm afraid so. Look at it this way ... this is a good way to end your life as a researcher and begin it as a field agent, which is what you are now."

"O.K. But first let's get down to business," Ross said glancing at a note reminding him of things he had to do and setting it down on his desk. "I need you to send out instructions to every local police department telling them that if anyone comes in asking to see their pedophile records to take them into custody immediately and contact me. This way if the guy uses the same M.O. we got him."

"No problem, Hug. I'll put it out right now."

"Thanks Don. When's my big interview?"

"Tomorrow at 1:00."

"O.K. I'll dazzle her with my good looks."

"You better find something else to dazzle her with Hug," Don chuckled as he walked out of Ross' office.

The next day at 12:45PM Susan Jensen showed up with a camera crew at FBI headquarters in Quantico to interview Special Agent Ross Huggins about the recent profile he had completed on pedophiles. The interview itself dealt mostly with the profile, though Susan did ask several questions about specific cases, only to get "I can't comment" to each one. But because of the talent she had developed over years of reading upside down, she came away from the office suspecting the FBI was investigating something unusual involving pedophiles. On Ross's desk was the note he had written on the plane back from Chicago reminding himself to instruct local police departments to hold anyone asking to look at pedophile records.

Ross, in the meantime, was glad to get the interview over so he could get back to work on his case. As soon as Susan left he began the preliminary work on his computer search. He knew that while he conducted this research he would just have to wait for the pedophile killer to either visit a police station or strike again. He also knew that there was no way of telling where or when that might happen.

* * *

Approaching the fork where Interstate 70 splits off from Interstate 80 and heads toward Washington, D.C. Dan began thinking about the two women in his life, Jan and Susan; both in the same city a short distance away. He suddenly got genuinely homesick for Jan and excited about the possibility of seeing Susan again. He knew he couldn't do both. It would be too dangerous and he would feel too much guilt. He didn't need anymore of that these days.

He flipped a coin.

"Hi, it's me, Eric," he said as Susan answered the phone.

"Oh, Eric. I was hoping you'd call."

"Are you still hot for me or did the fire go out?"

"Go out? It's a raging inferno."

"Well, we'll have to do something about that," Dan said, "what're you up to?"

"Oh, I'm going to San Francisco to shoot something. It's a profile on a family whose son was kidnapped a while back. I don't suppose you could meet me there could you?" she asked with hopeful anticipation.

"Man, I'd like to, but I can't. I'm on my way to Detroit to do some more research," he lied. His decision had just been made for him. He would visit Jan.

"I'm only going to be there for three days. Do you think you could come here when I get back?"

"I don't think I'll be done in Detroit. But let's just play it by ear," Dan said, not wanting to commit to anything and realizing that he shouldn't be pursuing the relationship anyway.

"I wish I could see you."

"I feel that way too Sue. But we'll get together ... we just have to have a little patience. How's the doc coming?"

"Great. I've really got some momentum going now with the shooting. In fact, I'm glad you called for another reason. I wanted to tell you something interesting that may be nothing at all. I interviewed an FBI researcher the day after I got back on a profile he put together of pedophiles and I saw something on his desk that might interest you."

"Well, don't hold me in suspense. Spill your guts."

"It was a note and it said to tell police departments to hold anyone asking to see police records on pedophiles. So, be advised big fella. They may be onto you."

"What ... what do you mean?" he was instantly paranoid and his heart jumped into his throat. How could she know?

"Nothing," she answered wondering why he sounded so shocked, "just that it looks like they may be trying to shut off information for some reason."

Immensely relieved he realized she didn't know. "Hmmm. I wonder why the FBI would want to do that," he said nonchalantly with false curiosity. He knew immediately they were onto him or his mission. He incorrectly guessed that he'd gone too far with the Guild House, which must have triggered an investigation into the pedophiles who had died in the last few months. He correctly figured out that the FBI now knew how he got the information on his targets and instantly realized that that method could never be used again.

"I don't know," Susan replied, "like I said, it's probably nothing. It was a handwritten note that someone might make to himself. It might not have even been official."

The rest of the phone conversation with Susan blurred as Dan contemplated the seriousness of what she had told him. He felt like an animal in a trap before the pain and struggle starts. Now that he might be faced with actually being caught, it all came crashing down upon him. He started to feel a sick guilt welling up inside him like an ocean wave building into a dramatic crest, which doesn't dissipate after it breaks. He needed time to figure out what to do now. He heard himself agree to call Susan in a few days. He said good-bye, hung up the phone and headed toward Wheaton where he hoped to find affection from his wife and a few good drinking sessions with his friend Jack Adams. He stopped at a motel to re-dye his hair, eyebrows, and mustache back to black. When Jan opened the door and saw Dan standing there she nearly passed out with surprise. "Dan!" was all she screamed as she threw her arms around him.

CHAPTER 44

It took a few very late nights but FBI Agent Ross Huggins completed his computer search for a list of parents whose child was kidnapped or sexually molested in the last few years and who had military experience. He was amazed at the large number and was now in the process of having regional FBI agents all over the country investigate each one to see if they could come up with a suspect. Seven of the names were on the east coast and those he decided to investigate himself. The first two sets of names turned up nothing; the four parents had been living with their grief but had not left the area since their child was abducted. The third name, however, Ross thought might be more interesting and he was right there in the Washington area.

* * *

"Got a spare room for a few nights?" Dan said as Jan hugged him in a desperate clinch.

She drew back slightly with a start, "I guess that means this is a visit, not a return."

"Yup. I missed you and needed a shot of Janny. Are you mad?" She looked more beautiful than ever to him with her long red tresses gliding down her back. He suddenly realized he still loved her, sex or no sex. Yet, in the back of his mind he couldn't ignore the intense passion he had felt for Susan just a few days before.

"No, I guess not. I'm just glad you're here so I can get my dose of Danny." They went inside the house where they both had spent so many splendid hours with Cole in much brighter days that seemed so long ago. Their conversation was easy, neither feeling the need to get re-acquainted. Jan told him about her job and friends and he made up a lot of lies about what he had been doing in his travels.

"How's old Jack?"

"Not too good. He had surgery and they got most of the tumor ... but not all of it. He's getting radiation and chemo and its wearing on him."

"How's his attitude?"

"Better than you might expect. Oh, he's playing the big, strong guy saying he'll beat this thing, but I know him and can see he's worried."

"Yea, who wouldn't be? I wonder what'll happen to the kids if he dies."

"Well, that's the really sad part. They don't have much in the way of close relatives who could take them. Jack told me there's only an aunt on Mia's side who could and while she's nice, he doesn't think it would be the best for them." Jan hadn't admitted it to herself, but she was subconsciously thinking about the possibility of them adopting Jack's children.

"Man, 40 years of cancer research and not even close to a cure. I guess we just hope for a miracle."

"Yeah, hope is about all he's got now. But you can tell by looking at him that he's really going down fast."

"This sucks."

"Dan ... uh ... this probably isn't the best time to bring this up, but maybe we should visit Cole's grave," Jan said apprehensively.

The comment was met with a deafening silence. Then, "Uh ... I don't think so." Dan still feared visiting the cemetery. Somehow, he felt that by not facing his son's tombstone Cole wasn't really dead.

"It might help you put some of this behind you."

"It also might dredge it all up again. I've been able to bury some of it and I don't want to have to start all over again."

"Dr. Simmons says sometimes you have to face your horror head-on to overcome it."

"I know all about that ... remember ... I've done that before. I ... I'm just not ready. Let's leave it at that ... O.K.?"

"O.K."

In spite of the depressing turn the conversation had taken, Dan and Jan ended the evening with some passionate lovemaking that lasted well into the early hours of the morning. "Honey, I've got to go to work in about four hours," she said as he began to maneuver her into their third session of the night.

"Call in sick," was his predictable reply, "tell 'em you have Dan-itus."

"Why not," was Jan's answer as she rolled over and hungrily took his love. While they were both surprised at how good their first night of sex was, she was probably the most surprised. Since Dan had been gone she had pretty much decided she could do without it. Up to this moment it had seemed to her that staying numb and ignoring her physical urges was the easiest path to take. Now, in the wee hours of the morning as she experienced her third earth-shattering orgasm she was re-thinking that conclusion. In the morning she called the hospital and arranged to work the night shift.

* * *

"Hi, I'm Special Agent Ross Huggins with the FBI and I would like to talk with you about an investigation I'm conducting," Ross said to Dan as he opened his front door. Jan was at work and Dan was stunned. His heart skipped a beat and he felt his sphincter tighten up as Ross explained who he was.

"Sure, come on in," he said with a practiced cool, all the while feeling the sting of intense anxiety as he and Ross sat down at the kitchen table, the same table he had sat at with Officer Jack Adams so long ago when this nightmare was just begin-ning. He was truly amazed that the authorities were onto him this quick, wonder-ing how much they knew and how they knew it.

"Coffee?" Dan offered.

"Yes, thank you. Black," Ross said as Dan poured two cups of coffee.

"What can I do for you Mr. Huggins?"

"Well, I'm talking to every parent whose child was kidnapped or sexually assaulted in the last few years and I would like to ask you a few questions."

"Sure, no problem. But what's the case?"

"It seems that someone is going around the country killing child molesters and I'm trying to get a handle on him. I'm thinking it may be an angry parent of a child who has been molested so I'm talking to each one to explore their feelings." Ross looked at him long and hard to see if he could get any kind of reaction. He got none.

"O.K.," Dan said calmly, "shoot." He knew instantly that the *explore their feel-ings* line was a load of crap. Huggins obviously had a list of parents of abused kids and was checking them one by one to find a suspect in the killings. Dan hoped that, so far, he had covered his tracks well enough so that he wouldn't become that suspect, at least for now.

"To begin with, have you or your wife traveled out of state in the last four months?" asked Ross.

"Yeah, I went to Colorado and the Southwest awhile back. But Jan hasn't gone anywhere."

"Was it on business or pleasure?"

"Actually neither. I just got away alone to try and get my head together. That's how I do it sometimes, by traveling."

"Where did you go in Colorado and the Southwest?"

"I spent about a month in Denver and a couple months in Santa Fe, Flagstaff and Phoenix."

"Did you make it to California at all?"

"No," Dan lied, "I lived there awhile back so it doesn't hold that much appeal for me. It's just got too many people ... otherwise it'd be a great place."

"I know what you mean. Did you go anywhere else?"

"No, I just spent some time in the Rockies and the Southwest and then came back here."

"Who did you visit?"

"No one actually. I just camped and stayed in motels when I needed a shower."

"Can you think of anyone who could verify that you were in those places?"

It was then that Dan realized the importance of his extra efforts to get his name on the motel registries in Denver and Phoenix and to make himself known to the motel desk clerks.

"Well, yeah, I guess the Blue Star Motel in Denver, Colorado would remember me and probably the Sun Palace Motel in Phoenix or the Mountain Inn in Flagstaff. Other than that, I stayed in a handful of motels for one night at a time that I don't remember the names of."

The interview went on like this for about forty-five minutes with Dan telling as few lies as possible and Ross not showing any outward signs of doubt or disbelief. But inside he found Dan's story of traveling aimlessly a little strange. He got basically the same information, however, when he questioned Jan at work later that day. He even interviewed Jack Adams and got his version of the same story.

The next day he had agents in Colorado and Arizona check the motels that Dan had mentioned to see if he had actually stayed in them. The answer was, of course, *yes*. Dan's signature was on the motel registries and the desk clerks remembered him. Good alibi, thought Ross, but his traveling story still seems odd. He then went on to investigate the rest of the names on his list, putting Dan down as a definite maybe.

Dan, meanwhile, realized that his mission was now about over. Actually, it occurred to him that he should quit now before he did something that the authorities could really trace back to him. But he felt strongly that there was still a lot of work for him to do. "So many perverts," he mused aloud, "and so little time." Besides, there was still the lingering matter of a certain kiddie pimp in New York

City who appeared to be responsible for a large number of missing children-turned-sex-slaves. And Dan couldn't rest knowing that this man was still out there ruining the lives of countless kids and their parents. But deep within himself he felt that one way or another, the New York mission would be his last. Before he could follow this line of thought much further, however, he knew he had to do one thing; visit his friend.

CHAPTER 45

The man Dan saw in the doorway didn't look much like the old friend he had seen a few months earlier. Wearing an uncharacteristic baseball cap, he was more gaunt and frail than the man he remembered. Jack Adams had dark shadows under his eyes and deep lines in his face.

"Danny me boy," he said with too little enthusiasm upon seeing his friend at the door, "come on in. When did you get back?"

"Just yesterday," Dan said as he tried to hide his surprise at Jack's rapid deterioration.

"It's great to see you buddy. Beer?" asked Jack as he made his way to the refrigerator and pulled out a can of his and Dan's favorite brew.

"Yeah, thanks."

"I regret that I can't join you, but it kinda' interferes with the chemo."

"What's happening Jack?"

"Well, I'm on medical leave and as you might've noticed I look like shit. The chemotherapy has been a little hard on me. And the radiation treatments haven't done wonders for my hair-do." Jack took off his cap to reveal his balding head. He had obviously lost much of his hair in clumps.

"You have looked better," Dan joked unenthusiastically, "but is the treatment working?"

"So far it is. They didn't get the whole tumor when they went in, but the doc says they might be able to kill the rest of it with these treatments."

"Well, that's good news," Dan said with half-sincerity, "what do the doctors say usually happens?"

"That it usually comes back bigger and better than ever. But I've got a plan ... I'm gonna' think the son-of-a-bitch away. I'm doing all the cosmic crap I can to keep it from coming

back ... you know, the power of positive thinking and all that. Hell, I'm even listening to these subliminal message tapes all night that have the sounds of the ocean with a voice underneath telling me that I'm healing myself and I'm spending several hours a day visualizing my cancer going away. I also pray a lot. It's about my only chance

Dan ... otherwise the prognosis is none too good and I need to stay alive for the kids."

"How are they handling the whole thing?"

"Pretty good, especially since they don't know what's really going on. I've purposely let them think this is nothing serious. Also, Dan, you better get ready for this because you might be surprised. Call it death bed repentance or whatever, but I've found God, or I guess He found me."

Dan was surprised to hear this from his whisky slinging, cursing friend, "What does that mean Jack?"

"It means that since I've been staring death in the face for a while now I have a different perspective on things. When you realize that you may not have much time left you really start to re-prioritize things and I have finally realized that out of all the philosophies of life you and I have discussed the only real one is right here in the Bible," Jack said as he picked up the Holy Book from the coffee table.

Dan took a long, pensive slug from his beer. "Well, I admit this wasn't really what I expected to hear from you, and if it was anyone else telling me this I wouldn't put much stock in it. But coming from you, I have to believe it's real."

"Well, it is. But don't get me wrong. You probably look at this as a philosophical choice I've made. It's a lot more than that. It's not intellectual ... it's spiritual."

"Uh huh," Dan said, seeing an opportunity for one of their philosophical discussions he had missed so much, albeit this one would be sober. "How is it spiritual and not intellectual?"

"Well ... it's something I feel, not something I think. I feel that God has filled my life and now I belong to him."

"I've always been curious about that though. The Bible says that to properly worship God you have to subordinate yourself to Him ... right?"

"Right."

"But we're all given an independent mind to make our own choices in life. So, why would God give us these free-thinking, self-governing minds if he just wants us to make them subservient to Him?"

"Very much a Dan Forester question. I think that by choosing to go with God you are exercising your free will and making an independent decision; a decision to turn your life over to him. That's your decision, no one else's… and you make it with an independent mind."

"O.K. But why does God need you to bend to his will and to worship him? I mean, I get this vision of a bunch of illiterate natives bowing down before an idol carved out of wood or throwing a young virgin into a volcano as a sacrifice to their god. It just seems so archaic that God would want to be worshipped. And besides, if He's really all-powerful why would he need to be worshipped?"

"That's the real clincher isn't it? I wrestled with this too and finally had an epiphany. The worshipping is for us, not him. We both know nothing's free in this life; we have to earn anything we get and salvation is no exception. I don't think God needs to be worshipped. I think that it's our worshipping Him that earns us a place in Heaven. In other words, this life is sort of like a test which, if we pass, we go on to the next grade or eternal life. God gives us the opportunity to earn our salvation by believing in him and worshipping him. It's not that he needs it … it's that we do … we need to earn our salvation. Besides, we owe Him because we killed his son. And, by the way … don't talk about young virgins … it'll get me hot."

Dan noticed that Jack looked a little better now than when he had first come in and felt almost as if someone else was speaking through him. "When did you come up with all this Jack?" he sincerely asked.

"Well, I've always thought about this stuff in my life and it was like as soon as I became saved it all came together. I know things now that I never knew I knew before. How's that for perfect English?"

"Great. Do you believe if you died right now you would go to Heaven?"

"Yes, I do. But that doesn't mean I want to die. I really want to stick around long enough to raise my kids."

"Yeah, I wish I still had a kid to raise," said Dan lowering his gaze to the floor in a melancholy instant, "now there's a question for your belief system. If God is such a loving God why would he let an innocent kid like Cole be abused and killed and let his parents go through such pain and agony?"

Jack looked at Dan with genuine sympathy and compassion and took a little longer to answer this one. "That's a little tougher Dan. The usual answer you'll get is that God works in mysterious ways that we cannot always understand. But my opinion is that while He created the world, he isn't actively running every part of it. In other words, I think He put us here and then sort of left us to our own devices; giving us that independent freedom you're talking about … the freedom to pass or fail the test. I think He provides us with occasional overt guidance like when He sent his son to earth and when He answers prayers. But I think He chooses not to run every minute part of our lives and that is why bad things like Cole's death happen. As harsh as this might sound, there has to be a bad for there to be a good. In order for there to be a positive there has to be a negative. If everything was good and nothing bad ever happened we wouldn't even know what good is. So, bad, evil things have to happen if anything good is ever to happen. Besides, what kind of test would this life be if everything went right and nothing went wrong? It's overcoming our trials and tribulations and maintaining our faith that helps us pass the test."

"Gee that makes me feel a whole lot better," Dan said sarcastically, thinking that this was more like the old philosophical Jack.

"I know Dan ... I'm sorry."

"Oh well ... I know what you mean ... I just wish it didn't have to happen to me."

"Me too. But who knows? Maybe you can take Charlie if I die." Jack had thought about it a lot and had concluded that the only people he would really want to take his son would be Dan and Jan. But he hadn't wanted to bring it up until he saw Dan again, face to face.

Knowing his friend well, Dan could tell that his remark wasn't totally spontaneous. He had thrown it out to see what reaction he would get from him. "Of course, we would take Charlie, Jack, but it's a moot point because you're obviously going to beat this mother," was the reaction he had hoped for and Dan didn't disappoint him. Dan also knew that the only way Jack's positive thinking, self-healing plan would work was if he and those around him really believed in it. And he realized how tough it must be to make oneself believe in such a plan when the overwhelming medical evidence says you're going to die. It also struck Dan how ironic it would be if he and Jan did take in Jack's son since Charlie was just a few years younger than Cole.

"Ya' darn right I am. I'm going to beat the statistics and you'll read about me in the New England Journal of Medicine."

"What's your treatment schedule like now?"

"Well, right now I'm on hold because my blood count is too low to take the chemo and radiation. See, the treatment itself lowers your blood count and then you can't get it again until it goes back up, so it's kind of a catch 22."

"How do you feel?"

"For the most part, pretty lousy. Some days are better than others, but much of the time I'm real dizzy and I have intense pain in my head. It's like I can actually feel my brain swelling up."

"Man tell me about it. It seems like I have a constant headache these days," Dan regretted the words as soon as they came out of his mouth. "I'm sorry. I can't believe I just compared my headaches to your ... uh ... condition."

"That's alright ole man ... I know what a sensitive son-of-a-bitch you are. But hey, want some of my Percocets for those headaches? I got a drawer full of them."

"Don't you need 'em?"

"Naw, they don't work much anymore and they just constipate me. Besides I'm on stronger stuff now," Jack said as he opened a drawer and pulled out a bottle of pills. "Here man," he said, "They're yours."

"Thanks Jack," Dan said, desperately hoping they would help his headaches and drive the black cloud away. How does the rest of your body feel?

"Oh man, you don't wanna' know. My right arm gets numb and then I get real scared that I'm about to have another seizure. I'll tell ya', once you've had a seizure you get scared to death of another one because you lose complete control of your body and that's one spooky experience."

"Yea, I'll bet."

"But in spite of how sad this whole thing is, it has made me see what this life really is all about and if I hadn't gotten sick I might very well have never seen it. We're just renting these bodies. You look at me and think this body is all there is to me, but actually it's just the present housing for who I really am ... my spirit if you will. Once this body is dead, who I am goes on in another form and most likely in a better place, so the body is nothing more than a temporary vehicle. It gets weird, but I'll tell ya', I've never felt so alive as now that I am supposedly dying."

"Did you read that somewhere?"

"Yea ... actually I did."

Dan came away from his visit to Jack feeling more confused and guilty than ever. While he hated to admit it, everything Jack said made sense. He had never been particularly religious, but the things Jack had said were forcing him to look at his mission with a strict moral eye. The cloud and the guilt were getting to be almost more than he could bear. Once again, however, he knew that if he were to accomplish what was probably going to be his mission's last objective, he was going to have to push these thoughts out of his mind.

"C'mon Danny ... stay here now," Jan said when Dan told her he was going to Florida for the last leg of his journey.

"I thought I could," Dan said, "But after seeing Jack I think I need one more trip alone. I'll be back soon ... back to stay."

Jan knew it was useless to try and change his mind so they kissed and said good-bye.

But Dan didn't go south to Florida. He headed north to New York.

* * *

Susan had not gotten to talk to Jan after she got back from Chicago. But as soon as she returned from San Francisco she gave her a call. It was the day after Dan had left and she was lonely.

"I got some juicy news to tell you," Susan said.

"Well, come over tonight and lay it on me," said Jan, looking forward to seeing her friend again. Upset by Dan's sudden departure Jan reflected on how drastically different her life was today from what it was when she had a stable family. Yearning for those days she got out some old home movies and was still watching them when Susan arrived.

"Hi Sue," Jan said as she answered the doorbell, "I was just watching some old movies. I'll put them away."

"Don't you dare!" said Susan, genuinely interested, "I want to see 'em."

"O.K., but I'm not responsible for your boredom," Jan joked.

The first movie was of Cole at three years old. The second one was a little more interesting for Susan, however, because it contained Cole and Dan. At first Susan just noticed a striking similarity between Dan and the man she had fallen in love with in Chicago. But then, as she watched she grew cold and her palms began to sweat uncontrollably as she realized that Dan was Eric Summers. Her first reaction was one of horror. After all, here she was at her best friend's house watching a home movie of her best friend's husband with whom she had recently carried on a wild, unabated affair. She was shocked and sad to find out that Jan was the estranged wife to which Dan had referred. She also wanted to get the hell out of there as fast as she could.

"Jan, I've been fighting this headache all day and I thought it would get better, but it's gotten worse ... I think I'd better go home and rest," she lied.

"Oh ... that's too bad," Jan said, "I was looking forward to one of our coffee klatches. But what's your juicy news?"

"Oh ... uh ... I ... I found a pedophile priest who will do an interview."

"Wow ... that is juicy."

"Yeah ... well ... I'll call you tomorrow. O.K.?"

"O.K. Sue. Get some sleep and I hope you feel better."

"Thanks. Bye." Susan cried all the way home, realizing that the only man she might have ever loved was married to her best friend. "It figures," she said out loud, "This is my life." But then as she sat in her apartment wallowing in her depression her investigative instincts started to play out and she tried to figure out how everything fit together. She speculated that Dan is really the distraught father of a boy who was sexually molested and killed. Then he turns up in Chicago right after the Guild House bombing.

"Wait!" she yelled, "What if he blew up the Guild House? Oh my gosh, I made love to a mass murderer!" She couldn't believe it, but it all made sense. Why else would he have posed as an author and why else would he have wanted to see the child molester files? And why else would the FBI have told police departments to detain anyone asking to see them? Suddenly the vibrant, pulsating love she had felt blooming inside of her began to turn into terror.

CHAPTER 46

Dan hatched his plan for the termination of kiddie pimp Ali Ban Hashemi on the drive to New York. When he arrived, he checked into a Hoboken, New Jersey motel where the rates were substantially cheaper than in the City. He was running low on money and realized that, if he had no other reason to quit, his financial situation was enough. He immediately got down to the business at hand, plotting Hashemi's demise.

* * *

Detective Derek Lindsay, meanwhile, had a different fate in mind for Hashemi, namely a long prison term even after plea-bargaining and ratting out all his pimp contacts. But he was running out of time and he knew it. He spent endless hours trying to concoct a plan to catch Hashemi in the act, only to come to the same conclusion each time. The guy was too smart. In the deep recesses of his mind Derek knew that he was probably never going to make any charges stick to Hashemi and it angered him.

* * *

Dan Forester, however, didn't have that problem. He was judge, jury and executioner and things were pretty much cut and dried where Ali Ban Hashemi was concerned. The first thing he did was call Hashemi's telephone number from his motel room and play the taped message he had made Tyrone Palmer record before his untimely death. It was Tyrone's voice saying that he had some extra special merchandise that Hashemi would not want to pass up. It
also said that an associate would call in two days to set things up.

Then, Dan drove to the airport and boarded a flight to Miami where he checked into a motel and spent the night getting very drunk and loud at the bar. So loud, in fact, that the bartender had to warn him to quiet down several times. That night he again dreamed about Cole trying to tell him something, and again he could not understand what he was saying. This time Cole was talking to him from inside of a subway tunnel with the bright headlight of a train behind him. The only problem was that once again the words were unintelligible. The next day he flew back to New York.

Upon his return Dan called Hashemi's number, leaving the message that he was the associate Tyrone had referred to and that he had a wholesale-priced lot Hashemi was looking for. He left a message to call him at the number of the cellular telephone he had just bought.

Hashemi, by this time, was sick of his side-line, even though it was making him much more money than his legal lobbying business, and he was ready to get out. His only problem was that to retire he needed a large amount of cash and right now he had the trips of four foreign businessmen to America pending, all of them wanting young boys and two of them wanting to purchase slaves. By that time several of his regular pimps had discovered that he was charging his customers twenty times what they charged him for one-night stands and up to several hundred thousand dollars per child sold into slavery. They didn't like it and were beginning to charge him higher rates. But this new call was from someone who doesn't know how much he charges. Normally he would never do business on this scale with someone he didn't know, so he called Tyrone Palmer in California to verify it was him who had left the message. He got a recording saying the number had been disconnected. This made him suspicious and gave him grave doubts.

* * *

"He's moving," Derek mumbled to himself as he jumped down the stairs to follow Hashemi. Another cab, another pay telephone, and another videotape recording, but no audio because the long-range microphone was broken. Derek thought he had broken it while climbing down the tree.

Apparently deciding a large payoff was worth the risk Hashemi was returning Dan's phone call from a pay telephone. He wanted to make his exit from the prostitution business with one big hit and big bucks and then retire altogether.

"I understand you've got something I may be interested in," he said in his shrewd, negotiating voice when Dan answered the phone.

"Yeah. What kind do you need and for how long?" Dan said matter-of-factly.

"Well, not so fast. I want to meet you first and then we can talk about specifics. Tomorrow at the Sassafras Tea Parlor on 163rd Street at 2 o'clock."

"O.K. I'll see you there. I'm five foot nine, with blonde hair and glasses. I'll be wearing a solid black suit with a black and purple tie. You can call me Philip."

"Tomorrow then," and Hashemi hung up the telephone.

Lindsay had already discovered that the number Dan left on Hashemi's answering machine belonged to a cellular telephone purchased by a Tom E. Jenkins. It didn't take Derek long to realize that the name and address listed for the telephone number were bogus and that there was no way to trace the phone's location.

* * *

The Sassafras Tea Parlor was an elegant restaurant decorated with silk and velvet curtains. Dan sat at a corner table studying everyone who came in, trying to figure out which one was Hashemi. By this time, he was so racked with guilt and misgivings over what he had been doing that his head and stomach ached constantly. Ever since his talk with Jack he had felt especially anxiety-ridden. His emotions were getting out of control, something that was quite foreign to him. He just wanted to get this one over with and then sort things out. That thought reminded him of his sergeant's favorite line in Iraq, "Kill 'em all. Let God sort 'em out." But nervous or not, he knew he had to stay calm and cool to carry out this last mission. Then he saw an overweight, foreign-looking man enter the restaurant and look around. Hashemi, of course, was looking for a five-foot nine-blonde-haired man wearing a black suit and a black and purple tie, not for Dan who was six foot one, wearing sunglasses, a brown wig and beard, a brown sport coat, and dark blue pants. It was 2 o'clock and Dan was pretty sure it was Hashemi, who was now sitting at the bar waiting. He discretely maneuvered himself out of the door passing Detective Derek Lindsay who was coming in. He had followed Hashemi. Dan waited outside in his rented car.

Gotta' be him, he thought 30 minutes later as Hashemi stepped out of the door and got into a taxicab. Dan followed, not noticing Detective Lindsay also following the cab. The taxi weaved its way through heavy traffic until it came to a stop in front of Hashemi's apartment building. As Hashemi fumbled with his billfold to pay the cab driver Dan knew he didn't have much time, so he pulled over to the side of the road and parked next to a fire hydrant. He ran up to the front door of the building, brushed past the doorman, and slowly walked toward the elevators with Hashemi close behind. Noting the security guard at the front desk Dan let Hashemi pass him and then entered the same elevator and got off on the same floor. Pretending to go to an apartment down the hall, he made a mental note of which apartment was Hashemi's.

Just one step behind Hashemi, Derek had seen Dan go into the building but didn't think much of it. Seeing Hashemi go into his building Derek parked his car and went back up to the stakeout across the street figuring this was just another routine and unproductive excursion. Then, turning the recording equipment back on he listened over the microphones hidden in the apartment. He first heard footsteps in the kitchen and a cupboard door opening and closing. But shortly thereafter he heard a voice that was not Hashemi say, "I'm Philip. Sorry about the restaurant but I have to be very careful about who I do business with." Dan had jimmied Hashemi's apartment door and entered unannounced.

"Well ... I don't appreciate you breaking into my home," was Hashemi's startled reply as his anxiety grew and he began to regret ever getting involved with this man, "and we certainly can't do any business here."

"O.K. You've got a point. I just need to know how many kids and what type you need so I can get the ball rolling." Dan only asked this question to make absolutely certain that he had the right man. Detective Lindsay, by this time was glued to the bug's headphones, barely able to contain his excitement while he listened to and taped the conversation. "I've finally got the bastard," he said out loud.

Hashemi, meanwhile, was debating with himself whether or not to answer the question. His shrewd instincts told him to deny knowing anything about what this intruder was saying, just in case his apartment was bugged or the man was a policeman. But electronic sweeps hadn't found Derek's state-of-the-art bugs and he knew cops didn't do business this way. Finally, his greed got the better of him and considering that this was to be his last pimp transaction he decided to take the chance and go for it. "I need four boys, preferably blonde haired, blue eyed and pretty. Two for one night and two for permanent sale," he said with sweat running down his brow. Hearing this, Lindsay literally clapped his hands together and shrieked with delight.

"I can arrange it," Dan said as he pulled his silenced gun out of its shoulder holster, "But first I want the names and addresses of the other pimps you do business with." He came up with this idea on the spot. Even though he had planned to make Hashemi his last victim he realized at the last minute that he might be able to get more out of this than he planned. In spite of his intense guilt he was getting greedy.

"Whaa ... why?"

"Let's just say I'm founding a pimp union. If you give me the list we can do business and make a lot of money. If you don't, I'm gonna' blow your head off and neither one of us is gonna' make any money."

"But..."

"You've got to the count of five."

"Well, I just don't see why you want this..."

"You don't have to see. Anyway, it's nothing that will hurt you or them in any way. But as I said you've got to the count of five. One..."

"Wait, I..."

"Two."

"I pledged never to give out their names."

"How noble of you. Three." Dan aimed the gun directly at his head.

By this time Derek, scarcely able to believe his ears, left the recorder running, shot out of the door, and ran full speed for Hashemi's apartment building.

"Please don't ... I ... I" Hashemi stuttered.

"Four."

"O.K. O.K. I'll get it," and with that he hurried into his bedroom to retrieve the list of names he had pledged never to reveal. He actually had two lists, one in his apartment with four names on it and another in his head with three additional names and numbers. He correctly figured that the man with the gun didn't know how many pimps he had so he planned to give him the list of four and act like there were no more. But he also correctly figured that there was a good chance this guy was going to kill him anyway. Dan followed him and waited at the door while he removed a brick from the wall and pulled the list out from behind it. Detective Lindsay had earlier searched the apartment, but had missed the removable brick.

"That's one list, the other one's in here," he said as he reached into his closet. But instead of a piece of paper he pulled out a .38 caliber pistol and quickly aimed it at Dan. But Dan was too fast for him and shot first, pumping two silenced slugs into his mid-section. Hashemi dropped like an old-growth tree, never getting off a shot.

Meanwhile, negotiating rush hour traffic, Derek charged into the building, flashing his badge to the doorman, and headed for the stairway. "The son-of-a-bitch better not have cheated me," he grumbled as he vaulted up the stairs three at a time.

Dan, meanwhile, with pimp list in hand, left the apartment thinking he had more work to do. He was calmly waiting for the elevator door to open and when it did he walked in and pushed the ground-floor level button. Just as the door began to close Derek came blasting out of the stairway door, running right by the bank of elevators. As he passed one he noticed the door closing and just for a millisecond the two men locked gazes just before it closed all the way. It was only a fleeting instant, but it seemed that in that ultra-brief glance each knew who the other was and actually may have felt a little unconscious sympathy for one another. Derek instantly reversed course and headed down the stairs the way he had just come, hoping to intercept Dan on the ground floor. Something also told him that he had seen this guy before, but he couldn't pinpoint where.

Realizing that the man he had just seen outside the elevator door was probably a cop, Dan got off the elevator on the second floor and ran to the stairway at the other end of the building. He dashed down the steps to the ground floor, left through the back door, setting off an alarm, and ran down the street leaving his rental car behind. Having rented it under an assumed name he wasn't worried about it being traced back to him. Lindsay, meanwhile, made it to the ground floor and stood with his gun leveled at the elevator door, waiting for it to open. It did, but it was empty and he knew he had been had. After walking about a mile through Manhattan Dan hailed a cab and took it back to his motel. For the first time he looked at the list of pimps he had gotten from Hashemi and was pleased to see it contained not only telephone numbers but also addresses. He lay down and tried to drift off to sleep thinking about how he would eliminate the first name on the list. He found that he hatched some of his best ideas while in the dreamy state between wakefulness and slumber. The only problem was that the dark cloud was now his constant companion and was beginning to interfere with his thinking. And now, to make matters worse, greed was poking its ugly head out of the blackness and further clouding his judgment.

CHAPTER 47

Detective Derek Lindsay spent the hours after he lost Dan going over his own list of Hashemi-connected pimps trying to figure out how he was going to get his captain to approve the number of officers it would take to stake them all out indefinitely. His list contained five names, one more than Dan's list, which he had accumulated during his surveillance of Hashemi's child prostitution dealings. He had enough evidence to get convictions on them all, but had been waiting to reel in the big fish: Ali Ban Hashemi. Now that Hashemi was dead Lindsay figured he would haul all five of the pimps in, but not until he caught the guy who was stalking them. By now he had concluded that the man he had seen in the elevator was on a self-appointed mission and would probably try to kill all of Hashemi's pimps.

Though he was devastated that Dan had cheated him out of his chance to nail the man he had spent countless hours pursuing, he was also a bit relieved. Captain Lewis had been making noises about shutting down the investigation and settling for his five pimps if Derek couldn't get more evidence on Hashemi. Also, Derek knew he would probably never have made the charges stick to Hashemi, even with the new tape of his conversation with Dan. Besides, he had to admit that he wouldn't even have the tape if Dan hadn't entered the picture. He also knew that even if he did arrest all five of the pimps they would probably be out of prison in less than five years to resume their filthy trade, and in the back of his mind he almost hoped Dan would succeed in killing them all. "That," he told his partner Sean, "would be the only way real justice would be done."

Derek then dug up an FBI report he remembered from several months earlier which alerted the police department to the fact that there was someone out there killing child molesters. As much as he hated working with the feds he felt they might be able to give him some information on the pimp-killer he was looking for, so he telephoned an FBI agent named Ross Huggins and told him his man might be in New York. The phone call got Ross's heart pounding fast and he booked the first flight to New York City.

Lindsay's immediate problem was getting Captain Lewis to approve the number of officers he needed to stake out all five pimps indefinitely. At first the Captain told him that he could only spare one man and instructed him to try and figure out which two names on the list Dan might hit first and stake them out.

"But Cap, this guy may be the pimp-killer the FBI has been looking for," Lindsay argued, "and if we get him it will mean big publicity for the department." Again, Derek figured the only way to get what he wanted was to appeal to Lewis' political ambitions, but this time it backfired on him.

"Yeah, but getting publicity for catching the guy who's whacking child molesters isn't exactly what I had in mind," Lewis said, "I can see the public making this guy out a hero. Then we would look like the bad guy. I'm not anxious for that kind of attention."

Derek knew he had played it wrong and that the captain probably wouldn't budge on this one. So, he resorted to the old reliable: bribery. It was something he only used when he absolutely had to since it always required a substantial sacrifice on his part. "Cap, if you give me four men I'll work the night prostitution detail for three weeks next month for no overtime," he said in a throwing-in-the-towel tone. Because of an approaching series of large conventions coming to Manhattan the mayor's office had ordered the police department to clean up the area's prostitution before the first one and Derek knew that Captain Lewis was having a hard time figuring out where he was going to get the manpower. Typical of the time, the department was being hit with budget cuts while at the same time being told to do more work. Derek saw his opening and took it, but somehow, he knew he was going to regret it.

Captain Lewis looked at him in silence and then said simply, "you've got three men for four days and that's it. Glad to have you on the prostitution detail." So, Derek got most of what he wanted, three men to watch three pimps. He would watch the fourth, and the fifth, he figured, would be left to chance with the odds of Dan hitting him first, remote at best.

* * *

Derek was right. Dan's first choice was one that the NYPD was watching. He decided that considering his visit from Ross Huggins and the fact that he was probably seen by a New York City policeman in Hashemi's apartment building he had better waste no time eliminating his four targets. This time he didn't have the luxury of watching them for a long time as he had with his other targets. And this time he also didn't have the luxury of making the deaths seem like accidents. He knew it was time to bring his marksmanship skills into play. The day after Hashemi's death Dan paid a visit to the high-rise Brooklyn apartment building of pimp number 1, Wesley Jackson. To make sure he could positively identify him Dan wrapped up a wristwatch with a note that said "In appreciation to a good friend" and delivered it to his apartment.

"Got a package here for Wesley Jackson," Dan said to the man answering the door.

"That's me," said Jackson and Dan had his identification. The key factor for him was that he lived in an apartment with a balcony. Once he identified which balcony was Jackson's Dan found a construction site about a hundred yards away on which work had apparently been stopped. Climbing up to a level on the network of steel beams which was nearly the same height as Jackson's balcony he hunkered down and waited for his target to venture out. Eight hours of staring at the balcony went by with Dan's joints stiffening up and his eyes falling shut, until finally a man came out. Squinting through the long-range scope of his 30.06 rifle, which he had placed on a gun tripod, he saw that it was his target. Jackson couldn't have been more cooperative. He stood motionless with his arms spread out, breathing in the foul Brooklyn air and forming a perfect three-point target. Taking careful aim, he thought it was almost like he knew he was out there and was trying to make it easy for him. He focused the scope and zeroed in on his target. "Plak. Plak. Plak." went the three shots as Wesley Jackson keeled over the railing of his balcony and sailed through the air. He was dead before he hit the ground.

Perfect, thought Dan as he packed up his gun and prepared to make his exit. But someone else saw Jackson's fall too. NYPD Officer Bill Ridley was parked outside of the apartment building and had a view of both the front door and Jackson's side of the building when he noticed something falling. It was the body of Wesley Jackson and Ridley tried to pinpoint where the shots had come from. By the time he did, Dan was long gone, leaving no evidence of ever having been there. He headed directly to the airport and arrived just in time to fly to Miami. As Dan was confirming his ticket at the airline counter FBI Agent Ross Huggins was getting off his plane from Washington and walked right by him. Dan's back was turned and the two men didn't notice each other. Getting into Miami at 11:00PM he went back to the same hotel bar he had been at before and acted quite drunk to make sure he was noticed and further establish an alibi in case he needed it later. He slept like a log that night even though he had his recurring dream about Cole trying to tell him something and not being able to get out the words.

* * *

Detective Lindsay had to admit that he was impressed with the clean hit Dan had made on Jackson, and with little time for planning and preparation. He wondered if, like himself, the man he sought was a Gulf War Veteran. Whatever he was, Derek knew instinctively that the rest of the hits would come soon. He knew that Dan was getting in a hurry and that that's when you make mistakes.

CHAPTER 48

"Detective Lindsay," Ross Huggins' voice came from behind Derek as he stood at his desk in the police station.

"Yeah," Derek said as he turned around to see the FBI standing there. He had hoped he could get whatever information he needed on the pimp-killer over the telephone and hadn't expected the FBI to send an agent, at least not this fast. The feelings of animosity between local police and federal agents were legendary since the locals usually felt that the feds were infringing on their territory and the feds often felt the locals were incompetent. But Derek was a pro and he realized that he was now saddled with Ross and decided to make the best of it.

Ross told Derek everything he had discovered so far, including the fact that he had narrowed his list of suspects down to four. He had pictures of all four, and held his breath as Derek looked at them, intensely hoping that he would identify one of them as the man he saw in the elevator. He was to be disappointed. Derek said none of the four was the man.

"You've got to understand though, I literally only saw the guy for a split-second before the elevator door closed. One of these guys could be him and I wouldn't know it."

"I know," said Ross dejectedly, "I guess I was hoping that for once things might be easy, but you know how that goes."

"Yeah, they never make it easy, do they?"

"That's for sure," Ross said enjoying the beginning of a newfound camaraderie with this veteran law enforcer. Derek, on the other hand, could tell that Ross was a rookie, but he seemed to be a decent sort. He then shared all of his information with Ross concerning Hashemi, the pimp lists, and Wesley Jackson.

"Which one of the four gets your vote?" asked Derek.

"If I had to guess, it would be this guy," and Ross held up Dan's picture. "He's got some pretty good alibis for several of the killings, like he was a thousand miles away at the time, but he just seems the likeliest to me."

"Why?"

"Well, for one thing, his son was raped and murdered by a child molester."

"O. K. What else?"

"For another, he was a sniper in the Army."

"Iraq?" Derek's ears perked up at this revelation.

"Yup, and a demolitions expert."

"Didn't the guy who blew up that pedophile house in Chicago use C-4?"

"Yup."

"Is there a connection?"

"Could be," was all Ross said enjoying having information Derek didn't have.

"What about the alibis?"

"I know. I know. I just have to say that when I talked to him I got this gut feeling that it was him. You know what I mean?"

"Yeah, cop's instinct."

"Yea, the guy throws his career away to be with his son and then some pervert takes that all away from him. Bad deal."

"Yea, but good motive."

"Well, we'd better get crackin'," said Derek, "you want to come along on a stake-out of one of the pimps?"

Ross's blood began to pulse at this one. Finally, he would be doing some real, honest-to-goodness police work. "You bet," he said calmly, trying not to show his excitement. The two men went to stake out one of the four remaining kiddie pimps.

* * *

Dan, meanwhile, returned from Miami. On the plane he had hatched a plan. The flight gave him a chance to figure out that if the man he saw in the elevator really was a policeman he had undoubtedly been watching Hashemi for some time and probably had the apartment bugged. That meant the police probably also had the list of pimps and were staking them out, waiting for him to strike. He knew he had gotten lucky with the first one, but probably wouldn't be so lucky with the rest. At least, he figured they didn't have balconies. In light of all this he knew that he couldn't go to them, so they had to come to him.

He drove to the Hilton Hotel in Manhattan, put on his brown wig and beard and took adjoining rooms on the backside of the building under an assumed name.

After dropping his bag off he took a cab to a pay telephone in Times Square and began telephoning.

"Hello," he said on the first call, "can I speak to Joe Barton please?"

"This is Joe," came the voice of pimp number one on the other end.

"Mr. Barton, I'm an associate of a foreign gentleman you've done business with in the past. He has met with an unfortunate fate and left instructions for me to call you and give you some information if he ever met with such a fate."

"O.K.," said the curious but suspicious voice, "go ahead."

"He wants you to know that it is quite possible that by now there are probably people who know of your business relationship and may be watching you. He warns you to be careful. Secondly, when he met with his recent misfortune he had several pieces of business pending which he left instructions to complete with you and two other people in the same line of work. The deals, I should mention, will earn you about four times what they have in the past and will undoubtedly be the last business we transact since, with the gentleman's exit this enterprise is over. Do you still wish to do business?"

Barton was silent only for a moment as he went through in his mind just what this was all about. His first thought was that it was a police set-up. But then he realized that the cops wouldn't do things this way. If they had the goods on him they would just haul him in, not play around like this guy was doing. Besides, if it were the cops they wouldn't warn him that the authorities might be watching him. Then he thought that maybe this was some sort of scam. But it then occurred to him that there was nothing for anyone to steal.

Finally, he concluded that it must be legitimate and it made sense considering that Hashemi had been making hundreds of thousands of dollars in past deals. In the end, the idea of making a huge profit was irresistible. "Yeah, I do. What's the deal?"

"Please go to a pay telephone, bearing in mind that someone may be watching, and call me at the following number at exactly 10 o'clock tonight ... then we'll arrange a place to meet," Dan said giving him the number of the pay telephone he was using. This is just in case your phone is funny."

"I'll do it."

"Very good then. I'll talk to you at ten. Good-bye."

Dan made the same call to the remaining two pimps, Jimmy Kozloski and Tom Hanover, but only found Jimmy at home. He also fell for the ruse and agreed to call the pay phone at 11:00 that night. Dan hoped to reach Hanover either later that evening or the next day. When the first two called he told them that to save time and effort he wanted to meet with all three of them at once in his Hilton Hotel room the next night at 10 o'clock. They agreed and he could almost hear them licking their chops over the possibility of big money.

He wasn't able to reach Tom Hanover until the next day when he called him early in the morning and obviously got him out of bed. Groggy or not, he also agreed to the meeting. The last phase of Dan's mission was on and he couldn't have been more relieved. His nerves were shot and he was no longer able to believe 100% in what he was doing. He needed a rest to sort things out. The funny thing was that he kept thinking about Jan and their home. Surprisingly, after his romance with Susan he still went back to Jan in his mind. *"She is home,"* he thought. It was as if after all the tumultuous sadness in his life over the past year she was the only stable element in his existence. He needed her kind of stability right now.

* * *

Derek Lindsay followed Joe Barton's car as close as he could without being noticed.

Dan's hope was that since he warned the three pimps that they may be under surveillance they would lose their police tails before coming to his hotel room. In fact, two of them did just that by driving wild on the New York freeways. One did not. Joe Barton was being staked out by Derek Lindsay and Ross Huggins. The two that shed their tails had only one policeman in one car following each of them. Barton, however, had Lindsay in one car and Agent Huggins in another. He managed to lose Ross, but Lindsay stayed with him and radioed Ross over a portable walkie-talkie.

Derek followed Barton to the Hilton and watched him go in. He was about to go inside himself to get a peek at where Joe was headed when he saw another Hashemi-connected pimp, Jimmy Kozloski going into the hotel. "What the ... ," he said to himself as he ducked behind a large planter in front of the building to avoid being seen. Why would these two guys both be here? Before he had time to think about that question he had to slip into the lobby to try and figure out where they were going. The best he could do was watch the numbers on the elevator Kozloski got into alone. It stopped on the second floor. At least he knew that's where he and probably Barton were going.

By that time Ross Huggins had arrived at the Hilton and joined Derek in the lobby.

"What's up?" he asked.

"Good question. I just saw two of the pimps. I followed Joe Barton here and saw Jimmy Kozloski go up to the second floor. I just don't believe in coincidences. There's gotta' be something going on. Let's go up to the second floor and nose around." Derek radioed for back up on his two-way radio and asked that an officer be stationed outside the hotel and wait for orders.

"Good idea," said Ross who was feeling growing excitement. The two of them walked along each side of the second-floor hallway listening for anything suspect.

* * *

Meanwhile, all three of Dan's guests had arrived and sat across from him in his suite. He knew what he had to do and that he had to do it fast just in case any of them were followed, so he did it.

"I asked you gentlemen here tonight to show you something," he said calm and coldly as he turned around and reached into the closet for something, "and here it is!" He instantly wheeled back with his .357 magnum in hand and fired three silenced shots, one at each man. They died in their chairs with surprised looks on their faces and the last one's hand halfway inside his jacket touching his gun. Dan threw his gun into a bag and ran into the adjoining room.

* * *

Derek and Ross heard the three shots from a room that seemed to be on Ross's side of the hallway. "Which room?" Derek yelled.

"I think this one," pointed Ross and without hesitation Derek drew his gun and shot the lock off. With his adrenaline at an all-time high Ross kicked the door in, leaped into the room and rolled behind a bed with Derek covering him. Poking his head around the end of the bed his eyes quickly scanned the room and came to rest on a slight movement just outside the window. It was Dan.

Thinking there might be one of the pimp's body guards or even a policeman out in the hall when he did the shooting, Dan had planned a quick get-away that would allow him to escape immediately. Earlier he had hung a thick, nylon rope from the window washer hoist on the hotel roof down to the window of his adjoining room. He gambled that anyone out in the hall would rush into the room where the shooting took place. By then he would be out on the window ledge of the adjoining room swinging his way to freedom. He had planned to swing to the roof of a lower building at the end of the hotel and he would have already done that if the rope had not gotten caught on a drainpipe running down the wall. He also hadn't figured on someone breaking in the door of the wrong room. Jerking the rope loose he accidentally smashed it against his face partially ripping his fake beard off. At this precise moment he glanced back into the room just before he pushed off into the dark night and he met Ross's eyes in a less than fleeting glimpse. As he had practiced earlier he swung in a perfect arc to the lower building and landed with a thud.

He quickly hung down from the building's eaves, dropped to the ground and ran off with Ross Huggins' surprised face permanently embedded in his mind.

Dan's impression on Ross was equally strong. He ran to the window just in time to see an indistinct figure scurry around in the dark on top of a nearby building. Their eyes had met only for a split-second in the thick blackness but Ross thought he might have recognized him. With the darkness and the rope, the curtains and the beard, he wasn't sure.

"Radio that he's climbing down a building on the east end of the hotel!" he yelled to Derek.

Derek shouted the orders into the radio, sending his outside man in the direction Ross had yelled. Looking back into the room, Ross noticed the open door to the adjoining room. Then he realized the shots must have come from the next room. "Check the next room, Derek!" he yelled. Derek shot the lock off of that room's door and he and Ross rushed in from different directions to be greeted by the three corpses slouched in their chairs.

Both men were stunned at the odd sight. Except for the hole in each head they looked as if they were sitting down for an informal get-together.

"Looks like the party's over, boys," Derek finally said to the three, and then to Ross, "did you see who it was?"

"I can't be sure, but it looked a little like Dan Forester. I just can't say, but I'm going after him," Ross said as he headed for the door.

"O.K. I'll stay and look around," Derek answered admiring Ross's spunk, but knowing that if the outside officer didn't get Dan he wouldn't be caught, at least not tonight.

By the time the officer and Ross got to the lower building Dan was long-gone. "It figures," said Ross, "but if it was Forester I think I know where to find him."

"Do you think he recognized you?" Derek asked when he got back to the hotel room.

"It's hard to say. It was dark and we only saw each other for a second. He probably didn't."

"What are the chances it was Forester?"

"Uh ... I'll have to get another close look at him to be able to tell."

"Well, then you go after him and we'll look for clues here ... and probably won't find any. I guess we'll just have to hope we can get him on the last pimp." Derek didn't know that the fifth pimp on his list wasn't on the Hashemi list. Ross was torn between staking out the fifth pimp and going to Dan's house in Silver Spring. And neither knew that Dan was now driving back to Washington instead of plotting another murder.

"My instincts tell me he isn't going after the fifth pimp," Derek told Ross. That was good enough for Ross and he decided to go back to Washington on the red-eye flight to get a close look at Dan and to investigate his alibis more closely. He wished he could be sure who he saw at the window. But the one thing he knew was that he was going to have to see him in person again soon if he was going to make any kind of determination of just what he saw.

CHAPTER 49

After jumping down from the roof Dan ran to his car and headed for the freeway to Washington. He knew Ross had seen him and was pretty sure he recognized him. "So, the game's over," he said out loud as he drove, "I'm about to be on the front page of every newspaper in the country." Then the reality of the situation started to penetrate his already troubled mind. He realized that if Jan had to go through the agony of being married to a serial killer it might push her over the edge. Susan's documentary would be compromised when it came out that she had an affair with a pedophile killer while she was producing it, and that will pretty much end her career. And worst of all, the liberal media will be all over this thing, portraying me as a monster, which will probably generate a little sympathy for the perverts I killed, hurting my whole cause. All these thoughts came crashing down around Dan like a collapsing building. The weight of too many murders was too much for him to bear. His sins caved in on him like heavy bricks of anguish as he suddenly realized that what he had done may be counter-productive and was about to hurt the people he loved. The guilt he had kept at bay for so long now saturated his soul. Guilt and remorse gave way to regret which finally and completely eroded the feelings of righteousness he had carried around for several months. He had dirty hands and he knew it. And it was all because he got greedy with his victims. Greed and guilt. It was a bad combination.

It was all so clear at first, he thought as he drove down Interstate 95. Kill the perverts and save the kids. He figured each of the pimps he killed would have been responsible for about ten pedophiles molesting their 24 kids each and that brings the total kids saved to over 2000. But now he wondered.

What was it Jack had said? You have to leave the big decisions up to God. He assumed that includes life and death decisions. Dan had mentally built a dam to hold back this river of feelings so that they wouldn't interfere with his mission. Now that the mission was over the dam crashed down and the river flooded, leaving him awash in a sea of guilt.

* * *

"Well, well, well," said Captain Lewis, "Look at what we've got here ... five dead pimps and not even a serial killer. So much for the great publicity."

"I know. I know," answered Derek sheepishly, "Not my finest hour."

Lewis continued to harass Derek until he had nothing more to say, except one thing.

"By the way ... there's a captaincy up for grabs and I'm recommending you."

"Whaa...?" Derek sputtered amazed that he wasn't being fired.

"You're a good investigator Lindsay. Now get the hell outta here."

"Thanks Cap," Derek said in shock as he left to call his wife.

* * *

Dan needed time to straighten himself out and plan his next move. He detoured into Philadelphia and checked into a motel. The next two days he did nothing but think and slip deeper and deeper into depression. The more he thought, the more depressed he got and the thicker the dark cloud surrounding him became. He knew how the criminal mind works and he knew he had become a criminal. He realized his growing guilt had led him to subconsciously hope he would be caught in New York so that he could do penance and pay for his sins. And yet, a nagging voice in the back of his head told him that he could never do enough penance for the sins he had committed. He simply had too much blood on his hands. He also realized it was time for some inductive, rather than intuitive, reasoning. The man of action had now been transformed into a methodical thinker who saw the need to think things through. It was then that he realized he had two options.

He knew that if he died they would probably drop the whole case. If the killer is dead why pursue it? Then no one gets hurt. It was a wisp of a thought at first, but soon started making sense. Then he thought of Jan, but realized that she would probably be better off with a dead husband and his life insurance money than with a live serial killer. Besides, knowing Jan, he figured she would probably donate most of the insurance money to the missing children's cause and that's a good thing.

Now it was just a matter of how to die. Should he kill himself and escape all this misery or should he fake his death and go somewhere far away and try to make misery his friend? He knew how to fake it. It was pretty simple to steal a body from the morgue holding area where there wasn't a lot of security. He would knock all its teeth out of its mouth and replace them with three or four of his own. Then he would put the body in his car and send it careening over a cliff on Skyline Drive in West Virginia with a lit gas can in the trunk to make sure it exploded and burned to a crisp.

Or there was the real thing: suicide. He could really be the one who goes over the cliff. He wasn't emotionally accustomed to this deep, dark depression and right now suicide seemed like a logical way out. As bad as he had felt about his son's death, this self-hate somehow seemed worse. He saw the irony in being the ultimate realist looking for the ultimate escape, but so heartsick was he that he wasn't sure he could go on with life in any fashion. Besides, maybe he needed the ultimate punishment for the ultimate crime. But the thought nagged at him that suicide was also the ultimate in selfishness. He had an epiphany that you don't really own your own life. Your family and friends own pieces of it and he knew that because they are so hurt by your death. In the end, however, Dan concluded that being arrested would hurt too many people and the only way out was for him to end it all and make it look like an accident, with him in the car or not.

He went to sleep that night planning to drive to Washington the next morning and get things in order. It had become almost routine for him to dream about Cole trying to tell him something. In tonight's dream, Cole was more emphatic ... almost frantic. From behind a bright light he waved his arms and tried to tell him something, but again no words came out.

On the drive to Washington the next day Dan planned out how he would straighten things out with two women and a good friend before he died.

* * *

Susan Jensen opened her door and clumsily carried two bags of groceries into her apartment. A can of beans fell to the floor and as she bent down to pick it up she heard a voice say, "Kind a' clumsy, aren't we?" It was Dan.

"How did you get in here?" she asked.

"I used to be a locksmith," he lamely quipped. When he had jimmied the lock on her door he noticed her smell everywhere. Every woman had her own smell and Susan's was particularly sweet and sensuous. Sitting in an easy chair, bathing in her scent, he had drifted off to semi-sleep and began daydreaming about the unbridled sex they had had in Chicago. It almost seemed like it had been someone else carrying on with her in that hotel room, not him. But then he began to feel it was someone else who had done all the things he had done in the last five months, not him, and that made him feel a little better. His reverie was interrupted by the sound of a key jiggling in the lock. It was Susan and the time to tell her the big lie had come. Their affair was over before it had begun and he was going back to his wife. He didn't know that she knew who he was and that he would have to convince her that he wasn't the mass murderer she thought he was.

"Well, I wish I could say I was glad to see you, but things have changed a little bit since Chicago," she said sternly.

That brought sweat to Dan's palms. He hadn't expected it and anxiously he wondered if she knew of his sins. "What's wrong?" was all he could muster.

"Not much, except that your name isn't Eric Summers, you've never worked in St. Louis, and, oh yes, your wife happens to be my friend. Isn't all that right ... Dan?"

With his cover completely blown there wasn't much left to do but tell the truth, or most of it.

"Yeah, that's about right," was all he could muster.

"Surely you knew who I was ... I know Jan told you about me."

"Yeah ... but I couldn't seem to resist you."

"I just hate being lied to."

"So do I. But I actually didn't lie about Jan. We really were separated."

"Uh huh. And why did you want to look at the police pedophile records?" she asked with both suspicion and fear in her trembling voice.

Dan knew instantly what was in her mind. She suspected him of the Guild House bombing. He also knew that if she found out he did it, it would jeopardize her documentary, which was her life's work. He knew this to be especially true since Susan was, first and last, a good journalist and would feel obligated to expose him. It was time for a good lie. "I really did intend to write a book on pedophiles and I needed the records for my research."

"O. K. then, why the ruse about being a newspaper reporter from St. Louis?" Susan's cold suspicions were already beginning to thaw.

"Well, I really was a journalist in Washington, D.C. but do you think they would let a Washington reporter whose kid was killed by a child molester see the files? I had to make up that story to see the records and then, since that was the role I was in when I met you, I had to go with it. I wanted to tell you the truth many times but, how could I?"

"Yeah, how could you."

"But I guarantee you," he went on, "Even though that part was a lie, everything I felt for you and everything else I told you was the truth."

Thinking of their time together, Susan started to melt, but it wasn't going to be that easy. All her years of reporting had made her skeptical of everyone and everything. Just because she had feelings for Dan didn't mean she was going to believe everything he told her. But then, enigmatically, there was that nagging report she had just heard from her old news director that the Chicago police had a suspect in custody in the Guild House bombing. If the guy was guilty that would let Dan off the hook and make his story believable. Besides, she found it hard to believe she could have made love to a serial killer. Then, she remembered how she felt when her sister was molested by her stepfather. She knew she could have killed him and that really got her confused. With all these conflicting thoughts running through her mind, she decided to drop the Guild House matter for now. But she still had to deal with her feelings for Dan, and as painful as it was, she knew what she had to do.

"I thought this was the one ... I could've really cared for you," she said with sadness and a solitary tear trickling down her face, "But now it's impossible."

"I know," was all Dan could say.

"You have to go now. Go back to Jan and try to make it work."

"Yea ... I guess so," he said as he got up to leave. "In other circumstances it would have been you and me making it work. I'm sorry Sue," he hesitated at the door and he was gone.

Susan sat staring at the door for a long time with tears now streaming down her face. She realized that Dan was the closest she had ever come in her life to genuinely loving someone and now he was gone. "He was probably my last chance," she sobbed, "now I go back to being the ice queen." What she didn't realize was that Dan had actually stirred up amorous feelings inside of her that she didn't know she had. Feelings that would not soon go away. For this she would be painfully grateful later in her life.

But for now, as she had discovered in the past, work was the best therapy. She knew the only thing she could do to cope with the situation was to pour herself into her documentary work; work, which would soon require her to move her base of operations to Los Angeles, California. It was there that much of the substance of her next phase of production, the kiddie-porn industry, was to be concentrated. Soon, she would leave Washington and Dan behind.

* * *

With heartfelt sadness the next stop on Dan's farewell itinerary was St. Mary's Hospital to visit Jack whose cancerous brain tumor had returned with incredible speed and was bigger than ever. "Jack my man," Dan gave him the normal greeting even though the man in the hospital bed was not the Jack Adams he had seen just a couple of weeks earlier. This was a wasting invalid who was now under the influence of nearly constant pain medication. Dan could hardly contain his sorrowful amazement at how far his friend had sunk in such a short time.

"Danny Boy," was Jack's weak reply as he held out his shaking hand for Dan to grasp. This was a man whose mind now routinely seemed to be somewhere else but who had rare glimpses of reality during which he seemed as normal as ever. The combination of steroid medication to keep the brain swelling down and painkillers had left Jack an empty shell. Never the less, Dan felt that seeing Jack was the most important thing he could do right now.

"You look like you've conned the nurses into giving you the fun drugs," Dan joked only half-heartedly.

"Oh yeah, between the dilaudid ... and the morphine ... I'm just one big narcotic lollypop. Only thing is ... with all these opiates I can't crap ... and you know how I always enjoyed a good crap." Jack was barely able to get the words out and with fluttering eyes he looked as if he was about to pass out at any moment.

"Yeah, I know."

"I've looked better ... haven't I Dan?"

"Yeah, Jack, you've looked better."

"I've lost buddy ... I'm dying."

The two men looked into each other's eyes with Dan's starting to water. It was the look only two warring soldiers could hold. Dan leaned down and did something uncharacteristic. He hugged his friend's wasting body. He then straightened up and walked to a table on the other side of the room to get some tissues. When he walked back to the bed Jack had a flash of clarity and hit him with the last thing he had been thinking about.

"Dan, I want you ... I want you to ... take Charlie." And then he was out, slipping into another morphine fog of semi-consciousness.

"Charlie," Dan didn't realize he was saying his name out loud. That was something he had forgotten about because he planned on being dead or long gone in a short time. He sat at Jack's bedside for nearly an hour waiting for him to wake up and thinking about his dying request. Then, he suddenly realized that Jan could use his life insurance money to raise Charlie and that it could actually be quite good for her. It would probably give her a new purpose to take the place of the loss of their son and her husband. *Or was that just a convenient cop out?*

Dan started to leave Jack's bedside and heard him murmur, "See you ... later Dan."

Dan couldn't resist answering, "Maybe sooner than you think, buddy." Now it was time to say his last good-bye ... to his wife.

CHAPTER 50

Dan drove down the familiar street and pulled up in front of his house, a house that had seen such good times in better days. He sat in the car for a few minutes reflecting on his life and his approaching death or mock death, he hadn't decided. Long ago he had realized that he had more past than future but now it was a lot more. He didn't notice Ross Huggins and another FBI agent sitting in a car down a side street. Ross had been waiting for him to show up for three days so that he could take him in for questioning and, most of all, get a good look at him to confirm whether or not it was him he saw on the window ledge that night.

"There he is," Ross said as Dan pulled in, "Let's get him when he comes out."

Dan got out of his car sniffing the air as he walked up the sidewalk. It was fall and it smelled like death. Death and rot of leaves and plants and it hit him that everything dies, but at least nature comes back to life. Who knows with man? Somberly he walked into the house. Hearing the front door open, Jan came out of the kitchen looking as radiant as she used to look before their tragedy.

"Danny!" she shrieked as she ran to him and smothered him with kisses. Sex was not on Dan's mind. Love was. He realized at that moment that he really did love Jan and always would. Something told him it was a more mature love than he was used to and he felt good about that. Instead of heading for the bedroom, Dan and Jan sat on the couch and silently held each other for almost two hours. It was at some point in this embrace that Dan suddenly realized he did have something to live for and he wondered if there might be another way out of this mess.

* * *

Ross was doing some thinking too while he waited in his car. Primarily he thought about whether or not Dan was the man he saw outside the hotel window that night in New York. In all the excitement he hadn't yet been able to take a critical look at Dan's face. He thought about the Chicago police sergeant who had told him that the man they arrested in the Guild House case was undoubtedly innocent and that they just needed an arrest. He went over his entire investigation to this point and thought about the right and wrong elements of what the pedophile killer had done. He thought about his own kids and what he would do if someone molested them. Stakeouts give you the time to think about a lot of things.

"What do you think?" Ross's partner asked, shaking him out of his reverie.

"Let's give it a little longer," he answered.

Just then Dan came out of the front door looking preoccupied. "I love you," he said to Jan on his way out, "but I have to do something ... then I'll be back ... for good." He didn't really know if he would or wouldn't. Jan, by now, was used to his strange coming and going and simply said, "I love you." Dan knew he needed to talk to one more person before he could make up his mind.

"I changed my mind," Ross told his partner as he watched Dan get into his car, "let's tail him and see where he goes." He didn't think it would hurt anything to wait and it might even give him a break in the case.

They followed Dan as he drove onto the Beltway and headed north. After one exit and several turns and stoplights Ross suddenly realized where Dan was going. "The cemetery ... he's going to the cemetery," he said, wondering why that surprised him.

Winding his way down the little cemetery road, Dan parked in the area Jan had described to him so long ago. Getting out of his car he glanced up at the clouds and noticed a storm was brewing. Then, preoccupied with his son's life and death and his own, he walked the rows of gray, black, and maroon, marble tombstones looking for the grave he had never seen. Suddenly his worst dread was realized. There it was and abruptly it was all too real. Cole's grave. Cole's death.

He stared at the black and gray stone for a full minute before he could speak. Then, as he had found it so hard to do so many times in his life, he found the strength. "I'm not sure if I can do it Cole," he said, "But whatever happens ... I ... I wanted to say good-bye. I love you son and ... I need your help." But before he could finish, a loud growl came blasting out of nowhere wrecking the quiet solitude of the cemetery. He looked up to see a motorcycle speeding over the graves and heading right for him. The rider wore a black helmet with a smoked glass visor. The bike slowed slightly as it got to Dan and a voice from inside the helmet said, "Now who's the fittest?" With that he pointed a gun at Dan and shot him three times. He crumpled into a heap on top of Cole's grave with blood spurting out of the three wounds. The motorcyclist popped the clutch and sped off. But with the helmet on he hadn't seen Ross and the other agent running up behind him with their guns drawn, both with a deadeye bead on him.

"Freeze. FBI," Ross yelled. But he couldn't hear him over the thunderous roar of the motorcycle and wouldn't have stopped even if he had. The two agents fired several times, hitting him with every shot and sending the bike careening over graves and knocking over tombstones. It then slammed into a statue of an angel on one grave throwing the rider 30 feet into the air. The agents ran up to him and Ross gingerly removed his helmet to reveal the face of Lee Santucci. "Nobody I know," he said as he checked for a pulse.

But as Dan lay near death, he knew. He just didn't know how. On that fateful day several months earlier, an ambulance crew had found Lee lying in a pool of blood and close to death. Apparently, his pulse had been too weak for Dan to feel when he had checked it. It was touch-and-go surgery for several hours, but Lee pulled through. When he recovered he had just one thing on his mind. Revenge. Revenge on the man he knew as Garrett Taylor. He hired two private investigators to track down an ex-reporter whose son was murdered by a pedophile.

It took a long time, but they finally came up with his name and address. Lee found Cole's gravesite and had been staking out Dan's house for several days when he saw him come and go. He followed him far enough to realize that he was going to the cemetery and passed him to get there first, apparently not noticing Ross and his partner through his smoked helmet visor on the busy freeway. If they hadn't been there, he probably would have gotten away clean. But they were and he didn't.

"Call two ambulances!" Ross yelled at his fellow agent who ran for the car's radio. Ross raced over to Dan's body. He was still alive and his eyes were open but fluttering. "Hang tough. The paramedics will be here shortly and you're gonna' be O.K.," he told him.

Dan tried to speak, but all that came out was blood, spittle, and a hollow gurgle.

"Don't try to talk. Just lie back. The ambulance will be here any minute," Ross said as he made a pillow out of his jacket and laid Dan's head down upon it. At the same time he clamped his hand down on one gushing wound to stop the spurting.

"Did you ... get ... him?"

"Yeah," Ross said, "we got him. Who was he?" He couldn't resist the question.

Dan had just enough consciousness left to know not to answer. All he could vaguely say was, "Saved me the trouble..."

"He's dead," said the other agent as he ran up to Ross and Dan after checking Lee's body.

All of a sudden Dan felt lighter than air as he rose up out of his body and hovered over Ross's head. It all seemed so natural as he looked at himself sprawled across his son's grave with Ross crouched over him. He then heard a sort of whooshing sound and began rising up in the air faster and faster. The sunlight turned to darkness as he felt himself entering a long, dark tunnel. At the far end he thought he could see a light. Behind him he felt the sadly familiar black cloud approaching. As he got nearer to the light an incredible, euphoric warmth began saturating his very being. When he got to the end of the tunnel he was enveloped in the light and felt the most pervasive peace and contentment he had ever felt in his life. Yet he knew the cloud was always lurking. Then came the voice ... but it wasn't really a voice ... more like a feeling.

"The lives were not yours to take daddy." It was Cole. "When you steal a man's goods," he went on, "You can pay him back. If you hurt a man you can heal his wounds. But if you kill a man, you can't make it up to him and you can't balance the scales."

"Cole!" Dan cried without words suddenly realizing that this was what Cole had been trying to tell him in all of his dreams. Then he heard the swooshing sound again in the distance. He felt himself being pulled away from the light and the celestial warmth began slowly leaving his being. He was lost in a turbulent eddy of emotions as he headed back into the tunnel with the burdensome earthly feeling creeping back in and the ghostly black cloud not far behind.

"Our lives on earth are like one grain of sand," Cole continued from afar, "The things you consider so horrible are horrible ... on earth. But the earthly life is just one tiny part of our overall existence." The swooshing sound was getting louder and louder, almost overpowering Cole's otherworldly message. The cloud was getting closer and Dan was experiencing pure anguish. "Your mistake was in basing your life and death judgments on only your earthly values, which are too limited," said his celestial son.

"Cole! Cole!" was all Dan could silently muster as he shot back through the tunnel at a blinding speed with the cloud chasing close behind him.

By this time the spiritual communication was barely audible as Cole said, "Jack was right. Life and death decisions must be left up to the one who created them."

Swoosh-swack went the sound and Dan was back in his body with his eyelids flickering open and shut.

"Yer' gonna' make it," Ross said seeing him come to with a look of confused anguish.

But Cole wasn't done. "Daddy," he said in a far away, ethereal voice, "If you look deep within yourself you'll see that it wasn't really about the children and it wasn't about protecting or avenging the innocent. It was about you, your loss, and your need for revenge."

It hit him like a bolt of lightning. What would normally take years of introspection and brutally honest self-examination, became a spit-second epiphany. It was all about him. Just like his whole life had been. Dan's eyes rolled back in his head as he coughed out a death rattle. Then nothing. Nothingness and darkness lost in a murky nether-world of swirling shadows.

Still there was another message from Cole as he said, "But, all is not lost. You will see a prophecy in your next life that will show you how to gain redemption by helping people and saving lives ... maybe even children's lives like mine. It's all part of God's prophecy and providence." And there it was.

But at this very moment, Dan was more concerned with living or dying than he was with any prophecy. *My next life?* he thought, trying to break through the haze to some kind of reason. *What does that mean exactly?* Cole must have heard his silent question because in one final admonition, he said, "You must wait for the prophecy to gain your redemption."

Somehow, peering through a slight crack in the black cloud that surrounded him, Dan got the impression that he might not be beyond some type of redemption like the cloud and all his headaches had made him think he was. According to Cole, he may still have a shot at redeeming himself and that got him about as excited as any dying man can get. But then, he felt the black cloud tighten around him and feared that it had finally won.

At that moment, Ross saw something that would haunt him for years to come. At the same time his eyes fluttered shot for the last time and that tears were streaming down Dan's cheeks, the beginning of a near-smile was trying to work its way onto his face. But it stopped at a look of profound understanding. No guilt. No remorse. No regret. Just instantaneous realization and acceptance. Then relief. Then satisfaction and almost contentment. He looked as if he had just discovered the secret to some age-old puzzle.

Looking down at him, Ross got the eerie feeling that Dan had just found something in death that eluded him in life. He stared at his face for a long time trying to decide if it was him he saw at the hotel window that night.

"Naw ... it's not him," he said as he laid Dan's head on his son's grave and stood up to meet the approaching ambulances.

A paramedic jumped out of one with a bandage wrap in each hand and slapped them both on Dan's gunshot wounds. They loaded him into the ambulance and hooked him up to an I.V. Twenty minutes later, fogginess surrounded him as Dan gloomily started to realize that he wasn't dead, not yet anyway. He faintly grasped that he was being wheeled somewhere, but he wasn't sure. Then he thought he heard a voice say, "If he lives, offer him the job and remind him that it's either that or prison."

And with that, he faded into unconsciousness as the monitor flatlined and sang its warning alarm. The last thing Dan heard was someone shouting, "Clear!" and then it was nothing. The half-smile remained.

THE END

Don't miss the second book in the Prophecy series:
Prophecy and Redemption

The search for the keys to heaven inadvertently births a program that predicts the future. Computer geek Mark Jacobs gets ahold of a copy and suddenly finds himself the target of governments and terrorists worldwide. As Jacobs avoids capture, Lt. Chuck Lansing is plagued by doubts about the Iraq War and his part in it. When these two come together, the fate of the world could rest in their hands.

Using a revolutionary, new computer program to search the world's holy books for predictions of the future, Jacobs gets much more than he bargained for. Climate change, disease epidemics, and nuclear war are just a few of the existential threats he finds while hunting for predictions of future terrorist attacks. Meanwhile, Lt. Lansing is in the midst of a moral dilemma over the war in Iraq. Mixing actual events with Historical Fiction, Prophecy and Redemption tells the real story behind the longest war in American history and the tragic missteps the U. S. made when it first invaded Iraq and in the years since.

Action/Adventure meets Creative Non-Fiction in this electrifying tale of war and intrigue with a little mortal danger and existential philosophy thrown in for good measure. Prophecy and Redemption is a roller-coaster ride of exhilarating adventure and thoughtful reflection with ups and downs that will keep you on the edge of your seat and wanting more.